Escapade at the Five Dollar Café

Escapade at the Five Dollar Café
The Adventures of Dick Phillips
-1-
Written By
Stephen Philip Means

Wisdomgame® - Published 2007

Cover by Stephen P. Means

ISBN 978-0-9792448-9-6

Previously . . .

I whirled the 44.80 and fired directly into Dr. Blood's forehead. The Gorgon jumped between us! Its brain exploded, but it was still alive. The spiked tongue lashed my face. The ladies screamed and tried to hide. Impossible! The hideous Gorgon too strong, too ugly, too fast. Fat Linda's white bra red and dripping blood. My debutante, Cynthia, wearing a fragrance called White Lotus, but I couldn't smell it. The room stank slaughter. Dr. Blood, his engorged blue vein pumping on the bald skull, watched and laughed.

"You're a dead man, Phillips!" Blood screamed and darted through the time portal.

"I'll get you Blood!" I cried and formed my hand into the Mandrake claw of death. "I'll get you if it's the last thing I do!"

The dying Gorgon lashed at me. Again and again it slashed and plummeted me. Its tentacles ripped my face and tore at my eyes. I couldn't see. Time stopped. Split seconds shattered. The red puss glands spewed acid on my face. Tentacles pulled my head toward the fletching stinger.

Mandrake claw form!

Slamming through the Gorgon's exterior metal plate, I serrated the spongy gut. My claw made a hollow sound, sluck! I pulled the spine through the warm green flesh and with one hard crunch, wrenched it, and crushed it.

The mutant puked and collapsed. The danger was over, but hundreds of innocent people and creatures died. At least, the ladies were still alive. Cynthia was safe, but I didn't know if Linda would ever recover.

"Blood!" I screamed. "Blood, you can't escape me forever. I'll get you! I'll rip your hideous mind from that pulsing blue vein!"

The time portal disappeared.

"Cross my path again Blood, you die!"

I wished I could have that evil time-master in front of me again. I pumped the slime covered Mandrake claw.

Be careful what you wish for.

Case Closed.

Chapter 1.

The Gorgon escapade finished bloody, but I knew someday I'd have my chance with Dr. Blood. It was another day. Whew! What a day, so many changes and yet it wasn't even lunch. I sat down and as the cool leather surrounded me, I thought about her kiss. Last night had been a long one. The fat broad, the shooting, all the blood, and then my young debutante. Her lips were so sweet. I sank a little lower in my brown office chair. My eyes shut for a second.

The holo-com startled me. I let it ring. Once, you were too eager. Twice, you needed the business. Three times, they knew it was going to cost them. If they didn't gulp when you told them the price, you bid the job wrong.

"Hello," I said, "Phillips' detective agency. Dick Phillips speaking."

No image. No voice. But there was something there. I heard a slight breath.

"Hello . . . hello!" I looked at the bandage on my arm. Still hurt a little. Gorgons bite deep. Probably wouldn't be any permanent damage.

"Hello! . . ." Damn it. Where was that holo-image?

An ancient creaky voice spoke slowly with a Chinese accent. "Is this the Phillips' agency? Are you Dick Phillips?"

"Yeah! This is the Dick Phillips' agency. Dick Phillips speaking. Who's this?"

"I have a proposition for you . . . Please listen carefully. Very important. It involves a great deal of money."

He paused. There was a long silence as if he couldn't find the energy to speak. "Exactly seventeen billion Yen. You meet me at the Five Dollar in ten minute. Do you understand?"

The old voice trailed off to nowhere, and my mind, which was usually in the same place, blasted into action. Seventeen billion Yen converted to a lot of dollars. I fumbled for the conversion rate. What was it? Was it seven hundred thousand dollars? Or was it seven million?

Still no image. I gave the holo-com a kick. Damn.

"The Five Dollar in ten minute," he repeated.

"Sure," I replied, "but how will I recognize you?"

Holo-com flash and the buzz. Disconnected. He'd hung up on me. I didn't like that. Not a quick flash. He wasn't pissed off. No, it was a single flash, a slow flash. What was the word? What kind of bird was he anyway?

"Computer," I asked. "Thesaurus. Reserved. Old. Distant."

The computer replied in his regular male monotone. "Inscrutable."

Yes, I thought. Inscrutable. Also stupid, weird, crazy, violent, ugly, insipid and vapid. I knew some words too. "Replication!" I commanded.

The holo flashed on. A fat old Chinese man appeared.

"More."

Another old Chinese man formed in the holo. Ageless, yet marked by time.

"Repeat com."

I looked at the inscrutable ageless replication. On the floor by my desk, a Big Mac wrapper seemed to be hugging the leftover sandwich, yesterday's lunch. Now, I was getting hungry. A slight hunger pang shot through my midsection, my loins. I thought about Cynthia, about last night. She was probably sleeping. Fat Linda crossed my mind, the Gorgon blood on her boobs and the stains on her white bra. It was funny how those huge melons heaved when I pulled my piece. I rocked forward in the chair.

"Repeat customer com."

The holo replication replied, ". . . The Five Dollar in ten minute."

"Customer voice analysis."

"Male," the computer monotoned. "Himalayan, age one hundred plus."

"Can you give me intent?" I asked, and then quickly corrected myself. "Please . . . intent. Customer intent?"

The Rex 1000 was a great unit, but sometimes it pissed me off. I guess the geniuses as the factory had a certain sense of humor. For some reason, down line on the string you had to be polite to your unit or it wouldn't respond. They must have the cybers working overtime programming themselves. Anyway, you just had to ask nicely. Hey, that's what relationships are all about.

"Rex, please. Customer intent?"

This time he replied. "The Chinese man wants to kill you."

That woke me up.

"Okay Rex." I replied quickly. "Please do voice analysis from the beginning. Perform sidereal access. Do vowels."

And what was that other term? I needed coffee.

Java Whiz was still warm, but it's dark brown liquid tasted bitter like poison.

"Ton toe!" I commanded.

"Side kick service," Rex replied.

"Reminder, clean, and drain, refill Java Whiz."

I sipped the stale coffee and laughed to myself. One look at my 44.80 hanging in its holster and the Chinaman would faint. Ha! He wants to kill me. It wasn't the first time. No way would it be the last. He wants to kill me! We'll see about that.

I jumped and kicked, slashed with my steel toe boots. Formed my hand into the magical Mandrake claw, adjusted my weapons belt, whipped around my 44.80, and checked my supply of bombs. Dr Blood crossed my mind. I wanted to explode his bulging brain head, and puncture that ugly blue vein. I hate him.

"Rex," I said as I formed open palmed Kung Fu. "Give me some resistance. Show the most evil warrior you can devise."

The Tartian flame devil appeared. My adrenal glands flared and raised the hair on the back of my neck. I made the Mandrake claw of death, but not soon enough. The monster lunged at me and struck my head, knocking my face, blurring my vision. It struck me again. Then again. I needed that.

"Image off!"

Whenever I felt a little spunky, I counted on Rex to produce a good opponent. But I was hot on the new case. I wanted to know more about the Chinaman. What was his reality?

"Sidereal access. Down line terms."

"Vowels? . . . Pauses? . . . Exhales? . . . Glottal stops? . . ."

"Terminate. Rex, please, customer glottal stops intent analysis."

The 44.80 slid out of its holster. I was quick. Sometimes too quick. At least, that's what Chief Parkenson said. I killed them too quick. I did and I didn't. My arm hurt. The blood smeared bandage would have to be changed. My arm hurt, that was for sure, but it wouldn't slow me down. I killed quick.

Too quick? No, not too quick.

"Rex," I repeated, "please customer glottal stops intent."

"Still computing."

Still computing? That didn't happen too often. Rex was equipped with Vortex Blaster Speed Straight. My heart took a jump. An exciting case was forming. I smelled intrigue.

"Masked intent," Rex droned. "First analysis possible mask. Glottal stops loop error. Ten per cent possibility he want you to kill him."

I raised my eyes. Boy, I thought. Sometimes I wished for earlier times before the war when we still had our wits. If he wants me to kill him, okay. How many kills did I have left?

"All right, Rex," I said, "I'm out of here."

The Five Dollar Café was down a dirty side street on the other side of town, and I loved it. I hadn't been down there for a long time, but it was always the same. I instantly made the shuttle from my office, and it flew me toward my meeting. The Five Dollar served pretty good food, dog, cat, I don't know. It was quaint. Same seedy old men talking to themselves. Same beggars making a living off spare change. There it was.

I pushed past the bags of garbage. The stench smelled green. They had to settle the strike. As I walked toward the door, I wondered if my old trick would work. Sure it was mean, but if I was going to be hanging out at the Five Dollar, I had to make a reputation right from the start.

The big one swatting by the door looked like he could take a joke. I wondered what he was doing begging. It appeared as if he could make a living on the docks. Broad shoulders, large arms, and the face reminded me of the 'Case of the Ugly Puss.' He was probably burn out. I turned away and lit up a smoke with my lighter. I perfected the technique. Perhaps, not the originator. You hold the dollar piece between two others and heat the first one red hot.

"Dollar for cup of coffee Mister?" he asked.

I smiled. "Sure," I said and dropped a red hot one in his hands. I could hear it sizzle as it hit his flesh.

He didn't flinch.

"Thanks," he said and smiled showing a toothless brown gap.

Hashish, I thought. Probably an opium freak too. I squeezed by and then it struck me. Too much muscle mass. Opium freaks didn't have mass. There was something about that beggar that bothered me. I fingered the 44.80 but let it slide back. Too quick to kill. Parkenson's words lingered in my mind.

The maitre d' at the Five Dollar was an old friend of mine. Kind of a wimpy looking Chinese guy. You wouldn't want to fight him, unless you knew Chi Kung as at least as well as me. Lee Tsing fought chicken style. He would pluck out your eyes before you could blink. Still, he wasn't' as fast as me. He'd seen me use the 44.80 and he respected me. He'd heard rumors about the Mandrake claw. I'm sure he respected me. In a fair fight I'd rather be on Lee's side than against him, but he knew when the curtain came down it was going to be him lying dead at my feet.

"Ah so, detective Phillips." Lee Tsing bowed and surveyed me with his tiny eyes. "What brings you to my humble house of chicken and rice?"

"Lee Tsing, good to see you."

I paused and looked him square. "Look," I said, "you aren't still mad about the last time . . . are you?"

He laughed. It wasn't a big howl or even a little he he, but I saw his eyes sparkle. I knew he wasn't mad at me. Sure, he'd kicked me out, but that was over . . . well, what was it? . . . At least ten years ago.

"Tsing, you know you haven't aged a bit. How do you do it?"

He shuffled his feet almost as if he were embarrassed. There seemed to be quite a bustle in the Five Dollar, I felt a presence. Tsing looked at me.

"China method," he replied. "Keeps me young. Also had to get a new young wife after last time you here. Nice girl, Kai. She treat me good. Good sex, brodder, you know it. Never you had that kind pleasure. Oh boy, now Lee brag too much. She fine, not like old wife. Old wife too straight laced, to much make up and dye hair."

Ah yes, 'The Case of the Frozen Madonna.' Well, at least Tsing was smiling. If he had a new young wife, of course he wouldn't complain. So what if I did kill the old wife. It was in the line of duty. After all, she was evil, and that's my job, to get rid of evil. Too bad, but once in a while it does happen.

"Say Lee," I said, "you have got to do something about the beggars. There's a big one sitting in front of your place. Better get rid of that scum. It doesn't look too good right outside your door."

"No beggars. Get rid of beggars years ago. Ha ha. Right when you leave. Ha ha."

He handed me a menu and spoke with a crooked smile.

"The special today is Instant Feast, duck. Enjoy," he said and walked away.

Now, the menu was the same as it had always been. The words were laid out in Chinese and English with the history of the Five Dollar Café. The private little booths, the wooden tables, the balcony, and the little waiters with pig tails . . . it was the same as it had been for years. Even the pictures that hung on the wall were the same old China. Butchering the chickens, coolies working the rice fields, bicycles, bicycles, every Chinaman on a bike. The countryside as it had been years before. Too bad they didn't find out about birth control five hundred years earlier.

I held my hand over my ear. "Rex, location: Five Dollar. Transcribe. Verify. Calls?"

Rex came on the transceiver in my ear. "Twelve forty pm. On line. No calls."

The ancient Chinaman appeared out of nowhere, right in my face. Perhaps he slipped in while I checked with Rex. Anyway, now, a small Chinese man sat in front of me. He was so tiny only his shiny face stuck over the table. His teeth were strangely like white ivory, and the eyes glowed black out of an old but ageless face. Inscrutable.

The smell of chicken and rice cut the air like a knife in a salted wound. The room filled with the sounds of people talking and dishes and pots and pans being cleaned. Waiters ran back and forth and a baby cried and a woman screamed. In the distance grunts, possibly men dying.

It wasn't often things got by me, but I was always prepared. I leaned forward toward the old man while at the same time I raised my right hand and snapped my finger.

"Waiter!"

That was the only diversion I needed. My left hand slipped the 44.80 out from its holster, pointed under the table at the gut of the China. I faced the old fellow.

"Name's Dick Phillips." I offered my right hand.

His green eyes burned me from between the slit lids. His face was old, very old. Long white hair touched his robe. My finger massaged the trigger. It felt cold, and it itched. Restaurant quiet. The baby stopped crying, and the whole place went silent. Vacant. My mind alert. Concentrate. A second more and there would be a bloody hole where he sat.

Still, he didn't speak. I held one hand out over the table to shake hands, and the other hand under the table tightened on the trigger. He reached in his robe. I could hear my heart pounding, twitching like my finger, and as I stared in his eyes I felt an old pleasant feeling. I was going to do him. My finger pulled at the trigger.

"For you," he said and removed a wad of green bills from his clothes. "Fifty thousand American. Yours to keep if you put away your gun and listen to me."

"Rex," I whispered. "Diction. Intent?"

Immediately Rex replied. "Deadly caution."

I eased the trigger, but kept the aim at the old man's solar plexus. "First," I said, "let's talk. What's the skinny?"

"Skinny?"

"The story. What's the story?"

He looked away as if looking into a distant past, and when his eyes returned to mine they were glazed. His hands seemed to grip an invisible ball of air, and his long fingers twitched as he spoke.

"Many, many years ago," he began. "I was a young man. Now I am very old. Much older than you or your computer can know. I have been trained in the ancient mysteries. I was on the Earth when the Pharaohs reigned. I saw Christ die. I have walked on the land for eons."

Sure, I thought, another freak, I've had my fill. I gave him five seconds before he ate death. I smiled,

"Continue."

The voice seemed to come from deep inside of him. "Every century I have rejuvenated myself with the sacred rite of Kala Kapa. From the beginning when I first became immortal I realized the existence of evil . . . and I have learned to fight it. By constant vigilance I have been able to keep it from overtaking the world. But now, my powers grow weak. Evil has established a hold and for the first time in eternity I feel fear. In my existence I have never felt it. I have always had power. I always moved with power and courage, but now, within me, I feel fear."

The old man slumped over, resting his sunken face on the table. He seemed exhausted. The waiter arrived with tea, and it was Lee Tsing himself. Lee nodded to me.

14

"Lee," I said, "we need two cups. One for me . . ." I motioned to the old sapient. "And one for my old friend."

Tsing replied in a strange way. "What old friend you talking of. You mean me? So sorry," he said, "I do not have time to join you, detective Phillips. Too much work now, thank you."

Lee Tsing looked directly into my eyes, and it was as if he had seen a ghost. He jumped and turned on his heels. Strange then, too, I noticed I was sweating. The 44.80 felt alive in my hand. It jumped, and I had to grip it hard to keep it from flying out and away. I concentrated on the ancient. He continued.

"I need your help. An object has been stolen. It must be found and returned."

I began to feel sorry for the Chinaman, and the money looked good. I poured a cup of tea and focused my left hand on the massive instrument under the table pointed at his gut. I felt sorry for him, but something in me said pull the trigger. My hand cramped with desire, but I thought about the fifty grand.

"First," I said, "take some tea. Then finish your story."

"No," he replied, "the tea is poison." He made a quick glance to the side. "Your life is in danger. We will talk again soon."

I felt it in my hara, in the pit of my belly. Indigestion? No, Danger! Danger!

Lee Tsing stood at the table with the big beggar who'd been at the door. He hunched huge and looked ugly. I could see my own eyes reflected on the mirror finish of the knife in his hand.

"Where is he?" Tsing demanded.

I felt that funny feeling. Time seemed to move like slow molasses. My gun pointed in the wrong direction. The old man disappeared. Gone. Vanished. I put my hand to my ear.

"Rex. Analysis"

That was wrong. It felt like a butterfly brushing through my hair, like ice sliding down my cheek. I looked at the beggar who smiled a brown toothless grin, and I turned my hand and tightened the trigger.

What was that sound?

Chapter 2.

My ear hit the floor with a thud.

You have to be careful at the Insta Med. Some of the interns there will sew your ears on upside down if you aren't careful. Lucky me, at the Five Dollar on the next table a bucket of ice provided cold protection for my ear. Didn't take too long to get to Med and get admitted and get my ear attached. Unfortunately, the Rex transceiver didn't make it. So no more coms until I get over to Nick's repair shop.

Just as the intern finished sewing back my ear, in strode laughing Chief Parkenson, who is one large cop. He's a big guy, and he has a big heart. You can't help liking him. Sure, he's tight, but me and him get along pretty well. I mean as well as any private can get along with the police. An Irish brogue came bellowing in. He kind of smiled when he said it.

"Too quick," Parkenson said. "Too quick to kill. You're just too quick."

Sometimes I wondered if he meant I killed too quick, or I was so quick that they couldn't kill me. Anyway, as always, thousands of thoughts crossed my mind. None of them seemed to make sense, but I knew I was quick.

"Huh?"

"Somebody give you an ear full?" Parkenson laughed.

"Look," I replied, "look at my ear. That guy wasn't trying to be funny. He only missed my jugular vein by a quarter of an inch. If I hadn't had the transceiver installed, I think he would have slit my throat.

"Rex saves Dick Phillips once again."

"That's right. We're a team."

"Don't pout, Phillips."

"Don't strain your high blood pressure, Parkenson. You aren't very funny! Except funny looking."

"Look son, don't get excited. It's just another time your computer saved your ass. You know you wouldn't even be a private dick without him. So I'm telling you son. . ."

"I'm not your son. I don't know why you keep saying that . . . wait. I do know why. You want to inspect me, err, I mean insect me."

"Bug you, son. It's 'bug' you. Settle down. Let's have the routine."

He held his hand to his ear. "Statement."

I repeated it as I had so often in the past. "Private detective, Dick Phillips, badge 324200."

Parkenson got cute. "Licenses please."

"You got them on file."

"Strike that. Phillips, repeat. Statement."

I went through it all again. "Private detective, Dick Phillips, badge 324200 . . . weapon, Johnson, 44.80, martial arts specialty, Mandrake; licensed to travel in all zones; death permit ten. Killed indigent in provoked attack."

In an ameba-like jelly movement Parkenson turned sideways. He was always doing that to make a point. Whenever he wanted to get on my case he would turn sideways, laugh with his Irish brogue, and make me pay more tax.

"Death permit ten. Death permit ten? Phillips, do you know what that means?"

Of course I did. "It means I'm allowed to kill ten people a month. I never kill anyone unless they ask for it. I don't want to lose my license. I follow the rules."

More sideways, and Parkenson had a way of gurgling when he talked. Sort of a brogue mixed up with a lot of cigars. "But Phillips, that thing you killed last night, and the bum just now at the Five Dollar . . . that makes eleven, and it's just the beginning of the month. Do you know what that means?"

I knew what it meant. Whenever Parky showed up I knew what it meant. It was a tax increase.

I took a look around. Our taxes paid for this insanity. The Insta Med was a mess. So many cases coming and going they barely had time to clean up the blood. Was that a head? It smelled like they never cleaned up. The long silver needles hanging on the wall always bothered me. Through the window in the distance I could see the head replacement factory. The checkered black and white tiles on the floor seem better suited to a pizza parlor. My ear hurt. I looked up at the fat chief.

"Okay, how much more?"

"By the book, son," he said. "I don't set the rules. The city council hires me to police you guys. I don't get the money. By the book."

He held his ear. "Computer. What's the price increase?"

As an aside, he said, "The costs are always going up." Then he laughed in his gurgling way. "It's only going to cost you fifty thousand . . . but that moves you up. Now you can kill fifteen people, or things, a month. You have four more kills left this month. That is, if you got the cash."

"Look," I said, "You know what I do. They go crazy. It's in my contract. I kill them. I don't do it because I like it."

Parkenson doted as I continued.

"I only do it to defend myself."

"Sure, sure."

"Really, honestly, I don't blow holes in people for the fun of it. My cases are important. I'm doing my duty, the same as any other badge."

"What about that creature you killed last night?"

"The Gorgon?"

"I guess."

"They don't count. They're already dead."

"Right," Parkenson said, and then he laughed. "Yeah, I guess it deserved what it got."

He paused. "Listen. If you haven't got the bucks, I'm going to revoke your license and take your Johnson."

I reached for my wallet and took out the fifty thousand the Chinaman gave me.

Parkenson laughed again. His belly wiggled. He could really loose some weight.

"Where'd you get that kind of money?"

"New case."

"What's that?"

"Oh, I guess I'll call it 'The Case at the Five Dollar Café.'"

"Huh?"

I looked up stoically. "No, 'Escapade at the Five Dollar Café.' That's it."

"What are you taking about?" Parkenson asked. "I mean that napkin. It fell out of your pocket when you got your wallet."

I picked up the napkin. It was from the Five Dollar Café.

"This," I replied, "is the first clue. The old man said the tea was poison. I took a sample on this napkin. When I get back to the office, I'll have Rex run a diagnostic."

"Who's this old man?"

A gurney flew by with a live head. We looked coldly at the garbage. It was headed for the factory in the distance.

"My new case."

"Always something. Son, and I use that word loosely . . . son, when are you going to learn. You ought to have a police job. Pushing paper is a lot easier than killing things and people. Say, why don't you come out to the country house and have dinner with me and the family? Come out sometime this week and bring your new girlfriend."

"You mean Cynthia?"

"Yeah, the debutante."

How'd he know about her? As we walked to check out, I wondered if he had a tail on me. Was I being set up by the fat man? Parkenson had to know everything about everyone. I looked at him out of the corner of my eye. Why was he always so jolly? A shuttle pulled up in front of Insta Med. Parkenson bent to me.

"Stay out of trouble, Phillips."

"Later Chief. I'll com you for that dinner."

The shuttle groaned away from Insta Med. Out to port I could see poor Parky was still filling out forms. The butt of my Johnson felt cold to my hand. Would these fingers ever be pushing pencils? I doubted it. I was glad I wasn't in the police. A badge was the only life for me, and my new case made me curious. How was the Chinaman rejuvenating himself? Why was Parkenson interested in getting me out to his country house for dinner? Was there a link between these two questions? Perhaps the poison napkin held the answers, but first things first. On to Nick's repair shop to get my transceiver repaired and com with Rex.

The city flew by. It was a tangled knot of lies and deception.

"Rex. . ."

I felt naked without him in my mind. What would he call it? "Imbroglio," a complicated situation? Outside, the ugly grey city marched from shuttle window to window. I felt the heat of my new case. There was going to be some killing, I sensed it. These thoughts only took a few seconds. Usually the shuttle was quite boring, and for some reason I couldn't go to sleep as I contemplated the new case. Sex, intrigue, killings. I loved it. Yet, only time would tell, and as I looked around the shuttle at the riff raff, I wished I had more than four kills left this month. These deviates all lived in their own world. If you caught the eye of an estranged one it might mean a slug in the heart, but I'm never afraid to look, because I'm never afraid.

An assortment of underbelly youths and shabby old farts, worn-outs, and burn-outs filled the shuttle. The drunk next to me stank like old cigar butts. His crusty beard was filled with artificial egg they served over on street five. It spoke to me.

"Sell me a smoke?"

I fingered my box. Fifty dollars a pack. The best smoke money could buy, Royal Fourteens.

"Okay," I said, "but it'll cost you a five dollar coin."

He flipped the coin in a familiar way, too quick, too easy. I looked him square in the face. Something about the deep brown eyes. I let the coin drop between us on the seat. A hot one! The plastic sizzled, and a burnt vinyl odor rose to my nose.

"Browny," I asked. "is that you?"

He put his arm around my shoulder and pulled me next to him. My reflex action shot down for my Johnson, but Browny's hand clamped like a iron fist on my arm, on the bandage on my sore arm. My ear throbbed. I was immobilized in a steel vice.

"Oh . . . oh poor Dicky. Does that hurt?"

It hurt. It was Browny. Long time no see. 'The Escapade of the Ant.' I thought he was dead. Good undercover man. The best. Always lived on the edge. He could disappear and reappear years later. I butted him on the head. As my forehead knocked him back, my left hand shot for the esophagus.

An old voice like that of the ancient Chinaman whispered, "Rip the throat."

But I released my hold. "How you been, Browny?" I asked. "I thought you were dead."

Through the messy brown hair and crusty beard his dark eyes smiled. "Ah Dicky," he replied laughingly, "I just let you win."

He opened his coat and taped his chest making a metal twang. "Look at this."

A sinking feeling in my gut. Somebody had done poor Browny, but the fools over at the Insta Med wouldn't let him die. A mechanico! I felt ill. Acid puke rose in my mouth.

"Yeah," he said, his eyes still flashed in the same old manner. "At least they saved my head. That's all that's left of me. Nice metal." He massaged his dark steel chest and closed his coat.

Now the puke rose thick in my throat and came up. Yuck, I wiped my mouth. I hated mechanicos. They were worse than good for nothing. The Insta Meds wouldn't let people die. They had to bring them back time and again. Broken souls that lived on and on until finally the heads went insane. They were hard to kill too. You had to shoot them in the brain. Good for nothing except menial jobs. Couldn't trust them, they went insane too quickly.

"What are you doing here?" I asked. "How'd you get out of menial service?"

"Ah, you know Dicky, I knew . . . that is, know too much. Can't see me cleaning dishes or washing shuttles, can you? Parkenson got me in the police on special assignment. You know how I know the streets."

Browny in the police! Now, I'd seen everything. It didn't seem possible, but then Parkenson was after me too. A badge in the police, that really didn't make sense. A mechanico on special assignment, it was absurd. Then again, since the war, it all was absurd. He looked me in the eye. Still had the old sparkle.

"You . . ." he said with a plaintive moan, "You . . . don't . . ." He paused as if to swallow if he could have. "It's not so bad being a mechanico." He looked away for a second. "Except they won't let me kill. They give you a body with special strength, extra fine hearing, special abilities . . . but they program you. It won't let me kill. It's the work of the Council, the Insta Meds messing in again."

A bit of spittle dripped out of his mouth. I wondered if he could feel it. His breath smelled rotten. He was deteriorating. How long would it be? A week, a month? I felt myself leaving.

Somewhere inside the crusted beard, he mumbled.

"What?" I asked.

"I want to kill so bad."

He stared at me for a minute without speaking.

"Dicky," he said quietly, ". . . they make these units without cocks."

Poor Browny, an ex badge, one of the best. Now, he was a mechanico with a few weeks or a month left. No one knew for sure. There were rumors some of them lasted for years. I even heard one lasted so long the Meds rewarded it with a real body. As if that were possible. Most went insane. I had to kill them. I'm a badge. It's my job.

I turned away from his stinky breath and looked at the scum in the other seats. How many of them we hiding steel bodies under their rags? How many were opium freaks? How many perverts? Deviates? Blood suckers? Animals? Freaks? Council members? Then it made sense.

"Dicky," he said. "I want you to do me."

"Can't," I replied. "I'm over my limit this month as it is. And besides, you know I only kill on perceived danger."

"Yeah?"

"That's right."

"Oh?!" His metal claw hand cut into my neck. "How about this!"

The story again. Listening to an old friend. Always the story and then the kill. My 44.80 slipped into my grip, and I shoved the business end in his mouth. Now, I felt my good smile, and I moved the Johnson from side to side. Was that the Chinaman's voice in my head?

"Go ahead, do him."

The claw at my neck. Couldn't breath. Gorge rose in my mouth. Air, needed air. Good by, Browny!

"Can't do it," he said, and let go. "My body won't let me kill. The programming . . . It's the shits, ain't it, Dicky boy?"

I caught my breath. "That almost worked. In one second I would have taken you out."

I would have, but I listened too long to that voice.

"In a second," I said, "your brains would have been outside the shuttle, blowing in the wind."

He just laughed. "Parkenson wouldn't like that. I'm your shadow."

A shadow. The worst sound a badge can hear. A shadow, an old friend, an ex badge and a mechanico to boot. Parkenson definitely knew what he was doing. Years ago he and Browny had been old friends. Now, the Insta Meds make Browny a mechanico and Parkenson sends him in as my shadow. Hell! You couldn't shake a shadow. You had to take them out. . . . And I would take him out. Browny knew it. Parkenson knew it, and I knew it. Should have done it just now when I had the chance. A badge couldn't have a shadow.

As the rumble of the shuttle moved me toward Nicks, I caught my breath and holstered my Johnson. "Browny" I asked, "remember the Ant Case? I took a hook for you in that one. Almost turned me mechanico. I barely made it. And you remember the night we got our badges? I gave you the red head."

"But you took the blonde. What are you getting at?"

"Remember when Dr. Marsall's brain blew up?"

"Yeah."

"I bought you dinner that night."

"So?"

"I, well . . . Browny, you owe me. Listen, I'll make you a deal. Give me twenty four hours before you start the shadow."

"Impossible!"

I had to offer him something he wanted. "Okay asshole," I said, "here's the deal. I get off at the next stop. You ride the shuttle for five minute and then start the shadow."

"Why should I do that?"

"Here's the kicker, Browny. The next time I see your ugly puss, I'll fire a slug right into your stupid brain. Bye bye."

His face lit up. "Deal!"

I hopped off the shuttle at the next stop with a sigh of relief. The Chinaman case was heating up, and I couldn't have a tail shadowing me. Especially one that reported directly to Parkenson. I wanted to get my hands on the Chinaman seven hundred thousand. Then I could move out to the country and retire. . . Nah.

I'd never retire. But I could live pretty well, even with inflation. A few subtle moves and I could keep Browny out of commission. I'd easily do him if we came to it. Better just to keep him off me. He'd go insane soon. By doing him I'd only be left with three kills this month. I don't need tax increases, and most likely I'd quickly solve this new case anyway and let Browny go nuts on his own time.

What would I do if I were Browny? If he gave me the five minutes we agreed on, he'd be minutes behind me. Would he follow me back here and try and pick up my trail, or would he head to my office and try to get Rex to help him? He knows that's impossible, but either way I needed more time. I twisted the long range extension on my Johnson, and as the shuttle pulled away, I fired a round in the energy system. It groaned and slowed to a halt. The emergency lock down would give me another twenty minutes. Enough time to stay one step ahead of him. I hailed a cab.

"Nick's transceiver repair."

"Where's that?"

"What!?" I screamed. "Impossible. The wizard of the east side? You never heard of Nick. You never met the wizard? East side. Quick!"

Chapter 3.

Well, I ditched Browny. No big deal. He'd catch up with me sooner or later, and when he showed his face again I'd put the sorry mechanico out of misery. Parkenson was really trying to jerk me around. Sure, we'd have dinner at his place this week alright, and I'd be sure to give him a piece of my mind, sending an old friend in as a shadow. A badge couldn't have a shadow. It was in the Council bylaws. Well, even if it wasn't, it should be. The thought of a badge with a shadow made me sick. Who the hell did Parkenson think he was? My ear hurt, and I felt naked. I had to get that transceiver back in stat.

Nick's is over in the seedy part of town near the Five Dollar. I felt like a boomerang, and I wished I would have eaten a little of that Instant Feast. Duck sounded good. My stomach growled as I jumped out of the cab, paid the cabby, and hit the sidewalk. Parkenson's investigative squad was just finishing up the mess at the Five Dollar, and I didn't want to spend any time with that bunch. They knew me too well. I lifted my collar and walked right by and turned the corner. A badge's life was a series of sly moves. As usual, Nick's bulb burned bright.

Good old Nick, he kept the same trade mark for the last twenty years. No light fixture, no globe, but that single light bulb always burning. "Fiat Lux," Nick would say. They didn't make Fiat's anymore, and Lux detergent was a thing of the distant past before the war. Nick kept saving it anyway. 'Fiat Lux.' Someday, I'd ask him what that meant. For now, I let it be. I had important things on my mind. I needed Rex to analyze that poison napkin, and I needed Rex back in my ear.

Oh, the smell! It was green and damp and putrid. I kicked a bag of garbage. When were they going to settle that strike? Damn it! My boot got wet. Now, what the heck is this?

"Mister, dollar for a cup of coffee?"

Another beggar. Could be the twin of the one I just put a slug into. I pulled out my lighter and lit up a Royal Fourteen. Flipped him a hot coin. Ha, Ha! The smell of singed plastic. Pitiful creature. He smiled up at me with a toothless brown smile. I pushed past him and entered Nick's.

Nick's place had the cluttered look of a never ending job. A little path led through cardboard boxes to a counter where transceivers were scattered about. Shelves were stacked with parts. The place smelled like burned metal. An old man with white hair and a white beard was squinting into a microscope. He didn't look up.

I cleared my throat but he spoke first.

"Well, if it ain't Dick Phillips," he said without lifting his head. "Did you read the books I gave you?"

What books?

He lifted his head with an excited look. "Do you now understand ionic transmutation? Wasn't I right?"

"I haven't quite finished those books," I replied. "Good to see you Nick. What's new?"

"I just got an X1017!" he blurted.

"What's that?"

He made a fist and pulled it to him. "Yeah! She looks almost real. She bang. She's so sweet!"

"Err," I replied. "I'll have to check her out later, Nick." I pointed to my ear. "See this bandage."

"Your transceiver busted again?"

"Yeah." I replied. "You know," I continued with a question, "what the hell is the world coming to? Just now, a big freak sliced off my ear and crushed Rex's transceiver. It was a big beggar, kind of like the one sitting outside your shop."

Nick removed his spectacles and looked at me. His face had fine crisscrossed deep lines, making him look like an old prune. He leaned over and squint at me.

"Yeah," he said. "That funny looking monster's been sitting out there all morning. He delivered some parts from my supplier and stopped working and started squatting. I'm guessing he's mechanico. They're using them for everything these days."

He stopped chewing tobacco and spit toward a pot on the floor. "Damn," he said, and spit again. "Looks like they'll be taking over soon. Used to be they only cleaned up. Now, they're doing delivery. Times are changing."

"I know what you mean," I replied, "Browny. . ."

He interrupted me. "Hell with them! I tried to chase him away, but he said he was being paid to sit, some kind of assignment for the D."

"The D!" I cried and froze.

No. It had to be a mistake. My side cramped. I clutched my 44.80. The sound of that name crippled me. The D! I lunged back through the cardboard isle toward the door. In a second the sidewalk would be covered with beggar brains.

The sorry mechanico had disappeared. One thought on my mind. The D!

Nick helped me back in his shop. "Please," I said, "you must be wrong. It's a joke, isn't it? You're kidding me?" My good kidney hurt.

"No, that's what he said. He worked for the D."

"Agh! The D!" Knee jerk. But it was only a moment of weakness. I always flinched at that sound. My lost kidney and four years in electro torture took a toll. I cramped every time I remembered the D. It had taken years of my life to rid the world of that evil organization, and now they were back. It was impossible. They were destroyed.

"No good," Nick said, and tossed my transceiver into a cardboard box. "The tele-crystal's wrecked. You have to have a new one."

"Nick," I replied, "I'm a little sore on a case right now. Can't you rig up a used one for me?"

"For a Rex 1000? You're the one who had to have the top of the line."

His eyes looked blank for a second.

"Wait a minute," he said. "Something came in this morning."

Boy, I thought, the D! I couldn't believe it. Nick reached beneath the counter and pulled up a new box. Probably diamond studded.

"Brand new," he said, "just came in right before you got here. Lucky too, transceivers for the Rex series are back ordered six months. He looked up. "It cost me three grand, but I'll let you have it for eight."

"Four."

"Six"

"Five"

"Deal. Five grand. . . You got the cash?"

Cheap for a transceiver, I thought. Nick was always doing me favors. He was like Parkenson who thought of me as his son. Well, not a son, but family . . . a nephew. I coughed up my last five G's, thought about the Chinaman. If he didn't come through with another deposit, I was going to be eating a lot of Instant Feast.

"Okay, fit it in my ear, but be very, very careful. It's touchy. I'm not going back to the Med."

"Yeah," Nick whispered, "You might end up with your foot in your mouth. If you get my meaning."

"Huh! What?"

"Nothing," Nick replied. "It's going to take a second to tune your frequency. Why not put it in the other ear, instead of the sore one?"

"Ah, you know, I don't hear so well in that ear after the 'Case of the Exploding Honey Pot.' That ear always feels stuffed up."

"Rex at your service."

"Rex," I laughed, nodded, and smiled at Nick, "it's me."

"Me? Who's me?"

Damn it. "I'm running late. Cut the humor."

I turned to Nick as I left. "Nick, I've got to get going on my case."

Fingering my Johnson if the beggar from the D had returned, or Browny had tracked me down, I left Nick's. At the street, a shuttle was loading. I sat down between an old fart and a smelly kid. No Browny. The ad windows were full of dancing women, butterflies, and robot boys singing that irritating repeating song. I communicate to Rex.

"No more humor. Please, Rex. Status?"

"Five calls," he replied.

"Go."

"Twelve forty . . ."

"This is Cynthia. Let's get together for dinner tonight at my place. I'm making a quick feast, Instant Duck. I loved what you did to me last night . . . can't wait for more."

"Two fifteen. . . "

"This is Parkenson. Just commed to let you know I want you and your deb to come out on Wednesday night. The wife says she's going to serve quick feast, Instant Duck. Bet you haven't had that for awhile. By the way, I ran into your old friend, Browny. He says he is looking for you, and will catch up on old times pretty soon. Ha, ha."

"Catch up?" Was that a Parkenson joke? He laughed, but what was funny about it?

"Three thirty. . ."

"This is Lee Tsing. You know me. Over at the Five Dollar. Heard you around by Nick's. Want you to come by for dinner real soon, possible big job for you, business proposition. Big money, chop chop Dicky. Special dinner this week only. We serving quick feast, Instant Duck. Very rare."

Instant Duck. Instant Duck. How'd Tsing know I was at Nick's?

"Three forty. . . "

"This is Instant Med admin. We need payment immediate. You're behind three operations. We need another payment. Access denied until payment."

Oh great. I rolled my eyes. Now what happens if I get shot up? I really needed another payment from the Chinaman.

"Four twenty. . . "

"This is Pella . . . "

"Stop," I said.

The shuttle driver turned to me. You know the rules. We don't stop in mid route. Only at designated stops."

"I'm sorry," I replied. "Com . . ."

I held my hand to my ear. "Rex," I whispered, "draw up a complete profile on the D and have it available when I return. Repeat four twenty."

"Four twenty. . . "

"This is Pella. Long time no see, my brute. Call me seven H R five six zero nine zero nine."

Pella, I thought, my beautiful fascinating one. My love . . . alive? No, impossible. She'd been killed. I buried her. How? Impossible? Together, we'd destroyed the D, but in the horrendous, rat filled underground she'd been killed. Now, just to hear her voice again, and the D back in operation . . . my tortured kidney ached. My side hurt. Puke!

"Stop . . . Voice analysis."

"Pella Sannow," Rex replied in my ear.

So. She was still alive. My heart skipped.

"Continue coms."

"Last, four forty . . . ," Rex continued and then paused.

"In progress, Chinaman speaking now. . . "

"Meet me at the Hotel Meringue at five fifteen. I give you deposit of hundred thousand American begin the search.'"

"I'll be right there, China." I replied.

"Rex, please give me intent."

"Masked."

I jumped off the shuttle at Center Seventeen thinking about Pella. How could I call her after all this time? I still loved her, but what about Cynthia? I waited for the north east shuttle to the Hotel Meringue to meet the Chinaman. Monkeys everywhere at this stop. We called them that. They all looked the same in their nice button down collars and three piece suits. Off work, they were headed toward local watering holes in herds. There was always too many of them at center Seventeen.

Could I even speak to Pella after all this time? Dare I even think about her? I was glad when the north east headed out. Pella alive?

The old sector was just what it sounded like. Old. If you lived long enough to become demented, they hauled you off to places like the Hotel Meringue. They used to call them old folks homes or convalescent hospitals. They were always just places to die. Nobody died at home. Death came in the street or in old folks' homes, in accidents, or with a bullet in the head. From what I'd seen of the old folks' homes, I hoped I took a slug in the head rather than die with a tube in my stomach.

Life's short. There used to be a song before the war. What was that line? 'Better to burn out than to fade away.' The Medicos were the faded old doctors from years before. Why the Insta Meds keep them alive, I'll never know. Politics . . . hard to understand. The Medicos against the Insta Meds, the Council against the Medicos. You were lucky to be a cop, privileged to be a badge like me.

As the north east shuttle ground along, my mind flashed back to Pella. Yes, she was a traitor. She deserted me, and I lost her. If I hadn't hated the D so bad, we would still be together. How could she still be alive? I couldn't figure it. I'd seen her buried, toes up. She wasn't coming back. Something was going on. The mystery around the Chinaman case was building. I could feel the intrigue. Pain shot through my kidney. I shivered. I wanted to dial up Pella immediate. I commed to Rex, but stopped. That was a rule I never broke. Business was business. Business before pleasure. When I worked on a case, I worked on that case. Yet, in the back of my mind I knew there was connection.

The money was very important. Now, if I didn't pay the Insta Meds, and somebody did me, they wouldn't even keep me alive as a pitiful mechanico. Not that I would want that, but occasionally, I did need my ears sewed back on. What if a Billy Boy was on the hunt for me? What if they canceled my credits? Without credits I wouldn't be able to ride the shuttle. How could I carry on with my debutante? I needed credits. The ancient Himalayan waited for me at the Hotel Meringue. He had the money, but who was he really?

It loomed through the haze. The Hotel Meringue's great tall green pillar stood erect, a tribute to the money of the faded Medicos. How often before the war as a young man had I drunk wine and gone crazy in those seedy rooms when the Meringue had been central?

Before the service, before the war, before becoming a speed racer . . . in those days I had been young and wild. Still young and wild, I thought and laughed. The scar near my left eye always hurt when I laughed. Young, ha! The Medicos owned the Hotel Meringue, but the Insta Meds controlled.

Dying old Medicos lived out their lives in tiny little rooms decorated with pictures of flowers. The Insta Meds kept the Medicos alive, probably for some nefarious reason like stealing their minds. Like the proud old dynamic Medicos, my youth and the Hotel Meringue had made similar transformations. They'd had gone from central to distant. Today, the Insta Meds and their head removal operation dominated the scene. As the shuttle pulled up, I could see some things were still the same.

"Jackson," I said to the doorman, "Do you remember me?"

"Well," he replied and pulled up his old body. The brass buttons straightened on his blue uniform. He brushed off his caplets and tucked his white gloves to his hands.

I lit a Royal Fourteen.

"Let me see," he said. "You be Mr. Dick Phillips. You smoke Black Knights and you drive Miss Pella to the park in the afternoons."

Not anymore, Jackson," I said and pulled hard on the fag. "Now, it's Royal Fourteens and Miss Pella's gone."

He nodded . . . kind of listening, kind of drifting off.

"How long has it been?"

"At least forty years," he replied. "Been here at the Hotel for forty years now."

I tossed him the pack. "Here, you smoke the rest."

"Same young Mr. Dick," he replied and held the door open for me. "You find the Himalayan behind the elevator between three and four."

The lobby was full of old Medicos. Most of them were wearing their white smocks over slacks and ties. Most of them were senile or demented. The Hotel had gone from the top joint to an old folks home in just a few years . . . perhaps, it had been more than a few years. It stank clean as a hospital. Unlike the Insta Meds, even in senility the Medicos never allowed any filth or stink.

I pushed the button on the elevator and the old door creaked open. How long had it really been? Could it have been that many years since I was Pella's driver? The war, the riots, the murders, things had changed, but somehow I knew our secret room hidden behind the elevator was still safe. Did it still smell like the jasmine flowers Pella and I collected from the living park that used to exist on street sixty five?

As the elevator jiggled slowly up, I thought about Pella. She and I had been in love from the first. The hidden room was our hiding place. I wondered if the yellow light bulb still glowed so brightly. What was the Chinaman doing there?

I stopped the elevator exactly two seconds after it passed the third floor. It groaned to a stop and lurched. For an instant I didn't think it would hold, and then it caught. The secret door unhinged with a shove, perhaps too easily. Someone had just used it. I loosened my Johnson and pushed through the door.

"Okay, Himalayan," I said in the darkness. "If you don't speak up, I'm going to dump my Johnson all over this room."

A fire flickered and a candle was lit.

"Put your gun away," he said.

He sat at the round table with a pot of tea warmed in a wicker basket. From the flickering candle light I could see the room was dusty but much the same as it had been years ago. He filled two cups.

"Come, sit with me," he said in his soft old voice. "Fifty thousand American just to listen. If you accept, it will mean seven hundred thousand dollars when you are successful."

"What if I'm not successful?"

His body seemed translucent. He smiled. "You will be dead. There is very little time. Evil now takes control of the world. Soon, everyone in the world will be under the domination of the D."

The D!

I put the Johnson back in my holster and sat down. The D, I thought. But what did the old Chinaman know about the D? "If it's the D," I said, "you won't have to pay me. I'll kill them all for free. I hate the D!"

He sipped his tea. "That, my young friend," he replied, "would probably be impossible. Listen closely. I have proposition. Listen to my story."

So slowly, so very slowly as if it were a snake uncurling its head, my 44.80 came out of its holster. No need to hide it. I pointed the pig nose directly at the head of the Chinaman. With both hands on the butt, I straightened out my arms and focused on his face.

"This better be good, China. Or you're dead."

It's the story. When it gets interesting, then you die. Not me.

I began to smile. It kind of came up in me from far away. The feeling was inside of me, inside my head. Not tee hee. Not guffaw. It was my smile of death. A story. I could feel the story. I had to be aware. I didn't trust that Chinaman. It could be a trap.

Death, dark, ugly, and stinking stalked the hidden room behind the elevator. The feeling was exactly the opposite as when Pella and I made love so many years before. Here was the old Chinaman, sitting peacefully in his robe, drinking tea and Jasmine seemed to fill the air. Yet now, now I was with Pella again. She was in my arms. The Chinaman was casting a spell. In a second he'd be a bloody corpus.

He had a funny way of speaking. He could look at you and kind of move his head around. He didn't do it so it looked like it was on

35

purpose. It wasn't on purpose, but immediately I saw he was trying to hypnotize me, or . . . he wasn't. But he wasn't, that was for sure!

I smiled. He didn't seem bothered by the presence of my large gun at his brain. He just kept on moving his head and telling the story. I guess it was the money. I know it was the money. Seven hundred thousand American meant a lot to me.

"Chinaman," I said, "if you move anything more than that yo-yo head, you're brains will be smeared all over this room."

"Money," he replied, "is very important."

He seemed to stutter.

"Money is very important," he said, and stacked a wad of bills on the table.

I felt a bead of sweat run down my cheek. There was silence.

After a moment he spoke. "You are Dick Phillips, master private eye and licensed killer for the Council. I am Da Mo, the Eternal. I have been an immortal man for over five thousand years. You can not kill me with a gun. Your Johnson 44.80 would jam, or the bullets would go around me. You can not defeat me with your hands. I am master of Tai Chi, Chi Kung, Iron Shirt Kung Fu, and all forms."

He lowered his head, and I had to lean toward him to hear him whisper. The story gets interesting, then you get killed. My finger itched on the trigger as the China whispered.

"But now I am dying," he said. "The Ching Da has been stolen from its sacred place, and my magic is slowly being drained . . . but now, still, you could not kill me."

I smiled at the old fart. Wearily, his head rocked back and forth. I must look a lot dumper than I am.

"You still think you can kill me," he said. "Don't you?"

At that moment I could have killed him with my body odor, a misspoken word, a stupid joke, my hands, the Mandrake claw, or the Johnson. He never saw the way I looked when I got up in the morning, or after a good night drinking, either. Yet, he may have been right. There was something about him. He looked almost too weak to speak.

"But you can't! Try as hard as you can, you can't kill me."

I couldn't be hypnotized. Many have tried. My finger . . . put pressure on the trigger.

"But you can't. You are a brave person, Dick Phillips. That scar on your face came from the 'Escapade of the Invisible Plant.' You were once in love with Pella Sannow. You used this room to make love, didn't you?"

I didn't nod. I didn't dare. Pella overcame my thoughts. I was alone again in the room with her. I tightened the trigger.

"You see," he stuttered, "I know you. You are me, just like me. I have killed. You have killed. I know you. That is why I have chosen you to save the world from Him. You must return the Ching Da to me. It is imperative!"

You couldn't help but like this guy, what with all the compliments he was giving me. But how did he know so much about me? It was tempting. I mean the situation. My saliva tasted metallic. The money on the table. All that green. Pull trigger. I heard it in my mind. Do it. Just pinch it off. I resisted.

All I had to do was pull the trigger. What the hell, I thought. A bird in the hand is worth two in the bush. The money looked good and green. Fifty thousand sitting right there in front of me. The money called out. Dick. Come and get me, Dick. Do him! What the hell.

Hell, it wasn't the whole seven hundred thousand, and I would be doing a client. It wouldn't be the first time. I tightened my finger on the trigger.

"Wait!" He shouted. "I have something to tell you."

I paused. "Go ahead."

"D! The D are at the bottom of this. They are still active. They have stolen the Ching Da. It is the magical vessel which holds my never ending elixir of life. Soon the D will discover how to use it, and evil will rule the world."

The D. I hated the D! I cringed at the sound of D-men. From this elevator room many plans had been made to destroy them. Pella screwed me on the plans. Well, anyhow, we did it in so many place we must have done it on the plans. I know we did it on the floor and the table and the bed. I started to cry inside. The memories! Oh, the memories.

The hidden bomb. The card trick. The invisible door. It took planning and perseverance, but we acted. Then the four years in captivity, electro torture, my lost kidney. The evil D killed Pella! The bastards shoved her in front of an underground train. On the tracks, her beautiful loins torn to shreds.

My head hurt. Pella gone! The pain of it. The memories. Hand to hand with D-1. Ah yes, D-1. His deformed face loomed in my thoughts. But finally I destroyed them and personally smashed his brains. So many years ago it's all some distant foggy, clouded memory. Until now, I thought the D were history.

Time seemed to stop.

My missing kidney hurt. The Chinaman looked like he was serious. I figured the hypnotism was just his way. Probably, some disease. I wanted the money on the table, but the seven hundred thousand was more inviting. I slacked off.

"Okay, old man," I said, and rocked in the seat across from him. "Let's hear your story."

The old sapient put his hand to his head and took a deep breath. With his eyes sparkling he started.

"I am Da Mo, the Eternal," he said eloquently, and then he paused and composed himself. "I was born an Indian prince. I was a Buddha. I taught secrets to the Shoaling Priests. In China, I discovered the magical elixir of the gods. It took time to develop a formula, almost my whole first lifetime, but I succeeded and I did it. I captured the eternal essence and formulated it into a liquid. It regenerates itself and it regenerates me. It is never exhausted. You drink from the Ching Da, and there is still more. The more you drink, the more there is of it. It keeps me alive."

The Chinaman's face crinkled. "Someone I trusted deeply," he said and straightened. He slammed his hand on the table, and his face turned bright red. "Someone I trusted has stolen the Ching Da!"

My stomach told me Mandrake style. I twirled to the left, the Johnson slammed into my right hand. My left hand formed the unmistakable claw of instant death . . . the Mandrake claw. There was no stopping. When I felt it in my hara, in my solar plexus, I automatically flew into killer mode. The feeling of hatred exuding from the eternal Chinaman set me off. In less than an instant, he would be dead meat.

"Calm down detective Phillips," he said as he slumped back on the chair. "I need the Ching Da to live. The world needs me and you to remove it from the hands of the Evil One. I feel their power building. Soon, the D will have its way . . . with everyone."

He looked at me with begging eyes. "You must help me save the world."

I don't calm down that fast, and out of the corner of my eye I noticed the green wad of bills on the table. Before the old man could react, I plucked the money from in front of him as if it were fruit on the end of a tree limb. The 44.80 slipped back to its holster. I picked up the money.

"All right," I said and reached out to shake his hand, but the Chinaman had vanished.

The little room was totally empty, like my brain. I didn't know what to think. It was imperative that I get back to the office. I could feel a slimy cold around me torturing me like the D had done. God, I hated them. I swore again to myself that if they were in existence, I wouldn't stop until I killed every single one of them. And if that monster D-1 were still alive, I would do him by firing a round directly into this brain. This felt like déjà vu. I'd sworn this twenty five years before. The D were history. Hadn't I done D-1? That old noise rose in my brain. His insipid laughter haunted me.

The room swirled mystically. First, it was pitch dark. Then, figures seem to project out of my twisted mind. The Chinaman was gone. I was alone with evil gnawing my brain. I pushed back the old door to enter the elevator, but it wouldn't move. The panel wouldn't budge. It was solid wall. What happened to the hidden escape route?

I don't know fear. But in the darkness, the slimy cold started to penetrate my inner core. The old sore opened for an instant, and face to face in front of me, Dr. Blood! His hideous face with the blue blood vein pulsing on his bald head caused me to writhe in pain. For about the time it takes to catch a train of thought, Dr Blood crossed my mind. Absurd! Yet, could he be behind all of this?

I knew that room behind the elevator. I'd made love to Pella in the old days and had lived there in hiding from the D. In desperation I struck out where the Chinaman had been sitting. My hand burst through a thin screen. So, it had all been trickery, a holographic projection. Intrigue surrounded me like a hot fog on a warm summer night.

I pushed through the screen with my 44.80 ready to blaze, but only the musty odor of dust and sticky tangs of spider webs filled the vacant hiding place. This was where Pella and I did the in and out many times in hot sweat, our young bodies coming again and again. A pain in my heart tore through me. I'd loved her and now she was gone. Reliving all the feelings I'd ever felt and then, suddenly, in front of me stood Da Mo.

I raised my Johnson. No one tricked Dick Phillips.

"You remember Pella," he said and waved his hand.

She sat on the tiny bed and called to me. She beckoned with her sly smile and motioned for me to come. Her fingers seemed to make symbols and intertwine. She was a tantric lover draped in diaphanous silk. Wet with sweat, she motioned to me. Animal. Goddess. Whore. Hypnotic!

It is always the story. Could be one line, or a vision, a trance. Everything was hypnotism. Dad used to say it. Look at that Dicky, then he'd slap me a good one. Again and again. When I moved my attention away from what was important, he'd slap me hard. Sure it was cruel. As a kid, I hated it. But it trained me. If the story took your attention, you were dead.

I didn't have to pull very hard on the trigger. The technicians at the Johnson factory balanced it. It was fine-tuned for my personal intent. The thought of firing it, and it would explode in multiple rounds.

I blasted the Chinaman.

It felt good. The 44.80 always heated up a bit. It was a nice little heater. What the hell, I did a client. That left me with only three more kills for the month. However, it might be a very long time before Parkenson and his boys found out about this one. I'd be paying a little more tax, but who had to know. I had fifty thousand. Too bad about the seven hundred grand. Nobody messes with me.

My mouth was dry and my skin felt prickly. For some reason Dr. Blood's ugly puss crossed my mind. I shivered and gripped the Johnson 44.80 . . . hard. Slid it in and out of the holster. If I ever figured out how he opened those time holes and escaped, I'd set his arrival destination to be my Mandrake claw. I'd remove the top of his skull and have a closer look at what made him tick. Someday I'd let that bad brain know who Dick Phillips really was. I had it with him. Now, no more nice guy. Not that I ever was. I flicked open my lighter and fired up a smoke. Yeah, a Royal Fourteen always tasted good after a kill.

Well, it had been an interesting, but short case. Didn't get the seven hundred grand but I might have enough to pay off my accounts. I'd be seeing Parkenson, that was for sure. And Browny . . . man! I was going to give Parkenson a wheelbarrow full. A badge could not have a tail. Nothing seemed to make sense anymore. Of course, really, it never did. What about those three humpbacks in the 'Case of the Stinky Tail?' Or the when the eyes blew out in the 'Case of the Rotating Mask of Death.' What about those two transvestite twirling dervish without underwear?

When I got the candle burning, the room lit up. I laughed to myself. Tiny shack of a place. The fragrance of Jasmine, a bed, small table, dust, and spider webs. I laughed. Evil? What a joke. Who cared? Did anyone even give a damn?

As the candle flickered, I could see that Da Mo's body was . . .

Chapter 4.

Gone!

There was no body. No Da Mo. Apparently it was all smoke and mirrors. In the flickering candle light I found the real trick door and worked my way out the secret shaft. I pondered the case. Sometimes, I am a little impulsive. Perhaps I did underestimate the Chinaman's powers. The shaft was a tight squeeze even for a young man. Which I wasn't.

Damn it! I pushed through the grate and landed in the lobby. Old Medicos wheeled about. Screams came from rooms down bleak hallways. Ancient doctors cried out, crying for help, for help with their dying. No one noticed as I fell from the ventilation grating. I crawled to a chair and caught my breath. If I would have been wearing a tie and a white smock, I might have been an old Medico.

But I wasn't. I was a badge.

Anyway, I needed to get back to the office. Big night tonight with Cynthia, my debutante. I hoped I didn't have to fight off fat Linda. Those tits were nice, but she was just too large. As I walked toward the entrance of the Hotel Meringue, it dawned on me that I was like an old Medico. The lights were on, but no one was home. I tried to kill my client. What was I thinking?

Not much. That's how disordered my thoughts were when I stepped out on the sidewalk in front of the Hotel Meringue. It seemed to be raining plaster. Then I heard the sonic.

Kram! The explosion of a Zeno miniature cannon.

More plaster. The hotel rocked and the ground shook.

Kram! Another explosion.

I jumped back in the doorway. Another blast. The Meringue was under attack. Another Kram! I leaped like a frog and ran like hell.

Jackson, the old doorman, looked at me with a kind, fatherly bent as his guts exploded. A warm red liquid splattered over my face and clothes. The poor man tossed his head back with a smile on his face, and his eyes froze as his head knocked down on the concrete. A portion of his gut and one hand came at me in slow motion.

Kram! Kram!

Nowhere to hide. Brick and fascia and plaster falling everywhere. People on the street being crushed, blown up. Rounds coming in. Only one chance, the underground.

Locked gate, I climbed over quickly. Then I heard it. A missile screamed over my head into the sealed opening of the underground. They were firing on me, trying to kill me.

Whoever they were, they were after me.

Kram!

The bricked up opening to the underground collapsed. The only escape route opened before me into the darkness of the dreaded underground.

You didn't go in the underground. The rails had been sealed long ago, but still the worst of humanity slept at the openings. The Zeno discharge blasted a hole big enough to climb through, and as I descended, I almost retched. It stank dank of years filled with piss and red wine. I hesitated. You didn't go into the underground. Creatures lived there. Inhuman creatures.

Kram! Another discharge.

Whoever was chasing me was gaining. In a moment they would be on top of me. If they had Zenos they also had shields. My 44.80 would be useless. No telling what I would find in the darkness of the underground, but I knew my fate if I lingered. I checked my pouch.

Luckily, I always carry proximities. These little beauties go off when anyone gets within ten feet. I set a megger and dove through the smoldering opening in the wall. Whoever came this way next would be . . . to use an old term, blown to smithereens. I raced away from the opening, running along a concrete ledge that had been a platform for the trains. I ran for about a hundred feet then too dark. Had to feel my way. Inching along, hand to foot, inching.

The megger blew. It knocked me off the cement. As I careened through the air, at least now, I thought, I would be safe. Of course, that was relative safeness. You didn't go in the underground.

Ouch!

The rail and the ground hit me hard. I felt like a straw going through a telephone pole in a hurricane. I hit with a thud. A steel rail punched my ribs so hard it made an impression like Big Hangus doing his imitation of an old queen on Level Seven. Hurt so bad just to be alive.

Who was behind this attack? Why had I been driven underground?

The stinking underground. You didn't go there. Yet, here I was. My head rang worse than after drinking ten super ionosonics and my side ached bad, real bad. I struggled to stand and tried to remember who I was and where I was, but my memory echoed in an empty bucket. The Chinaman, the Hotel Meringue, Jackson blown up, I dove into the opening to the underground. Darkness. The heart of darkness in an empty bucket.

I came to, and I came to fast. I could feel them stalking me.

"Ouch!" I put my hand to my neck. Searing pain.

Darkness everywhere. Still, I could feel them.

Newt! Flesh eating lizards. Red eyed Saurians. Fangs. Eyes that glowed in the darkness. They were all around me. I could feel them waiting, checking me, salivating, ready to attack and eat if I should stumble. Skink everywhere. But there in the darkness a small flickering glow. I crawled to it.

Walking, thinking . . . lizards, genetically produced to cure the world of disease, the experiment had gone sour. They were driven underground. Deformed Saurian! Now, as I dragged my bruised, broken body toward the growing glow at the end of the tunnel, I could sense the Newt everywhere. Saurian. They ate human flesh and soon they would be on me. They never ate the body, just the flesh. They peeled you like tin can laser. Too many of them. Thousands of red eyes. I was dead flesh.

Then I heard it, the high twine of a mobile generator.

44

A rough voice commanded, "Switch it. Switch it now!"

I hunched behind a pile of iron tracks as a bright glow lit the tunnel. Thousands of lizards, rough skinned, fang dripping, and salivating, ugly . . . saurian retreated to the darkness. I would never be a meal for them.

"Hit the transformer. Now!"

D-men!

With muscles bulging under red and black uniforms, they worked with slow deliberate movements. These weren't the D-men killers. No, they were the technicians. They all looked the same, replications of D-1, but the technicians moved slower than the killers. Of course, even the slower technicians could rip out your heart.

Hate them. I squinted. Hate them. They hadn't spotted me, and in the open they were sitting ducks. I fingered my 44.80 and stepped into the glowing red light.

"Die!" I screamed.

The first one flung his wrench, and the second one jumped at me, flipping over and over. The other two took fighting formations. The first one froze in tiger style. The second one raised his palms in monkey style. But it was too late for all of them.

The Johnson snaked alive in my hand. I liked that. I smiled. Now, I felt good. I laughed as the first D-man's chest blew up, and then as the other's head blew off. A clean shot through the neck of the third one, and the forth one's guts emptied on the ground. Four perfect shots. My aim was swift. Like oil and water, a badge and D-men didn't mix. They had to die.

No time to gloat over perfect shots. The magna generator lit the platform. All around strange instruments fluxed, pinged, and vibrated. Then it hit me. Unbelievably, I'd stumbled on a D-man time-space continua. Sure, I'd read stories about this science, about Scaler waves, free energy and time displacement. But they were always rumors, until now.

An orange glowing portal about ten feet in diameter floated in space right in front of me. A portal to some time and space . . . I wasn't sure. It could be a death trap. If it opened to the underground when trains ran, it would mean certain death. To land on the tracks at the wrong time. Squish!

The sound came in stereo. From both ends of the tunnel, from the darkness, came the sounds of D-men and their red mongrel hunting dogs, bred specially to rip out badges' hearts. No time to lose. I set the timers on my two final proximity bombs. When the D-men squads arrived, the whole lot of them and the time travel machinery and the rest of it all would be blown to hell. That meant there would be no returning. Where ever and whenever the destination, the glowing time portal was my escape, but I'd be stuck there. Most likely there would be no return. My arm and my ear and my neck hurt. No time to be a crybaby. I raised my Johnson.

"Mandrake claw form!"

Now, I was ready for anything. The squads of D-men closed in. I took a deep breath and jumped. The orange portal flashed.

Sonabitch!

Diarrhea!

Cosmic diarrhea!

Then ram, flushed through the tube, a bag of bones and blood and all the memories of the lives of every poor mechanico whose life Dick Phillips ever snuffed shoved up my brains and twisted and pulled out with a sharp stick . . . so hard, so hard, out the black hole of the universal rectum twisted backwards double flip and falling.

The ground hit me like a ton of steel fists. I froze. Dazed.

Flashing lights. Roaring trains. A long whistle. Bright lights from a platform. Women screaming. Sparks flying. Metal grinding on metal. Fireworks. A hand pulled my arm.

"Help you up, mate?"

A strong young man wrenched me to the platform. It was Browny.

I flashed the Johnson to do him as promised, but quickly returned it to its holster. He was a younger Browny, a Browny I'd known many years ago.

We walked quickly through the crowd on the landing, through the turnstile and as we rounded a corner and made the stairs an explosion closed the time portal. Smoke followed us onto the street. There were cars, and people walking, and trees. It was a time before the war.

"Say mate," Browny asked. "What's the skinny?"

"About ten inches, and it ain't skinny."

"No, I mean with that orange glow and that explosion. What were you doing on the tracks?"

"Thanks for helping me up. Oh, you know, I work for the city. It was a gas leak. It's a risky job. Hope nobody got hurt."

I wondered if the past held the solution to the Chinaman case. More important, how was I going to get back to my time?

Browny had a question on his face. "Don't I know you?"

We were safe now. The explosion sealed the D-men time passage. As we walked, I noticed the neighborhood looked familiar. In fact, we were right around the corner from the Hotel Meringue. We walked and talked.

"What?"

"I wonder," Browny said and paused. "I know your name, but I can't remember it. What is it again?"

"I haven't changed much," I joked, "since the last time we met. I'm Richard Phillips. Dick Phillip's dad. You remember me, don't you? I look a lot like him . . . a little better looking, don't you think?"

"Try not to," Brown replied. "Gets me into trouble."

"You're a friend of his, aren't you? If I remember right, he lives somewhere near here. Doesn't he have a place at the Hotel Meringue? He's Pella Sannow's driver."

Browny smiled his wide grin. This was before he lost his front tooth and his teeth were white as ivory.

"That's right," he said. "You're Dick Phillip's dad. Pleased to meet you, err . . . again."

"What's your name?" I asked rhetorically.

"You can call me Browny."

We walked past shops and little bistros. It was pleasant before the war. We walked east toward the Hotel Meringue.

"Where'd you get that name? You been sticking your nose someplace funny? You a candy ass? What?"

"Yeah," he replied, "I been looking for love in all the wrong places." He hesitated.

"You really are Dick's dad, aren't you? You got the same warped sense of humor. Seriously, they call me Browny because I always carry a chocolate brownie. Want one?"

As he handed it to me, I started a brown study, or it was a Brownian movement. We walked and talked and nibbled our cookies. Deep in thought, I started feeling depressed. I knew this fine young man would end up with a dying head on a mechanical body. And I knew I'd be the one to give him a final curtain call.

Yet, the air was unpolluted and there were real trees everywhere. Men and women were holding hands, birds were flying. On leashes, dogs barked. The air smelled clean. It was a fine feeling being with young Browny, like the good old days when we were pals. We walked, and talked, and soon turned down the alley of the Hotel Meringue.

"Say," he said, "why don't we play a fine trick on old Dicky. You and me can sneak up the back way to his flat and spy on him. He's probably making it with Pella right now. We can catch a peek."

"Browny!"

"What?"

"That's rude. Very rude."

"Come on, we can use the fire escape."

He jumped up and pulled down a rope and then the metal ladder followed.

"You go first," he said. "It's a good joke. They won't even see us. It'll be funny."

Rung after rung, flesh on steel; we climbed toward the eighth floor apartment. I couldn't remember being surprised by my older self and Browny. Therefore, I knew at this time I would not run into my younger self. The generator and the time gate had been destroyed so I knew the D weren't following us. The path of least resistance led to my old apartment. From experience, I know when a clue will appear. I could feel it coming.

At the eighth floor landing, we crouched near the window. I touched Browny's arm and looked at the young man. Poor son of a bitch. All we had gone through when Dr. Marsall's brain blew up. I felt the puke rise in my throat at the thought of Browny being a mechanico. He cleaned the window with his cuff.

"Look," he said.

Inside, I was lying on the bed with Pella. That is, a younger Dick Phillips and Pella were lying on the bed, talking. And excuse me, but boy was that one good looking Dick. I could hear them.

"I love you," Pella said, "but this is bigger than our love. No matter what, the D must be destroyed."

"Absolutely!" Dick replied and embraced Pella in a passionate kiss. He began to unbutton her blouse.

Browny seemed embarrassed. He started back down the ladder, and motioned for me to follow and then tugged at my pants. As he descended, I gazed through the window, fascinated by the lovers. I didn't remember ever meeting an older me. I had never been surprised in my apartment by myself. Should I go down, I thought. Follow Browny? For a second, my mind was blank. This caused a reflex action and my hand shot for the Johnson, but it seemed to move in slow motion.

What if I knocked on the window? What if I busted in on myself and Pella? Would I be changing time? Was this the reason circumstance had brought me to this moment? Would two Dick's in one room be one too many? Would the Cosmos explode?

Whatever. It had to happen fast. As I stared at the young couple, Dick saw me peeping at them. I had to move fast. At that time, as a young man, I carried a Sterling 16 strapped to my leg. I was quick then, so there was no choice. In a second young Dick would be firing through the widow. Instantly, it occurred to me young Dick and Pella's plan had failed. The D still existed. A new plan formed in my mind. I was going to need a partner. I pushed open the window and moved to the side, out of gun range.

"Dick! Pella!" I said. "I need to talk to you."

The reflection of my face in the dirty widow was like waking up in the morning from a dream with a hot poker in your underwear. It's real. Something sets off your mind and the memory rises to the surface. I remembered everything.

I'd been brain-washed. Pella hadn't died. She was still alive, alive in my time. The D wiped my mind clean. They brain washed me and caused me to forget that an older me visited me. I'd been captured and my mind altered to help them with their evil plans. Or, then again . . . not! It was a kind of déjà vu. My memory returned. Or was I creating that memory now? It didn't matter.

I jumped in the window with my 44.80 alive. My exact aim blew the Sterling out of my younger hands. I remembered it all. I remember thinking, whoever this guy was; he was a damn good shot.

"Freeze!" I commanded. "I'm you! I mean, you're me!"

Time seemed to stop.

"I've come from the future, thirty years from now."

The younger me whispered to Pella. "I can take him. He's old."

Her green eyes flashing, Pella jumped between us with hands akimbo. "Get out!" She yelled at me. "Whoever you are, get out!"

She was beautiful, even more than I remembered. Her fiery green eyes erupted out of a Malaysian brown face circled by long dark black hair. Her nipples pointed up through clothes that clung tight to her body. I stared at her for an instant but kept my Johnson pointed at my young head. I wondered. If I killed my younger self, would I disappear?

"Don't move, Dick." I said. "Or, I'll blow out your brains."

Pella studied me. "You are Dick Phillips." She looked at both of us. "You're both Dick Phillips." She turned to the young me. "It is you, Dick. It really is you."

"Nonsense!" the younger me replied. "It's a trick of the D."

The more he looked me over, the more he seemed to withdraw, to loose energy and fade out. It was as if his energy was being channeled back to me. Perhaps my maturity sucked his life energy. Or when you see yourself as you really are, it's impossible to focus on yourself, especially your older self. It didn't bother me. I liked looking at me.

The D hadn't been destroyed, but how did the Chinaman fit in all this? Was evil really taking over the world? I had seen Pella killed. Were my memories real? Was Pella actually was alive in my time? Was it the older or younger Pella who commed me in my time? This case was developing to equal the 'Case of the Rotating Mask of Death.'

I sighted my young self and Pella over the nose of my Johnson, while these thoughts crossed my mind; then a new thought struck me like lightening on a rainy summer night. Steam furled out my ear. Why hadn't I thought of it before? I commed to Rex.

"Rex," I said, "messages?"

Perhaps, if there were another time door somewhere in this time, I would be able to communicate with Rex.

I waited. No response. Then I corrected myself. "Rex, please, any messages?"

"Two thirty," he replied, "Parkenson."

"Pick up a bottle of wine before you come out to the house. We'll be eating at seven thirty sharp. Harriet says don't be late. Remember, it's duck, Instant Feast."

Yahoo! Rex on line. That meant there was another time opening somewhere in this time and I could return. Then another thought crossed my mind. Why return? Seven hundred thousand green American cancelled that thought. I needed the money. Besides I was a badge. I was sworn to fight evil.

Time seemed to stop as I faced Pella and my younger self and Rex commed my ear.

"Three fifteen," Rex continued.

"This is Cynthia. Hi baby. I'll be ready at seven wearing my see through like I promised. . . . Later. you can do me good. Toots."

"Four forty five."

"Kee Man Laundry. You shirts ready."

My finger itched. No one moved. Rex continued.

"Four forty six."

"Instant Med. No more operations until you pay your bills."

"Five."

"Da Mo. Desperately need your help. Have more money. Meet me at the five dollar in twenty minutes."

Okay. There was another opening back to my time. Had it recently opened, or was it part of a D-man transport system from this time to my time? Since Rex was on line, somewhere in the underground or the city there was an open time portal.

"Listen!" I commanded my younger self, "I don't have much time to explain. Your plan to defeat the D won't work. In the future, in my time, they are still active. We have to work together. It's the only way."

My younger Dick was overwhelmed. It wasn't like me at all. He, I mean me, seemed to shrink back from myself, but Pella moved closer to me. She moved into my space and wrapped her arms around me and kissed me a long wet kiss. While we kissed, she rubbed her hand down my legs, and I started to get big and hard. I kept my eyes focused on my younger self. It had been years since I had Pella, since those dark red lips touched mine. I longed for her. I wanted her. I wanted it bad.

"I'm going to the future with you," she cried. "You're the Dick I always loved. I don't know why. You're bigger and stronger. You're real! I want you! I love you!"

"Bitch!" my younger self cried.

She looked at the young me and then looked at me.

"I want you," she panted. "It's immediate. It's you I've always loved. We'll defeat the D together."

She ran her fingers over the scar on my face. She touched my hair. "Older, meaner, more attractive, powerful."

This was an unusual turn. If she wanted to come to the future with me, she was coming. Together, we could finish the D. Perhaps I could save her from the fate I knew waited for her under the steel wheels of the train in the underground. Had I already changed her fate? I looked deeply into her beautiful eyes, and again I smelled her scent so dark and musty. How long had it been? I felt a twinge in my loins just as young Dick lunged.

Chapter 5.

Like a mad dog with a snarl on its face, its back straight up, bloody fangs extended, glazed red eyes, Dick Phillips dove at me. One fist of iron and the other of steel, he showed his blood lust smile and gave a familiar demonic cry. This was before 'The Escapade of the Magical Hand,' before I obtained the Mandrake claw. Young Dick didn't yet know he would be trained in the mysteries of Ryang-jin. He didn't know yet half of what I had learned. Compared to me, in my rage, he was a baby. He flew at me like a wild pup deprived of a bone.

I bitch slapped him, pushed him down, and pulled Pella to me, and barked at him.

"Don't try and stop us! Don't follow us!" I added. "Damn it, you know I'll kill for her."

Holding Pella's sweet meat near me, and holding my 44.80 on young Dick, we backed out the little window onto the landing. My mind felt muddy. I wondered if it would ever get clear since I was removing and creating fresh memories at lightening speed. Why did Pella come so quickly with me? I knew I was attractive, but I didn't remember it happening. No wait, that's right, the D wiped my mind. She did leave me when I was young. Or did she? It seemed I was creating a new personal history. It didn't matter. The sound of our feet on the metal landing and the feel of the steel rungs of the ladder, her breath next to my face, the warmth of her breasts on to my chest, the fresh air, these were real. As we descended hand over hand down the fire escape, I balanced the Johnson in one hand, Pella close to me, and one eye on the window above. In a second young Dick would have his Sterling.

I remembered that Pella and I defeated the D with the help of Browny and Parkenson. Then I discovered she was a traitor. But now I realized that those memories weren't true, that my mind had been brain washed, and the D were carrying out an extraordinarily sinister plan to rule the world. Pella wasn't a traitor. She hadn't died in the underground under the wheels of a train. She was alive in my time, waiting for me. Was this all true, or was I changing history?

Spring! Sprang!

Bullets ricocheted . . .

Sprang!

. . . Off the grating of the landing above us.

Sprang!

Another shot rang off the metal. My younger self was willing to kill me to get Pella back. But could I take the chance of killing him? If I killed myself, I might disappear from time. Private eye investigation in time is very complicated. My Johnson, for once, was silent. I could have dumped it on the younger me, but I dare not. It was a risk I couldn't take.

Pella jumped to the pavement.

"Which way?" she screamed.

We hit the ground running. "Get to the underground."

Out the alley, we rounded the corner and ran along the street through the smell of fresh brewed coffee, past the small umbrellas, and past the tables with little cups and hot rolls. There, ahead, the opening to the underground.

Pella shot me a look.

"Dick will be right behind us," she said.

As we came to the opening of the underground, I put my hand on Pella's shoulder. We faced each other. Over thirty years younger than me, yet somehow the love was intense and immediate.

"Look," I said, "this is going to be dangerous. Not only will young Dick be chasing us, but in my time things have changed."

"What do you mean?"

"There was a war. The streets are different. There are mutants. They give people mechanical bodies, then they go insane."

I looked down. "I'm a badge. It's my job. When they go nuts, I kill them."

"What about the D!" she screamed. "We have to stop them! What's your plan?"

"Kill them all!" I replied.

"That's it?"

"That's it. We start with D-1. We find the time portal back to my time, search them out, and kill them. Are you in?"

". . . Maybe." She looked up to the right in her thoughts and then, "Might work! She got close. "I'm in. . ." She whispered and planted a wet kiss on my lips. "Fascinato! Sexo! You are the meanest, bravest man alive. I love you."

She spewed. "You're my dad, my lover and my boyfriend combined. Compelled! I must go, see the future."

"I'm not your dad!" I cried, and yanked her toward the smoky dark hole of the underground.

I hoped the trains were still running. As usual, Parkenson's squad was cleaning up the mess I left. Strange to see young Lieutenant Parkenson, all spit and polish, actually doing the dirty inspection. I almost couldn't resist the urge to stop and joke with him, but I knew young Dick was right on our tail. They were allowing the first train to pull out, and it might be the last one for awhile. We pushed our way to the front of the line. Suits, high fliers, reefs, faros, radicals, young she-he, and Billy Boys. These were the travelers on the underground of my youth. Pella tossed in a couple of coins and we jostled through the turnstile. The doors closed us in like sardines. In the window I could see young Dick struggle through the crowd. A flash from his Sterling. Glass broke around my head.

Pella made the middle and as the crowd shoved me back, I grabbed a pole. The train was stinking crowded with scum and business elite. Silk ties and woven tweeds mixed with black leather. I laughed to myself. The Council and the Insta Meds in the financial district, it was humorous. Right in front of me, between me and Pella, two black men, Billy Boys with their baseball caps turned backward. They stared at me.

"Ah smack, mon," the big one said.

"Rack scarack, ee's da wan."

Billy Boys talking about me in their strange Jamaican language. What was this all about? I needed to be close to Pella.

"Vasta remon vordox!" I shouted.

The Billy Boys jerked like they'd been shocked. The first one looked me directly in the eye and the second seemed to raise and grow larger. None of the suits looked up, and everyone else's eyes seemed go down. Time stalled. The train swayed and rocked. I went for my 44.80. These black religious freak Billy Boys might waste you for talking to them. In an instant they would be empty.

But they moved aside, the Johnson fell back, and I stood next to Pella.

"Where'd you learn to talk like a Billy Boy?" she asked.

"The Case of the Cunning Linguist," I replied and put my hand to my ear. I commed to Rex.

"Rex, triangulate the signal. How far to the time opening?"

Rex didn't answer. Damn it! I hit the side of my head.

What was I thinking?

Ouch! My ear really hurt. Why do I always hit the side of my head? When was I going to remember? My ear was still sore.

"Rex," I said, "Triangulate the time opening. How far?"

Rex didn't answer. I hit my head. Memory. Memory!

I repeated myself. "Rex, please triangulate the time opening. How far to the portal?"

Instantly, Rex replied. "Five thousand, two hundred and twenty eight meters. South. Southwest."

The Capitan came on the loudspeaker. "Next stop, Village Eight."

Village Eight! That was good. That would give us some cover. I couldn't remember chasing myself, but there were large gaps in my memory. I knew I would chase myself. I knew I'd do anything to get Pella back, but I couldn't add two and two to make a fiver. Now, it equaled three. I had the edge of experience, and I had a Rex-1000 in my throbbing right ear.

Why did Pella come with me so easily?

Her kiss jerked my memory, and also the big bone in my pants started to throb. It had been too long. I wanted her. She could really make love, that I remembered. To tell the truth, I didn't care why she came with me. I wanted her clothes off. We kissed long and deep as the train slowed.

I commed to my Rex-1000. "Rex, please triangulate our location with the last transmission, interrupt that with the time since the previous transmission. Determine the exact location of the time continua."

Rex replied in his sanguine tone. "You are eight hundred meters from the opening. Proceed at a thirteen degree vector south by ten degrees west."

We entered Village Eight. This was going to be fun. The time continua was hidden in the most outlandish group of apartments in the city. It had grown from rubble. Apartment after apartment, built on, lavished on, invested in. Built and rebuilt year after year, first they were apartments, coffee houses, then bars, whorehouses, dance halls, and opium dens. Actually, that might be reverse order. No one knew the real history of Village Eight. The war, the pandemic, redevelopment. There was one constant. You could find what you wanted in Village Eight.

We emerged from the underground to a small park-like setting with some flashing lights. Signs pointed to all kinds of amusements. Blow. Smoke. Crank. A dollar a spank. Head. The Twist-a-twirl. Doggy-Dong.

A man in a hat with puffy sleeved shirt called, "Come, watch Fatima pick up a silver dollar!"

A midget whore in a yellow dress gave head to a thirteen year old fat boy wearing striped blue pants. A big red neon sign announce the dog and pony show. Next door, a flashing purple sign blared 'El Diaz De Los Muertos,' the day of the dead. A social couple, in white dress and a tux, whizzed in on a jet taxi. They were gays ready for a night on the town in Village Eight.

"Pella Sannow," I asked, "how old are you?"

She seemed surprised. "Why do you ask?"

"I'm just trying to remember . . . err, that is, my memory seems a bit cloudy."

"Don't you remember us?"

"Of course," I replied and lit up a Royal, offering one to her.

"What is it?"

"It's a Royal Fourteen."

"It doesn't look like a regular cigarette. Are they narco?"

I scanned the area for the time opening. Strange, in a way, from thirty years ago to my time a lot had changed, but Village Eight stayed the same, same park, same buildings, same traffic, same Pleasure Palace. The little stairway, then the landing, it was all familiar. We followed the gay social couple down the wooden steps to the café that led into the Palace.

Pella turned and looked at me. I sensed a question.

"These Royals," I said "are a special blend. They amplify your feelings."

She took a drag.

"Yes, oh wow!" She said. "I see what you mean." She started giggling.

We slid in with a group of seedy looking wasters and high deviates playing hide the salami. The air reeked of old jizz, panties that'd been fingered one too many times, toe jam, smegma, and also some fresh ripe fig, some young puss that I just had to have . . . that was Pella.

"Rex, please triangulate."

Black dancers and red sparkles, red, white, and blue silk. Thirty years later it was still the trade mark of the Pleasure Palace. I wondered if any of the old gang were drinking here tonight. Jay, my sniveling little sidekick in the 'Case of the Uncle Ant,' would just be beginning his career. Maybe I'd even see Talbot before they broke him. What a case that had been. The Crime Master almost took me down.

Rex replied, "Thirty meters north."

I looked at the stage. Of course. If D-men were traveling from time to time, what better camouflage. The music blasted from the stage where free-form dancers were madly gyrating. Weirdly decorated fiends, midgets, half nudes, big brains, and towel heads danced from the mashe pit to the stage and back. This happened twenty four hours a day so it was the perfect place for a time opening. In the crowd of dancers no one would see you disappear. And, of course, you would simply reappear in the Pleasure Palace thirty years from now in my time. That might explain why there were so many freaked out dancers. They were out of time. But I jest.

"Hey Dicky!" Pella shouted in a strange high tone. "These Royals really do the trick. I'm retro-blasting. Rockets. Trails. Stage... I'm going up."

"I'll be right up," I replied, and made my way to the bar.

"What'll you have bud?" Sam, the bartender, asked.

"Give me some chew. Cannabis thick." In the old days, before Royal Fourteens, the gum they sold at the Pleasure Palace would get you high. I peeled the stick and made a few quick chews. I commed to Rex.

It was a big risk, but I had to take it. "Rex," I said, "I'm leaving your transceiver in this time stuck under the bar. I won't be able to communicate until I get back to the office. Please be prepared to analyze a poison napkin and have complete file on the D ready for me. Set max amplification and record all conversations. Over."

Boy, my ear was sore. I popped out the transceiver, pressed it securely into the gum, and secreted it under the bar as scum and transvestite crud closed in on me. Busted one in the chops and grabbed a handful of who knows what from the other. Stepped over a couple doing the sixty nine, and just then someone big and fierce breathed foul breath on my face.

I shoved that ugly decomposer to the side, smashed him once in the gut, shoved him down, and stepped on his face.

Pella motioned me to come on stage. Some things you don't even want to touch. Yeah, it was the Pleasure Palace. I followed Pella up on stage, and we gyrated. It had been awhile since I danced on stage at the Palace, but the dancing made me think about later at

my mod. What's that they say, "Can't dance, can't slam banger."
And that brought up Cynthia. I pumped my hips, and thought about
my deb. It had been a couple of days since I'd bone-danged her.
Could I made our date tonight and do Pella too? Intrigue. Sex.
Lust. Killing. I loved it all. Then I saw the opening.

A subtle orange glow on a black curtain, not much to notice,
some wavy lines in the dark curtains, some chiaroscuro . . . it
appeared to be a place where shadows dance with themselves. The
time gate! We dance toward it. I moved close to Pella.

"Don't be afraid. I love you. No matter what, we'll always be
together."

"What's happening?" she whispered. "I feel strange. I'm all
tingly."

"It's going to be okay. I'll hold you. Don't worry. Dance close
with me."

We swirled around in a dizzy dance step, going faster, turning,
and turning, melting together. I lifted her and we spun around and
around. I pulled her close and kissed her neck and put my lips over
her ear and stuck my tongue inside.

"Oh Dick," she whimpered, "I'm hot for you."

I pulled her face to mine and kissed her lips and jutted deep in
her mouth. Our hot lips fused.

We spun and jumped into . . .

Chapter 6.

The time portal pulsated.

We rotated into an orange spiral. Our bodies fused. Time stopped and then sped forward like a bullet. I didn't know where we would end up. Just in case. I pulled the 44.80, wrapped Pella tightly in my arms, and lunged through.

I jumped through the time opening with Pella in my arms. It was like falling on the floor, nothing more. The D-men perfected time travel. There was no tube, no feeling of being squeezed, and no cosmic explosion. Going forward was easy and backward was hard. It didn't matter. No time passed. We were in the Pleasure Palace on the stage with blaring music and wild dancers all around. We hit the floor with a dull thud. Pella's tits were real.

"Owe, Dick. Not so hard!"

We were just another weirded-out couple who had too much to drink, and smoke, too much sex stimulator, and by God we were wild. But falling on the floor anytime at the Pleasure Palace was accepted behavior. In fact, the flesh beneath us squirmed. We landed on a young couple. They were making it. I saw the glazed look in his eyes, the veins in his neck engorged. Her lips parted, panted. She panted, "Ouie! Ouie!" They moaned and slapped meat. Anything was possible in Village Eight. His big butt humped up and pushed us to our feet.

"Pella . . ." I said, and pulled her. " We've got to get out of here. Da Mo is waiting for me." I paused. "It's my new case."

"Whoa," she whispered and pulled me back to the dance.

Her flesh was hot, and her breasts pressed my chest. I could smell the warm scent of her sweat mixing with the strange, odiferous flavor of her Jasmine perfume. Blue and red and green lights flashed all around. Dancers gyrated, jumped, and pounded. The heavy back beat of new music filled my head. Her fingers touched my face, and Pella danced like a whore, motioning me toward her sex. The Royals were affecting her, but I had to find Da Mo. The case called. She needed an ion. I grabbed her arm and pulled her off the stage. Reluctantly, she followed me to the bar.

Everything changes, but life remains the same in Village Eight. A tough Nellie dyke lounged her fat butt at the bar where I secreted my transceiver thirty years ago. I needed that device, and I knew they never cleaned up. The place was open twenty four hours a day. Was my transceiver still secreted in the gum under the bar?

While the Nellie eyed Pella, a gigantic freak dressed in an orange dress tried for the opening at the bar. As I brushed off the he-she, a shaved wire-head tried to squeeze in, but I whacked it. The air smelled like cum and the floor was sticky. At last, we edged through the scummy crowd and arrived at the old wooden bar. The Nellie chirped and brushed her tits on Pella. I reached under the bar and felt for the gum.

"Sam," I said, "two Planetary and a couple of ion backs."

Feeling under the bar, I must have brushed the dyke's leg. She shot me a look. I knew what was coming next.

"You want to suck on this, mother fucker!"

Up came her blade. The knife sprang open with a quick slit sound, and the silver blade reflected colors on Pella's face stuck in a silent scream. My eyes drifted to Pella's nipples, which stood erect through her shirt. . . A moment. The Nellie's eyes followed mine, and lingered a bit too long.

An instant is all a badge needs. I shot out my hand, snatched the blade away from her, and continued the follow through. My elbow broke the bitch's nose. Just to make sure, I slammed her head down on the bar.

"Ah," I said, "I'm sorry Sam. She had a little too much to drink. When she wakes up, send her over to Insta Med. Tell them to give her a nose job on my account."

"Dick," Sam said in his familiar rasp, "you'd better take care of this yourself. I don't want Parkenson down here. Too many violations, you know."

"Parkenson," I replied, as I dug in the gum with the bitch's knife, "doesn't care about broken noses, especially with some old Nellie."

The tip of the blade hit metal. The transceiver! I pried it loose along with a solid old putrid wad of gum. My joy was short lived.

"Parkenson cares about this bitch," Sam rasped. "That's his sister, Sara."

I picked up her head by the snarly scuff she called hair and looked at her pathetic pasty face, red smeared lips, and false eye lashes. She smelled like beer and looked like she's been on a two week bender. But something. Oh shit! It was Sara. She really let herself go. Only been a few years since she was a pretty young woman, socially on the rise with a bunch of young boy friends. What the fuck was the world coming to? Then it hit me. She was on an assignment for him. Damn that Parkenson! Now I'd done it.

"Pella," I said and handed the planetary ion to her. "Drink this. It'll bring you back to your senses. We have to get moving."

I tossed the spritzer on Sara's face. Pella and I dragged her to a booth away from the action, and she woke up.

"Dick Phillips," she muttered and wiped the blood from her face with her sleeve. "I should have known it was a badge. That was dirty trick you just pulled on me."

The story. Then they kill you. Might be Parkenson's sister alright, but you'd be dead just the same. I put my hand where she could see the 44.80.

Pella sipped the Planetary. Her eyes brightened as the effect of the Royal wore off, and the ion stimulator took over. She moved next to me and rested her head on my shoulder. We listened to Sara who spoke in low tones.

"Thought you were dead," she said. "Heard rumors about you getting it in the underground. Good to have you back. My brother wants you in the force. We need you here. I'm on stake out now. Behind those other scum, see that Rasta over in the corner."

"Just a typical Billy Boy," I said, but something in the look of his black face reminded me of someone, somewhere, in another time or another case.

"No," she replied, "not typical. We think he has a direct connection to Billy himself."

"Who's this Billy?" Pella asked.

"It's nonsense!"

"No Dick," Sara responded, "It's true."

"No way!" I said. "Billy's been gone for ten years. Got enlightened, then disappeared. Anyway, he was just a pathetic old baseball player. He was the leader of a few violent Rastas, but he couldn't take the pressure. He disappeared without a trace. That's old news."

A drop of blood came out of her nose, and as she licked it off her lip Sara smiled a funny smile. "You've got something of his, they say. And he wants it back. They say he paid for the operation . . . at least the hit."

I shook my head. "Nonsense. He's dead I tell you!"

Pella put her hand on my arm. "Dick. Take it easy."

Sara held her bloody nose. "They say he might be a mechanico, or enlightened, or who knows what. He's mad at you, Dick, that's for sure. He's probably gone insane but somehow figured how to keep from deteriorating. Now, he runs the Billy Boys. We proved that."

"That is utterly stupid," I said. "Billy was a poor excuse for a saint ten years ago. He wasn't a hero then, he was totally incapable of doing anything. He was a lackey of Medicos. And I should know."

Sara kind of giggled. "We've all heard the stories. From what I hear the rumors are big and thick. Can't tell for sure, never had the pleasure, but your girl friend must know all about it."

"I haven't the faintest idea what you talking about." Pella replied tersely.

I looked back at the Rasta, but he was gone. "What the fuck time is it?" I said. "I have to meet the Chinaman."

Sara's eyes lit up. "You coming out to the house later?"

Parkenson's house party. I forgot all about it.

As we exited the Palace behind a threesome of transvestites I could hear Sara sputter through her nose. "Don't forget your debutante," she laughed.

Hard to believe, still, with all the fighting and killing and muck around, everyone magnetized the social scene. I guess the diversion is what made life tolerable. I'd forgotten about the party at Parkenson's. Of course, there was no way I was going to miss it. Cynthia, my debutante, would be on my arm, and we would really make a nice couple. Then, really, fat Linda would probably beg me to take her too. Parkenson always tried to do a little side work. Linda and Parky could bump a little when the ugh, Mrs. Harriet Parkenson, oink oink, had her head in some puffy pussy, I mean pastry.

Now, this did present a special kind of problem. With Pella back in my life, how was I going to do both her and Cynthia? Not that I couldn't handle both of them. I laughed to myself. Lord and Billy knew I had the equipment. Was the artificial environment the answer? The silence outside Village Eight shook me.

Pella shattered her own cold stare. "Who is this debutante?"

"What? Did you expect me to live alone after you were gone?"

"You mean, after I went to the future with you?"

"Yeah." I lied. "Yeah."

I could see it was going to be difficult explaining to Pella that I had seen her killed in a train accident in the underground. I didn't know how to talk about it. Maybe it wasn't going to happen this time.

The cold street and dirty buildings led us out, and as we turned down the last dark alley toward the shuttle landing. I saw him. The Rasta. The same Billy Boy from the Pleasure Palace. I forced Pella behind me, and my hand flashed on my cold steel, the 44.80.

"Don't move, Billy Boy. Or you're dead."

As he stepped out in the light, I recognized him. The scar. The distorted smile. Now in the early morning light, the shadows, and the color of his dark face, I could see it was the same Rasta Billy Boy from the underground, from where we'd escaped from young

Dick Phillips. But the Rasta was older and looked about fifty times meaner. His side-kick was probably behind us a few yards away hiding in the darkness. I only had one round left in my 44.80.

A glint of light. The Rasta flicked out a twenty inch blade.

I whisper to Pella. "If they do me, don't let them take you alive."

The Billy Boy strode toward us, his blade swishing through the air in front of him.

"Strass morka resta!" he shouted.

"I'm sure you only want our money. . ."

He moved toward us.

I gunned out the 44.80. "Kamrama or deck!" I ordered.

His wet eyes glazed and seemed to drip a smile. "I speak very good English, mister. We will take your money too. Give us your girl friend and we will let you live to watch."

Something didn't feel right. He didn't seem like he cared much about dying. I took aim. What Billy Boys did to women, it wasn't funny. The way they cut the flesh turned my stomach. He was dead. But the Rasta was too bold. Instead of the fine feeling I always got before a kill, I had a sickening puke feeling. My gut hurt.

"We're going to do your girl friend," he said, and put his hand on his crouch. He jiggled his organs. "Give her to us now, and we'll kill you quick. If you fight, we kill you slow and still make you watch."

"I knew Rasta Billy," I cried. "Yeah, I knew your little Saint. And you know what? He wasn't' a Saint. He was an asshole traitor. You know what? He sold you boys out to the Medicos. That's right. Billy sucked up because he was afraid. He was a coward! You wouldn't be living on the streets now if it weren't for him. I saw him on his knees begging for his pitiful life. I saw him lick shoe."

The Rasta Billy went off. He lost cool. He moved into a fighting stance, threw his arms around like a chicken, or a rotating windmill, some kind of bastard dragon style. Striking the air, punching here and then there, he called in a high pitched voice.

"I and I and I and I!" he screamed.

Encircling us from the darkness, out stepped four huge Billy Boys, each one larger than the one before. The first one had small eyes as round and bright as diamonds. The second's muscles bulged, and he had shivs in both hands and his eyes were like five dollar coins. The third Rasta snarled and laughed like a hyena, and the fourth was gigantic. He blocked the sun. They made Rasta Billy look weak. They were really big and really mean.

"Now," the Rasta said, "I and I and I and I are going to take off your girl friend's clothes and fuck her. . ."

He flashed the giant blade. " . . . And after that we will cut off your toes, then your fingers, then your arms and your legs. We save the head so you can see us cut off your dick and take it back to Saint Billy."

I laughed to myself. Hump! So Saint Billy was still alive. All this time. He must really hate my guts. We were in a pickle, for sure. Only one way out. They wanted Pella, so I grabbed her and pointed the Johnson at her head.

"Don't be afraid," I whispered. "Struggle, but don't worry."

"Rasta," I shouted, "You want her. Let's make a deal!"

"No deals mon. The dick is going back to Billy. He smiled and closed his eyes for an instant.

That was all the time I needed. I shifted the Johnson and fired directly into his brain.

Holly Shit! I couldn't believe it. The plaster exploded behind him. His image wavered slightly. He cracked an even bigger smile. A hologram! The image wavered again, and as he disappeared I heard him make a command to the four Billy Boys.

"She's yours! But I want him to watch. An extra thousand credits to the Billy who brings back the dick."

I pushed Pella to the ground and stepped forward to meet the four huge Billy Boys. I had no doubts they were real. Four giant Billy Boys against a badge in hand to hand combat. The odds were in my favor.

"Mandrake claw form!"

The first one flung himself at me like a giant bear. His massive arms rose up to crush me under him. Cha Chang! My Mandrake claw ripped off his face, and he went rolling over and over holding the hollow where his eyes, nose and mouth had been.

I picked up his face and held it up. "Next!"

From the void came a call. "Two thousand credits for the dick!"

A giant fist struck my chest. I stumbled back, planted my left foot and kicked a three sixty into the air into the Adam's apple of the next Billy Boy. My steel tipped boot, crunch! Blood erupted from the neck. It writhed and puked red bubbles of air and blood.

Instantly, one of them had me by the arms. His iron vice grip tightened around my neck. I couldn't move. My back was about to break. We struggled, and I saw the really big one, the ugly one, pull down his pants, and bend over Pella. His mouth dripped saliva. He hunched over her and quivered the beginnings of the Jamaican sex ritual.

The giant Billy Boy holding me had arms like steel. He moved me from side to side as if I were a puppet. My brain began to explode. I couldn't move the Mandrake claw. Pella! Pella!

"Kill him" Cut off the dick!"

Darkness. Then at the last moment, my hand brushed my pocket. The gum, the transceiver, Sara's blade. With the final energy of my being I fumbled in my pocket. At last, the blade!

I grabbed the blade and jammed it back into the stomach of the Billy Boy.

"Pella!" I screamed and dove forward, driving the blade into the neck of the giant on top of her. Slashing his jugular vein, I kicked him off her.

I turned to the last Billy, the one who had held me in his vice grip. Still alive. Bile spurted out of his side. He didn't have long to live, so I took pity.

"Saint Billy!" I cried. "If you're watching this, I have a little gift for you."

I rammed the Mandrake claw down the dying Billy's throat.

Purple red blood dripped down my wrist as I held the still beating warm heart over my head.

"Come on Billy! I'm waiting for you!"

Chapter 7.

The smell of death, like a Billy Boy's heart, is as ripe and green as the stench of putrefied garbage, wine, and piss. At first it fills your nostrils and mouth tasting warm and good, and you inhale it inside with a full breath. Then you puke it out until your guts hang out on a line to dry. Revenge tastes sweet, at first.

"Why?" Pella asked, as we made our way to the shuttle stop.

"Why what?"

"Why did you have to do that to that dying man?"

I closed my steely eyes to slits and looked her up and down. She was young, full, and ripe. I felt a pounding in my midsection. The old lust for her wouldn't quit.

"Remember," I replied, "I told you the world had changed. It's tougher here. You never know who's or what's watching. The satellites. They're watching. Everyone sees everything. Billy has to know what he's up against. Dick Phillips doesn't cave in to threats."

We were quiet for a minute. Bad moods, but calming down. One look at Pella, her tits stuck thorough the blouse, more than just buttons on her shirt, each one a mouth full. They attracted flies. Old-men at the shuttle stop glared at us. Old lechers sitting on park benches watching her, thinking of pretty pants dripping juice. I knew what went on in their minds. It was the same thing that went on in my mind. I fingered my 44.80 but dropped it back. Out of ammo.

As we pushed through the human garbage toward the landing, I wondered if I was ever going to have her to myself. I shoved an old fart to the ground and stepped on it. Now, I was in a better mood.

"Out of my way scum! Badge coming through!"

The shuttle had a magnetic lock. Systematically it scanned your iris, took a digital facial reading, and analyzed your voice. As far as I knew it was impossible to break into. Of course, badges had certain rights. Part of my tax was access to the shuttle. However, I knew Pella would be denied. I had to use an override.

"Badge 324200, Phillips and guest. Personnel command override female twenty four years."

The magnetic field released us into the shuttle. Of course, this meant I was going to be seeing Parkenson before too long. He'd probably pin those last four Billy Boy kills on me and raise my taxes again, so I desperately needed my next draw from the Chinaman. If I could find the Ching Da and get it back to him, the seven hundred thousand would be mine. I could retire to the country, or maybe not.

We sat down. As I caught my breath, I noticed Pella was shivering.

"What? What is it?"

"I'm scared. I didn't think it would be like this."

"What did you expect?" I replied. "It's been thirty years. There was a war. Society went to hell and didn't come back. Things got worse."

"I know. You told me. "But . . ." she paused. "I thought it would be better. More advanced."

I remembered the D.

"It's worse than you think. Evil has a grip on the world. When I encountered the D in my time, I knew our original plan failed. I was chased into the underground and discovered a time portal to your time. Now I see some mysterious hand has been guiding me, I mean us, toward a destiny beyond my previous conception. Something strange is going on. Bumping into Sara, killing the idiot Billy Boys . . . someone doesn't want me to meet the Chinaman."

Pella's eyes grew large. She seemed frozen, stuck on a single thought. "You mean," she said with her voice fading in the realization, "that our plan to rid the world of the D . . . that our plan failed?"

"Yes," I replied. "Don't you see? You coming with me. Us returning so easily. It's too simple. The D aren't gone. If I could just remember who the leader of the D was, but they've wiped my memory."

"What!?"

"Exactly!" I retorted. "What, who, when, where and why?"

"You mean you really don't remember?"

The shuttle groaned forward, and the gray buildings and dark sky filled the ports. We moved like molasses on a hot pancake toward the stark out city and my mod.

"Verily," I said.

"Why don't you remember?"

Why, I thought. What kind of childish question was that? Why does the Earth turn? Why does a waterfall fall? Why do lovers love? Why didn't I remember? Shuttle rides seemed to do that to me. Time slowed down so much. They were so boring. The scenery so nondescript that conversation looped and looped.

"I do remember," she ejaculated. "I know why. I remember it perfectly. It was the second or third case after I met you. The Mystery of Dr Blood. We discovered that Dr. Blood was the head of the D."

"Of course." I ejaculated back. "Dr Blood!" There had be some sort of connection between Dr. Blood, and Saint Billy, and the Billy Boys. I wondered what it would be like to be in the same room again with Dr. Blood and Saint Billy. If there were a next time, they would both eat death from the hand, that is, the claw that fed them . . . the Mandrake claw.

Pella lunged shivering into my arms. "Oh my God!" She cried. "Dick, hold me!"

"In my mind," she said, "just now, the picture of that huge Billy Boy on top of me with that hideous instrument. I can't stop shaking. Make it quit! It's sick here! I want to go back. Take me back!"

"Oh sweetheart . . . it's okay. We're almost home. You'll be safe at my mod."

73

Pella and I were from different worlds. Thirty years ago, as shitty as life was, it was better than now. The Medical Politicos ruled then. The Hotel Meringue was central, and we made love so many times. Now, the Insta Med were in command. Mechcanicos were everywhere. What the hell! I was a badge. It was a job. The Council told the Meds what to do. The world, society, sat on the brink of revolution. Good and evil waged constant war. Parkenson and the cops tried to keep it all under control. The badges did the dirty work. It was a job.

As the shuttle ground along, my brain went dead again. We were quiet for a time. The strain of the magneto vibrated heavily in our souls.

"What you did to that dying black man back there, Dick. . ." Pella whimpered. "Why?"

"Billy Boys are evil. I'm a badge," I replied. "I fight evil."

Every whine of the magneto seemed to fill the hallow of my head. We droned toward the outside of the city where my mod sat at the end of the line. It was a quiet, non-descript, relatively clean area. Here, you wouldn't find too many creep or scruff. Still, you kept the steel shut. My mod was only a few feet from the shuttle stop.

I put my hand in the imprint, and the massive steel slid open. The high intensity security scan flashed and we entered.

"This is it."

Exactly as I left it. Your standard kitchen, shower, bed, and artificial unit.

"Nice," she replied.

"Yes. Clean and nice. It's on the artificial too."

"What's that?"

"The artificial?"

"Yeah."

"Oh, that's right. We didn't have that in your time."

I poured a couple of Solar Eclipse.

"You wouldn't know about the artificial. I subscribe. It's less than a couple of credits a month. Not much."

"But what is it?"

"It's holographic," I replied and touched her arm. "Here, drink. You'll feel good."

The Solar Eclipse were filled with ion stimulator and tasted great. Instantly, we both felt better.

"Come here!" I commanded and pulled her to the bed.

We rolled on the bed.

"The artificial can wait. First, I want to fuck you."

We rolled over each other like children. I got turned on. She caught her breath and pushed me up and looked me in the eyes.

"Is that a cattle prod in your pocket, or are you very, very happy to be with me?"

As I pulled off her pants, I noticed her panties were wet in the middle. Her love tunnel waited for me, wanted me, and I put my face between her legs and my nose in her underwear. I rubbed my face back and forth on the wet spot and chewed it. I tore at her panties with my teeth. I couldn't stop myself. I dug my teeth in and tore her panties to shreds, threw my head back and then reared down into her wet mansion. My lips locked on her nethers, and my tongue shot around like an eel in a washing machine. My cock got hard as a geode.

I pulled down my pants. I had to have her!

"Eee! Owe!" she screamed. "Where did you get that big black thing?"

My stomach rippled hard, my legs like iron steel springs, my massive arms, my giant muscular neck and head. . . perhaps I jest. Well, a little hyperbole. I was turned on.

"It's a long story. Hee hee," I laughed as I forced her legs apart, ready to insert my magic wand. I laid the massive head on her engorged brown lips and lubricated her by swishing the giant Priapus on her sprouting clit. I worked the mouth open.

"Ieeee!" she screamed. "It's too big!"

"No." I laughed. "Just right."

I got it in a little bit. Then, a little more. The hole absorbed my whole, and as I got it in a bit more I pulled myself on top of her and put my arms around her back and pulled her shoulders down. I pushed my hips between her legs, and it slid in. It slid in and out, in and out. I slid in and out.

I kissed her dizzy lips and burned. My tongue swished across hers, and hers shot into my mouth. She grabbed my ass with her hands, and I rammed my big wad into her again and again.

Moments, hours, days, months, years, eternities drew from one stroke to the next. I was gentle. I stroked her sweet little pussy. I brought the end of the dick out and rubbed it on her clitoris, and gently slid it back in again. Up to the lips. Then . . .

Slammed to the hilt!

Resting for a moment, I withdrew and curled my finger and got her G spot and worked it. In and out and around and down and across and over and on, then to the clit, around the stem. Careful here. The pleasure comes. Careful touch. Back to the lips.

"Corkscrew!" cried Ahab . . . "and he fan-tails like a spit jib in squall. Death and devils! Men, it is Moby Dick yea have seen . . . Moby Dick . . . Moby Dick."

And young Pella, Damn! Did she . . . She spewed!

And when at last inside again, with sweet and sparking purple orgasms, both our bodies were vibrating and shaking and trembling, I rammed home a gigantic explosion right into the bottom of her ripe dripping fig. Zam, ram, bam!

Later, as we curled and spooned on the pillows and shared a smoke of a Royal, she whispered to me.

"Dick," she asked, "could you talk dirty to me. Touch me like you used to and talk dirty to me."

I really don't know dirty words. That was a long time ago. I was young then. If all the dirty words I forgot were stacked together, it would be like the tower of Babel. Where to start? I guess I put my finger in a labia pie.

"Dark clouds and darkness," I said as I caressed her pussy lips. "One white horse in the mud. One maniac with a knife. A simpleton riding on a jackass. Three old hags in dirty rags. A happy man who is now sad. Apple pie on a new black tie. A turban stained with bourbon."

Pella panted and gasped. I kept on babbling.

"Big hump, the midget bumped the fat lady's rump, took a jump and pumped and pumped till his rod, red hot, blew up and spewed over dripping, gooshy red hot clit to wit, in slashes. . . It trembled and came cosmic colors orange and purple-red atomic flashes."

I bit her ear lobe. "Hot cum," I whispered. "Dripping, hot pussy cock mouth fuck me fuck me, hard. Deep! Heavy, deep, and hard!"

I moved my finger to the G spot.

"Corkscrew!" she cried, and fan tailed like a spit jib in a squall.

And she spew again and again.

Well, the next morning was business as usual. I had to get back to the office. I could feel evil penetrating the world. It was my job. I needed to check in with Rex and get to the Chinaman. I got dressed, and as I expected to run into Browny anywhere at any moment, I reloaded my 44.80. From the sheets, Pella smiled up at me.

"You were wonderful," she said. "But where did you ever get that big cock? I don't remember you every having anything like that?"

"Ah," I mumbled, "it happened about eight years ago. Me and a whole bunch of Rastas got in a big fire fight. No one was left alive. There were body parts all around. The Medicos put me back together. That was right before the big revolution, before the Insta Med started making mechanicos, about the time Saint Billy disappeared. I guess if it happened now, I'd have a crazy brain walking around with a metal body. But anyway, some of the less important parts got mixed up in the mess. I got some poor Rasta's black cock. Who knows where mine is?

"You got to understand, it was a ghastly time. The revolution and all. The Politicos were losing power. Dr. Blood got driven into exile. I came out looking bad. The press tried to link me to Saint Billy. Rumors were going around that I took a payoff from the Rastas. They said that's why I came out alive. It looked bad for me.

Without Parkenson's help, I wouldn't have made it through. Eventually, I got my badge back. You know what? I didn't get paid on that case either. If I ever catch up with that lying female hunchback, I'll make her wish she never sucked me.

I pulled my cock out of my pants and swung it around like a pendant. "It's awfully big, but it works good."

I turned on the switch.

"This is how the artificial functions. Whatever time and space you want to be in . . . it recreates it for you. Nothing new or original about it really, but it'll be fun for you while I'm at work."

"No," she wailed. "I want to be with you."

"Can't. Too dangerous. You need to rest. We'll get together tonight after I have more information. Then you and I can work on our plan to defeat the D."

She shook her head. "No Dick! I'm going with."

"No one can get through the steel so you'll be safe here. You can go anywhere in the artificial and it'll tell you all about the war and the revolution. Or, you can be back in your time."

"Dick. . ." She pleaded.

I pointed at the large external disconnect. "One thing. I had to reprogram the voice override. The artificial always want to be activated. They jammed the voice override, so I had to install this manual switch. Just give it a quick pull."

"Dick," she exclaimed, "it's central. We have to work together. I want to come."

"Look," I said, "I have a lot to do today. You're exhausted. As soon as you get rested, when you catch up, we'll start the attack on the D. Today I have to meet with Da Mo. It's a hectic day. Get some rest. Catch up on your history. Make a plan. The artificial will entertain you. Whatever you do, don't go out. It's violent, terrible, and evil."

"I'll be bored!"

"No you won't."

I lit a Royal and handed it to her. She took a hit and giggled.

I pushed up the switch to the artificial

"Rome, two hundred BC."

Dressed in a loose toga, a young Roman stepped into the room and spoke in a high eunuch's voice. "Your service guide."

I tossed her a full pack of Royals. "Take a break. Have some fun. Take a tour of history and get a going on a plan."

The steel slid open to the morning haze.

"I love you," she pouted as the steel slid shut behind me.

The shuttle arrived on it's time, as always. I had a lot of things to work out. I'd missed my appointment with Da Mo, and I really needed a payment on that case. My arm was healing but my neck hurt where the big Billy Boy jerked me around last night. Yet, somehow, I felt wonderful. Doing Pella vitalized me. I knew she would enjoy the Royals and the artificial. Defeating the D was central, but getting more money from the Chinaman was the only solution. We needed credits. The Royals would take care of Pella until I returned tonight. She'd have a plan ready, and I'd take care of her again.

Sex with Pella was wonderful. I felt lucky . . . too lucky. Why'd she come so quickly with me? Couldn't be anything but my extreme magnetism, could it? Anyway, she was back with me, and that was the way it was going to stay. I only wondered now, how was it going to work out with Cynthia, my debutante? I might have to go back to injecting myself in the butt with vitamin E as I had done in the 'Case of the Nuptial Night of the Twins.'

The lump of gum in my pocket reminded me to stop at Nick's later today and get the Rex transceiver cleaned and reinstalled. I had to get back in touch with the Chinaman and his money. Nick wasn't cheap. It would cost to rebuild Rex's transceiver. Even if it just need a cleaning and a battery that was at least a grand.

The shuttle groaned toward the city. My mind filled with nothingness.

Suddenly!

Chapter 8.

Like sliding into home, feeling all alone, diarrhea! My mind woke up with a purge. I had a lot of thoughts, but they went away.

The shuttle ground to a halt in front of my office, and I stepped out of the field lock. Was I ever going to open a file on this case? Could I get some clues going? What!? The distinct whir of a magna jet caught my attention.

Simpson, Parkenson's black driver, stood next to the magna jet with a disgruntled look on his face. His paralyzer 18 Z-6 seemed to have a life of its own. His hand moved from possible victim to victim, jerked up and down, not shooting, aiming, jerking, aiming, quivering, aiming. Sometimes, Simpson scared me. He never exposed his hidden rage, but it was there.

"Simpson," I said, "long time no see. How's it hanging?"

"Big and thick to you." he said. "Same old shit, Phillips, different day. You know, there was a minor uprising last night."

"No. I didn't know that. Really? What happened?"

A sweaty pungent odor, he needed a shower. He puffed his chest and pursed his lips. "Seems as if the Billy Boys went a little nuts. Some kind of revenge action for killing of Saint Billy's henchmen."

He rubbed the stubble of his unshaven face. "Haven't been to bed yet. Cleaning up the mess. The damn fools tried to storm the Council. Idiot Billy Boys!"

"What are you doing here?" I asked.

"Parkenson's upstairs waiting for you."

I took the force field to my office. I hoped Parky didn't link me to the four Billy Boy kills last night. I was out of money, and with another tax increase I could lose my badge and my Johnson. I wasn't sure what to do. No escape. Couldn't dance good, but still had to face the music.

Parkenson sat back with his feet on my desk, and he had a very disturbed look on his face. In his right hand he poked at Rex with a silver disrupter pen. I held my breath. If he touched my computer with the tip of the disrupter, I'd be on the streets begging for work. Without a Rex, a badge didn't have clout. I'd be in the gutter, my reputation gone.

"Last chance, Rex . . ." he said.

"Excuse me," I interrupted, "can I help you, or am I interrupting?"

He laughed in his roly-poly way. "Uh, not really. I was just about to send your Rex back to the factory for repairs."

He waved the disrupter pen back and forth, awfully close to Rex's eye.

"For some reason," he continued, "your Rex won't grant me access. You know, that's against the law. That will cost you."

"Rex," I said hurriedly, "have you denied access to Chief Parkenson?"

Rex didn't answer.

"Now Rex," I said, and added, "Please Rex?"

Rex replied in his monotone. "Access accepted."

"See," I said, "no problem. Just a typical Rex. Got to ask nicely."

"Humph!" Parkenson grunted and swung his feet off my desk. "Please Rex, please Rex," he said. "Please, or I blow you the fuck away. Give me the whereabouts of Dick Phillips between two and seven a.m. this morning."

"Transceiver malfunction at 1:10 am. Unable to locate between those hours."

Parkenson looked at me. His eyes were more piercing than usual. "We had a report of you entering the shuttle with an unauthorized at 3:26 last night. Have you anything to say?"

I looked at the ground. "Got to have a little fun once in awhile."

"You dumb fuck! How old are you? Don't screw with those illegals from Village Eight, son. You'll end up in a mess of trouble." He paused for a second. "Now, we also have a report of four Billy Boy kills in that general area. Your style too. Did you know there was an uprising last night?"

"Yeah, Simpson."

"Did he tell you it was a reaction to those four Billys killed in a style much like yours? What about that?"

I kept quiet.

"Look Dick," he said and walked around the desk and put a hand on my shoulder. "You're almost a son to me, right?"

Parkenson was more like a critical uncle.

"I want you to be more careful. You got a good thing going with your debutante, Cynthia. Who knows, someday you two can tie the knot like Harriet and me. I can get you into the force. You might be able to move to the country with us, but you got to be careful. You can't be messing with that slash at the Pleasure Palace. Oh, I know it's more bang for your buck than anywhere in town. You can't be taking those unauthorized on the shuttle."

So, he didn't really have anything on me or he would have hit me with a tax increase. I breathed a little sigh of relief. And, he wasn't digging into Rex to find out about the Chinaman. I was getting off the hook.

"Now, about my sister."

His grip tightened on my shoulder. I gulped. He pulled me close to him. The tip of the disrupter pen rose close to my face. One false move and I thought about the hole, the operation, the metal body, my brains going insane . . . puke. He put his other hand behind my head and looked me straight in the eye.

"Had you going for a second. What you did to my sister . . . was great!

As if he were a digit-programmer, he shoved the pen back in his shirt like a geek. He looked off in the distance.

"She was headed in the wrong direction. You know, she was really going down hill. But last night at the Insta Med she got a nose job. She got hair implants and liposuction. You wouldn't recognize her." He laughed. "You two should get together. You know if she wasn't my sister, Sara. . . She's beautiful."

He laughed again. "So what's a few Billy Boys and an attack on the Council? Let's just call it even."

As he was leaving, as he neared the force, he stopped and turned. "See you tonight, at the house around seven thirtyish. Bring Cynthia and what's her name, that fat one?"

"Linda." I said, and muttered to myself. "Son of a bitch."

I slid into to my big leather chair. That's a strange turn of events. I thought I'd missed the party at Parkenson's. Hum. Must be working too hard, or somehow time-travel messed my brain. Could be both. No tax increase and a party tonight!

"Rex!" I commanded. "Let's please have the calls for the last twelve hours. No, wait a minute! If the time door were still open, then my transceiver is still under the bar in the previous time. Let me hear the transmissions in real time coming through the time portal. Err, please let me hear the transmission?"

"Hold on," Rex replied. "Clearing out static."

A strange whine, but I could hear some voices. One of them was familiar.

"So anyways I says to him, Dicky, for just a hundred I can get you the information you needs. And for a thousand I'll guarantee you gets your man or woman, hee hee."

"Sure," replied another voice. "Since when has that wimp Dick Phillips ever had a thousand bucks?"

"No, no. He is on one big case. He told me about it last night. He calls it the escapade of the Varicose Vein."

"Dr Blood?" The voice cried.

"Now, I wouldn't say that. Pssst. In fact, it might be better not to say anything like that. See that guy down at the end of the bar? He's got connections with the Medicos. Never mention Dr. Blood's name again, and listen, Dough Dough, if you wants to work on this case with me, we'll split sixty forty. "

I squinted and thought back. 'Dough Dough' was a familiar term one of my sidekicks used to use. Yes, the case of the Varicose Vein. That voice was familiar, but it was so many years ago. Could it possibly be my ex-side kick, that sniveling jail bird, Jay? I saw him hunched over the bar, wringing his hands, planning a way to get me to give him some credits. But who was that other voice?

"Rex," I commanded, "please identify voices."

"First voice, Jay Fallow, informant. Second voice, unable to identify. No known data on that voice."

"Okay Rex," I instructed, "keep tabs on the conversations, and break in and alert me if the opening closes, or if you identify any other voice patterns. Record all conversations, we'll run through them later. Now, give me all the calls that have come in since my last check in. Wait a minute."

I made a little joke with myself. Rex didn't like it too much. I took the poison napkin from my pocket. I placed the sample I'd taken from the Five Dollar Café, and put it in Rex's mouth. That was the joke. I called Rex's port his mouth. I didn't mention it often, he couldn't digest it.

"Now," I said, "while you give me those calls I want you to chew on this and let me know the composition."

"I don't have teeth. And I don't have a mouth!"

"Don't take it personally. It was just a joke. Please let me have my calls."

"Five twenty five. This is Da Mo. Where you? Have money. Need to start case immediately. Please come to Five Dollar now."

"Seven thirty. Dick, where are you? Our date was for seven sharp."

"Eight forty. Dick, this is Cynthia. Where are you?"

"Nine forty five. You fucker! Screw me and then stand me up on a date. You're an asshole. Where are you? Call me when you get in. You know my number."

Cynthia's pissed, I thought. I liked that. I didn't know she cared.

"Ten forty six. Hey Dick, it's me Pella. Long time no see. Shoot me a call, seven D-568900."

"End," Rex monotoned.

"Please Rex," I asked, "can you give me a voice analysis on that last message?"

"Pella Sannow, Malaysian."

"Give me the age."

"Pella Sannow. Malaysian. Age fifty four."

Fifty four. The last time I was with her a few hours ago she was twenty four. Now, it was thirty years since I'd seen her. So, she survived. She didn't die in the underground. There were two Pella's in this time. One back at my apartment and one at Seven D-568900.

"Dial up the last number."

"Ringing"

"Hello. This is Pella Sannow. I'm not here right now. Sorry I missed you. At the tone, please leave your message."

Poor. Can't even afford the hologram interface. I wondered if she still had her looks. Time seemed to be harder on women as they got old. Ah, what the fuck, it was hard on me too. The truth was I really had to start taking those shots of vitamin E in the butt. I rested back in my chair. Could I do young Pella, Cynthia, and older Pella at the same time? That would be a trick. Sex. Intrigue. Women. I loved it.

As my mind drifted in that ocean of reverie, a noise like a cat's paw on rice paper woke me to attention. I slammed out the 44.80 and twirled around in my chair.

"Easy," Da Mo said and bowed. "Mr. Phillips, I did not mean to scare you."

"Greetings," I replied, "sorry I missed you the other night."

"So am I. Have you found the missing Ching Da?"

"No. not yet. I haven't had time to get on your case. I start working on it tomorrow."

"Start today! Start right now!"

Da Mo seemed indignant. I wondered what the big deal was. I hadn't even had time to make up a case file, much less get started. Besides, he'd only given me a retainer. Money makes the world go round.

He slumped, barely able to hold himself, and put a hand on my desk. He looked sick. His yellow skin looked parched and dried out. When he started to choke and make a gack sound, I thought he was going to croak. I kicked a chair toward him.

"Are you alright?"

"Find my Ching Da," he whispered. "I feel evil everywhere, and I have lost the energy to fight it. If I die, it will take over and forever rule the world. Time passes. Soon even the Ching Da will not be able to save me. You must find it and return it to me."

I fumbled through some old contracts on my desk, turned over some notes, and pulled out a new pack of Royals. Nonchalantly I slammed one out and lit it up.

"Well, you see," I said, "it's like this. A new case came in last night, and I'm pretty sore on it. So I guess I'll have to refund your money. Don't really have time to help you out."

"Money!? That is no problem!"

"You got some?"

"One hundred thousand American. . . ." He reached in his robe and pulled out a wad of green Americans.

"Okay, now we're talking," I said, and blew a nicely formed smoke ring that floated out and circled the money.

"What the!" he cried, and before I could blink he snatched the Royal out of my mouth. He sniffed it, and then he took a long drag.

"Hey!"

"Charachunga," he replied with a large smile as he exhaled a long puff.

He took another deep drag and a look of sublime satisfaction rose on his face. He stood erect and his whole appearance change. He grew younger in front of me. In fact, his voice changed. He stopped speaking with a clipped accent and began addressing me in elegant English.

"This cigarette is wonderful," he said in perfect English. "It contains refined essence of my Ching Da. It is Charachunga."

I looked at the hundred thousand American. Green cash to be sure. It was time to get to work.

"Alright Rex, open a new file. Let's see, what will we call it?"

I thought for a second and looked at the old Chinaman who now seemed reborn and much younger. I remembered our first meeting.

"Let's call it the Escapade at the Five Dollar Café."

Da Mod nodded, and his eyes sparkled.

"Chinaman," I said, "you'd better tell me the whole story."

Now, Da Mo seemed more relaxed. I had a couple of packs of Royals stashed in the top drawer of my desk, and I figured when he took me uptown for lunch on him I could pick up a few more. As long as he had, what did he call it, his Charachunga, he wasn't so uptight. He seemed relaxed and at ease, but then all of a sudden he was on his feet, smoking and pacing back and forth across my office.

"Where to begin? Where to begin?" He asked himself.

"Begin at the very beginning," I said. "Don't leave anything out. I'll stop you if I don't understand. Rex will keep track if I need to go over anything. Just one thing."

"Yes?"

"We're going to need a written contract."

He stopped pacing and as his eyes grew twice their size, he spoke. "Trying to trick me again. You want my soul?"

"No. No tricks. Sometimes my bigger clients want written contracts, but as far as I'm concerned, if you got the cash I'm doing the work. Don't go retro."

I could see the strain of the missing Ching Da was getting to him, but the Charachunga kept him going.

"Look," I said, "I've got to be over at Nick's later to get my transceiver repaired, but we have all morning. We'll break for lunch, but let's get started. Simply begin from the beginning."

Da Mo sat down, and as he started talking his head rotated and bobbed and rolled in his hypnotizing manner. At once he seemed ancient and also young. With each drag of the Charachunga he spoke more and more elegantly. I took a drag on my Royal, shifted down to low gear, and listened to his amazing story.

"I was born in India near Azar," he said with a sophisticated air, "near the Plateau of Tibet, twenty four hundred years before the birth of Christ. My family were peasants. They were poor rice farmers who had nothing. I was born the third male child. My sisters who were born before me, as was the custom, had all been put to death. My mother and father were overjoyed to see at last they had another male son to help them with the farm. Needless to say, my brothers who were three and five years old were happy to see me. Although I was another mouth to feed, soon, like them, I was helping with the daily toil of rice farming.

"However, all was not to be as happy as my family had projected. In the year 2,450, when I was five years old, a great winter overtook the plains of Tibet, and we were forced from our rice farm to the City of Dzong, which is an evil place full of men who resemble maggots and merchants who look like worms. At Dzong, we were forced to live in a single room on the edge of town. To keep warm we thawed out animal bones by the fire and burned them. My father was weak and dying, and for money for food my mother and my brothers sold themselves to the rich maggot merchants.

"One night my father began to tremble and shake and demanded I put more bones on the fire. But we had none. First he would sweat, and then he would shake. In desperation I ran to the shack next door. No one was inside, so I went to their bone stack and stuffed my clothes full of bones. Right away someone opened door, so I hid.

"It was my mother and a fat maggot merchant. Both of them were drunk and laughing. The merchant pulled down my mother's clothes, and he began to hump his body on her, and she laughed and screamed in drunken delight. Right then I remembered my father, and I ran to our shack. I put the bones on the fire and held my father's head in my arms. He jerked and jerked and then his eyes got wide and stopped moving. He looked at me but didn't see.

"When my brothers came home they whipped me for letting my father die. My mother came home, and as the custom, we cut my father into small pieces and ate him. Spew! Ugh! Right then I swore on my soul I would never eat flesh again.

"Later, when I was seven I began to make my way by selling myself to the traveling merchants who came from all parts of the world."

I stopped the Chinaman. "Un . . ." I asked, "what exactly do you mean by selling yourself?"

"Sex you idiot!" he screamed. "I laid down on my stomach for them and they put their things in me. I did what they wanted me to do. I did it all, you see. But unlike my older brothers who squandered their money on women or younger boys, I saved mine. And I was better looking and younger than my brothers, more prized by the maggot merchants. I did everything for them. I let them beat me, and I also beat them many times. I was their favorite. And soon, by the age of fourteen, I was able to buy my first boy and right away I was running a large stable of boys. I was able to buy fine clothes and a horse."

The old man sucked in the smoke of the Royal. He held in the long drag and then exhaled. Looking younger and more alive, he spoke in the most elegant English.

"At sixteen I traveled to Kanphur where immediately the local king took notice of me and invited me to his court. Almost as soon, his daughter, the Princess of Shigatse, fell madly in love with me, and coincidentally while hunting pheasants I saved the king's life and he crowned me prince.

"As a prince of Shigatse I had complete freedom and I happened to meet a penniless idiot who was actually an enlightened being. This enlightened wanderer taught me secrets that had been handed down from generation to generation, and soon I also became enlightened. When news of my enlightenment reached Emperor Liang of China, I was invited to teach my secrets to him.

"However, the imbecile Emperor Liang did not understand my enlightened words, and he attempted to have me killed. Instead, I withdrew to a Shoaling temple. There I saw that the priests were weak and could barely take care of themselves. So I meditated for nine years and sat staring at the same wall over and over, year after year, searching for a way to rejuvenate the priests.

"It was there, in the Shoaling temple, deep in meditation that I came to the realization that evil was real. You see, often I traveled on the Astral plane, leaving my body behind. I explored the universe and learned all the knowledge and magic of antiquity. I appeared before the Lord of Light, and the Lords of the Solar Ring. I met and mingled with Lords of all the planets. I traveled to the zone of Jupiter. In the zone girdling the Earth, I discovered evil existed, and in that plane I almost lost my existence to Him."

Da Mo jumped up and slashed his long fingers in the air. Then he pointed directly at me, the red tip of the Royal in my face.

He screamed. "There is no room for that kind of thought! You think evil is some kind of mental construct. You think evil is just an opinion of mine."

"No," he shouted. "Evil exists. He is as real as you or me. I have seen Him. I am telling you, now he leads the D. The monster D-1 is not the leader of the D. The leader of the D is the Dark Prince himself. One look at his face and you will turn to stone."

Stone? What a goofball this Chinaman was. "Take it easy," I said. "Get on with your story."

"Since I discovered evil," he said in an elegant manner, "He has tried to trick me into signing away my soul, for He knows if I should die, He could easily rule our universe. That is why I formulated the Charachunga, for it rejuvenates my spirit which is always, even now as I speak, doing battle with the Evil One."

A goofball and actor. He slumped down for effect. "But I am growing weak. If I should happen to slip, to stumble, to lose control, a darkness would fall over the world like a void. A drain would open and life would flow away from the world. . .

"To counteract evil I taught the Shoaling priests the arts of Kung Fu, Tai Chi, and Chi Kung. When His forces, disguised as Emperor Liang's army, attacked the temple we were able to defeat them. Through my superior fighting techniques we withstood the onslaught and I had time to formulate the everlasting fluid."

Da Mo stuttered and faltered. "But now . . . now it . . . now it has been stolen from me."

I looked at Da Mo. The pathetic old Chinaman had gone a little off his nut, but the American green looked real. If he had the money, he could do all the talking he liked. I took a long drag on my Royal.

"Go on," I said. "When did you first discover this so-called prince of darkness?"

Da Mo got in my face. "He is not so-called."

I wiped the spit off my forehead with my shirt. "What the hell is he then?"

"Do you think?" Da Mo said, making motions with his hands and bobbing his head. "Do you think? . . . "

Chapter 9.

"I try not to," I interrupted. "I let Rex do that for me."

"Do you think . . .?" he repeated, "that Evil is bound by shape. Does It let form bind It? Is It held in time? Would you recognize Him if He were standing in front of you now? Did you know when you think about Him, He comes close to you? Is He behind you right now? You're a damned fool!"

I grabbed the 44.80. Who the hell did this old Chinaman think he was talking to anyway? The last man that called Dick Phillips a fool is now walking around with a mechanical body, a head that's going insane, and the knowledge that when he shot his mouth off to me it wasn't worth a penny for his thoughts. Then, on the other hand, sometimes if you let your client spew you can see deeper into them where the real clues are the lies they tell. I would let him rant, but I didn't take compliments lightly.

"I didn't have any brothers or sisters and my mom raised an idiot who was a simpleton, but didn't raise no damn fool!"

Da Mo stood erect and paced back and forth. He rung his hands and took a long drag on his Royal, only to snuff the butt on the palm of his hand.

"Look, you fool! I have conquered pain. I am the eternal man! Quit joking with me. This is serious, very serious. Evil can take any shape, any time. I could be evil for all you know. But I'm not, and I know you're not. You too much of a nonsequential ignoramus. That's why I chose you to help me. Now, give me another Charachunga cigarette."

"You're right," I replied sheepishly, "enough joking around."

I hoped he was joking around. I was going to get Rex to define those two words after the Chinaman left. I wondered what he meant. Was that a compliment? What was a 'nonsequential ignoramus'? It sounded like a bass-ackward non sequitur.

"If this prince of darkness doesn't have a shape, or that is, doesn't take the shape of a man, or can take any shape, . . . then what shape does he or she take?"

Da Mo sat down, but his voice rose to a high falsetto like a guru. "You see," he said, "I was in deep meditation. It was a positive meditation. I was living in the holy city of Shamballa. Oh, my body was in the Shoaling temple, but my spirit was in heaven in Shamballa. And I tell you I was full of love. The true star was there, and I was part of the Holy one, I am was I am, the Tetragrammaton circled the square and I was at peace with the universe. Immediately in this space I united with nirvana and then .

I bent close to him. "Yes . . . and?"

"And then . . ." he whispered.

"Yes. . . "

"Then . . ."

"What. . . ?"

He put his face next to mine.

"Then . . ." He spewed on my face. "The mosquito from Hell!"

I jerked back and wiped my face, while he jumped up and started pacing.

"That damn mosquito wouldn't leave me alone. It kept buzzing around my head. I couldn't meditate. I tried to return to Shamballa, to Nirvana, but my spirit became disturbed. I tell you that mosquito was evil."

I laughed. "Why didn't you just kill it?"

He crinkled his face and gave me a funny stare. "You don't see at all, do you Mr. Phillips? I was an enlightened prince. Even to kill an insect was a terrible act. But the mosquito was itself evil. What could I do? I believed it was my karma, so I sat and tried to meditate. But I couldn't. It kept buzzing and buzzing around my head. Finally, I could stand it no more and opened my eyes. My spirit left Shamballa and returned to my body. The mosquito landed in front of me on the edge of my ancient tea cup.

"Instantly I shot out my hand to capture it, but I missed and the beautiful cup sailed away and smashed against the wall. The mosquito buzzed around my head while I sat patiently, without moving, waiting. Finally . . . it landed on my face."

He slapped his face.

"I slapped at it, but I missed and slapped my face instead. Then the mosquito landed on the other side of my face, and I slapped it."

Da Mo slapped his face again and again.

"This side, then this side. That side. Then that side."

The Chinaman looked blankly in the air.

"Get out of here you damned mosquito!"

"So I thought I would trap it. I poured a little honey in a jar and set the jar on its side. The mosquito buzzed around me, but soon it became very curious and landed on the lip of the jar. I didn't move. I sat quietly, and as the buzzer entered the jar with a single slap of my fist I smashed the jar to bits. Honey flew everywhere."

"Honey all over me! Then from the corner of the room, buzz, buzz. The damned thing was still alive."

The Chinaman sat down and took a long draw on his Royal. He was silent for a moment, and a smile came on his face.

"So I devised a fantastic plan. I pulled the cord and rang for my faithful servant who came instantly to my side."

"Darjeeling," I begged, "clean up this mess. I want you to go down to the creek by the reeds and find something."

"The creek, master?"

"Yes," I said. "Find me the largest frog you can and bring him back to me. Chop chop!"

Da Mo stared at the floor.

"That was the first mistake of many. When Darjeeling returned, he was wet and covered with mud. He held the finest, most spirited bull frog you have ever seen. I would have laughed, if the mosquito from Hell were not buzzing in my ear at that very moment.

"You may go now," I said, "but leave the frog."

"Now do your stuff, Froggy," I whispered. "The mosquito landed on my hand to inject me with pure evil, but Froggy's tongue shot out and with a quick jot, gulped down that insect. I was at last free of the insidious buzzing."

Da Mo stared at the floor. "That was my second mistake."

"As soon as the mosquito got inside the frog, Froggy pissed in my lap and the most vile crocking sound came out of him."

The Chinaman looked me in the eyes and must have hypnotized me for the next thing I knew his was right next to my ear.

"Rack, rack, rack!" he screamed. "The worst sound you have ever heard. He wouldn't stop no matter what I did. Finally, I called in Darjeeling.

"Get his frog out of here."

"Rack, rack, rack!" screamed the frog.

"What should I do with it?" Darjeeling asked.

"Squish it with a mallet, grind it up, and bury it. I don't care. Kill it!"

Darjeeling became indignant. "Master, you know we are sworn not to take the life of a living thing. This is a beautiful creature, one with Nature."

"Then throw it back in the river!"

"That night was a very good meditation. At last, I was free of the mosquito from Hell. Again, I returned to Shamballa, and there I visualized the formula for eternal life. I returned to Nirvana and the square circled the Tetragrammaton. Sound, number, feeling, and thought combined. I united with the Holy of Hollies and then. . . "

"Yes," I replied and leaned forward.

"Indeed yes," he said. "Then . . ."

"Yes, what?"

Again he spewed in my face. "Rack, Rack, Rack. The slimy croaker from hell!"

"I couldn't sleep. I couldn't meditate. The formula for eternal life was right before me, right on the tip of my tongue so to speak, but every time I tried to return to Shamballa that frog interrupted me. And it wasn't from the creek either. He was right outside my door, somehow knowing exactly when I would meditate. Rack, rack, rack. I rang for Darjeeling.

"Darjeeling," I said, "we have to do something about that frog. It is driving me crazy."

"What is?" he replied.

"Don't you hear it?"

"Yes, isn't it beautiful?"

"Kill that frog!"

"Oh no, master. You know I can not."

"Then bring me the kitchen knife."

"I walked resolutely to the pond and began to slaughter the croakers one by one. At last, I had the large ugly one in my hands, and I laughed insanely as I stabbed it again and again. I admit it. I sinned. I lusted for frog blood."

"Soon I returned, worn out, wet and bloody, but I had done it."

"Master, you do not look well."

"I know." I replied. "I have killed every frog in the creek."

"My meditation that night was wonderful. I reached Shamballa again, and I could read the mystical incantation. It was right in front of me."

Da Mo whispered. I could not quite hear him.

"It said . . ."

"Yes . . . ?"

"Rack, rack, rack!" he screamed. "That frog was still alive! Day and night, night and day. My sleep was ruined. I couldn't meditate. I couldn't think. I became distraught. Finally, I called Darjeeling.

"Darjeeling," I said, "go into town, to the home of the bird master and buy the strongest and meanest owl you can find."

My office turned gray with smoke from the Royals. In a few minutes I would have to have Rex open a portal. For now, it was cozy.

"Soon, my servant returned with a very fine wise bird. Its wings were strong and its talons sharp. When Darjeeling uncovered its head, its eyes flickered, and it had a razor sharp beak. We were be kindred spirits. With him on my arm, we walked to the creek where I unsheathed his head. From the side of the bank came the unmistakable rack, rack, rack of the frog."

"Go get him owl," I commanded and cast him off my arm.

"With a few bold strokes he soared into the air, and as a streak of light he dove straight at the frog. One strike and the frog was no more.

"That night my meditation was wonderful. I heard the sound of the universe, the music of the spheres, and in those sounds I deciphered the formula for eternal youth. Almost as if guided by a mystic force, my hand wrote the symbols in the dust on the floor. I entered Shamballa, conquered nirvana, brought the mystical formula back with me. Then . . ."

Da Mo slumped over in his chair. He didn't speak for a long time. At last, I got up and went over to him and shook him. Nothing. I put my hand in front of his nose. No breath. He was either dead or in deep mediation. I shook him again. I bent close to him.

"Hey Chinaman."

"Hoot, Hoot!" He screamed in my face. "The owl from Hell!"

I jumped back, and leaned next to my computer. "Rex?" I asked. "Are you getting this?"

"Hoot! Hoot!" Rex replied.

"Thanks a lot"

Da Mo beat his arms in the air. "Hoot! Hoot!"

"Hoot! Hoot!" Rex responded.

"Calm down!" I shouted. "Take it easy. What happened next?"

"I was going nuts," he replied. "Here I had the formula for eternal life, but it was just a bunch of hieroglyphics written in dust on my floor. The stupid owl was flying around the room and wouldn't leave me alone, and to make it worse no one else seemed to mind. They all liked it. The Shoaling priests thought it was beautiful. Darjeeling gave me strange looks. There was only one solution. I knew I must seek the council of the Old One.

"It was a long pilgrimage to the Old One. There were many perils and always the owl followed me. Several times I felt my life was in danger. Once, along the cliff path it flew around my head, and I slipped, but I was able to gain my footing. At last the path gave way to a broken down hut.

"Inside an old man sat naked, cross legged on the hard dirt floor. He mixed a bowl of rancid blood."

"You have come about evil," he said.

"Not exactly," I replied. "I've come to find out how to get rid of that damn owl. No matter what I do, I fail. The hoot, hoot, hoot is driving me crazy."

"The old one threw bones on the floor. His long yellow finger nails turned red as he mixed the bones and the blood."

"Say," he asked, "are you hungry?"

"No! I'm not hungry," I answered. "I've got to get rid of this owl. You have to help me!"

"The Old One grabbed my hand and with incredible strength forced it into the blood and bones. He then pulled out a rice paper with ancient symbols on it."

"You want to be free of the owl?"

"How many times do I have to say so?"

"He stamped my hand on the paper. Little did I know it was the contract of the Evil One, and I was trapped."

"What is this?"

"A simple oracle," he replied. "I will read your future. Very strange. Yes. Oh no. No. No it can't be! Interesting. This is interesting."

"What! What?"

"The oracle."

"What does it say?"

"You are mine now!"

"I don't understand."

"The old one scratched his head and again looked at the bloody rocks and bones. He held up the stained rice paper."

"It says here you must be hungry."

"I told you already I wasn't hungry."

"The owl was now right at the opening to the Old One's hut."

"Hoot. Hoot. Hoot!"

"No, no." The Old One replied. "It says you must become very, very hungry."

Now, Da Mo had a funny look on his face. I almost thought I saw a tear in his eye. He seemed very far away.

"Stuffy in here," I said. "We could use a little air. Please Rex, open a port."

I walked to the wall. "Window!" I commanded, and the wall opened to a window facing the street below.

Holly shit! The street below was crowded with Newt, giant lizard Newt. Filling the streets in every direction there were thousands, millions, of snarling lizards. Men, women, and children were being devoured as the lizards used their razor teeth to rip the their poor victims to shreds. Blood and guts spewed forth from human and lizard . . . but the green monsters were getting the upper hand. Too many. They lusted for human flesh. No one was safe. An old street vendor tired to escape but a lizard jumped on him and bit off his head. A little girl ran from the crowd but a big leathery creature unzipped her skin with slash, and her poor skinned body twisted and rolled on concrete. Then I saw them.

Below in the middle of the street, Parkenson and Simpson were single handedly defending themselves from the hordes of Newt. They were cut off from their Magna Jet and it look like they had less than a minute before their hides were lunch. Soon, their quivering fleshless bodies would do the dance of death, twisting and genuflecting in the hot noonday sun. Could I save them?

Chapter 10.

"Weapons!" I screamed, and immediately the cabinet opened.

I scanned the assortment of killing instruments. My Johnson 44.80 would be practically useless. From here I could take out a chunk of them with the long range cannon, but Parkenson and Simpson would go too. A proximity bomb would do the trick, but that also would detonate too soon, not leaving us time for escape. Only seconds separated Parkenson and Simpson from their fate at the razor sharp teeth of insane lizards.

I had to do something. Piercing cries of human death reached up to me. Newt and man fought tooth and nail, and I knew defenseless humans were getting the worst of it. I could smell ripe flesh.

In my collection, from years ago, the antique concentric atomic caught my eye. An old weapon to be sure, outlawed before the war over twenty five years ago. It had a range of a thousand yards. It evaporated every living thing in a giant circle, except at the center in a three foot radius. Clean, an old neutron model, it didn't leave radiation. Of course, if you weren't in the center of the blast it took you out too. You got ten thousand neutrons up your ass. Goodbye.

Did it work or not? It's not the kind of weapon you test. I'd traded it for a simple investigation. What was the case? The Rubber Glove Fiasco. Or, was it the 'Case of the Blown Blue Balls?'

No time for thinking. The green monsters closed in on my two friends, and they were running out of ammo. The concentric was their only chance. I grabbed the atomic and made for the force, hit the pavement running. Switched the 44.80 on automatic, fired at will and dove through the spewing blue green slime sputum. As I dumped the final rounds of the 44.80 into the lizards between me Parkenson and Simpson, I could see it was now hand to hand. I cocked the concentric. Slimy lizard bodies crunched under my boots.

Mandrake claw form.

Lizards eat death!

But so many of them. . . At last I made the inner circle.

Sharp razor teeth were about to rip Simpson from crouch to throat, but I caught the lizard with the butt of my Johnson and knocked it off the big man.

"About time you showed up!" he cried, and tossed a big green one off my back.

Parkenson looked at me with a pitiful smile. "Should' a stayed upstairs you young fool! Know how to dance without your skin? We're done!"

My Mandrake claw sliced the head off a huge green monster.

"I ain't so young, and that's the second time somebody called me a fool today. I'm getting mad!

I held the little beauty where they could see they could see it.

"Concentric Atomic!" Simpson shouted. "It'll kill anything within a thousand yards."

"Except us!"

"Fire that mother fucker! Parkenson cried.

I pulled the trigger and the hammer slammed against the cartridge. Time stopped, but nothing happened. I cocked it again. The trigger slammed. Nothing happened. The Newt closed in. One of them had my claw in its mouth. Rip!

That is, what used to be its mouth. But too many of them. We fought bravely.

I cocked it again, and then a strange thing. Something flickered on the edge of my consciousness. Some strange darkness, more like a feeling, like something dank, something evil, moved in the corner of my eyesight.

The Newt were on us. The three of us, me and Simpson and Parkenson, and perhaps what was left of humans in the city for all we knew . . . we fought side by side, tooth and nail. We flailed. Our weapons were empty, so we pounded the lizards with our guns.

"This is it, boys!" Parkenson voice broke. "We're out of ammo. In a second we're gonna have our skins peeled off of us like ripe oranges. I'm not going out as a quivering mound of meat without my flesh."

He held the pocket disrupter pen to his forehead.

"No way!" I yelled and grabbed his hand and rammed the pen into the cartridge of the concentric atomic.

KARAM!

Circles of death spread five, ten, twenty, a hundred, and a thousand yards, radiating in all directions.

Being inside a concentric atomic discharge was a very exciting experience. Fortunately for us, everything outside the radius was completely fried by neutron rays. At first, it was as if everything just stopped, sort of frozen in time. Slowly, as if we were the center of time itself, everything around us disintegrated and disappeared. The Newt were wiped out. It did take out a few street vendors, but they weren't going to be selling too much without their skins.

In the end there was no way of telling if the humans or the Newt got the worst of it. An empty shuttle floated along with no one in it. Most of the street people had already been skinned before they were evaporated. Their money lay in the street for other beggars. That reminded me. I'd left hundred thousand American sitting on my desk. And what about Da Mo? Did he escape? Was he evaporated?

Back in my office, Simpson was hyperventilating. His chest rose, expanded, and contracted and blood seeped from the rip up the center of his body. His empty Z6 jumped in his hand. The rounds were gone, but he kept firing empty shots.

"Simpson," I said, "calm down. We won."

He tried to speak. "I, I . . ." but he couldn't. He was shaking and jerking. "You s, s . . . saved my life."

He paused. "Got anything to drink?"

"Yeah," Parkenson inserted, "you got any of that Scotch you been peddling."

The Chinaman was gone. Vaporized? I didn't think so. He was a tricky old bastard. A case like his would wait, especially when action called. And the money was still on my desk. I pocketed it before Parkenson noticed and recovered enough to start doing his typical questioning. That's when I saw the note.

'Meet me at the Five Dollar in twenty minutes,' signed Da Mo.

Parkenson held his hand to his ear. "What!"

"Simpson," he commanded. "Get downstairs and start up the jet. We've got to reboot. There's another riot in Sector Four. D-men have been spotted in different parts of the city. The council's under siege. We may have another revolution on our hands."

He turned to me and pointed. "You better hide out, Phillips. The D are back and it looks like they're gunning for you."

"D-men!" I cried. "I ain't afraid of no D-men!"

"It's Dr. Blood!" Parkenson screamed. "He's at the bottom of this."

"Blood." I said. "Finally . . . finally, I get my chance to pop that vein! Bring him on!"

Parkenson laughed. "Listen, whatever happens, remember the party at my place tonight. Bring Cynthia and Linda. Don't be late."

As he and Simpson exited into the field, I thought I heard him say "I'm sorry. It's not my fault. It's politics. Bad blood in the council."

Or did he say, "Dr. Blood in the council?"

It had been six years since the Insta Meds took control, and no one knew where Dr. Blood could be found, but then no one was looking for that blue vein. At one time he and his powerful Politicos ruled. I had mixed feelings about that. No one, especially me, liked Blood and his torture chambers. But his iron hand did control the streets. If that were the only way to live, I'd rather be dead.

I knew Dr. Blood was the head of the D. And if D-men had been seen again in the city, Dr. Blood was somewhere to be found. It was a bitter sweet idea. I wanted his hide, and he wanted me dead.

Still, I had a job to do. If our paths crossed, D-men would die and so would Blood. I'd get him this time.

Mandrake claw form!

I slashed the claw through the imaginary head of Blood and popped his giant vein. Die Blood!

Still, Blood or no Blood, I had a case. I was on the trail of the missing Ching Da. If I found it, I might take a long drink of that Charachunga.

"Take a break, Rex." I said.

"A break?"

"I'm joking. I know you're never off. Listen! I'm going down to the Five Dollar Café to get the skinny from this Da Mo character. First, what is the analysis of the poison on that napkin you been chewing on?"

"Ninety two percent H2O," Rex monotoned. "Six percent green tea and two percent One Daktara. And I don't chew."

"One Daktara. Where's that grown?"

"California City."

"California City?"

I hadn't been out there since rot kissed scum. Before the change it was prime resort. Now the Ozone desert crept toward it, eating it bit by bit, changing what had been a grand resort into a hovel for ski bums and itinerate surfers. It was the world's worst resort.

"Book a seat on the Link." I thought for a second, which was usually a little too long. "No, book two seats."

I tossed half the Chinaman's American into Rex's mouth, I mean port. I could never quite figure out how Rex digested cash and turned it into credits. But what's that they say? "You don't have to know how a magneto works to drive a shuttle." In times like these I guessed the only thing you could trust was the computer system. Somehow, the cash turned into credits, and that meant I was back on line at the Insta Med, just in case I needed a stitch or two. Or a metal body. I hoped not. I reloaded my Johnson. Ready for work.

The street smelled about as clean and fresh as I could remember it. No shuttles running yet. The neutrons cleaned the place pretty well, but although it's a long walk to the Five Dollar Café, by the time I reached Nick's, street bums, beggars, and scum were pulling at my pants just like usual.

I looked over at Nick's for an instant. Inside the shop sat old Nick, and I'd pay him a visit later after I interrogated Da Mo. I crossed and headed down the street to the Five Dollar. I needed to get the gum cleaned off my transceiver, but I also needed to eat. Some of that Insta Feast sounded good. At the Five Dollar, Lee Tsing greeted me at the door as he always did.

"Welcome to my humble bowl of chicken and rice," he said. "Ah Mister Dick Phillips, I see you got my message yesterday."

"Message?"

"Ah so," he replied and bowed. "I leave telephone message on your computer. Big, big proposition. I want you work for me."

My ear was still a little sore. There were no big beggars at the door, but he must have noticed the scowl on my face.

"So sorry," he said, "about ear. But you know old Chinese proverb, 'Man who shoot first wife find ear on plate.'"

"Lee . . . you made that up."

"Maybe, maybe, ah so . . . now, we even."

You can't blame a guy for being mad about loosing his wife. Still, there was something a little slimy about Lee Tsing that I didn't like because he looked a lot like a squid, because his smile wasn't real, because he never looked quite right. Or, just because.

"Give me a back table, will you?" I asked. "Say, you having Insta Feast today. I'd love a little duck."

"Duck? Ah so. Duck. Insta Feast coming right up."

He guided me to a back table under the balcony near the stairs. Same old Five Dollar Café. It didn't change. Wooden tables, pictures of China, Chinese boys with pony tails. Drummed my fingers on the wooden table. Where was Da Mo? Put my hand on the cold steel of my Johnson 44.80. My trigger finger itched. Come on, Da Mo. Where are you? I was hungry and hungry to get started on the case. Then Cynthia came to mind. I'd be doing her at

Parkenson's tonight. I wondered how it was going to be with Cynthia and Pella. Could I do them both?

"Insta Feast!" Lee shouted, slid the plate and a cup of tea in front of me, and then sat down.

One Daktara will kill an ordinary man. I wasn't ordinary. I'd had it at least twenty times and developed immunity. I drank some of the tea. Tasted more like mint than One Daktara. What was Lee Tsing's game?

Tsing smiled his broken yellow tooth smile, and I took a bite of the food. Fabulous! Better than I remembered it. The duck was wonderful and the potatoes perfectly firm. Tsing rubbed his hands impatiently. I beat him to the punch.

"Okay Tsing, what's the deal?"

"Big case for you," he replied and pulled out a stack of American green. "Very mean man in town. You must find and kill."

"You know I don't do that," I said. "I'm not a hired killer. I'm a licensed badge." The money looked good.

"No, no, no!" he shrieked in his high voice. "You find. That all. Then we kill."

I picked up the bills and fingered them. Twenty five thousand American. Nothing like Da Mo's but a lot for Tsing, who was rich compared to the average, but still this was a lot of green. The bad man must be somebody big for Tsing to come up with that kind of cash. I tossed the money down on the table.

"Give me the details."

"Perhaps," he began, "You did not know, but the Five Dollar Café is an international chain. I am proud to say this is number one restaurant of all time. But now giant corporation from China tries to buy us out. Even my life has been threatened. I not want to sell my part. If sell, have no where to go. Money no good today. Only property, only power. Big Chinaman wants to take restaurant away from me. You find him. We get rid of him."

I ate some juicy bites of duck. Umm. Well, what a twisted set of events. Of course, twenty five thousand wasn't much, and Da Mo's case was number one, but I might fit in a side job. I wondered if I could milk this cow.

"I'm not sure I have the time right now, Tsing." I said. "You know your Insta Feast is really good. What's the secret?"

He leaned over and whispered. "Instead of Duck, we use Newt."

The lavatory stank. In the first stall, I drove the white steering wheel. There was a crack in the floor stained red. The wall board was rotting. The mirror frame needed paint. My face looked old and ashen. Aging too fast. Nothing new. I needed vitamin E in the butt. It had been too soon after the firefight with Parkenson and Simpson, too soon to eat Newt. As I turned to go, from another stall a hand shot out and grabbed my shoulder.

The wall burst in an explosion. My right hand caught nothing but air, and the follow-through punched a section of sheetrock wall. I whirled around and faced Da Mo.

"Easy," he said and put a hand to defect my second and third blows. "We must talk. It is too dangerous in the café. We are safe here."

"You almost died, Chinaman!" I screamed. "The last man to attack me like that left his face on the road."

"Relax Mr. Phillips! The forces of evil mount, but we have a little time. You must find the China Da and return it to me."

I was beginning to respect the Chinaman's fighting ability, but I didn't trust him. I didn't like men touching me in bathrooms, so I whipped it out.

My Johnson pointed straight up at his head.

"Alright," I said, "let's hear the rest of your story. But if you make a move toward me, you're history."

"First Charachunga."

We lit up a couple Royals. He inhaled deep and again spoke elegant English.

"I was in the hut of the Old One," Da Mo said in an elegant but resigned manner. "The Old One's face made a contorted smile as if he'd just won a long battle. I looked at the blood on my hands and the stained parchment in front of me, but only the "Hoot, hoot, hoot!" of the owl outside filled my thoughts.

The Old One mixed dirt and blood with his long yellow fingernails. "You must become very, very hungry." He licked his lips and laughed.

"Ha, ha, ha," he laughed. "Eat me . . . I mean, eat meat. Ha!"

"The way back to the Shoaling temple was very difficult. I stumbled many times. A great fog clouded my mind. It was cold, and I couldn't find my way. The path changed to steep rocks and thorny bushes. At last, drugged with exhaustion, I found a niche in the mountain and closed my eyes.

"But as soon as my eyes closed, 'Hoot, hoot, hoot!' the owl swept at me and pecked my face. It wouldn't let me sleep. I'll get you, I thought, and picked up a large rock and threw it. But the owl dodged it easily and my foot slipped. Right then, I realized my predicament. In my deranged state I had wandered on a ledge some hundred feet above a raging river. I teetered on the ledge and grasped for a tree limb to hold to, but the owl swooped around my head and pecked at my hand. I lost my hold and slipped. I fell a hundred feet to sure death in the raging torrent below.

"Luckily, for me, I fell directly between two large rocks, and the raging torrent buffeted me about like a leaf. Hours later, dirty, exhausted, cut, and bruised, I crawled out of the river at the pond next to the Shoaling monastery.

"Master!" Darjeeling shouted as I dragged myself inside.

"Yes, Darjeeling," I replied, "it is I."

"What has happened?"

"Nothing," I replied. "I have just been for a swim. Bring me some food."

"But when Darjeeling entered my room with rice, I could not eat. The words of the Old One kept entering my mind.

"You must become very, very hungry."

"Darjeeling," I said, "Go to town and bring me the Bird Master."

Da Mo inhaled another deep drag on the Royal. I put away the Johnson and sat back on one of the toilets while the Chinaman continued his story.

"I had to repeat myself."

"Darjeeling," I said, "Listen to me. Go to town and bring the Bird Master."

"Oh master," he replied, "that beautiful owl has just returned."

"Bird!?" I cried and flung open the curtains.

"Hoot, hoot, hoot!"

"Isn't it beautiful?" Darjeeling said. "How it welcomes the day."

"Go get the Bird Master!" I said and pulled shut the curtains.

"When at last they returned, I greeted the skinny old Bird Master."

"Bird Master," I said, "welcome to our temple. I have called you here to solve a problem for me. I need you to dispose of the owl you sold us a little while ago."

"He stroked his long nose. His beady little eyes darted as he spoke. "Dispose?" he asked. "What you mean?"

"Get rid of the damned thing!"

"You want sell him back to me?"

"No. No!" I screamed. "Kill it!"

"I no kill bird, is impossible."

"Alright," I replied. "Answer me this. What is the natural prey of the owl?"

"Why," he said and looked toward the ceiling, "that be Great Eagle, the giant sky bird."

"You must sell me one of those."

"But have none."

"What! Then where can I find one?"

"There only one know of," the Bird Master stated. "Must go to Gartok. The Bird Master of Gartok point to its nest."

Again Da Mo took a deep hit of Charachunga. I didn't know how much more of the story I could take. The restroom smelled like piss and throw up, and I could hear some men behind the door waiting to get in. The Chinaman begged me for another Royal. He was chain smoking them worse than me. He continued.

"In Gartok the Bird Master was a shapely young woman. She beckoned me to enter her tent, so I sat down in among the large and small cages holding various birds."

"Show me your hands," she said.

"I have come about the Great Eagle," I replied, "not to have my nails done."

"I know. Come closer," she whispered. "Place your hands on this rock."

"I wasn't falling for that one, not after the Old One's tricks."

"Now, wait a minute," I said. "Why do you need my hands?"

"The Great Eagle is very powerful," she replied, "and will kill you easily. However, if he sees you have claws like him, he will listen to your request."

"I set my hands flat on the rock that separated us, and without warning she smashed a big rock on top of my fingernails. The Bird Master then inserted new longer nails on my fingers and sewed up my hands.

"It was a hard hike to the home of the Great Eagle and the owl kept pestering me, and my fingers were killing me, but as I neared the great nest, the owl turned and flew away. It was quiet there, and at last I felt a peace I had not known for some time. There, in the shade of the giant nest, I was able to meditate again. The directions for eternal life came to me. I discovered how to create a formula which would recreate itself, forever renewing itself and keeping its owner alive for eternity. I memorized the formula and burned it into my mind.

"At that moment I heard a sound like ten thousand wings beating, and my heart quickened as I looked up to see the Great Eagle land in its nest."

"Great Eagle," I said, and held up my claw hands. "I beg your forgiveness. I have come about the owl that is pestering me day and night."

Bam!

Da Mo stopped speaking. We turned to the bathroom door.

Bam! Bam! Someone pounded on the door.

"What is it?!" I said.

A man's voice. "I have to poop."

"I'm a badge. This is important business. Go next door in the woman's."

Da Mo whispered in my ear. "Be quick now. Meet me later at the Hotel Meringue. Bring Charachunga cigarettes."

Then I heard it. Ka lick. The unmistakable sound of a shell entering the firing chamber of a Zeno Fourteen sawed off cannon. I hit the floor and held my ears.

Blammer! Rama Kramar!

The door blew open in three foot hole and part of the wall behind was demolished. The Johnson flared hot in my hand. In their red and black uniforms, three D-men stepped through the bathroom door. The first one took it in the eye, and his brains splattered red lumps on the wall. The second caught a direct shot through his teeth and his head blew up. Less than a second separated three shots. The third D man seemed to freeze in mid air, then jerked and fell limp to the floor.

Back at the table, Lee Tsing was animated. His eyes darted back and forth, and he made his hands into fists and then relaxed them. He looked at me and his head jerked. Finally he blurted it out.

"D-men. D-men. See, they trying to kill me. They want restaurant!"

"Calm down Lee. Parkenson's squad will be here soon to clean up. It's just an isolated incident. Some trouble in the Council. They won't be back."

"Better not be. Better not."

I squinted at the little worm. "Let's get back to your case."

"Twenty thousand American if you find the evil man."

"Now wait a minute, Lee," I said, "a few minute ago you said twenty five thousand. What's the deal?"

He tossed a piece of wallboard on the table. "Five thousand to repair bathroom. Twenty thousand to find evil man."

"Okay, okay," I said, and pocketed the American. I couldn't refuse. I knew I'd soon be paying Parkenson more taxes. "You got a deal. I'll find him, but you got to do him. Now, give me the details."

"Long story. . ," he said.

I rolled my eyes in my head. Not another long story. First Da Mo, now Lee Tsing. I hoped he didn't ask for one of my Royals.

"It's a long story," he continued. "But I make it short. The one we want you to find is the legendary fighter Kang. He fought his way to the top in China and became very rich. Now, he has come to America and is trying to buy the Five Dollar."

"Well," I said, "describe this Kang."

"That's the problem. That's the problem."

"What."

"No one's seen him. Only big stories."

I took the bait. "Let's have the stories."

"They say if you try to hit him you could not. He is like mosquito. When you try to strike him, he is not there. They say he has large eyes and can see in the dark. They say he has springs in his legs and can jump thirty feet."

"Can he fly too?"

"Yes. Yes. They say when you fight him, he has long talons like a bird and fangs like a tiger. He is a devil. He has horns that grow out his head. They say he has bright red eyes, and if you look at him, you turn to stone."

I pulled out the Johnson and set the 44.80 on the table. A waft of smoke came out of its shaft. There was a quiet moment, a moment when the hustle and bustle of the restaurant became background music. It was the music of glass breaking, babies crying and Chinamen slurping soup.

They were eating chicken and rice and bowls of egg flower soup. Odors of food filled the restaurant. A small baby nursed at its mother's breast. A old man pounded the table and threw a hand of

Ma Chung. A waiter crossed with a tray of steaming vegetables. I leaned close to Lee.

"Does he eat lead?"

Chapter 11.

So now I had two cases going. I was working on the finding the Ching Da for Da Mo, and I was looking for this ex-fighter, Kang, a big time corporate raider. As I walked up the street toward Nick's, I retraced some of the events of the past few days. There was no doubt about it; D-men were after me. Them trying to kill me was just sport for me. It didn't bother me. It wasn't the first time. Then again, who actually was the leader of the D? I knew that the D-man army were just the lackeys of someone or something bigger. It had to be Dr. Blood.

Hump! I thought, Dr. Blood. His big brain was always thinking, making that varicose vein on his forehead pulse with plans to conquer me and the world, or to torture hapless innocents. I wondered how Saint Billy fit into all this. I'd soon find out once Nick repaired my transceiver. I tapped on his window.

"Nicholous," I said as I walked in, "good to see you. Nice day, isn't it?"

"Well, well," he replied and looked up from his scope. "If it isn't my old friend, the badge, Dick Phillips. Weren't you just here yesterday? Already break that new unit?"

"No, it's not broken. Just worn out. Needs a new battery."

I reached out to shake his hand. "How are you buddy?"

"How come you in such a good mood, Dick?"

"Nothin much. I got started on two new cases, and just shot dead three D-men over at the Five Dollar."

I took out the wad of gum holding my transceiver. "Here it is," I said, and tossed the chunk of gum on the counter.

"Question is, what is it?"

I laughed. "Hee, hee . . . It's the transceiver you sold me yesterday. It's buried inside this hunk."

He held it up. "That's impossible," he said and adjusted his horn rimmed reading glasses. "This hunk of I don't know what to call it is at least twenty years old."

He looked at me. His eyes stared over the spectacles, "How is that possible? You been time traveling again? I told you that's not good for your spleen. You're not getting any younger, Dick."

I lit up a Royal. "Yes I am. It's these Royals. They got a special quality. It's called Charachunga."

"Bull shit! You just get high off of them. They're narco."

He held up the lump of gum to his high intensity light. "Poof," that is some stinky old crap. How'd your Rex ear piece get buried in it?"

"Classified."

"Bull shit again! I do all the work and you have all the fun."

"Okay then. You're right. I traveled back to my youth, secreted the transceiver under a bar in Village Eight in that time, and got it back in this time. Satisfied?"

"Sure you did. What's the real story?"

"No really. Young Pella's back at my mod waiting to fuck me again."

"Again!" He slapped the counter with his hand. "When am I going to get some of that young tang? Why do you get to have all the fun?"

"Nick, you need to get out."

I put my arm over his shoulder. "Nick, just get the scent. That's all you need. Just get the scent. You're not too old. Dip that thing in the honey. It'll all come back. How long has it been?"

He held up two fingers.

"A couple of months? That's not too bad. Why you complaining?"

"Decades, Dick. Decades!"

"Gad Nick, I didn't know. You ought to get over to Village Eight. They got illegals that'll take care of you."

"Ah fuck all," Nick said. "Let me get to work."

Even if he was way behind on getting pussy, I liked the way Nicholous worked. He was a true wizard, somebody that liked their work, a joy to watch as he quickly trimmed off the gum. His laser snapped, and in an instant he cleaned my unit and checked the voltage.

"Battery's dead."

"Go ahead," I said, "put in a new one, and while you're at it, make sure everything else is working."

"Tune up will cost a thousand."

"No problem." I tossed the money on the counter.

Nick looked up and smiled. I was paying his rent. That was for sure.

"Wait a minute," he said and paused. "That's strange."

"What!"

"This transceiver has been set for dual frequency."

"Dual frequency?"

"Yeah, hold on a second." He touched his control board and the computer spoke.

"Frequency 1240876-9907899, Dick Phillips, badge 324200."

Nick touched the control board again, and the computer spoke again. "Frequency 124-876-9907899, Council chambers."

I looked at Nick. We both seemed to have a question on our faces.

"Somebody over at the Council wants your ass."

Ugh. Now, I was hot under the collar. What was it Da Mo called me, a nonsequential ignoramus? Badges are sacred. The laws are specific. Once you get your badge your communications are not to be tapped. I felt violated. Someone in the Council set me up. They sent me through time to get inside my head. Hell, they didn't have to go to all that trouble. There was nothing there. I could have told them that. Then an idea came to me.

"Put a battery in for a second, then when I give it back, take it out."

"No problem."

I held my finger to my lips, and motioned for Nick not to speak. I held the transceiver in front of me.

"This is Phillips. The hidden bomb in the Council chambers should explode in minus ten minutes."

I handed it back to Nick who flicked out the battery.

"That should get them going. Take that other frequency off, and fit it back in my ear. I've got a shuttle to catch. It's been a long day. Still have to meet the Chinaman at the Hotel Meringue. And Pella's waiting for me at home."

As I walked out to the shuttle I heard him call.

"You're a magnet for women, Phillips. Damn you!"

But compliments didn't placate my agony. The shuttle wait never seemed to be over, and the only solace I found there in front of Nick's was that perhaps Browny would be on board. And I could do him. I let the Johnson slide back to the holster.

As I edged through the lock, the shuttle stank full of underbelly and weirdo but no Browny. I wondered where he was. Poor mechanico probably went out of his mind quicker than I thought he would. It wasn't like Browny. He should have caught up with me by now . . . unless he lost the trail in the underground, or he waited for me around the next corner. The gray city moved slowly through the windows of the magneto portal, and at last the Hotel Meringue loomed in the distance.

I commed to Rex on my now secure channel.

"Please Rex, give me any calls."

"No calls," he replied.

"New voices from time opening."

"No new voices."

"Good man."

"Insults won't get you very far," he replied.

The shuttle ground to a stop at the Hotel Meringue, and I jumped out. Kind of quiet. They'd already patched up the underground from the fire fight yesterday, and things seemed pretty normal back at the old Medico's Meringue Hotel. Jackson was out in front as usual.

"Jackson?"

"Master Phillips, Master Dick Phillips."

"Jackson, I thought they got you?"

"I took one pretty bad," he said and tapped his chest.

"Nice metal, huh?"

"You're not . . ?"

"A mechanico," he said. "Yeah, but it's not so bad. I only got a few months left. But you know, son, at least I still got my head."

"Here," I said, and handed him a Royal.

"No thanks you, Mister Phillips. Don't smoke no more. Just messes up the machinery."

I found Da Mo in the little room behind the elevator between the second and third floors. He was slumped over with his head down on the table, slurping tea with his tongue like an animal. He looked exhausted, a real mess.

"What's the idea?" I said. "Did you set me up with those D-men?"

His long fingers reached out to me. He could barely lift his head, and when he did his parched dried face showed yellow skin crinkled like paper. He could hardly talk.

"Cigarette me!"

"Listen you pathetic old sapient," I said, "there's another revolution going on. The Council's in danger." I flicked out a Royal and handed it to him. "Give me the whole story and don't leave anything out."

"You want it all?" he asked.

"Give it all."

We lit up . . . and after he took a few puffs . . . smiled, and became animated. At last, he lifted himself to his full height and moved about the small room, gracefully describing the events of his life. He looked younger, yet also moved with distinction. He thanked the Great Eagle.

"I looked up at the Eagle and waited, but all I could hear was a "chomp, chomp, chomp" sound like bones being crushed. Some brown feathers fell from the nest. Owl feathers! The Great Eagle had eaten the owl. All my problems were solved. At least, I thought they were.

"As I bowed in thanks to the Eagle, the giant bird dropped from the nest and swooped down toward me, only missing me by inches as I bowed. The Great Eagle was after me. It flew about me enraged, biting, and snipping at my head.

"Squawk, squawk, squawk!" it shrieked.

"Instead of simply pestering me, as the owl had done, the Eagle was trying to kill me. I was sure of it. As fast as I could, I ran back to the Bird Master's hut."

"Bird Master," I cried, "you have to help me. The Great Eagle is trying to kill me!"

"Nonsense," she replied, "he only wants to show you his appreciation for the fine meal of the owl."

The Eagle beat at the Bird Master's door, tearing at the hut. "Squawk, squawk, squawk!"

"See, he is only showing how strong you have made him. He wants to thank you."

"Yes." I said. "And I want to thank you also. Please, while the Great Eagle is here with us, will you walk with me to the edge of your fine city of Gartok?"

"Why of course," she answered.

"You know," I said, "I am the Master of the Shoaling temple." I touched the fine robe I was wearing. "I want you to have this."

"I took off my robe and gave it to her, and she tried it on and smiled. I took one of her old blankets and covered my head."

"Please . . . walk me to the edge of town?"

"We started walking toward the edge of Gartok, toward the bamboo fields, and I looked for the Great Eagle. He was nowhere to be found, but I noticed a small dot very far up in the sky. As we walked into the opening before the bamboo where the trail led to the forest, I stopped and thanked the bird master. The dot in the sky grew larger.

"Bird Master, you are very beautiful. You look so nice in my robe."

"I covered her head with the robe. " Keep yourself warm," I said. "Thank you for saving my life."

"I entered the safety of the bamboo and scurried along, hidden by the tall plants. Soon, I heard the horrible sounds of bones crushing and the high shriek of the young Bird Master as the Great Eagle tore out her heart.

"I returned to my temple, and thinking I had at last defeated the curse that was upon me, I called my servant to my room."

"Darjeeling," I said, "I want to have a wonderful celebration. Call all the monks together, and we will make a great party."

"Oh yes, Master," Darjeeling replied. "We will celebrate that the Great Eagle has come to live with us."

"Darjeeling," I said and held my head, "the Great Eagle is not here."

"Oh yes, Master." He interjected. "He has just arrived this morning. Isn't it wonderful?"

"Go into town and bring back the Beast Master."

"The Bird Master?"

"Are you deaf? I said the Beast Master."

"Unlike the Bird Master who was tall and skinny, the Beast Master was an ugly dwarf who normally I wouldn't be seen with, but this was an emergency. His little hump was repulsive, and the way he twisted his face when he spoke made him hard to understand. But he had a certain way with animals.

"When at last they returned, I had Darjeeling make a fire and serve wine on our finest tray. As I held the wine down to the dwarf, he smiled, quickly took the glass, and drank it down in a gulp. Three more glasses and he turned his face from the fire and looked up at me."

"What want of me?"

"I need to know if the Great Eagle has a predator, and where can I find it?"

The dwarf pushed his eyes together and crinkled his mouth. "Predator?"

"Yes. Yes." I screamed. "What animal will kill the Great Eagle?"

He thought for a minute, and then replied. "More wine."

"First, tell me"

"Kill the Great Eagle?"

"Yes, you simpleton. Quit repeating what I say."

"Quit repeating. More wine? More wine?"

"More wine. Darjeeling!"

After the next glass of wine, the midget was ready to speak.

"More wine?"

"Damn it, listen."

"Squawk, squawk, squawk!"

Da Mo fluttered his hands in the air and grimaced. "The Eagle," he screamed, "has been eating babies and stealing farm animals. Listen, midget! Even now it tries to break in and kill us. We have to kill the Great Eagle before it kills us."

"Hold it!" I yelled. "Hold it. Stop the story!"

"What is it?" asked the Chinaman who took another casual draw on his Royal.

"I'm bored of this damn story," I replied. "Not enough sex, no violence. Where's the pussy? How about some intrigue? What happened to adventure?"

The poor old man got a strange look on his face. Well, I mean strange looks. First, he seemed indignant. Then he was pissed, and I thought he looked like a slimy reptilian. He went to his tea and slurped the liquid. He flapped his arms and bobbed his head and pecked about. Finally, he snarled at me.

"Do you want to hear the story, or not?"

"Sure, sure I do. But spice it up a bit."

"Okay," he said, "I'll act out the parts."

"Don't . . ." But it was too late.

The old Chinaman moved about in his hypnotic manner looking a little like his servant Darjeeling, then the Great Eagle, and finally squatting down and hunching up like the little dwarf Beast Master.

"Kill the Great Eagle?" muttered the idiot dwarf.

"More wine, Darjeeling!"

"After several more glasses the Beast Master was drunk. He jumped and ran to the fire and poked his hand in the flames. He poked and poked and stirred the fire and laughed. He turned his twisted little face, and the light cast a demonic red color on his squished features, and created a gleam in his eye."

"The snow lion of Yangtze," he laughed.

"That night," continued Da Mo, "I gathered together the other priests in the grand hall and made an announcement.

"I am going on a very dangerous mission," I said. "And I will need volunteers to help me."

Tozan and Kora stood up.

"You will need to wear my robes and travel by day to the south and the west. Meanwhile, under the cover of darkness, I will make my way to the snow covered mountains of Yangtse."

The Chinaman spoke softly. "That was the last time I saw Tozan or Kora . . ."

"With much difficulty, after many days, I arrived at the village of Yangtze. As the dwarf instructed me, I stopped at the cave of the Beast Master of Yangtze. But unlike the dwarf of our village, this Beast Master was himself a beast. He was a monster, and his hump rose far above his back and constantly bumped on the ceiling of his cave so that as he moved about he had to stop and squat. Then he would forget himself and again bump his hump. Hump bump; hump then bump. He was far uglier then than our village dwarf."

"Welcome," the Beast Master said. "I have been waiting. You wish to visit the Snow Lion. Is this not true?"

"Yes," I replied.

"The Beast Master ground his hump on the top of his cave, smoothed his long mustache, and stroked his beard."

"Make a big smile."

"Now wait a minute," I said. "This is not a laughing matter."

"Smile!" he demanded.

"All right," I replied, and smiled a giant smile. Just then, before I could react, the Beast Master jammed a pointed rock between my teeth and broke my front teeth."

"It hurt like hell. A gong seemed to explode in my head. I felt the presence of evil inside of me."

The Chinaman shouted. "Evil pain! Pain and evil!"

"It really hurt."

"To greet the giant Snow Lion," the Beast Master said, rubbing his hump on his cave, "you will need long teeth like fangs. Otherwise, when he sees you he will eat you with one bite."

"The Beast Master sharpened my teeth and rubbed a fluid on them and they grew larger. There was a terrible pain, but not as great as the ever irritating sound of the Great Eagle outside. Squawk, squawk, squawk!"

"Now, when the Snow Lion sees you, he will listen to your plea."

"As I climbed toward the cave of the Snow Lion, at least the blizzard kept me hidden from the Great Eagle. I was very cold, my hands hurt, and my mouth ached. My brain was filled with the gong of evil, always pounding, and I moved slowly up the cold mountain. I hadn't eaten for a long time and the words of the Old One filled in the spaces of my thoughts. "You must become very, very hungry."

"Snow Lion," I pleaded, "hear me. I need your help."

"But there was no animal in the cave. It was too cold outside, so I went inside and waited. Soon, I fell into a great meditation. The circle rotated around the Tetragrammaton, and I returned to Shamballa and entered nirvana. It became clear to me that the sacred formula for Charachunga would have to have a receptacle to house it. In the cave of the Snow Lion, I discovered the formula for the perfect holder of the rejuvenation fluid. I visualized the perfect timeless container, and I burned that formula into my mind."

"Then I saw him. The sleek Snow Lion was returning from the hunt, and in its mouth he held the Great Eagle."

"Rahh!" the Snow Lion growled as he devoured the Eagle."

"I held my giant finger nails in front of me and smiled with my fangs and thanked the Snow Lion."

"Thank you, Snow Lion," I said, but the Lion growled at me. Rahh. Rahh. Rahh! Its eyes glowed bright red and it looked evil."

"Yet, as it ate the Eagle, it took little notice of me. While it devoured the Eagle, I counted my blessings that I had finally gotten rid of my troubles. I crept out of the cave and made my way down the mountain, back to the cave of the Beast Master of Yangtze."

Da Mo stopped talking for a moment.

"Wake up!" he screamed.

Then he kicked me in the side. "Wake up you idiot! There's a clue in this. I'm paying you to listen. Now wake up!"

"I am awake! I thought you were talking to the Beast Master. Get on with the story. I am not an idiot!"

"Yes you are! Now, where was I?"

"Beast Master."

He hit a drag on the Royal. "Somehow I made it back to the cave of the Beast Master and ran in."

"Beast Master, help me. The Snow Lion is after me."

"How do you know that?"

"Trust me, Beast Master. I am the Master of the Shoaling temple. Trust me; I know danger when I see it."

"Sir," he said, rubbing his hump on the top of the cave, "you are being silly. You are the Master of your temple. I am the Beast Master. You are simply out of your silly little mind."

"Little, I thought. Everything was little to that giant humpback!"

"You're safe with me!" he commanded.

"Of course," I lied, and started running toward the low land. As I rounded the giant rock, I heard him scream.

"Why are you leaving?"

"A silent pause, then I heard him scream again.

"No. No. Get back! I'm your Master. Get back." Then came terrible screams and the sound of meat being ripped. I knew it was over for the Beast Master."

"Soon, I made it to the river and I worked my way back along the rocks and disguised my tracks by walking in the water and hiding in the brush. I knew the Snow Lion wouldn't follow me to the low lands. After much time, I trudged through the pond near the temple."

"I sat in my room and Darjeeling came to comfort me."

"Wonderful news, Master," he said, "The ancients have blessed the town today. A friendly giant Snow Lion has graced us with his presence."

"I didn't even look up."

"Get me the dwarf Beast Master, and when he comes, bring lots of wine."

"When the little dwarf arrived, he was elated. " You seen him? The white Snow Lion, never see before. So beautiful."

"Shut up you little twerp!"

"Shut up you little twerp!" he repeated.

"Many glasses of wine later, we talked."

"What's bigger than the Snow Lion?"

"Bigger Snow Lion."

"You fool, what's stronger?"

"Stronger."

"The little man looked into his glass."

"More wine. Yes?"

"What's stronger?"

"He smiled his demonic look."

"The Mammoth Brahma Bull of Kanphur."

"That night, at the meeting of the priests, I explained the problem. It's like this, I said. The Snow Lion is a menace to the town. Tomorrow morning I want a group of eight, the bravest of you, to go to the town and capture this Snow Lion.

"That was the last I saw of those eight priests. That night, I started the long journey to Kanphur. It was very difficult, and I was very hungry, but I did not eat. The words of the Old One rang in my ears."

Dick Phillips is hungry too, I thought, for a story that had more vibrant descriptions, more sex. What happened to the plot? This damned Chinaman was more long winded than a hurricane, and the way he was dancing around like a tornado, bobbing his head and acting like dwarfs and lions. . . he was nuts as far as I was concerned.

Hungry? He hadn't seen Cynthia's boobs, fat Linda's ass, or Pella tight little puss. Nor, would, would he, see my woody, which was a big one. That's what they were hungry for . . . my big woody. Ah fuck, look at him dance around. This fucking story is a real drag. When his he going to give me some clues? Why isn't there more sex in this story? Come on you old yellow bastard, get to the meat.

"Meat!" cried Da Mo. "Eat me. . . I mean eat meat." That's what the Old One had said."

He pointed at me. "Listen up, Phillips. Stop dreaming," he said and took a deep drag on his Royal fag, smiled heartily, and with a gleam in his eye continued his diatribe.

"In Kanphur, I made my way to the Beast Master's temple. There the Beast Master was a giant of a man, far bigger than the one in Yangtze. He was bigger than a hut. I felt humbled by his size, and instead of one hump he had two mounds on his back. I felt like a peanut."

"Beast Master," I said, "I must find the giant Brahma Bull. I have a request to make of that animal."

"The huge Beast Master flexed his muscles and his two humps grew large and thumped like drums as he spoke."

"To visit the great Brahma Bull is a grave task. He is unlike any animal in existence. He only eats meat, and he may swallow you whole. If he thinks you are tasty, he will eat you."

"Can't you give me something for protection?"

The giant did not hesitate. "Yes," he said, and grabbed me by the neck. "Don't struggle. It will hurt less. You will need these horns to approach him."

Da Mo slapped his forehead with his fist, "With that, he screwed two horns in my head. There was horrible pain, but I withstood it, for I knew somewhere right behind me the Snow Lion stalked me."

"Slowly, I crept out on the grassy plain of Kanphur. My fingernails sprouted long talons, my teeth were long fangs, and

126

now I had horns growing out of my head. The evil gong in my brain shattered all thought. I truly had not eaten for days and days.

"The Brahma Bull was no where to be found. I waited and waited, and in a short while, night fell. There, while waiting, and even though in great discomfort, I fell into a fantastic meditation. I discovered how indeed I could formulate the magical rejuvenation fluid, the Charachunga, and create its receptacle, the Ching Da. I made the plans. It would take many, many moves. It was a horrible, horrendous plan, but necessary. I resolved no matter what to accomplish it, if I could just talk the Brahma Bull into buying me more time by destroying the Snow Lion.

"A strange gnawing sound woke me from my meditation. I sat not more than ten feet from the great Bull himself. It was twice the size of the largest hut. Its head seemed to be in the clouds for one of its hoofs was larger than my whole body. I was almost covered by the strands of its shaggy brown mane, which I brushed out of my face to see there in front of me the carcass of the Snow Lion. The Brahma Bull had saved me.

"I moved away through the grass, slowly making an escape, but the Bull must have smelled me."

"Bra-ha, bra-ha, bra-ha!"

"It brayed at me and charged. There was no escape. I was done. So I lowered my head and bowed. My death was certain. At the final moment in my plan to cure the world of evil, to attain everlasting life, I had failed. Ironic now, being very hungry, I would eat death. But then a strange thing happened. As I lowered my horned head, the Bull stopped in its tracks and returned to the carcass of the Snow Lion. I ran back to the Beast Master."

"The Brahma Bull is after me!"

"The horns protected you, didn't they? The Bull looks like a monster, but he is only a pussy cat. You wait here; I will go and talk to him."

"I made my escape down the path from his hut and heard the sounds of bones being crushed and heard the screams of the giant Beast Master, but I didn't look back. I made the trail, and although it was a difficult journey and many days passed, I finally returned to my temple. Darjeeling looked at me as if I were a stranger.

"Baphomet?" he asked, shivering with fear.

"I had forgotten the horns, fangs, and talons.

"It's me you fool!"

"But," he replied, "You do not look at all like the Master. Are you hungry?"

"I looked at him with a suspicious eye. " Why do you ask that?"

"Because," he replied innocently, "we are having a big feast for the Giant Brahma Bull that has just wandered into town."

"Bra, bra, bra!"

"I could hear the animal in the distance."

"Darjeeling," I said, "we have no time for celebration. Set up my laboratory, and after you are done I want you to go into town and gather all the young baby boys."

"Baby boys?"

"Yes, we will have to fill the ranks of the priests who have disappeared recently . . . and Darjeeling, don't forget the castration kit."

"That night I made real the formulas I had found in my meditations. It was a simple matter to compound Gold, Sulfur, and Mercury. One by one I held the screaming little babies and cut off their gonads. Then I purified the seed and added it to the compound. There was a large explosion. The eternal receptacle, the China Da was created and inside, the sparkling eternal fluid. The Charachunga glistened.

"Immediately, I drank it half empty, and just as soon it returned to fullness. I had done it! I created the everlasting rejuvenation fluid and the eternal receptacle. I took another drink and the talons on my fingers changed into fingernails. My fangs disappeared and the horns fell off my head. I felt young and strong. The gong of evil was gone from my mind and I knew what I must do.

"However, right then came a pounding on the temple. It was the Brahma Bull, butting on the wall. The plan came quickly. I knew what I had to do, and I escaped out the secret side door while the Bull trampled the temple.

"When I reached the cave of the Old One, he sat in the same place as before, naked as a bird."

"Welcome, he said, "you have come about good and evil."

"Yes," I replied.

"And," he asked, "Are you very, very hungry?"

"I am."

"Insects?" he asked and placed in front of me a handful of festering bugs."

"No, thank you."

"Fish?"

"No."

"Bird?"

"No."

"Lion?"

"No."

"He looked perplexed.

"Oh, I know," he said and pushed a strange looking platter under my nose.:

"This," he said, "will become very popular in years to come. See, it is a cooked piece of ground beef muscle and gut, some pickles, and tomato between baked sesame buns. You want eat?"

"No."

"Wait, I know." He held out his arm. "Human flesh. In the future, neighbor will eat neighbor." He laughed and smiled. "You can start now."

"He sat in front of me, dirty and naked, with long matted hair and a toothless smile. His one good eye seemed to gleam. I knew I had found Him."

"In my reign," he said, "the only food will be your father, your mother, sister, and brother. Neighbor will eat neighbor. Men will eat women and women will eat men. Everyone will eat. There will be one slogan and only one slogan. Everyone will tell each other. Eat me!"

"I knew what I had to do. I saw my prey. I knew the reason I couldn't find peace. I realized. I knew. I understood. My fate had been seal after I killed the first mosquito. It was my karma. There was only one way, one path, and I took it. What can I say? I admit it.

"I was very, very hungry. The first bite was the hardest. It didn't scream or flinch. In fact, he drooled in pleasure as I ate. Afterwards, I drank the whole bottle of Charachunga, and the China Da immediately refilled itself."

Da Mo sat down and slumped over in the chair, exhausted. Telling that long story had exhausted us both. I lit up a Royal. It was getting to be quitting time. I inhaled a long puff, thought of the meat of his long story, and wanting to get back to Pella, stood up. The Chinaman grabbed my cigarette.

"You see," he said, "Charachunga changed me back to my old self. I no longer had the fangs, the claws, and horns. As long as I continued to drink the fluid, I lived eternally, and good and evil were perfectly balanced."

I puffed on the Royal. "Interesting story," I said, "but how'd you lose the China Da?"

"Well, he continued, "as everyone around me aged and died, I took up residence in the Old One's cave. For many, many years no one paid me any attention. At times of world disorder, I would lend a hand, but that's another story. Centuries of peace and war came to pass, and then about eight years ago a black man showed up at my cave saying he had a vision."

"A vision?"

"Yes, he said he had a vision that he would save the world from evil, and he said he was looking for enlightenment. Frankly, I told him to go to hell. But he stayed on. He worked well. Of course, he knew nothing at first, but he asked a lot of questions. He cleaned the cave and kept it orderly, so eventually I taught him many things. I trusted him. The years went by. We became friends . . . at least as much as we could . . . considering the differences in our thinking . . . and then one morning he was gone, and so was the

Ching Da. I looked everywhere. It was gone. He took it. I'm positive of that. I chased him here. I need that Ching Da. I'm loosing my power. I have to find him . . . so I hired you."

"Can you describe this black man?"

"Ah yes. A big lanky black man, he was a Jamaican. He talked with an accent. What do you call him, a Rasta?"

"Did he have a name?"

"Yes, he called himself William."

"Saint Billy!" I cried, and then thought for a second . . . which was usually one second beyond my capacity.

"Now, there's just one thing. What really happened in the cave? What happed to the old man?"

"The Old One in the cave?"

"Yes," I said. "Tell me the truth. You said you ate something. What did you eat? You didn't . . ?"

Da Mo licked his lips and took his time to reply. "That is unimportant. What is important is that you find my Ching Da immediately."

"What's the hurry?"

"Look at me," he said, and suddenly his face morphed. Hair sprouted all over him. Horns grew out of his head, and fangs erupted from his mouth, and talons sprouted from his fingers. His tongue lashed around his mouth, and his eyes glowed red. His voice filled the room.

"I am evil!" he screamed.

Then he shrank back to his original self. "And I am good too. I am the eternal man. I balance good and evil in the world. But I must have my rejuvenation fluid. Without the Charachunga, I will no longer be in control. Find the Ching Da!

"Of course," I said. "Now, there's just the matter of the money."

"Money! You're a damned fool. The world is being destroyed even as you flit around like a bee looking for a little honey. Evil is taking control. The clock is ticking. We're at the end of the line. Time is genuflecting on itself. There is no turning back."

He reached in his robe. "Here is two hundred thousand American. The final four hundred thousand when I get the China Da."

"No problem," I said. "I'm out of here."

"Phillips," he called and I turned around.

"Yeah?"

"Promise me this. It is very important. Promise me that no matter what I say or do the next time you see me, if you have the Ching Da, throw it at me as hard as you can. You see, the Evil One in me wants it so he can destroy it. If he is in control of me, he will trick you. You will pay with your flesh and bones. He will eat you alive. Whatever I say or do, don't listen. Just throw it on me. Make sure it covers me."

I looked at Da Mo, but I couldn't focus. He vacillated back and forth between a human being and a monster. First, he was the Chinaman. Next, he was a bird, a lion, and then a bull. I tossed him my pack of Royals.

"Keep smoking these," I said.

"Promise!" he demanded.

I turned and nodded my head. "I promise. Throw the Ching Da. You got it."

On the way out of the Hotel Meringue, I stopped at the concession and bought a couple more packs of Royals. Something on the pack, some writing under camel, caught my eye. It said, 'Made in California City.'

"Made in California City!" I said aloud.

Synchronicity. The napkin was tainted with One Daktara which was produced outside California City. Royals were made in California City. It might not make sense to the average Joe, but to a badge clues fit seamlessly together. Like machined gears messing, the wheels of my finely tuned mind ground from first to second. Next stop, California City. Then the party tonight crossed my mind.

All work and no play make a Dick dull, boy. Besides, I had to get the skinny on what was going on at the Council. Parkenson was the only with that inside information. I could squeeze him easier than a one legged milkman.

Jackson opened the door. "Did you get to see Mr. Kang?"

Kang?

The gray blue sky told me it was about four o'clock, and for once the shuttle arrived on time. That was it for today. I wondered if Pella was enjoying the artificial. How was I going to do both her and Cynthia? I'd already promised to take the debutante out to Parkenson's place tonight, and she would not stand for another woman, besides her friend Linda Hoarse. Did I have enough time to get a vitamin E shot? Really, I didn't need one. I felt great. Two hundred thousand American, not bad pocket change. I'd get Parkenson to do some investment for me.

Who was behind all of this? Dr Blood? Kang? What connection did Da Mo have with them? And Parkenson, was he part of the power play? I looked for Browny on the shuttle, but he didn't show his sorry face. Next stop, transfer at Fifth, and then the long haul back to my mod. My loins craved Pella. All the way home I rested one hand on my Johnson and one hand on my woody. I pondered the significance of a one legged milkman, and remembered the old joke about the horse who goes in for a drink and the bartender asks 'Why the long face?'

That's how I felt as the shuttle pulled in at my stop. Not so much long-faced like a horse, more like I needed a good shot of ionizer just to get rid of the blues. That is, to get rid of the blue balls I had from holding my woody all the way home. It throbbed in my pants and poked up like a baseball bat.

I slapped big Johnny a few times to make him shrink just to get out of the shuttle and into my mod. I'd have a nice present for Pella. Yum, the thought of her luscious body caused several thumps between my legs. I couldn't think of anything but her as the shuttle neared my stop and my mod.

It was a short walk to my door and as I put my hand on the steel door, it felt cold, too cold. Something was wrong. I sensed it. The love of my life waited for me. In my mind's eye I saw her beautiful

133

body, dressed in a silk nightgown. I could hear her moan. As I placed my palm in the security imprint and the steel slid open, I heard her moan.

Oh my God, no. Pella!

Chapter 12.

Pella lay face down, pinned on my bed by a huge half naked Roman gladiator hunched over her, his erection pushing through the chain mail wrapped around his loins.

"Get off of her," I screamed. "Damn it, get off of her!"

The gladiator didn't respond, but Pella turned her head toward me and whimpered. "Help me!" Her blank eyes told me she been abused, and I shifted my gaze to the giant on top of her. He edged his thing toward her wet mansion.

I dove at him and knocked him off. He was thick and real. An artificial with mass? How was that possible? No time to ponder.

Another soldier came from no where and took a long swipe at me. Normally, I would have laughed, because the artificial weren't real. But the gladiator was real, too real. I ducked, and the blade cut a swatch of air over my head and destroyed a table illuminator. Now, things had gone too far. They were programmed against damage. I had it.

I jumped on the first one's shoulders. As we twisted round and round, I rode him down and ripped out his eyes. Before the second gladiator could move, I rammed my fist into his nose, broke it, and drove it into his brain. A third one came out of the air with his short knife drawn. Too late, my karate kick broke his sternum.

What!

From behind the walls of my mod a coliseum emerged. Around me were hordes of Roman soldiers. There were thousands of them, each waiting to do battle with me. The disconnect switch! Our only hope! But two massive Romans stood between me and it, and the wall and the switch were morphing quickly into the coliseum hologram. Only seconds until we would be absorbed. Had to get to the switch. A giant Roman jabbed his spear at me, but with a swift chop I broke his wrist. Another monster drove his fist into my face, but the blow glanced off. A solid kick to the groin and he was down. The phalanx descended on me. The switch! I had the switch in my hand.

But it was stuck. It wouldn't pull down!

Swords and blades entered my body. The shroud of death covered my face. Darkness overcame me. With one final effort, one last pull with all my strength, I yanked the handle.

Saved! The scene evaporated. The swords disappeared.

I rushed to the bed, and though alive, Pella was exhausted. Her pulse was slow.

"Sweetheart?"

She couldn't speak. They'd done her, done her good, almost done her in.

The holograms were programmed never to hurt, never to do damage, never to attack. It was supposed to be entertainment. The holograms were never designed to be real. I couldn't believe it, but it was true. Evil was taking over the world.

I held my warm love in my arms and then covered her and let her sleep. Perhaps evil was taking over the world, or perhaps the holography had simply malfunctioned. Philosophically, I wondered if things weren't as they always had been. Was there a meaning to life, or was my life simply nonsense? I felt the same emptiness I'd know in the 'Case of the Paradigm Paradox.' That was a maze on the third order. There was only one recourse.

I lit up a Royal and sat on the edge of the bed. Poor Pella. I brushed my fingers over her brow, kissed her warm forehead, and inhaled her sweet fragrance. Well, I guessed, this solved the problem of who was going out to Parkenson's tonight. Too many, too fast, she was exhausted.

I dragged the fag and thought about the whole turn of events since I'd first talked to the Chinaman. Deterioration, killings, lust, depravity, avarice, gluttony. Perhaps I was the only respectable citizen left, unless hubris was a sin. I laughed to myself. The Chinaman's investigation was becoming as philosophical as the 'Case of Beatrice's Dante,' and that was a hell of a case.

With that thought in my mind, I got up and pulled the brain from the artificial and tossed it in the incinerator. Even if somehow maintenance got it working again, it could never be trusted. I wondered what was happening to the other subscribers who couldn't fight as well as me. Ah well, I wasn't a socio-political. I was a badge, a horny badge. I stepped in front of the interconnect.

"ZR-234-009-0," I said and dialed up.

Cynthia's beautiful young face came in the hologram. "Dicky," she cried, "why didn't you intercon with me? Where have you been? We had a date last night. I'm very mad with you. Where were you?"

"Sorry babe. It was a hot case and my dates got mixed up. I'll make it up to you. It won't ever happen again."

"Look," she whispered and opened her robe, showing her full ripe young breasts. Her nipples stood up on large pink pads, and I almost thought I could see a droplet of milk at one of the teats.

"Cynth," I said, "you know better than to do that on the intercon." I wanted to cup those beauties in my hands, but someone might be hacking the line. I didn't want the police or anybody to see. I wanted her visage just to myself as I felt the blood pounding in my cock and a big erection coming on. I thought of Pella for an instant, but no. I couldn't do that to her, could I? I looked over at her, exhausted and sleeping.

"Is someone there?" Cynthia barked and closed her robe.

"No, of course not."

"Then who were you looking at?"

"Oh," I replied, "I had the artificial on. Look at the mess they made. It went haywire. I turned so she could see the room, but not the bed. I moved back into holoview.

"Beautiful," I said with a smile, "you remember we're going out to the big party tonight at the Parkenson's country estate. It's going to be a long flight. Can you be ready by six thirty?"

"Know what," she said, and leaned forward. Her long blonde hair moved a little over her face, and she brushed it away. "I'd really like it if we could take Linda with us."

"Horse!" I cringed even though I knew she was coming, and I knew I'd give in.

"It's Horace!" A voice called out.

"Please," Cynthia begged. "I'll hum the Anthem."

"Get down? Get down and hum the Anthem?" That was my favorite thing.

"Can you ask her?"

"Yeah, err . . . now?"

Cynthia smiled and left the holo, and fat Linda Horace came on. Her orange hair and fat fleshy face took up most of the view. She waited with her goofy smile. It was probably the first time she'd ever been asked on a date.

"Linda," I reluctantly asked, "we simply have to have your presence out at the Parkenson's party tonight. Will you please join us for a wonderful night of friends, fun, and passion? Can you be ready at six thirty?"

"Is it formal or casual?"

"It's high society."

"Let me check, Mr. Dick," Linda said. "Oh, now, I'm not sure. She looked through a small black appointment book. "I may have to cancel with the foreign minister. Oh no, that's tomorrow night. Six thirty it is. Toot a Lou . . ."

"Wait, put Cynthia back on."

Too late. Off. I wanted to tell her to wear that see through black lace outfit; the one Mrs. Harriet Parkenson hated to see on the young fanny I always brought out to her house. Anytime Harriet got upset, I had a good time.

Back at the bed, Pella slept peacefully. I stroked her hair and pressed my forehead to her warm forehead. Deep inside her head were plans to defeat the D, and we would begin our quest tomorrow morning after she woke. First, we would take D-1. After I fed his meat to the dogs, then one by one all of the D-men would be history. If Dr. Blood got in the way, cha chang! The Mandrake claw would cut his brain in two. Pella and I would cure the evil that was taking over, but first she was going to need at least twelve hours sleep. And this worked well, because I would be getting rest and relaxation out at Parkenson's with Cynthia and the horse. I ordered up a jet taxi, took a shower, shaved, douched, and got in my clothes.

The jet taxi got me to Cynthia and Linda's student mod at exactly six thirty. Not too many riffs or squatters in the University sector, but I carried my Johnson 44.80 to be safe. Passed through the magnetic field and took the force to their apartment. Cynthia stood at the opening, and much to my happiness she was dressed in her black lace see-through.

"Sweetheart," she asked with a twinkle in her eye, "you like?"

Her long blonde hair curled up at her shoulders, lightly touching the black see-through net gown. Beneath the net, her nipples stood up, and lower I could almost see blonde hairs at the v of her legs. My cock flicked around in my pants, and in my lust for her I wanted to eat her ripe fig pie. My hips started to quiver, but then out of the bedroom waltzed fat Linda Horace who also was wearing a red see-through, which I wished she wasn't, because I never ever got stanky with fat girls. Well, I did in the case of the 'Secret Chocolate Pie,' but it was only because that giant black woman made me do it.

"Like it? I love it."

I turned to Linda. "Swell outfit," I said, "but listen ladies, we have to get hopping. It's a long haul out to Parkenson's. We only have ten minute before the last flux."

I kissed Cynthia on the neck, and in my patented quick move I opened her net gown, spread her pussy lips, and fingered her clit. "You're coming, aren't you?"

"Not now!" Ejaculated Linda. "And please Mr. Dick, would you please think a little bit about others. I am a woman too, you know."

"Stop calling Mr. Dick." I railed. "My name's Dick, not Mr. Dick."

"Shush, you too," Cynthia instructed. "Let's go."

The polished steel and rock of the flux station at the farthest edge of the city created the image that it was alone and remote. And it was. It rose above a moving, living jungle carpet. As the last station for a hundred miles before the massive expanse of green inpenatratable forest, it jutted out. It held the hover craft that waited patiently for us. Unless you could buy a sanction to the magnetic hover, you couldn't get out of the city. The Politicos planned it that way. After the radiation wars, they planted the jungle. It grew out of control, and they stocked it with wild animals to protect their country estates. Without a security clearance there simply was no way to get out of the arm pit we called home. There were no roads through the jungle, and unless you were the privileged rich, Insta Med, or a positioned cop you didn't leave the city. Even badges didn't have access unless you were on a list for a party. The iris scan locked on to my left eye, and I stepped into the magnetic field.

"Badge 324200 and passengers Cynthia Dantus and Linda Horace to the Parkenson estate."

There was a few seconds delay while the iris scan processed the information, but immediately the field released us and the hover lifted off and started to glide above the dark green of the forested jungle. A cool breeze blew through my hair, and the warm dark smell of vegetation rose in my nostrils. A dark green carpet spread before us as far as the eye could see.

"Tell us more about Parkenson's."

As the flux soared over the jungle, and we relaxed into the deep brown leather cushions, our drinks automatically appeared. I lifted my glass with a silent salute to the ladies, while outside in the jungle a large creature chased a human-like shadow.

"Well, Cynthia," I replied as I sipped the blue ionizer, "it is wonderful. Why, it's got a swimming pool, and green lawns, and a creek, and a waterfall. He's even got his own stable of horses." I got close to her. "But enough of that. Let's sing the Anthem, or you know that other one, 'Tulips on my organ.' Can you hum it?"

"Puddst." Linda laughed.

"No, I'm serious. It'll take up some time. We can harmonize. See, I'm not such a serious guy. How does the Anthem go?" I started, "I am . . ."

And Cynthia followed me. "I am . . ."

Linda came in last. "I am . . ."

Then we all joined together. "I am a medical student without no head. The Insta Meds cut it off, but I still ain't dead. I study all day from nine to five. I ain't dead, but I ain't alive.

We laughed and then sang the second verse. I started.

"I am . . ."

In came Cynthia. "I am . . . :

Next Linda. "I am . . ."

"I am the baseball Rasta who didn't throw. I might be a saint, you never know. Rasta's big and mean and don't carry a gun. And if he gets you down, you won't have no fun."

We laughed and finished. "I am I cum, I am I cum, I am, I am I cum."

Oh, the Anthem was a silly song. The students made it up for the next revolution they were all talking about. The song went on and on about how Dr. Blood would kiss Saint Billy's boot someday and how the world would change, and how peace and love were coming back. Cynthia taught it to me. She could hum it very well. The students dreamed up these crazy songs. I laughed and nudged Cynthia, and motioned my head and looked down at my crouch.

"I want you to hum it."

"Dicky, sweetie, not now. Later, after the party. Look. . ."

Parkenson's estate loomed beyond the edge of the jungle. The castle grew larger on the horizon. Our tension grew too. These parties at Parkenson's were world renowned. For young students, for these two young debutantes, this was a life changing event. It was high excitement. They'd never seen this dog and pony show, and little did they know they'd be presenters. I touched Cynthia's hand. Not this one. This one was mine. I'd let horse, I mean

Horace, be the pony. Parkenson already was a dog. I took the last drink of my blue moon ionizer and gave the girls a warning.

"Look," I said, "what's important here, whatever you do; stay on the good side of Mrs. Parkenson. Harriet's . . ."

But there she was. As the port opened, there stood Harriet Parkenson herself, wearing an outlandishly tight silver blue elastic dress. Her red hair was moussed to a point on top of her head, and her face was spotted with red and blue sequins. She looked a cross between a body builder and a fire cracker whore. As she strode over to us, she reminded me of a Tork 284. Solid, built to last, strong, just don't let her blow up on you.

Oh, we'd had our good times. That was for sure. I'd seen her get down, and even seen the clown go down on her, but I'd never done it. Not even Parkenson could control that bitch when she went to town using an embossed credit card with your name on it. We never got that far, our relationship was mutual. We loved not liking each other.

"Dick Phillips. . ." she announced, and wrapped her arms about me.

I whispered to her. "Harriet, you're a fucking slut. Tonight's the night. I'm going to do you good."

She pushed me away and looked me over. "Oh, I love it! She cried. "Then what?"

"And after that I tie you up and whelp you until red butted you beg me more, more!"

Her body jiggled. "And . . ?"

"And then you get down on your hands and knees and bark like a dog, squeal like pig, and squirm like an eel."

"Oh, I do that anyway," she said and looked over at Cynthia and Linda. "My, you have some beautiful ladies with you. How do you do it?"

"Well," I replied, "I just asked them three simple questions."

"Which are?"

"I'll ask them to you."

"Shoot," she replied.

142

"Do you like chocolate?"

"Yes."

"Do you eat choc-o-lat?"

"Eh, yes."

"Will you eat my cock-a-lot?"

"Dick," she screamed. "You're bad. Now, introduce me to these sluts."

Linda stepped right up. "Dick, she asked, "Is this the famous Mrs. Harriet Parkenson that you've told us some much about?"

I looked back at the Magna Flux. The doors were closing and the magneto was charging. Why did I bring horse? But, it was too late. These two were like oil and water. Or, so I thought.

Linda kept talking, as always. "Mrs. Parkenson . . . Harriett. You're so young and athletic. What diet are you on?"

I interrupted and pulled Cynthia next to me. "This is my debutante, Cynthia. Cynthia, Mrs. Parkenson."

"Pleased to meet you," Cynthia said with a courtesy.

Harriett looked Cynthia up and down with a cold stare that probably had defrosted many frozen Instant Feasts. She knew her husband too well, and so did I. Cynthia was mine and none of the Parkenson family, including the sister, Sara, was going to eat any of the pie I'd brought to the party. I'm sure Harriet didn't know I'd brought Linda out for her old man. Then again, as those two waddled together on the path, I had to chuckle. Harriet herself probably would be riding the horse, the Linda Hoarse, later that evening.

From that moment on, those two were inseparable. They had a lot in common. And I had a lot to think about as we walked up to the castle. I put my arm around Cynthia and her sweet Jasmine perfume filled my being. The evening was beginning to cool and her flesh felt warm and soft. As we walked, she rested her head on my shoulder and nuzzled my neck. We watched as the fat butts ahead of us waddled back and forth. Harriett and Linda were talking up a storm. What a damn place this was. A giant castle rose above the lawns and stables. A deviate sex crazy party, and more, awaited us

But first, as usual, we had to go through a security check with Simpson doing the honors. He stood by the massive wooden doors with a hand held device. I guess it was necessary, but I always felt naked without my Johnson. Then again, it allowed the parties to be a lot more fun. This far from the city, insulated like we were, the partiers, these sojourners, could breath easy. It was better to get down when you didn't have to worry that some Rasta might cut off your head or some D-man blow you away with a miniature cannon. I handed Simpson my piece.

"Take care of this buddy," I said, and then I did a double take. "Simpson, you need some rest. Have you been to sleep since I saw you last?"

"Yeah," he replied. "I will later. After I get a some good tail at the party. I'm the star tonight."

He smelled randy. I knew it had been at least a few days since he'd taken a shower. I held my breath and stepped up to be scanned.

"Bleep!"

I backed away. "Oops, forgot these," I said, and handed him two proximity bombs I had hidden in my coat. You just never knew when you might need a quick get-away, especially with the D everywhere.

As Harriett went ahead, Linda emptied her purse, and I had a little chuckle. A Silvia Huntsmith fell out on the table. Those had been outlawed for a few years. Simpson picked it up, and looked at it with an amazed quizzical look.

"It's not what you think?" Linda said abruptly.

"What is it again?" Simpson asked rhetorically. "A vibrator?"

Linda seemed to blush. "It's a Huntsmith. A Silvia Huntsmith."

"Oh yes," Simpson replied and deposited it in the rest of his collection. "The most criminal trick ever pulled on a rapist. What was that they called them, 'The Huntsmith Destroyer'?

He turned to Cynthia with a devilish smile. I could see Simpson might give me a little trouble later on, once the party got underway. I cracked the knuckles on my Mandrake claw hand. No one was going to mess with my debutante.

"Miss, you're next." Simpson said, and then scanned her up one side and down the other. As he reached the soft area between her legs the scanner went off.

"Bleep!"

Simpson laughed. "You'll have to declare that, miss."

Cynthia squat down and reached between her legs. The disrupter pen rolled across the table.

"It was only set on low."

My fingers ached. A dirty trick. To think, awhile back I almost got some stinky finger. I could see myself eating Instant Feast with my left hand. Now, I really had to watch this so called sweet young thing. University medical students were full of tricks. I guess she was trying to get back at me for missing our date last night. Ah well, this party would make up for it. I couldn't be mad.

Already the main hall was filled with socials and medicals. Several ex-politicals moved about wearing their distinctive high hat, while flag wavers pranced through the crowd. Drums and a bass hammered out a beat, and the high tone of flute cut the air. The smell of fresh cooked meat seemed to be coming from a giant fireplace, and the aroma of hot bodies filled the room. A naked statue came alive and then froze in a new pose. A line of young girls dressed only in red and purple flowers held hands and danced like a serpent through disguised people, wedging together, pretending.

Dressed in long flowing red and blue silks, entertainers sang out songs, juggled, and played old time string instruments. Some older couples moved about, dressed as in centuries past, with white wigs piled high on their heads. Some of them walked with the distinctive movement of having worms up their butts. In the center of it all, wearing nothing at all but oil and tiny belts, two naked sumo midgets grunted. Still dressed in his police uniform, the massive body of Parkenson greeted us.

"Dick?" He asked in his brogue, and looked at us.

"Dick?" He said again, as he moved closer to Cynthia and drooled. A white orb of spittle fell from his chin, and he looked down her dress.

"Dick . . ."

"Dick Phillips," I shouted. "Don't wear it out."

"Sorry," Parkenson replied, looking past Cynthia and me. He stared at Linda. "And who is this?"

"Do you have a gerbil in your pocket?" Linda asked and put her hand out to greet Parkenson.

"What?"

She pulled him to her. "Something's dancing around in your pants. Looks like you got a lion that's ready to roar."

Parkenson whispered something in Linda's ear, and her whole body glowed red through the lace dress. Lucky for Parkenson, the Tork, I mean Harriett, was busy with the diner preparations. The Parkensons would be riding the horse, err . . . Horace, later tonight. They would play a game called 'Hide the Salami' and Linda would understand the meaning behind fulfilled. Or, not, but anyway there was sure to be some squealing, a whole bunch of puffing, a pillow fight and if everything came out alright, Parky would have a new young squeeze in the city, and Harriett wouldn't have to know anything. On the other hand, if she caught them, Parkenson's dick would end up on that spike on the Tork's helmet, and she would parade it around every night before bed just to prove to him she was more of a man.

My succulent thoughts were interrupted by the piecing blare of a French horn. Twirling dervish sexophants danced about the room. A loud bell rang, and then tiny symbols rang out a sound that crescendo like a waterfall. In the center of the ring, where the midget sumo wrestlers had grappled, Harriett Parkenson, now dressed in a long red silk dinner gown, stepped between the ropes, and spoke into the hanging microphone

146

"Ladies and gentlemen, thank you for coming tonight."

A great round of applause greeted her. "No, no. Thank you. Thank you. This is important. Quiet now."

A hush fell over the room. Harriet bowed. Her full body seemed to sink to the mat, and as she rose she moved her hand toward the massive tables overflowing with plates and glasses and flowers. "Dinner is served."

Parkenson and Harriet took their places at each end of the grand dinning table, and we all took our seats. Cynthia sat next to me, then Linda wedged in between a high hatter whose face was painted with red and blue sequins. Next to him, a transparently dressed transvestite played with his and herself, and then there was Parkenson's sister Sara, whose operation had healed, and who smiled at me. Her eyes had a diamond twinkle in them, and that made me think I might be eating more than one ripe fig tonight.

I wondered what the evening held for all these crazy people. What did the old poofster sitting next to the young Elvis impersonator think about the jewel masked boy in loin cloth who French kissed his hand? What about the midgets, the giant, and that singular man dressed in blue and green wings whose buzzing upped the conversation level to an unbelievable din. Right then the sound of a spoon tinkling on crystal brought us to attention.

Parkenson stood up. "Ladies and gentlemen and others," he said. "Before we eat tonight, get real loose, before the dances, the ritual, the performance and game boy, before we eat, I want to make a toast." He looked over at me with a smile, and he held his wine glass toward me. "Let's all drink to Dick Phillips, the last of the great badges. He was the greatest."

I stood up. "Thank you. I'm happy to be here."

Everyone clapped.

I put my hand up. Okay, that's enough," I said, "No, no. . . just kidding more . . . more . . ."

"Dick and I saw a lot of action." Parkenson continued. "The case of the rotating mask of death, the explosion of Dr. Marsall's brain, the invisible enforcers . . . to name a few."

147

He chuckled and spoke sideways with his brogue, "Of course, I always stepped over it, while Dick ate it."

Parkenson looked casually at the midget to his left. "Then again," he said, "there was a short side to some of the cases. I bailed him out. He never paid me back for any of my help. I invited him into the force, but he always refused." He glanced quickly at Harriett. "I offered him the best meat. Oh well, I guess he just wasn't a meat and potatoes type of guy." Finally, he looked back at me, paused with a resigned look, and he smiled.

"Thank you badge 324200. Thank you for your service."

I felt humbled. It sure was nice finally getting the recognition I deserved. All these years of fighting in the trenches, working hard for the man, defeating evil, doing good. Yes, now I felt my life had meaning.

As the applause died down, my butt started to feel the hard padding of the chair and the wood up my ass. I wasn't retiring. This was a crazy sex party, a much welcomed break from the grind, but not a Dick Phillips roast. What did he mean, "last of the badges?" The other badges might have something to say about that. What was going on? The Council met today. Could Dr. Blood have something to do with all this? And what about Kang? My butt did hurt. I was doing too much considering when the butler leaned over my shoulder and locked up the breaks on my train of thought.

"Instant Feast." He said, and lowed a plate of meat and mashed synthesize.

"Browny!" I cried, and slapped for my 44.80. Of course, it was checked at the door and I only slapped leather.

I held my finger to his head. "Bang, bang!"

He laughed, "I lost you in the underground. Where'd you disappear to?"

"Time travel. Browny, what are you doing here?"

Browny's lips were smeared with chocolate. "Oh," he said with a twinkle in his eyes, "Parkenson's got a special job for me tonight. I'm the game boy. You can make good on your promise."

Browny, the game boy! Well, that was cold. He'd be a tough one all right. Probably lead me halfway through the jungle before I nailed him. Mechanicos could run like hell, and one like Browny could lead you on a lot of goose chases. The wild animals wouldn't bother him either, only a shot to the head could kill him. He would make the perfect game boy. Yet, I knew how he thought. I'd do him tonight riding my favorite steed, Spur.

He put a little chocolate wafer on my plate. "Here's a brownie for you, for old times. Do me good tonight; my mind's starting to go."

Okay, I didn't know exactly how he thought . . . then again, my mind was gone too. Browny was a mechanico. It was too bad, but he had to die. I was a badge. I did my duty. I'd made the choice long ago, and I didn't regret it. Besides, sitting with all these beautifully dressed people, eating tasty Instant Feast, and my lovely Cynthia by my side, what more, I thought, could a man want?

"Here love," Cynthia said as she cupped a handful of mashed white synthetic in her hand and held it to my mouth, and moved her mouth over mine. As we French kissed, mashed synthetic moved from my mouth to hers, and I thought, what utter delight, like the salutation I just gotten. It was warm, thick, and like her tongue it lingered for a long time. But I had to let it go.

After dinner, and before the hermaphrodite dance, Cynthia and Linda mingled with some of the Insta Meds who were trying on different rubber devices, and I sat on the couch next to Harriett.

I lit up a Royal and put my feet on the coffee table.

"Excellent dinner, Mrs. P." I said. "It's been a long time since I had Instant Feast that tasted that good. What's the secret?"

"My dear Dicky," she said with a sly smile. "Don't tell anyone, but we get Newt shipped directly from the Five Dollar Café."

The bathroom was sparkling clean. After a few minutes, Newt came up on me. So, okay, I drove the porcelain steering wheel again. But at least while washing up, my face didn't crack the mirror. I was aging awfully fast. When I found the Chinaman's Ching Da, I would help myself to a long drink of Charachunga. I wasn't too bad looking. Actually I loved the way I looked. I wiped off my face. Simpson stepped out of the shower.

"Simpson, what up?"

"Oh, about ten inches every time I look at your girl friend."

I politely moved the Mandrake claw hand in front of him, but didn't bring it out. "I'm sure you know enough not to mess with her."

"You don't scare me, Phillips." he replied, and stepped into his panty hose. "Because you saved my ass with those skink lizards, I'm going to let you in on a little secret."

"Yeah, what's that?"

Simpson pulled on his halter top and slipped in his tight dress. He fit the long blonde wig on his head, moved next to, and checked it in the mirror. He spoke in a falsetto.

"Parkenson had to make concessions in the Council today. A lot of things came to a head after they got your message that in ten minutes a bomb would go off."

"What!?"

"Yeah, you didn't know it, but the Council was intercepting your Rex transmissions. They evacuated the chambers. One of the members had to go to Insta Med and came back with a different face."

"It was just a joke," I said, "I was at Nick's. Nobody's supposed to audit a badge. It's the law."

"Well, they changed that. This new member, Kang, got power."

"Huh?"

"Yeah, you probably don't even know. Dr. Blood returned, and he wanted your head." Simpson stuttered, "But that's not the half of it. Kang's more powerful than Blood. Blood is Kang's slave! Even Saint Billy returned from California City, but could do nothing. Kang put him in a trance too. Parkenson couldn't do anything. The vote went against you."

I stared at Simpson, and found it hard to focus on him. He looked utterly fascinating and terribly silly at the same time. He made the perfect bitch. Now, I understood why he'd looked so lustfully at

Cynthia, why Harriett was so happy to see me, and why Parkenson had roasted me at dinner. They wanted my spoils. A titanic feeling sank in my stomach. The Council sentenced me!

"How much time?" I muttered.

"Tomorrow night."

"Who's going to do it?"

"D-1 volunteered."

D-1! So, Da Mo was right. Was it possible? Could evil have gotten control so soon? My side hurt. That monster D-1 almost killed me before, took one of my kidneys with his electro torture. My mind went blank, but immediately a plan formed.

I smiled my little smile of death. This time I would do D-1 for good. I would defeat the D, take care of Kang, and rid the world of Dr. Blood. I would need Pella and Saint Billy. Somehow, I had to make my link to California City tomorrow night. That meant staying alive. I clinched my fists. They would all pay.

"Good luck at the performance tonight, Simpson."

"Thank you," he replied. "Don't I look a good fuck?"

"Yeah, sure you do."

"Say, Phillips. No hard feelings?"

"Never!"

I lied. At the moment I felt revenge tasted like a thick pastrami sandwich on rye bread stacked with pickles and Swiss cheese. I could eat a slab of that with Simpson's and Parkenson's names on it. Even though the big black man was dressed to kill in his tight dress, dressed as a queen with his cock tied tight in his halter panties, he couldn't hide his shame at betraying me.

"Can you do me a favor, then?"

"Sure Simpson, what?"

"Parkenson," replied the big stupid mother fucker transvestite whore-like slut "is going to have a little talk with you later. Do me a favor, Dick. Don't tell him I told you everything."

The living room stank of expectation. Glasses raised. One of the sexophants spun uncontrollably from person to person, rubbing and massaging and swapping spit. I slid in next to Cynthia on the couch. On stage, a tiny hermaphrodite dressed in a pink ballerina costume was slowly removing its clothes. Simpson, in the bitch fuck costume, trotted across the stage from a side curtain. I slumped back. A sentence! My time was up. I couldn't concentrate. Besides, I'd seen it all before. First came the tease, then the chase, the eventual struggle, and finally the exposure and the audience participation.

"Dick," Cynthia said as she touched my arm, "you don't look well. Have a drink of Deep Purple."

I pushed way the ion stimulator. No, I wasn't feeling too well. A sentence! And D-1 my executor. How was I going to get out of this one? My Johnson was locked up at the door, and it was a long way back to the city. I had until tomorrow night. After that, even if I survived they'd cut off my access. They'd get me. There was no escape. California City was a possibility, to hide out, but that was only postponing the inevitable. My number was up. Goodbye, 324200. Goodbye, Dick Phillips. I wasn't religious but I wondered that if now I were living in purgatory, what the hell was hell like? This time tomorrow I would find out. I slumped, but then my spirit raised. I would not give up without a fight. I would defeat evil!

"I'm sorry sweetheart. It's just something I ate. What going on now?

"They're arguing," she replied. "The hermaphrodite is squatting on the big whore's foot, squirming on its big toe. The transvestite demands that the illusion of sex is more real than the act of sex. Right now, he is holding the little being in the air and forcing it onto his sex. Oh my!"

"What is it?"

"Can't you see?"

"My eyes are a bit misty."

"Dick are you crying"

"No! Badges don't cry." I lit up a Royal. Too smoky. What's happening?"

"Now, the hermaphrodite is making a soliloquy."

I could see the tiny creature turn its face to us. It puckered its tiny lips and rotated its eyes and moved its tiny hands about in front of its face. It looked at the black man and then out to us. One small finger touched its lips, and a tear ran down its face.

"You try to make me do this thing. I can not refuse. But I am woman! I love. I am man! I love. My mouth slips over your huge erection, and I see you look up into your head in pleasure."

The little hermaphrodite looked up at the big transvestite. "Look at me! The pleasure is not in your head. It is here in my mouth. I am pleasure. Look at me!"

The little he-she ripped off the remaining vestments of the torn ballerina costume and spoke loudly to us. "You are the fools. I am everything. My sexes intertwine, and I come in me. You are nothing but illusion. I am the real. I am woman! I am man!"

The little creature paused for an instant, and then beckoned. "Come up. Come one, come all. Come to me and partake. Take the seed of this black man dressed as a woman. Take my vagina in your mouth. Take my large erection. Shit on me, piss on me and I will do anything for you. Squat on my face. Kiss my body everywhere. Rub your body on mine. Salute me with your cum. Feel me. Love me. Heal me. Come up now!"

Cynthia pulled me. "Come on Dick."

"No, you go ahead. I want to save my strength for game boy."

Harriett pulled Linda on stage and they started to kiss. Some socials and Insta Meds flew about each other rubbing, stroking, sucking and hugging and kissing. Cynthia got on her knees in front of Simpson, and I thought I heard her hum the Anthem. A high hatter yanked down the bird man's pants, and the young boy seem to fold into the arms of the poofster. Everyone moved to the stage while the smell of sweat and cum filled the air, and a room full of moving bodies rotated around me until out of the corner of my eye, I noticed Parkenson motioning from the door of his den.

Time froze . . . then jumped.

The big antlers hanging over the fireplace set off the desk and chair, and the books that lined the shelves implied that the big man was not only a gentleman, but an intellect. He grimaced as he gazed at his desk, avoiding my eyes.

"Dicky," he said "we been friends for a long time."

"Ah come right out with it, Parkenson." I said. "Simpson already told me."

He breathed a little sigh. "Yeah, it's true," he said. "The vote in the Council went against you. I tried to help, but there was nothing I could do. They sentenced you."

"And . . . ?"

"Twenty four hours."

"But why?"

"Oh," he said in an offhanded way, "They linked you to the Newt attack. They had reports about you going in the underground. That's totally illegal! Then there was the explosion of the concentric atomic and a bunch of other stuff. Most of all, that bomb threat. I knew it was a joke. Dr. Blood showed up. He wanted your head. Amazingly, Saint Billy appeared. For some reason he begged us to save your hide. This new guy, Kang, why . . . he just took over. We couldn't resist him. The vote went against you. "

"Don't I get to plead my case?"

"Sorry Dick, the Council is phasing out badges. The D-men will be taking over your jobs."

"D-men!" I shouted.

"That's right. I know it's crazy after all we went through, but I don't make the rules. Why, I'm just a cop. D-1 is now in control of the badges. He's going to wipe them out, make them join the D-men. Even if you could get a reprieve, you'd have to start wearing red and black."

A badge wearing the uniform of the D, it wasn't possible. "The other badges aren't going to take this lying down. They'll back me up."

"I don't think so," he responded, "D-men are out right now, collecting Johnsons. It's the end of an era."

I knew a great fire fight exploded throughout the city. The badges were tough. They wouldn't give up with a fight. Then again, if it were an edict of the Council, the tide eventually would turn. All access would be cut off. The computers shut down. The badges wouldn't have any power. One by one, the D would take them. My head felt like it was in a vice, bad brains squeezing out.

"Twenty four hours," I mumbled.

"Yeah," he said, "I guess after game boy tonight, we'll have to lock you up. I know you want to do Browny, so I'll give you back your Johnson with one round for him. You got to give it to him, right in the head, you know."

I looked at Parky, a stupid fat man in his too tight clothes. My mind, as always was pretty blank. At least I was going to be able to do my friend, Browny, before he went insane, and before my time expired. Well, it had been a good life.

"What about Cynthia and Linda?"

"After the chase tonight, Simpson will make sure Cynthia gets back safely, and I'll personally escort Linda. You won't have to worry about a thing. I'll download your Rex and take care of your mod. I'll keep it as a spare." He pause for a second, "I'm sorry son. If you would have come into the force, I could have protected you. Too late now. The Council doesn't want badges around anymore. Don't take it personally."

I didn't think about it for long. A plan was working its way from some remote region of my thoughts where emptiness created reality. Either that or I had to again drive the porcelain steering wheel. Anyway, back at the stage, it was all over but the mop up. Simpson, still in his dress, the hermaphrodite in jeans and a t-shirt, Harriet, Linda, and Cynthia were all relaxing, taking a smoke.

Harriett Parkenson sat down next to us and wiped her sweaty brow on my shirt. "Where you boys been?" she asked enthusiastically. "It's time."

"Not yet," I cried.

"Well, yes Dick, it is time for . . ."

The room froze in expectation. Everyone magnetized toward her. She leaned close to my face. I could smell her cum laced breath.

"It's time for game boy."

Chapter 13.

I ducked out of the dining room before the revelers changed into their riding clothes. I needed a moment to prepare, a moment to compose my thoughts, to find the plan in the infinite empty space of the hollow halls of my brain. The stables were quiet except for the shuffling sounds of horses and a big black fly that buzzed around my head like the mosquito in the Chinaman's story. Huh! Da Mo, I wondered how he was doing. Did he find a good supply of Royals? Most likely he was already dead, dried out like a prune.

As I walked the quiet row of horse stalls, the green aroma of fresh hay hit my nostrils and mixed with the warm smell of horse piles. A chill ran up my back. How many times now had I been the champion? Was it nineteen? Could this be the twentieth running of game boy? What steed would I choose this year? I looked down the rows and rows of stalls. Each horse, a friend of mine from younger years, held fond memories

Bay whinnied and shook his head at me. On the other side, Lothario kicked his stall. He knew me, but no, the old boy was too slow. Further on, I came to Mambo's stall. The black mare could run, that was for sure, yet she couldn't jump. In the very last stall, my favorite, Spur, stuck his head out of the paddock, and with a laugh curled his lips over his teeth.

"Come to me."

"Spur, when did you learn to talk?" I asked.

"Come on, baby!"

"What?"

"Come in my mouth!"

"Spur!"

I stopped in front of Spur's stall. "Who's there?"

Parkenson's sister Sara popped up and began to brush the shank of Spur. She looked beautiful. The transformation at the Insta Med had changed her from a Nellie Dyke to a fetching young lady.

"Horses sure got big whangers," she mumbled and swallowed. "Jacked a big one."

Well, you can take the Nellie out of the dyke, but you're going to have to plug up the hole or the filthy ocean will spill back in.

"What are you doing in Spur's stall?"

"Getting him ready for you. You wouldn't want to be riding a horny young boy like him what with all those mares in the field. Would you? And besides, after breaking my nose at Village Eight, taking away my livelihood as an undercover, and making me live back here with Parkenson; don't you think I owe you?"

I knew right there I was going to have to teach this little girl a lesson, Parkenson's sister or not. Then again, I'd been sentenced. Did I have time to do her? I looked at the nipples sticking up through her shirt and her long blonde hair and her sleek riding pants. Those legs must end up in a tight little pussy. Her rhythm as she brushed and the way she moved her chest against Spur's coat, entranced me. The metal catch on the half door to the stall felt cold and unlatched with a click. I felt a throbbing in my pants, but as I neared her, the trumpet blew. Now, there was no time.

I heard the high voice of the midget and the shriek reply of the hermaphrodite followed by the bellow of Parkenson directing the crowd. With only seconds to discovery, I put my hand behind Sara's neck and pulled her face to mine. As I wrapped my arms around her and pulled her on to me, her hot lips melted in mine. Horses bayed, people laughed, the stables became a den of party noises. Another trumpet blew.

"You'll always be mine," I said, and spit. She tasted kind of horsy.

"In your dreams!" She cried and walked past me.

"Sara," I said, "I've been sentenced. So, we could . . ."

"Sentenced!?" She raised her right hand in a spirited salute. "Yes!" she screamed and walked out.

I patted my stallion. It was up to me on this final run to take out the mechanico. If I had to do Browny, so be it. He'd be insane shortly anyway. No one knows what the future holds. You have to do your best. That's all I could do, I thought, as I tossed the leather saddle over Spur. I buckled and hitched him.

"Sometimes life ties you up, puts on a saddle and reins, and rides you hard in the dark night. What do you think Spur?"

Parkenson stuck his big head in the stall. "Horses don't think son. They eat, they poop, and they run. Come on! Game boy's starting. You gotta get in the line up."

"I'm coming."

"Wait a minute," he said, and handed me my Johnson. "There's one bullet in the chamber. Shoot Browny in the head, do it at close range just to make sure."

Outside, the warm summer night sky held a brilliant bright white moon that cast shadows from the horses and riders and from a small cage where the form of a man meshed with steel bars. Parkenson and his wife Harriet sat in their saddles. On their right were the two midgets and the hermaphrodite. Cynthia and Linda were on the left hemmed in by a socialite and a high hatter. Around them with different colored scarves, flags and hats . . . riding costumes, Sara and the group eyed the man in the cage.

The mechanico beat his metal claw hands on the small cage while the riders led their horses to the line. The tiny cage rocked back and forth. He beat his head on the bars and white sputum formed on his lips and chin. He growled, ranted, and snarled at the crowd. But they really didn't have to cage Browny, he was a good sport, he wanted to die. He wasn't going anywhere. It was just a ritual, and Browny was acting out. He wasn't insane yet, and no one was really afraid of the mechanico. Well, some of them were. One year a crazy mechanico did kill several horses, a bearded fat lady, and the legendary half wit who'd been Parkenson's stock broker.

"Ladies and bent little men," shouted Parkenson. "When the next trumpet is blown we will release the mechanico. He will be given a ten minute head start. Then, when the second trumpet blows, we go." He lifted up his rifle. "Check pistols and your rifles now. Remember, it takes a direct shot to the head. Get yourselves ready. Naturally, he'll run to the jungle. If he runs this way, plug him! This mechanico's pretty smart, so you have be careful. Don't let him double back, or get behind you. The moonlight's to our advantage. Let's put the poor sucker out of his misery. Get him into the shoot!"

I flicked the reins and Spur ambled out to the line. My poor ex-partner Browny, I thought. All he really wanted out of life was a hunk of chocolate in his mouth and the scent of a good case under his nose. He didn't deserve to have a metal body. If there were only a way to bring him back, to give him a human body, I would have given anything for that. But I had to do him. It was my duty, my last act as a badge, and though I wished things were different, deep in my soul I needed to kill him. Badges killed mechanicos. We did it quick, efficiently, without candor. I lifted my Johnson. One round sat in the chamber. I wouldn't miss. Browny's brains would soon stain red the green moss. The living darkness in the heart of the radiated jungle beat a call to me. We all felt it. The jungle itself needed a sacrifice. It was my duty.

Cynthia edged her horse up next to me. "Why so serious?"

"Do you feel it?"

"What?"

"The anticipation. Everyone's ready to ride. Look, the shoot's opening."

The first trumpet sounded. Horses surged, and down the line a black stallion reared and came down to paw the line. As Browny sprinted toward the trees I eyed him over the top of my Johnson, but Parkenson shook his head."

"Calm down."

"Don't get in my way Parkenson," I said, "he's mine."

"Okay, everybody," Parkenson barked. "Hold your horses. Give him his head start. The second trumpet is about to go off. Check yourselves."

At the opening to the trees Browny stopped running and turned toward us. "Hey, all of you!" He shouted, turned around, and pulled down his pants exposing his metal butt. He bent over and hung out his ass. "Suck on this!"

Bang! A shot rang out from Parkenson's rifle. The bullet ricocheted off Browny's behind. This was the signal, and the second trumpet sounded. It had all been planned. I dug my heels into Spur, and the line of horses gave chase.

Shoot him in the head!" Cried Harriett.

"Head! Get head!" The crowd shouted behind me. Spur and I accelerated toward the dark opening, leaving the others to eat their own dust.

The dark jungle opened. I reined in Spur. We stopped, and he turned and reared on his hind legs. I raised high in the air and waved at the approaching stampede of riders, and a bullet whizzed by my head. Then another cut through my hair. Those drunken idiots, I thought, I'm not the game boy . . . am I?

"Giddy up!" I cried and drove Spur into the jungle where we sped along quietly, quickly as the blood pounded in our veins. Branches of trees and vines beat at my face. A flock of birds sprang to the air. Moonlight cut through the trees. For several seconds the air filled with the sweet heavy fragrance of night blooming Jasmine. A fallen log. Spur jumped over it and flew along the trail. Deeper and deeper we drove into the heart of the night.

Somewhere in the darkness a mechanico ran for his life. Somewhere behind me drunken revelers were riding around in circles shooting off pistols. In a few minutes when they took a break, one of the women might look up at the moon and cry for a man. She'd get that wish granted . . . if I knew Parkenson and Simpson. Damn, I wished I was there. But even as I drove Spur along the trail of broken twigs and leaves that Browny left for me, a plan formulated. It was an escape plan, a plan to get to the Link, a plan to retrieve the Ching Da and to save the world. It would

161

have worked too, but before I could think a tree limb knocked me off Spur.

Darkness.

"You alright?" A man said as metal arms dragged my body along the ground.

We stopped, and I regained my senses. "Where am I?"

"Look around." He replied. "Look, the full moon is overhead. We're sitting on a small log in a clearing. Isn't the air fresh? Even in the moon light, isn't that grass green. Can you hear those song birds? The crickets? Don't you feel alive? Isn't it great to be with a friend? Isn't life wonderful?

"Here," he said, and put a wafer in my mouth. "It's a brownie."

I pulled out the Johnson. "I'm going to do you."

"Hold on a few minutes. The others are hours behind us. They may never catch us. I been on a few of these hunts too, you know. The party's much more fun than the shoot."

"It's my duty."

He pulled his arm up on his knee and rested his forehead in his metal palm. He still had the twinkle in his eye, and I thought he smiled through his beard."

"If you got to do your duty, get over behind the tree. Only a dying animal shits where it lives."

I pulled out the final of pack of Royals, flicked out the last cigarettes, and lit one. I crumpled the empty pack and tossed it at him.

"What are you saying?"

He stood up and walked into the moon light. Even though his motions were jerky and mechanical, he still had that shy boyish manner. He hemmed and hawed and turned his palms around like always.

"Dick . . ." he whispered. "Dick, I got a family. Yeah, I been married for a few years and me and the misses got a couple little ones. They're so pretty. I call them Sweet-tart and Cookie. I miss them so much. The misses is a beautiful woman. She's retarded, but I don't care. At night, when we sleep together, it's like we were

162

parts of a jig saw puzzle. We fit so nice, and her skin feels so good."

He brushed his metal hands down his sides. "I want to touch her all over again. I want to hold her and the kids. I want to make brownies for them on Sunday morning. I want to hold them in my arms and kiss them again and hug them all over."

"Damn," he cried, "It's not fair. I didn't do nothing wrong. I just did my duty! I don't want this metal body no more. Help me, Dick. You're a smart guy. There must be a way to get a body back."

He sat down next to me, and when he leaned close to me I could see a tear in his eye. He spoke in a low quite way. "I don't want to die."

"It's my duty."

"Duty! You ain't got no duty. You been sentenced."

"How'd you know that?"

"I'm the best," he replied. "I saw it in Parkenson's eyes. The Council wants you dead. What did they give you, a week?"

"Twenty four."

He laughed. "We're both dead. Say, why don't you give me your body?"

"No can do, pal." I replied. "I've got a plan."

"For me too?"

"Yeah," I said. "Yeah, that's it. For both of us. If you get me out of this jungle, and if you haven't gone insane, I'll find you a body."

"What's going back to Parkenson's going to do? He'll kill me and lock you up."

"No," I said, "not back to the estate. We go though the jungle to the edge of the city. From there I'll find my way. The answer is in California City. You in?"

"Yeah," he replied slowly, "I can get you out, but where am I going to get a body?"

"Well, you can have Dr. Blood's, D-1's, or Saint Billy's. Even Parkenson's."

"Agreed!" he shouted, jumped up, and headed to the darkness." We've got our work cut out for us. Let's go."

Partners again with Browny. I slapped Spur's behind and sent him back the trail toward the revelers and the estate, and had a little laugh. Imagine, partners with mechanical Browny. Oh he'd gone insane, that was for sure. Mechanicos would say anything to keep you from blowing their brains out. And that story about a wife and kids, it almost made me cry. He didn't have a wife and kids, and he wanted his body back? Hell, I didn't know if the Insta Med could put bodies back together. At the most, the heads they put on mechanical bodies only lasted six months. Knowing them, they would probably sew his head between his legs. Well, anyway, then he'd be back to normal.

Spur couldn't come with us, which was good, for by the time I caught up with Browny we crouched down, hacked our way through overgrown vines, and mushed in a green swamp up to our knees. While mosquitoes attacked me and leeches stuck to my hands, these were minor annoyances. As we rounded a bend at the edge of the swamp a fantastic buzzing filled our ears.

"It's fire ants! Browny cried. "Get into the swamp!"

A giant mass of flesh eating ants rolled toward us as it devoured a hunk of flesh at the center of its rotating ball. Consuming every living thing in its path, the insatiable mass flew over us. Although we escaped in the mucky swamp, Browny was exasperated.

"This can't be too good for my machinery."

"These leeches ain't good for me either. Let's take a break."

"Don't step on that!" He screamed.

I looked at the small brown log on the ground in front of me. "What is it?"

He bent over and put his face close to it. "Get down here. Smell this."

I bent down. "It stinks like poop."

"Yes," he said, "It's about ready to explode. There is an animal," he whispered, "that eats only the ripest berries, the most succulent fruits, and the most alive worms. It's the Gugupu, a surly large beast, a squatter. They run in pairs." He looked around. "This looks like a little log, doesn't it? But it's not. If you step on this it could ruin your day. No . . . if it explodes it will ruin . . . your whole life." He tugged my arm. "Come on, just watch out. Where there's one there may be many."

Browny had gone insane, that was for sure. Now, I didn't know if he were leading me around in circles. Sometimes he had me running. Sometimes we crawled along. We seemed to be getting no where. All night we trudged along, our only companions were the sounds of mad monkeys, the screams of jackals, and the insane laughter of the hyenas. The spider webs were hideous. The rotten stench of decay burned our noses. My matches were wet. My Royals damp. I was feeling sick when the dark tunnel we were crawling in opened to a clearing in the dawn's light

"Look," I said.

"What," he replied.

"Next to that big log."

"What is it, more exploding Gugupu?"

"No, you stupid fool!" I cried, "It's the crushed empty pack of my royals. You've led us in a circle."

"Well, what did you want to do?"

I raised the Johnson to his forehead. "I want out of this jungle."

"Look," he said, and pointed as the dawn's light illuminated a chain link fence, and beyond the fence, a road, and beyond that, the city.

"Which temple do you want it in?" I asked.

"Dick!" he cried. "We had a deal. You promised if I got you to the edge of the city you'd find me a new body."

He had done what he said he was going to do. Perhaps Browny wasn't as insane as I thought. I guess Parkenson had been selling off parts of the jungle to pay the rent. The city was right next to us all the time. All I could do was lower my gun. I didn't do him. He didn't matter anymore, and neither did doing my duty. Who'd I owe anyway? Certainly not the Council, nor Parkenson, or the rest of the badges. Badges were now on their own. What did my word matter? The only truth I knew was there was a clue in California City that might solve the Chinaman's case, keep evil from taking over the world, keep my head off the block, and make me some more cash. These thoughts and more, some more polished than others, rolled around in my lapidary tumbler as I climbed the chain link fence to egress the jungle.

I looked through the fencing at the poor confused mechanico. "Browny, you coming or not!"

"I can't," he whimpered.

"Why not?"

"When I became game boy they installed an explosive chip inside. If I leave the perimeter we'll both be blown to smithereens."

I heard some music playing soft and low, coming from a bar down a side street. "So what are you going to do?"

"They'll never find me. I'll hide out in the jungle until you find me a new body. Then you and my head will go directly to the Insta Med."

Sweet cabaret music drew me down the street. Browny was insane, there was no doubt about it, so as I crossed the alley, I dropped all thoughts of him from my mind. I moved past several dumpsters full of wine bottles, and from a dark enclave, from behind a small white door with a brass knob, music beat a slow sad tune. I twisted the knob and entered the darkness.

At first, until my eyes adjusted, I couldn't see. The walls were smooth and cool like polished marble, and then at the end of the hall, I saw a light and could make out couples slow dancing, embracing, and kissing. A light focused on a rotating mirror ball and music came out of an old time juke box in the corner. I shimmied up to the bar and sat on one of the stools.

A huge woman stuck her face in front of mine. Her giant tits rested on the bar, and as she spoke through broken teeth I could see the stubble of a mustache on her lip.

"What do you want!?" she demanded.

"Ionizer any flavor and some information?"

"Do you mind some advice?" she asked. "Get fuck out of here right now."

"What?"

"Men ain't allowed in here."

"Why not?"

"This is Dhog."

"What's that mean?"

"Dykes on Hogs," she said and then called out. "Ladies! We got a man here."

Before I knew it, five of them were on me. Big ones, bigger than me, they held me with their vice grip strength and spun me around. Before I could command the Mandrake claw, the bartender cupped her hands on my mouth and then duct taped it. Steel wires wrapped my chest and arms and legs. I struggled but couldn't move.

"Hit the lights!" the bartender commanded.

The first one was a giant of a woman wearing blue jeans and a tee shirt, a shaved head and blue tattoos on her bulging biceps. The next one was black but shorter than her and much wider. She was gigantic, girdled with a kind solid fat mass. The third's face was pocked with festering sores and her eyes stared from hollow sockets. She looked mean. The forth one was thin, with long red hair. She wore black stockings and a black dress with a slit up the side. Her blade came out of no where and poised beneath the soft flesh of my nose.

"What you looking at sucker!"

The fifth one was a beautiful young blonde girl holding a riding crop, standing in riding boots and wearing riding clothes. My eyes opened wide.

Sara!

"Sara," the red head said. "You know this pee pee."

"Yeah," Sara laughed. "He's a badge. It's Dick Phillips."

They stepped back and eyed me, and then the big shaved-headed one got right in my face. "Phillips," she spewed, "you got a reputation. They say you don't like lesbians. They say you don't like homos. Are we too gay for you?"

She turned her head to the fat one and then bent and kissed the mean skinny one. "Are we too queer for you? You too much of a stud for nice ladies like us? They say you got a big one in your pants. Let's see it."

"Pull his pants down!"

Now, an ordinary man would have pooped his underwear, what with five Dhog, pronounced dog, standing in front of him with knives, and tied up like I was. But not Dick Phillips. Out of nothing, I mean my thoughts, came a plan. From the time I spent in India, working on the 'Case of the Shrinkee,' I mastered the technique of withdrawing my genitals into my body.

They pulled my pants down and then my shorts. "Let's look!"

At that instant, with an act of intent and will power, I sucked up my genitals.

To a man, I mean woman, they stared in amazement.

"He's one of us!"

Later, at the bar, Sara toasted me. "How does a girl like you pull it off?"

"It comes easy."

"What?"

"You know, acting like a man. Men are so stupid."

"You're telling me! . . . Dick . . . can I call you Roberta?"

"Sure."

"You know," she whispered, "back at the paddock, you should of told me. I never would have guessed. We could have made it then, but now the dance floor's open, you want to try again?"

"Sure," I said, and downed the last swig of a deep purple ionizer. I had to play my cards right, time was running out to get on the Link. What was my next move?

Soft music . . . and little spots of light circled on the floor. The big shaved headed dyke held pocked-face in her arms and swayed back and forth. The red head and the fat black one waltzed slowly around us. Sara pulled me close, pushing her breasts into my chest.

"Give me another kiss, please?" she asked.

I moved my face over her and planted my lips on hers. Instantly, her tongue shot into my mouth and swished around my gums. She started sucking my tongue hard into her. Oh, oh. The Shrinkee technique had been taught to me in a monastery full of men. I felt my big throb start to jerk and grow, and right then Sara grabbed my ass and pulled me to her.

Sara pushed me back and looked me in the face and screamed, "Dhog!"

It wasn't the first time I'd been thrown out of bar. I guessed Sara saved me, for later, for when we could truly be alone. Or, she figured she still owed me a favor. They tossed me out. Oh, I could have battled them with the Mandrake claw, and I did have one round left in the Johnson, but the clock was ticking. Now, there wasn't much time left. It takes time to battle dykes, and these dykes were real fighting men, and besides I knew where there were Dhog, there were jet air bikes. And as I flew through the bar's double doors, through the air, across the street in front of the bar, there they were. Five large air hogs sat parked right in front of me.

So who could I trust now? The Council sentenced me. The badges were being wiped out by the D. I only had a few hours . . . Pella crossed my mind. If I could get to my mod, reload the Johnson, get iris blockers, and fake identities, and then if we could take the Link to California City . . . we could work out our plan to defeat Dr. Blood, D-1, and the D-men. It didn't seem humanly possible. Then again, I was Dick Phillips.

Five huge air bikes . . . hogs . . . leaned on their kickstands in front of the Dhog bar. But these weren't ordinary air bikes; they were modified jet flux, like the ones I used to race when Pella and I were living at the Hotel Meringue. Sara's name was written on the biggest one. She must be the leader of the dykes. I rammed my claw into the ignition, hot wired it, stepped over the seat, kicked it once. It fired and revved with a gutty roar. The magneto lifted off the ground and we rose above the street.

Before firing the jets I hovered for a minute, put my hand to my ear, and commed. "Rex, this is Dick."

"Who else but?"

"Quit kidding around. Please."

"We have some problems, Dick."

169

"What?"

"It's too quiet in my brain."

"Me too."

"Seriously," Rex said, "the other Rexes are off line. I'm getting lonely."

"I'm in the air now. I should be back to the office immediately. Please prepare two sets of iris blockers and two matching fake id. Copy that. Roger. Over and out."

"The name's Rex. Why do you always call me Roger?"

Whatever Rex was saying didn't seem to make sense, and I didn't have time to reply. I waited too long. Below me, the dykes screamed. Sara shook her fist, and pointed at me, but I couldn't hear her over the flux magneto. The other dykes ran out to their bikes. Almost as a group they kicked them over, but the big shaved headed one rose first to hover next to me.

"You gonna die!" she screamed.

I rotated my bike around and fired the rocket into her machine. An explosion trailed me as I lifted above the buildings and headed west toward my mod. One toasted faggot queen wouldn't need to keep shaving her head.

The city moved about below me, and I was glad to be flying. The cool morning air blew my hair, my pants fluttered in the wind, the magna jet hog roared. The ride was peaceful, except for sound of hogs. Magna jet hogs! The other three dykes were right on my tail.

The fat dyke ran up along side me, and as I bent lower to the metal, down to the handlebars to lower wind resistance, I felt the swipe of a blade over my head. I turned to look.

"Got damn it!" the fat black dyke yelled, stood up on her bike and poised to jump.

I down shifted. She sailed toward me and latched on the handlebars. Too much weight and she wouldn't let go. We started spinning down and around in a slow spiral between two buildings until we were almost on the road.

Again and again I planted my fist on her face. "Get off of it, get off you fat bitch!"

But she wouldn't let go.

We were almost on the ground, when finally I knocked her off and she slid down the road. Then from my left, over the top of a burned out shuttle, the red head emerged and roared her bike straight at me. I gunned mine directly back at her.

Inches to collision . . . time stopped . . . then we collided with a thud of metal. I went flying over and over and landed on my back, rolled over, and jumped up.

She reared up on her hog, rotated three sixty, and roared at me, but I sprang on top of her and threw her off. I grabbed her machine, mounted it, twisted the throttle, and raised high over the city. I roared west toward my mod, when from nowhere the final leather dyke, the one with the pocked face and sunken eyes, dropped out of the sky onto my back.

She slapped her cupped hands onto my ears.

"Yee owe!"

And I felt a thin piano wire loop over my head.

But I caught it in time. The wire cut my hand. I threw my other elbow back into her ribs. She pulled tighter. I jammed back again. Again! And again! Finally, she went sailing off. I gunned the machine toward my mod.

Full throttle!

I pushed the big pig up to the clouds, and at last, I was free of the dyke leathers. Soon, I would be back with Pella at my mod, reload my Johnson, and stop at the office to get new identification papers. Then on to California City where we could lay low for awhile, and I could search out the Ching Da. It only took a few minutes at red line, and as the clouds thinned I could see my section of the city spring up. Seconds later, I set the hog down in front of my mod.

The heavy steel door slid open.

"Pella!" I shouted.

I reloaded my Johnson and took one look around. Nothing had changed in the mod.

"Pella?"

Where was she? Why did I leave her alone? Gone! What happened to her? I hoped the D hadn't been here. If D-1 had her, I feared for her very soul. Could Rex answer those questions? No time even to com. I ran from my mod, climbed aboard the jet hog, revved it, and gunned red line back to the center of the city, back to the office.

Far below at the shuttle stop, people were pushing and shoving. I couldn't quite tell what was happening, but it looked like several couples were copulating. Next to a building there seemed to be a pile of dead bodies. A jet taxi smashed into another. Nothing unusual was going on, except that my bones felt different. Was evil taking over? Why had the Council given in to Dr. Blood? How did this new figure, Kang, fit in? Where had Pella gone? Had Parkenson turned bad? My stomach growled. Was it time to eat? Rex might have the answers. The city blurred beneath me, but at last, my building appeared. I rode directly up the force, and parked the jet in my office.

"Rex," I said, "please let me have two sets of iris blockers, the ID's and are there any calls?"

"One call."

"Repeat."

"Pella Sannow. Dick, why don't you dial me up? I've been calling for two days.'"

I knew that voice. I was Pella, but it was the older Pella. Damn, I'd forgotten about her. She knew the whole story. Of course, she knew where the younger Pella had gone, and she might even know the reasons behind the Council's actions.

"Com her."

"All satellite's down."

"What!"

"Normal communications are out of order."

"It's going to get worse. Rex, I may not see you again for some time. I'm leaving. What's her address?"

"Sector twenty eight, one G, apartment forty six."

"Okay. Listen. After I leave, use auxiliary power to keep a channel open, and go into chameleon, keep the building at tenement level until I return. Whatever you do, don't allow access to either Parkenson or the D . . . Roger?"

No looking back. I jumped on the jet hog, gunned the pig down the force to the street, then up, up and away to open air. Turning for one last look at my office, I was glad I gotten the Rex series as my building was morphing to a run down tenement, but I was also a little irritated as a voice came in my ear.

"My name's not Roger. It's Rex!"

I couldn't quite understand what he said over the roar of the jet flux. It didn't matter, with less than an hour to make the Link to California City, there was no time to joke with my computer. Sector twenty eight was the poorest, lowest part of the city. In the thirty years since I'd seen her, I imagined Pella had gone through tough times. I prayed to God they didn't blind her or maim her. If she were living in sector twenty eight there was a good chance she was an amputee, or at the least, disfigured. She was poor, for sure.

With less than an hour to make the Link to California City, I roared through the clouds toward that sector and computed the time table. If she could walk and I could get her moving and out of the apartment in ten minutes, possibly we could make the flight. Surely, if the D-men were on to my escape I would have encountered them by now. I fingered my Johnson. No matter what, D-men were going to die.

I slowed in the sector and the air got thick. The old buildings were rotted, and a stench rose over my face. It smelled like termites, rot, and damp sewers. Street one G had piles of furniture, trash and old refrigerator units piled high. I cut the flux to neutral and drifted to level forty. Her apartment sat near a balcony railing.

I jumped from the jet flux. The wood beneath buckled, but held. I knocked.

"Pella," I called. "It's Dick. Dick Phillips."

A pretty Malaysian woman opened the door, and I recognized her. It was Pella alright, but she was older, very attractive, and somehow more beautiful. Her breasts were fuller and her hips a bit wider, but her eyes still held dark mystery. The gargantuan guardian of delight between my legs leapt about like a young boy on a trampoline, but there was no time.

"We've got to go."

"Right now? Where?"

"Get your things. There's no time. Our plan to defeat the D failed. California City is our only hope."

"It's been thirty years."

"I know. What happened to you? I was just at the mod. You, I mean the younger you was gone. What happened?"

"You came from the past and took me back to our time. Don't you remember?"

"No."

"We lived together until you got obsessed with Dr. Blood. You sure you don't remember?"

"The D wiped out my memory. I thought you'd been killed in the underground."

"I survived. Don't you remember?"

I put my hands on her shoulders and turned her. "Look," I said, and pulled her soft warm body to me and held her tightly. "All that doesn't matter. We're back together." I moved her out and held her head in my hands. "You're alive. You're whole. I love you, but I've been sentenced by the Council. We have reservations on the Link to California. D-1 and the D are in control of the city. All the badges and anyone associated with the badges will be killed. Our only chance of survival is to get out. We must leave now!"

She got her stuff and the hog's jet fired right up. As we lifted up Pella sat behind me and held her arms around my waist like she had done so many times thirty years ago at the Hotel Meringue when I was a speed racer. I gunned the pig at full rotation and red lined out to the Link launching spire.

I felt her warm breath in my ear. "Dick . . ." she whispered, ". . . what's that thing in front of us?"

"What thing?"

"There, through the clouds, it's floating in the air."
"Where?"
"It's got a weapon!"
"My god, it's . . ."

Chapter 14.

Ugly.

Pella gasped and tightened her grip around my waist. "What's that black thing!?"

"Where?"

"Right there, in front of us, floating in the air."

I beheld a vision in front of me, and my eyes began to burn. We hovered in the air and gazed at the dark being in front of us which seemed to be half man and half machine. The monster floated in the air while fire belched from its rear. It carried a gleaming sharp sickle in one hand and a long piece of steel rebar-like a spear in the other. The black monster had a face like a man but breasts like a woman. Smoke rose from its mouth. As it spoke, we heard a shrill voice.

"Come! The scales are now balanced. The Angle of Darkness seeks revenge!" The jets fired and it began to speed at us. The spear poised to rip through us.

"Oh, sweet Jesus," Pella whispered.

"The seventh of the seven churches are on fire. Justice will be mine!" It cried. "Stand and deliver!" The being hurtled toward us.

It was the big shaved head faggot from the Dhog bar. I recognized her voice. Her and her bike were burned, and she looked like the dark messenger of death. She must have been tailing me all this way and finally caught up when I stopped at Pella's apartment. We didn't have time for a fight. Our machine was double weighted, and we couldn't run.

"Dick," Pella wailed, "It's going to spear us!"

"Lean hard to the left!" I shouted.

The rebar spear shot over our heads and cut the air near my face. That was it; I had enough, and reached into my holster and pulled out the 44.80 and a shot into her machine. It sputtered and slowed, and in one last attack she hurled the sickle, but it sailed over our heads. As the burned out Dhog hog descended through the clouds, I heard her cry.

"God damned man! I'll see you in hell!"

I gunned our bike toward the giant space needle in the distance.

Soon, almost in no time, we arrived, and it was an easy matter to ride the force to the boarding area.

The great space needle rose above us as we parked and headed for disembark. With Rex's prearranged reservations, false identification, and iris blockers it was a simple matter to pass through inspection, enter the magnetic, and be whisked on to the Link. Our seats were toward the front, near the coils. As we prepared for blast off, I turned to Pell whose face was flush with excitement.

I smiled. "I didn't think it would be quite this easy."

"I know," she replied. "It was smooth sailing after we got past that sooty knight. What was that thing?"

"Oh, that's a short chapter of my life," I replied, "that we don't need to review. I want to hold your hand again. Let me look into your beautiful eyes. It's been so long, thirty years I guess, even though it seems like yesterday."

She looked pensive. "It was yesterday for you, the older you. That is, I don't mean you're old, I mean you, now, older. Wow, I'm getting confused." She looked up the aisle over the seated passengers. "Could we get a Deep Purple or a Clear Head? You want ionizer?"

"Yeah, see if you can flag an attendant."

"They seem pretty busy, there's a lot of people on this link." She turned to me and smiled, but had a question on her face. "Dick, again, why are we going to California City?"

"It's a long story," I said. "Most of all we need to get out of town. Pretty soon it's going to be awfully hot for anyone connected at all with me. If they figure out a way to interrogate Rex. . ."

"You have a Rex?" she interrupted.

177

"Now, now. I am a professional investigator, and I don't boast much, but I am somewhat successful, you know."

"But a Rex!"

"Anyway, you know California City used to be the recreation capital of the world before everyone discovered Iceland. It's relatively easy to hide out in California City. We could be ski bums, surfers, or race magna jets. The chances are it's going to take the D a lot more time to find us there. It's beyond the Ozone Desert . . . very hot, but we could hide out in migrant camps."

"Migrant camps?"

"Yeah, um, I mean that's the last resort. We have reservations at the ah, Hilton, of course, penthouse, top floor."

She relaxed. "Yes," she whispered.

"Then," I continued, "Our first venue is the Skyview shopping mall. We'll eat at the Pinnacle, and we'll dance that night at the Silver Slipper. Afterwards, total rejuvenation at the Cucumber Slice where we'll be revitalized, re-aged, and realigned." I paused.

"Yes," she sighed.

"Look Meaty!" I always used to call her Meaty.

"Ionizer?" The attendant set down a couple of spritzers.

Pella's eyes came alive, and we clinked the glasses.

"Look, Meaty. Evil is taking over the world. It doesn't matter what life is like for us in California. We must find a way to defeat the D."

"It's immediate! Let's drink to our plans. What were they?"

"Somehow I know it's all connected with my Chinaman case. This new devil, Kang, has gotten control of the Council . . ."

I pulled out a pack of Royals.

"No smoking sir," the attendant barked.

"No, no," I replied and continued. "Royals seem have some substance that keeps evil at bay. And Royals are manufactured in California City."

She lowered her drink, lifted her eyebrows, and turned her head. "That's a pretty thin thread of evidence."

"Well," I said, "Somebody tried to poison me with Daktara. And that grows outside California City. That's a clue too."

"That's all."

"It's not much," I replied, "but I've been sentenced. They gave me twenty four hours. Which is almost up! We should be safe in the air in a few moments, so we don't have to worry about that. But if we're going to make a plan, we need more time. That's the real reason for California City."

"Dick."

"Yeah?"

"I think I left the water running in the bathroom."

"Listen," I said, "your old life is over. You're with me now. Don't worry about the old stuff from the past. Help me figure out a way to defeat the D." Then it dawned on me. I'd beaten the Council. Their twenty four hour sentence failed. I stood up and clinched my fist and looked at my sweet Meaty."

"I did it!" I shouted. "We did it sweetheart! We escaped the Council."

"Sit down, sir," the attendant said. "Fasten your seat belts."

As the shuttle blasted off, the gravitational force slammed us back in our seats, our ears popped, our brains pounded, and we couldn't breath. Out of the corner of my eye I could see Pella's face contort. The engines rumbled for at least thirty seconds and then peace. We entered outer space and drifted free of gravitation. A chunk of spittle drifted by my head toward the purification intake, and a voice spoke on the intercon.

"We will be in space for thirty minutes. This week's holo movie is the musical, Destruction of Planet Demitar, staring Tal Madge and C. It runs twenty eight minutes. Enjoy the flight and the show. Thank you."

C I thought. Now, she was a real slut. She'd defined the word with her singing road show and the National Basketball Association. Still, she was a great performer."

"Pella, what do you think of C?"

"I don't know, but look, she's doing 'Get down Bitch.'"

179

In the holo, C pushed the blonde locks off her face, rolled over on her stomach and ran her long finger nails up her black net stockings. She did the splits and shot her hand between her legs. Tal Madge tried to kill the four faced queen of Demitar, and C moved into her song. "Get down you bitch," she sang. "Get down you fucking bitch. Stretch and drip the bloody slitch. If you got it, then scratch bitch the itch! If you can't scratch that itch, you gotta get down, bitch."

The four faced queen of Demitar bit Tal on his neck, but Tal countered with a series of quick blows to her heads. C jumped up and pranced around them and seemed to dance down the isle toward us. Making her fingers into little guns, she pointed this way and that. "Get down bitch. Get down on your back and pitch, down on your back with your dirty ditch. Get down, get down, get down bitch!"

The holo movie wavered, and static interference destroyed the image. To our amazement a new image began to form. A face filled the holo. Greasy black hair, bushy dark eyebrows, penetrating beady eyes, a bulbous nose, the scar that ran the length of his face, and the hideous harelip, it was D-1. The face laughed.

My hand shot for the Johnson 44.80, but who or what could I shoot? The holo image wasn't real. My shot would pass through the image and blast the Link. Our air would be sucked out, and we would explode to space. I let it slide back to the holster.

"Ha. Ha. Ha. Ha!" D-1 Roared. "Phillips, we have you now. In exactly twenty six minutes the Link will enter the atmosphere. Since I control the guidance system, you won't be landing smoothly. In fact, you won't be landing. Ha ha!"

The way he laughed . . . that lisp always irritated me.

"Since I ate your kidney, I've always wanted to cook the rest of your meat. You and your brown little girl friend are gonna burn. This is an invitation to your cremation."

I jumped out of my seat. "Wait a minute," I demanded. "You can't kill all the people on this space craft just to take me out."

He kept laughing. "People, what people?"

One by one, in the seats about us, the people faded out. Pella and I sat alone facing the huge face floating in the holo.

"Artificials!" he spewed with his lisp. "You dumb badge. You don't get it. We save the people . . ."

His image morphed. The dark eyes sunk deep and glazed over. From behind the curled lips, long white fangs sprouted. In the center of his head, a thick horn grew. Baphomet! The devil laughed again, and his crippled harelip-smile savored the words. ". . . We save the people, so we can eat them. But not you two." His voice clipped Chinese like Da Mo's. "You gonna fly," then was back to normal with his lisp. "Wait, not fly. You gonna fry."

I looked at Pella. We were alone on the Link, just me and her and the hideous image of D-1 in front of us in the holography. Pella's eyes were glassy, and then a single tear curled over her eye lash and ran down her face, leaving a trail on her cheek.

"Dick," she sobbed, "I don't want to die."

She grabbed my hand. "I want, can I say it? I . . . I wanted to have a family with you."

"A family?"

"Yes, us. A family. But look what you've gotten us into."

"We aren't dead yet," I replied. "Still twenty six minutes until the Link re-enters the atmosphere. I won't give up."

The holo image appeared right in front of us. "Give up!?" D-1 screamed. "You're already dead! There's nothing you can do. Say you're prayers, and if you know what's good for you, pray to Kang!"

"Dang Kang!" I yelled and ran to the holo com. I took out my Johnson and smashed the projector. The machine, D-1 and his hideous laugh died with a sweeping sound.

"That will keep that monster quiet. Now I can figure out a way to fly this baby."

Pella moved next to me. "You know how to fly the Link?"

"No. It's all electronic. There's no pilot. The controls are all in front, through this port. Give me a hand."

Pella grabbed the latch, and I put my arms around her on to the cold metal. A primal passion which I hadn't felt for thirty years welled up in my loins. There was no time for that. Less than twenty five minutes separated us from instant incineration. Still, as our bodies twisted and pulled at the door and our sinews strained against each other and the odor of her sweat rose in my face and the warmth of her skin penetrated my pores, my big waddy wanted a taste. But the door wouldn't budge.

"What are we going to do?" she pleaded.

"First of all don't panic. Don't panic. Don't panic. Don't panic."

She slapped me. "Stop repeating."

"We still have lots of time." I said. "All we have to do is get this latch open and figure out how to reset the controls." I twisted the short range on the Johnson 44.80. "This ought to do it." I said, and fired a clip into the lock.

Together we yanked and twisted and pulled. It still wouldn't budge.

"Times running out," Pella screamed. "We have to do something!"

"Mandrake claw form!"

I tore into the metal with my claw and ripped the door open exposing banks of electronic brains, lasers pulsing, hot diodes and tiny flashing lights.

What was what? I was badge, not an electronic wizard. Out through a port, the stars and the moon floated peacefully. The Link drifted like a leaf in the wind. There really didn't seem to be any hurry. Space was so calm.

"Do something!"

I froze.

"I don't know what to do. If I change any of this stuff we might explode. For all I know we could fire retros and head for the moon."

We looked blankly at each other for a moment.

"Look through those drawers," I pointed. "There's got to be a manual in there."

The Link's computer voice came on the intercom. "Five minutes until re-entry. Please return to your seats and prepare for re-entry."

Five minutes! My God, we should pray to dang Kang. What had I gotten Pella into? I looked at her beautiful face. She appeared to be an angel. I loved her, and if things had been different, I would have married her and had a family. Would have been nice to have some kids running around the house, a dog, and some cats in the yard. Life could have been as peaceful as space. One more look out the window. How beautiful. Stars like diamonds rotated around the bright broach moon. We were drifting slowly. No worries. The beautiful orb of Earth below looked like a blue marble floating in a dark pool. Why worry?

"Four minutes to re-entry. Please fasten your seat belts."

"Dick! Dick!"

"What! I don't know what to do."

"Please Dick!" she screamed.

I put my hands to my ears. "Help, help!"

"Roger. This is Rex, Roger."

"Rex?"

"Rex on line."

"Rex," I commanded, "please patch me in with Nick."

"Ringing"

"Come on. Come on."

"Ringing."

"Hello, this is Nick's repair. Who's this? I thought all lines were down."

"Nick," I said, "This is Dick Phillips, we're on a Rex isolated circuit, listen closely. I can only tell you this once. . ."

"Three minutes to re-entry."

"Nick," I said, "I'm on the Link. The controls are jammed. We're reentering the atmosphere on the wrong angle. What do I do?"

"Where are you in the Link?"

"We're in the control panel?"

"Let me think. . ."

"Two minutes to re-entry."

"Come on!"

"Don't rush me. Let's see, you could reboot the controls, then you'd land okay but you'd be way off course. Where you headed?"

"California City."

"Oh, that's fun. I had a nice vacation there once."

"Nick!"

"Theoretically, you could land in the Ozone Desert, but it's pretty hot out there."

"Not as hot as in here, we're burning up!"

"One minute to re-entry."

"Hurry up Dick! Pella screamed. "We're gonna fry!"

"Come on, Nick!"

"Okay, you see that first panel. The one under the three contiguous flashing lights?"

"Yeah?"

"Open it up. What do you see?"

"There are four tiny transceivers."

"Four? Oops."

The Link computer voice cut in. "Beginning re-entry procedure. Thirty seconds to landing."

"Come on Dick," Pella lamented, "I can't breathe!"

"Dick," Nick blurted, "take the Rex transceiver out of your ear and change it with the transceiver in the first portal. Rex will relay apogee changes. Have a safe landing. Keep cool."

I quickly followed Nick's instruction, and we jumped back to the first seats and strapped ourselves in. I grabbed Pella's hand, and we held each other tight. If we got out of this alive, I was going to make it up to her for dragging her along. She smiled at me, and her hand was warm. Too warm. I hoped it didn't get too much warmer as the Link slammed into the atmosphere.

We were accelerating!

The hull shook and moaned. The air grew hot, too hot to breath. Flashes erupted outside the hull while inside, the Link began to glow orange. My heart beat in my head faster and faster. I couldn't get any air. Our seats shook and vibrations shot through the craft. I prayed that I had inserted the transceiver in time.

Relief.

Damn, at last I felt it. We were banking into a turn. Rex controlled the craft. Soon we would be landing safely. Thanks Rex, I thought. Saved me again.

Suddenly, the bottom fell out.

We dropped in free fall toward incineration. Pella's eyes rolled in her head. Her face screwed and twisted. The G-force pinned us in our seats. My head shook and my neck bones cracked. My guts jumped up. Pella's face stretched over her skull. I retched. Spew came out of my mouth. We fell faster and faster.

I gasped and called out. "Rex! Rex, pull us up!"

Straight down. Free fall.

The control booth exploded orange. Red flames erupted from the electronics.

Crushing sounds. Safety belt cutting me in two. The floor ripping. The seats and our bodies pitched.

Darkness.

Sometimes a dream happens right before you wake up. Sometimes, you wake up several times, and have the same dream every time you wake. D-1 tortured me in the electro machine, and he took out my kidney. That wasn't as bad as seeing him eat it. Over and over he chewed it. Again and again, as I tried to bring myself back to consciousness, I relieved that nightmare. How he licked his lips, and how he savored the flavor. I couldn't wake up. When I did, the real nightmare started.

When I finally woke up, the Link was quiet except for the automatic fire extinguishers. A warm body rested beneath me. I crawled off of her and held her face. A three inch gash cut across her forehead. She was alive, but unconscious. I had very little strength.

"Sweetheart," I said, "Stay with me. Please don't die."

She was out of it, but alive, and I didn't feel too well either. It's a sin for a badge to tremble, but my hands were shaking. I stared blankly at the smashed electronic controls. The Link was motionless, and in the quiet I could feel my heart pounding like a sledge hammer on an anvil. I pulled out a Royal and tried to light one, but my hands wouldn't behave.

Finally, I got one lit, and I sat back on a torn out seat. We were lucky to be alive. I took a long drag. We were safe, but I knew we were a long way from California City, probably in the Ozone Desert. We didn't have a chance to survive. The Ozone desert was too treacherous. If the burning sun didn't fry off your skin, if the heat didn't boil your blood, then at night a wild beast would surely devour you.

Damn! I'm a badge. I will save her and I will save the world!

I made up my mind; right then and there no matter what . . . we would get to California City, find the Ching Da, and defeat the evil that had taken over the world. I smiled my little smile and flexed the hand of my Mandrake claw. D-1 was a dead man. This time, this time I was going to rip out his guts.

I glanced at Pella. How I was going to get her across the hell hole of sand and rock and brush? The Link only carried minimal food and water. How far was it, and how were we going to transverse the desert without shelter from the sun? I checked the Johnson, only three clips, that wouldn't be enough. We would be facing animals, terrible dangers. Who knew what monsters lived in dark holes behind rocks in dank caves. I didn't want to think about it.

I stroked her face. She was still so beautiful. She hadn't changed, and she wanted to be my wife . . . what a laugh! If she regained consciousness, we probably wouldn't be alive after a week. A feeling ran through me. Almost a chill. It turned to resolve. I clinched my fist.

"Babe," I said, and bent and kissed her face. "I'm getting you out of this, and when I do, we'll make that family. No matter what! I won't let you down. We're going to make it to California City."

But which way was it? I walked around the shuttle in a daze, absent mindedly checking for what we would need. The control panel was still a smoldering mess with heat radiating off the blown electronic panels. No luck, Rex's transceiver was fried. Well, we were lucky, if being stranded in the middle of a sand bowl of death was lucky. Nick must have barely gotten instructions through to Rex and he altered our course down. Inside the control box, pieces of charred metal fused with the transceiver. We would be hiking across the desert blind.

I puffed on the Royal. At least, I had my Royals, and they got me feeling a little better. California City rotted out there somewhere, but which way. It was in the west, but which way was west? I twister my rubber neck around and looked out the port. A full moon shone brightly, and I could make out the outline of cactus in the moonlight. I saw something large, strange, dark, and vicious. Big, it moved with stealth and speed. Was it a jackal, a big cat, or a monster? My eyes played tricks on me.

Through the port I could just make out a few bright stars. We didn't see those much in the city what with the haze, the lights, the advertisements, born-agains, replicants, and the regressives they projected. 'Buy, buy, buy,' the mantra of the age. Holography spoiled the night. Those few stars made the desert floor seem quiet and lonely. If we survived the next days, we might have a slim chance of survival. But it was a chance. I got a blanket from one of the stations and covered Pella.

"We'll make it, honey," I said.

I lay next to her, and our bodies formed a spoon with her warm rear end next to my loins. She was out of it, but breathing in a natural way. I loved her so. I thought about all the times we rubbed our naked bodies, smeared them with grease and squished around on plastic sheets and got our naked bodies hot and heavy with sperm, and like Moby Dick, we spewed. Her beautiful breasts weighed heavy on my mind. Could I touch them a bit without disturbing her? Could just slip in for an instant? No. No! What was I thinking? The crash must have hurt my mind. Maybe not, but still I felt disturbed. I thought about what we'd be up against in the next few days. I couldn't help it. My body trembled.

Didn't sleep much that night. Daylight broke too soon.

187

Pella breathed smoothly. She couldn't wake up, but finally the gash on her forehead stopped bleeding. There would be a deep festering wound. I got up and stretched. Out the port the early morning light cast long shadows over the rock and sand. Here and there scruff and cacti grew next to each other. The early morning sun was behind us, so that way was east. The hatch would open to the west. I turned the lock and cracked open the hatch.

The pain shot through me like ice falling into molten metal. The skin on my hand began to evaporate. It hurt like living hell. Immediately I withdrew it, and large boils rose. Pain. I fried the flesh on the top of my hand. . . The Ozone desert.

Yet, inside the Link we were safe. Pella was alive but couldn't wake up. I moved slowly, in pain, and collected all the food and water, but it was a poor excuse for nutrition, mostly snacks and ionization stimulator. More pain. Seconds drifted to minutes. Minutes added to minutes and became hours. Night came.

The lonely walk from Pella to the controls, from the controls to the back of the Link and back again to Pella. Over and over. Not much else to do. Pacing, the lonely walk, my guts craved action. God damn it! Why wasn't I with Cynthia? Why wasn't my debutante humming the anthem? Why wasn't I drinking a Blue Ionizer, relaxing on Parkenson's estate? I walked the walk, but in my head I wasn't talking the talk. Wake up, Pella, wake up! But she wouldn't. Commander Dick Phillips, you can command all you like, but it won't do no good. I poured small sips of water in her mouth and nursed her hour by hour, but she would not wake up.

In a few days my hand was feeling much better, and at night, by starlight, I was able to scout around the scuttle and check the damage. My hand hurt like hell, but I could move some small boulders and the rubble. The shuttle was damaged beyond repair and pieces of the heat shield were scattered all around. I dared not make long reconnaissance missions any distance from the ship for fear Pella would slip away, but I did discover cacti everywhere. When I opened one of them the meat crushed to yield a yellow fluid. I drank it and felt alright. Several times, at night, I was able to catch small insects, and I noticed that while the sand seemed to be dead during the heat of the day, at night it teemed with life. Soon, I found ways to capture different kinds of food. Not Insta Feasts, to be sure, but it kept us alive.

On the tenth night, Pella woke up.

"Oh, my head," she moaned. "Where am I?"

"We're alive, honey. We made it," I said and put my hand gently to her face. "The heat shields saved us, but we crashed and you hit your head. You're going to be fine."

"Thank God for the shields," she paused. A tear rolled down her face, ". . . and for you."

Those were first human words I heard for ten days, and my heart rejoiced. Then I understood why Nick had a light bulb burning over his door. A switch went on in my head, and a ten thousand watt bulb exploded. The heat shields! They were the answer. They would save us.

"Baby," I said. "I thought I'd lost you." She smiled at me and my heart fluttered, and I pulled her to me and we rocked back and forth.

"Where are we?" She asked.

I looked out the port. The desert looked lonely and barren and something moved and flickered on the edges of my vision. Where were we? I didn't know. Like a piece of material, worn out over the years, our luck was threadbare, torn, and shredded. We were alone in the heart of darkness . . . two stranded souls on a night flight to nowhere.

She was warm. Her eyes lifted to me.

"Sweetheart," I said, "It doesn't matter. You're with me and that's all that counts. I was lost, but now I'm found. And I know the answer."

I pulled her close.

"Dick, you're trembling."

I relaxed.

I gave into the weight of the moment, and pulled her closer. I didn't want to think of what lay ahead, the disgusting desert and the unfathomable danger.

"No," I said and pulled a blanket over us, "I'm just a little cold."

Chapter 15.

The days that followed blended one to another. Pella grew stronger as each day passed. Soon, she was on her feet, and we made the Link our home. We slept during the terribly hot days. When darkness fell the nights were long and still awfully hot, but we made good use of them.

Pella occupied herself with fashioning blankets into ponchos by sewing them with control wire. I collected insects, lizards, and rodents which we ate or dried for later. The cacti provided us with enough water to sustain our thirst. We slowed down, and like molasses in a frying pan we seeped on the Link from one position to another. In this routine, we lost all track of time.

My main job, besides searching for insects and lizards, was to collect the thin sheets of Moliboron Carborinium which had been the heat shield of the craft. To think of the plan was easy enough. We would simply carry our heat shields with us. At night we would walk toward the west, carrying the shields. Before morning we would build an igloo structure with the panels and sleep all day. Perhaps, if we figured it a bit more, we wouldn't have even tried.

One night, I drew a little plan. "See," I said to her. "It'll be easy. There's plenty of separated shields. All we have to do is tie them together and we have a perfect place to sleep during the day."

"Why don't we just stay here? They're bound to rescue us soon."

She still wasn't clear, and I didn't want my anger for the D and Dr. Blood to spill on her. "Meaty sweetie," I said, "No one's coming after us. They wanted us dead and I'm sure they think they succeeded. But I won't let you down. We're getting out of here."

"Are you sure we can make it?"

"Come here!" I pulled her close. "Let's go out and look at the stars."

Outside in the warm night air, something in our diet or the radiation from the desert floor . . . we both felt very alive. In the extreme heat we'd both been going shirtless from the start. Now, Pella's bosoms were full and her nipples stuck up like little fingers on her breasts. Her whole body had become tight, taught, thick, and resilient."

"Honey," she said, "lay those ponchos on the sand."

As we lay next to each other, a shooting star cut across the sky.

"What is that thick band of stars?" I asked.

"Silly," she replied. "Don't you know the Milky Way?"

"No, I don't think I've ever noticed it before."

"Silly, city boy. It rings around the Earth."

"It's your wedding ring. Marry me?"

We pressed our chests together and kissed.

"Ouch!" she cried, "Must you always carry that gun?"

I unstrapped the holster and the 44.80. Silently, I made sure the safety was on.

"I think I'll shove this up your cunt!"

"Oh Dick! Yes. Talk dirty to me like you did thirty years ago."

I gripped the metal. "Lick this." I said and held the pistol to her mouth.

She turned away.

"Lick it!" I demanded, grabbed her hair, and forced her head around.

"Stick out your tongue!"

"Eh," she whimpered, closed her eyes, and stuck out her tongue while I tossed the Johnson to the side. Her long snake came out a little farther and I put my lips over it and sucked it in my mouth. I sucked her tongue hard. At first she resisted, but then released and the full thickness came in my mouth.

She sucked my tongue back in her mouth and pulled on it. We kissed, and the spit ran from my mouth to hers and I licked her lips and her tongue shot in my mouth and flicked in and out. I felt my cock get big as it ever had been and jerk and strain against my pants.

I lifted my legs as she unbuttoned my pants and held my massive protuberance in her hands. Then she found my balls and squeezed the left one hard. Next, she gripped the right one and tightened down on it. My blood vein grew bigger and bigger, and my hips jerked and a shutter rippled from head to toe.

I forced her face to the side and took her whole ear in my mouth and stuck my tongue deep inside her.

"Oh please fuck me!" she screamed. "I want you inside of me. Fuck me!"

I moved over her face, leaned close and kissed a short kiss on her lips and whispered. "No, not yet."

I pulled down her pants and put my hands on the wet spot in her panties, gripped the material and pulled them off and spread her legs. In the starlight from the Milky Way I could see the juicy bulging red lips and purple interior meat of her fig. Hunching back on my knees, I crept before her delicious shrine, bent my face in her wide open puss, but first I licked the crack of her ass. I flicked a slick lick in that tight crevice, and then aimed my nose and buried my full face in the wetness of her hairy mansion.

I licked her long twang clit with sweet slow lip flicks, then another wet slick kiss on that finger that trembled and wouldn't quit. As my tongue shot sideways and back in her little mouth, between my legs, my penis hard as a rock, began to jump, thump, and twitch. With my face in her puss, we pitched forward and back.

"Aiee!" she screamed. "I want that cock inside of me!"

I pulled myself along her body, kissed her neck and lips. "Not yet," I whispered. My middle finger lingered in her wet hole and circled the inner lips then lightly brushed the clitoral mound. As if it were there, then not there, my finger softly brushed the shaft. Her body shuttered, rose, and stiffened. A bolt of energy rippled from the back of her neck down to her knees.

She shoved away my hand and pushed me over on my back. "Let's ride!" she cried, and climbed on top of me. With a swift little motion in a squat, she slipped my cock into her juicy cunt.

193

Um, I thought, as I lay back on the poncho and gazed at the Milky Way. So many stars. The down slide was a wonderful feeling. Millions . . . no, billions of stars. So many stars.

Oh, the up sliding feeling. Must be people living on those stars. A million lovers, on a billion stars. The push down, the suction up. Lovers, making love.

"Yes," she whispered, "yes."

As I lay on my back on the ponchos between the ruined Link and the piles of heat shields, caressed by warm cacti blossom-scented night air, with the Milky Way above us, a new sensation overcame me. At first, it just felt good. Her warm puss pushed my cock away, then sucked it up. Up and down. Up and down.

My dong got big and very hard. She slammed against me. Harder and harder she pumped. Her body pulled me up, and slapped me down. She sucked me up long and pushed down hard. Long and hard, up and down. I felt a strange new feeling. It was as if I was no longer inside her, but she was inside me. We were no longer two, we were one. Too perfect, the unity could not exist in this universe and in a mighty blast, a giant explosion erupted inside of us.

We jerked and jerked and heard a cracking sound that we could not hear and saw a blinding light that we could not see. A door opened to a white and purple translucent arching fecundating flashing strobe universe that could seal the door where evil dwelled and existed, but did not exist as the singularity or the many, and we knew not when, why, or where we were or were not one. We came again, and again. Then again! And again!

I saw it. Behind Pella, behind the stacks of Moliboron Carborinium. Its eyes glared red. It had giant horns, and long fangs, and sharp claws. Blood dripped from its paws. Saliva frothed in its mouth. Its distended tongue hung in the air. It panted and scratched the ground and lurched forward. Its huge body heaved up, and it jumped over a large pile of heat shields. Its hideous face stretched over its sharp teeth, and it seemed to smile. In an instant would be on us.

My hand shot for the Johnson. Where was it? It wasn't on the poncho. I searched on the sand. The monster was right on top of us. Now its giant claws extended from cloven paws. It was right above us with hot fetid breath. The beady red eyes erupted with hot flashing light. The mouth bared long fang teeth, and saliva dripped on my face and scalded me.

There, at last in my grip, the cold heat of my Johnson. I aimed. I fired. It wouldn't fire! The safety jammed. It wouldn't fire!

"Dick!" Pella shouted and pulled my arm. "Dick. Wake up. You're having a nightmare. Come on, we've got to get inside. The sun's coming up."

Just a nightmare? I wasn't sure. Had we had sex last night, or I had I lowered my guard for an instant, and had evil impregnated me? Was an evil being growing inside of me? It didn't matter. It was time to get moving.

My plan was easy enough. Simply, we would carry the lightweight Moliboron sheets as far toward the west as our strength would allow. At that location, we would build a small protective igloo and spend the rest of the night collecting cactus water and whatever food we could find. During the day we would sleep in the structure. The small igloo would take about twenty pieces of flexible sheeting, so if I carried four sheets and Pella carried two that would mean several trips back and forth to the new location.

The night we were set to leave, Pella tied her hair back. Her eyes looked wild, and she grabbed my arm.

"Dick, are you sure this plan will work?"

"It'll work babe. I know it will?" I lied again. "We've been planning it for weeks now. I don't see how it can fail. We have enough cactus juice and food for quite awhile, and we can find more. The desert is alive. California City shouldn't be too far away."

"How will we know which way to go once we're away from the space craft?"

"We're headed west. We know the sun sets in the west. All we have to do is follow the sunset. We'll get there soon, and when we do we'll start a new life. You'll see. I've still got the two hundred thousand American the Chinaman gave me. We'll live like royalty. Don't worry. We'll make it, but it is going to be hard."

It was much harder than I imagined.

As the sun set we marched west across the wasteland away from our quiet little homestead. I carried four of the lightweight shields and Pella carried two. We moved along until we were about a half mile from the Link, then we walked back. Three more trips and we were ready to set up the shelter. It lashed together easily, and we left small vents at the bottom for air. It was a tight fit for two, but the ponchos made a nice floor. The morning came too soon.

Exhausted, but secure, we sat in the darkness and waited for the sun. We were safe and secure. If I hadn't been a badge and experienced every kind of torture, I might have gone crazy. At first, it didn't seem bad. In fact, it was comfortable. Then the sun came up.

"It's too hot," Pella remarked.

"It'll get hotter," I replied. "Let's try and sleep. . ."

At last we fell asleep, but my mind was racked by the same dream. The monster attacked us again and again. It tore our flesh, pulled my insides out, and ate my guts in front of me while a succubus grew from my torn guts and formed into the same ugly monster that kept attacking us over and over. At the end of the dream the face would grow larger and larger, more and more real. It was D-1.

Our igloo felt less like an oven and more like a sauna in hell. We were literally being cooked. But we slept, and finally the sun set. The night, compared to the day, was cool. But it was still hot. We sweated as we tore down the heat shields and carried them as far as we could before rebuilding the igloo. Inside, again the day broke too soon. The sweat, the heat, the dreams of dying, and the fear got to me. Night after night we trudged through the rock and sand toward a new life in California City. Soon our supply of food and water was depleted, but luckily, at night the radiated desert teemed with life. Outcrops of cacti, bugs, and small rodents supplied us sustenance. At night, the radiated desert cared for us and protected us.

Back and forth we went, each night breaking down the old camp and by morning setting up the new one. Sleeping in the daytime, we moved and foraged at night. At first, we only made a short distance, but soon, perhaps due to the radiation, I was able to double my load and carry all the panels. This allowed Pella to search for food and water, and we made more distance each night. Yet, while the nights were pleasant and we advanced, the days were hell.

One early morning, before going to sleep, Pella looked at me with a blank smile on her face.

"I can't take it anymore," she said. "Look at my skin. It's turning white. I've lost all my color. My hair's a mess. We stink. We haven't bathed for weeks. Your beard's matted. I'm sick of the darkness. I want to feel the sun again. I'm going out."

I grabbed her arm. "Look in my eyes." I shouted. "Look at me, in my eyes! My beard is matted and my hair's long, but I'm still me. I'm Dick Phillips. You're Pella Sannow. You can't go out. You'll burn. Pay attention! We're almost there."

She tried to jerk away, and I slapped her face. "I'll kill you woman!" I pointed my Johnson. "I won't let you open the igloo to the sun." That shut up the bitch.

It wasn't the heat. It wasn't the sun. It wasn't the work. It was the routine. Night after night we trudged. Sand got in our food. Our clothes became rags and hung tattered around us in torn threads. We were both white as ghosts. My beard seemed to be alive with insects and my hair tangled on its own. Like trapped animals, we started acting wild. While I carried the shields Pella would stalk me, and we'd growl at each other like primitive beings. But we moved on. We forgot time. We didn't talk. We lived for our small nightly movement over the desert floor. It didn't matter that we were eating insects, lizards, and rodents. It didn't matter that I had to carry the shields. Time didn't matter. Evil didn't matter. We forgot about the Ching Da. We forgot about California City. We followed the sun. The only thing that mattered was moving on, simply moving on.

Toward the morning of another day, who knew what day or how many days we had been in the same routine, as we set up the igloo and got inside to avoid the sun, I looked at Pella. What a damn mess, I thought. If I didn't steal her out of time, if I paid more attention to her instead of being so caught up as a badge, perhaps we could have had a family and a life. I touched her arm.

"Grr," she growled and brushed me off

I pulled out the Johnson. Light sparkled off the barrel as here and there a streak of light cut through. The sun started showing through the cracks. I guessed this was it. I'd just do her. Put a bullet through her scraggly hair and then finish myself off. In a thousand years someone would find our bodies, pressure cooked and mummified. I pointed the Johnson, but I couldn't form an intent. I couldn't pull the trigger. Even in this desolation, I still loved her. She was my meaty, my baby. I let my 44.80 drop to the grass.

Grass? Grass meant something. I couldn't focus.

Thud!

Something heavy beat against the igloo.

I picked up the Johnson. Pella and I shrunk back against the hot metal. My hands shook. I couldn't concentrate. Should I kill both of us before the monster broke into our shelter and tore us from limb to limb?

A voice called out. "Ey mon, who is dat en dare?"

I whispered, "It's us."

"Hey!" cried the voice. "You can no park on the field. We wants to play."

Chapter 16.

"Hey inside!"

Weakly, I unlashed the wires that held together the Moliboron Carborinium shield. Pella brushed the matted long hair from her face, and I stroked my hand over my beard and pulled a knot from my stringy hair. Streaming in on us now, the sunlight was less intense. Was this California City? We gathered ourselves up to face the voice as I released the final wires.

At first I couldn't focus. The sun didn't burn us, but the light was bright. We seemed to be on a green soccer field. A group of black soccer players gathered around us, and one black man with long stringy hair and a bushy beard stood in front of them. He looked at us and his eyes grew large and he laughed.

"Will you look at that, mon," he said to the others. "White Rastas!"

"California City?" I asked meekly.

"No brodder. No California City. This is Billyland."

I still had my wits. I looked at Pella and then hugged her. "Billyland," I shouted and danced a little jig. "We be saved. We be saved." I got down on my knees and kissed the grass. "Praise Saint Billy. We made it, we be saved."

Billyland? Oh sure, I'd heard the rumors. A protected place where the water was so pure you never got old, where fresh fruit and vegetables grew wild, and where the air was filled with love. No one really believed those rumors. I figured it was just a hoax the Rastas started to promote Billy as a Saint. Now, here we were in Billyland.

Beyond the playing field, rolling hills lead to orchards overgrown with fruit. Under the trees, large vegetables hung from row after row of trellises. In the distance was a small village. Here and there black children were playing. One ran on the field pushing a hoop. He ran on a path toward a group of houses, and a dog ran along with him, barking at the hoop.

"Come. Come with me to the fountain and drink. You will be refreshed."

The Rasta led us along the path toward the group of houses, and I put my hand over Pella's shoulder. "We're safe, baby."

"Where are we?" she asked in a whisper.

"I'm not sure," I replied. "Either we're still in the igloo asleep and I'm dreaming, or this is paradise."

"No paradise." The Rasta said and lifted his hands to the air. "This is Billyland. This is de land of milk and honey, de land of love."

The path circled through small white finely landscaped houses to a bubbling fountain where a manicured park was lush and green with grass and shade trees. A cup hung from a peg.

"All is love here in Billyland. Come mon, come womon, drink of da water of life. Be free. All is free in Billyland. Welcome to de land of free love."

He dipped the cup in the water and handed it to Pella. "Beauty first."

Pella sipped the water and changed. Her whole body became more supple and fuller. She emoted a youthfulness. Her hair changed and glowed. And when I drank, I felt vigorous and strong. I flexed my muscles and stretched. The last weeks in the desert had been a strange dream. I looked at Pella.

"Sweetheart," I said, "we're home."

"Oh Dick," she cried. "I love you."

"Me too," I replied.

"Dis water," said the Rasta "is da sacred water of Billy. All is love and wisdom and devotion in Billyland. It is written. We welcome the white Rastas. Tonight at meeting, we give you house to live in and love work devotion."

He nodded to Pella. "Peace to my sister." Then he nodded to me. "And for you, my brodder, more peace."

"Brother," I said, "I am called Da Phil. And this is my wife, Da Pella"

"I am called Ro Nes," he replied, and motioned to a small white house. "Come and be refreshed, clean yourself and rest in ma home."

Ro Nes' house was filled with posters of lanky baseball stars from years ago, some of them seemed familiar, but I couldn't quite place them. We showered, and boy, that felt good after all that time in the desert. We were given fresh white robes and then we were led to the center of the little town to the main hall. Black men and women dressed in Jamaican costumes, with hair braided in dread locks, were laughing and playing. Ro Nes stood in front of the assembly.

"Da prophesies have come true," he announced. "The white Rasta have arrived. Dis day is da beginning of the new order. Soon da light will arrive. We will be with him again. All join hands for the invocation. May Billy return."

Next to me, dressed in an orange flowered muumuu, a large black woman grabbed my hand. On the other side of Pella a muscular black man took her hand. I held Pella's other hand, and we completed the circle of Rastas. Ro Nes chanted, and the group followed him.

"From the point of light within the mind of God, let Billy have de power. From the point of power within the throat of God, let Billy have de strength. From the point of love within the heart of God, let Billy have de love."

Ro Nes stepped into the middle, and still holding hands, the group began to circle him. In the center of the circle, he turned round and round and held his hands in the air. Everyone stamped their feet and the hall filled with noise. Then it stopped.

Ro Nes looked at the ceiling. "May Billy seal de door where evil dwells!"

The room grew silent and he spoke quietly. "Now Masalla will lead us in the Anthem."

A beautiful young Jamaican girl took his place and the group followed her in song.

"I am . . . ," she sang.

A female in the circle broke in, "I am . . ."

Across the room a male came in, "I am . . ."

Then the whole group sang.

"My name's Billy, ma love makes me a saint. You know I am, but they say I ain't. My name's Billy, ma love makes me a saint. Rasta says I am, but they say I ain't."

The young girl again took the lead.

"Evil's time will someday be through. On the day Blood kisses Saint Billy's shoe. Three times four words will be chanted too, 'cause righteousness came when Billy threw."

The group again sang the refrain, "My name's Billy, ma love makes me a saint. . ." And while they were singing I tried to remember who Billy was. He was associated with something I was working on before when we were in the desert, but I couldn't remember. My hand reached up to pull out my gun.

Gun? What was I thinking? We don't carry guns here in Billyland. This is the land of love. And how I loved them all. The circle of love was complete. My heart opened, and I felt a wave of understanding and acceptance. I loved them all. Pella and I at last could relax. This was indeed where we belonged. We were home.

That evening we all got acquainted and Pella seemed to fit right in. They all gathered around her and talked and talked. Pretty soon I was on the outside of the group, and I don't know why, but I started craving. I wanted a cigarette. I walked out to the fountain and held the cup.

"Help yourself," Ro Nes said.

"Thank you."

I drank from the well and felt much better. All the cravings were gone. I felt wonderful. I was at peace. Zip a dee do dah, an old tune hummed in my mind, and I skipped about.

"I love it here."

"I know. But come," Ro motioned, "it is time for instant replay."

Back inside the hall, the lights were dimmed and everyone sat on pillows. A distant humming sound told me an old style holography machine had begun, and soon we sat on a large baseball field surrounded by a huge crowd. In the stands people cheered and jostled and yelled. A banner announced the game. It was a World Series ten years ago.

The crowd went nuts. Everyone screamed. Half of them were drunk. A women took off her panties and threw them at the players. A group of men fought. The scoreboard read the top of the ninth, and the score was three to two. On the mound, a lanky black pitcher checked his glove. As the catcher tossed the ball back to the pitcher, the batter threw his bat and kicked the dirt. One out. Two to go.

Another great cheer from the stands. Tied three games to three in the series, the last inning of the last game, the score of that game three to two. The winning pitcher ground his mitt. On the mound with only two outs left to win the whole series, he adjusted his hat; again ground the ball into his mitt, looked at the catcher and ground his ball into his mitt.

"Throw da ball, Billy!" the catcher shouted.

The pitcher looked like he was in a trance. He shook his head. He looked at the catcher. He shook his head.

"Throw da ball, Billy!" shouted the catcher.

The pitcher stood immobilized for several seconds.

"Throw da ball, Billy!"

Suddenly, the pitcher was a blur. His windup, his motion, and his pitch were instantaneously delivered. He moved so fast you couldn't focus on him.

The ball scorched across the plate. "Strike one!"

Now, the catcher looked familiar. I tried to remember who he was, but I couldn't. Then we were back on the mound with the pitcher, again in his trance. The catcher screamed. The pitcher shook it off. The catcher screamed. The pitcher shook it off.

The crowd waited breathlessly. The catcher screamed a third time.

"Throw da ball, Billy!"

This time the pitcher exploded, went into a blur, and the ball crossed the plate on fire.

"Strike two!"

The ump moved out of the way, and this time I got a look at the catcher. Even behind the mask I could tell it was a younger Ro Nes. I looked over at him in the hall as the holography whirred around us. He was reliving the moment and had a big smile on his face.

Then in holography the young catcher, Ro Nes, was screaming. The crowd hushed. The pitcher, baseball Billy . . . in a trance, in a blur, he threw another smoking fireball.

"Strike three, yer out!"

The crowd went mad, jumping and screaming and pounding their feet. A giant wave rolled across the bleachers. Women disrobed. Men poured buckets of beer on each other. Hundreds of baseball hats flew on the field.

My memory was returning. I'd seen it all before. They used to play it in the bar at the Pleasure Palace. We would get a laugh. It was one of the strangest happenings in sports, that day that baseball Billy became a saint.

The tension of the crowd mounted. It was the final out. A lot was riding on the next three pitches. Billy's team was up one run. All he had to do was strike out the next pitcher and his team won. Everyone held their breath. Casey McGraw, the all time home run king, stepped to the plate. His huge muscles rippled as he pointed his bat toward the bleachers. He'd hit Billy's fast ball many times. The crowd became deathly silent.

On the mound in front of us, the lanky pitcher tipped his hat. He ground the ball in his mitt, threw it back in the mitt, and ground it again. He tipped his hat, shook off the signal, and let his hand drop by his sides.

"Throw da ball, Billy!"

"Strike one!"

Casey McGraw stood there looking. He looked at ump, and he looked at Ro Nes. He got a mean snarl on his face, and took several swings and again pointed at the stands.

"Throw da ball, Billy!"

A fireball whizzed passed McGraw and he stood there looking.

One strike to go and baseball Billy would go down in the record books as the greatest pitcher of all time. His team would win the series. He would walk away with the money and the reputation. It all hinged on the next pitch.

"Stop the holo!" Commanded Ro Nes, and as the lights came up in the little hall, he stepped in the front of the group. "You watch now, very careful. Da next part is de best part. It show exact when Billy become a saint. Run holo."

Back inside the stadium the crowd was shouting, "Billy. Billy." Then a single voice called out, "Hit the ball, McGraw!" Part of the crowd raged and the other ranted. Together they raised a great din.

"Throw da ball, Billy!" screamed Ro Nes and a rocket ball ejected from a blur on the mound. McGraw took a swing, tipped it, and the ball went flying back into the neck of Ro Nes. The ump bent over, said a few words to the catcher, then took the ball and tossed a new one out to Billy.

Billy looked at the batter. He raised his frame to its full height and ground the ball into his mitt. He seemed to be waiting for something. He tipped his hat, looked at the catcher as if waiting for some signal.

For an instant, he turned and looked at the bleachers. He looked at the sky. He turned around and looked back at Casey McGraw. The cameras moved close on Billy's face. His eyes were blank. Billy looked at the catcher. Tipped his hat and waited. The catcher was silent.

On the mound, Billy's lanky arms dropped next to his sides. He turned around and looked at the sky. He dropped his glove and dropped the ball. He stared at the sky. His body quivered and jerked, and his eyes grew wide. His face took on a look of utter amazement.

And in the hall, his face seemed to fill the little room. "I see God!" Billy cried and pointed. "He's there in the sky above us."

His eyes came alive and his face took on a beatific smile. "God is love. God is beauty. God gives instruction for all of us."

The crowd hushed, and then some began to boo. A terrible noise rose in the stadium. The camera focused on the pitcher's face.

"Quiet!" Billy demanded.

"Quiet!" He shouted, and his voice broadcast over the crowd. "God told me the world will end in ten years. The Evil One is coming! He will try to destroy us. There will be a war between good and evil, but he has chosen me to protect you." Billy motioned with his hands. "Come to me, my brothers. Join me in the fight. Rasta brothers and Rasta sisters, join me. Help me save the world."

He stretched his lanky frame toward the crowd, "Love your neighbors."

Billy walked around the field dodging thrown objects until finally the officers lead him off and the image focused close on him. He turned back to the belligerent crowd. "I am love," he shouted. "I am the truth, the light, and the way. Follow me and I will protect you."

Ro Nes switched off the holo and the images were over about as fast as Billy's career. His team went on to lose that inning, the game, and the World Series. It seemed a lot of people didn't like him proclaiming himself a saint. Eventually, in a few years he found a big following, but after a skirmish with the politicos in the Council, Dr. Blood forced Billy to step down. They never made him kiss Blood's boot, but he was forced into hiding. No one knew exactly what happened to him. Some of his city Billyboy Rastas became quite violent, and there were those rumors about a sacred protected enclave of eternal youth and love. It had always been a legend to me, but now my love and I were living in Billyland.

That night, in the little house they assigned for us, Pella and I wrapped together and slept in each other's arms like snakes. But in the middle of the night I woke with a violent start. In the darkness, two blood red eyes focused on me. I blinked and sat up cold rigid. Whatever it was, a dream or my imagination, I was now wide awake. I couldn't sleep. Thoughts of the Chinaman and Kang flashed in my mind like a broken holo, repeating and repeating. I became hyper. I must find the Ching Da. I must!

Yes, it was imperative I find the Ching Da. Time was running out. This little village was protected by the water, but I knew in my heart that the rest of the world was in the throws of destruction. We had to get to California City, even if it meant again braving the desert.

I couldn't sleep, so I put on my robe and walked through the village. Here and there doors were open and couples and families curled up. There was no crime here. No one wanted for anything. The land of love. Hard to believe it really existed, but here I was living in peace and harmony. I wandered around Billyland as I wondered.

Soon, I found myself at the entrance to the main hall where only several hours ago we viewed the holographic testimony of Saint Billy's conversion. Funny, how things change when people are about. Before, it had been filled with happy souls. Now, it turned into an empty and forlorn place. My bare feet made a hollow sound on the cool wood floor. I needed more information. The holography held a clue to where I would find the missing Ching Da.

I energized the old machine, and as it began to hum, Billy was on the mound. No, we just saw that one. I took it out and inserted the next one. The machine whirred and the empty hall became the center of the village at the fountain. Some of the houses were being built and around the water a group of black men and women were sitting before Billy. The lanky baseball player held a small glass container that sparkled in the sunlight.

"I bless de water, now and forever," he said and poured a fluid from the glass.

"Praise Billy," came a cry from the audience

My suspicions were confirmed. He poured Charachunga into the well. That was what was making me feel so good. That was keeping us all young and protecting the village from the evil that was overtaking the world. It was true. The William who had lived with Da Mo was actually Saint Billy on a quest for enlightenment. He stole the Ching Da!

In the holo image, he held the receptacle to the light and the container automatically refilled itself. He took a sip, and as he swallowed he grew younger. I figured all I had to do was find Saint Billy, get the Ching Da back to Da Mo, and the world would be saved.

But time was running out.

"Praise Billy!" chanted the crowd.

I removed that disk and inserted the next one, walked over and sat on a large stuffed pillow. The machine hummed and the scene changed.

At the edge of the village, Billy boarded a shuttle. He walked on the ramp with Ro Nes. They turned and waved to the Rasta crowd, who cheered as Ro Nes turned to Billy.

"Saint Billy," Ro Nes asked, "when will you return?"

Billy patted his hand on Ro Nes arm. "Tank you, ma friend." He paused and put his hands up in salutation to the crowd. "I am going to California City. When the work is finished, I return."

"What sign will there be of your return?" asked Ro Nes.

"What sign?"

"How will we know to prepare for your coming?"

"Before me, out of the desert will come two white Rastas. One will come with a heart of love. One will come with a violent fist. Love them both. Dey proclaim my coming."

He waved and stepped into the magna craft. But I knew he wasn't going to come back. Simpson told me Saint Billy sat on the Council when they sentenced me. He was probably Blood's slave. Was Blood already in control of the Ching Da? Or had Billy taken the Charachunga to the Royal factory? Was evil taking over the world? I didn't know for sure, but I did know Pella and I had to get out of Billyland. The fate of the world rested on me finding the Ching Da. Time cranked like a sonic locomotive. If evil took complete control, only heaven knew if it could be stopped.

And, my sentence had to be revoked. Of course, there was the other matter of the Chinaman's money, the five hundred thousand American. More than money, I wanted revenge. I'd rip out D-1's throat, I thought, and make Dr. Blood eat it. Why I'd . . . but my thoughts wondered. Here I'd been chasing the Ching Da for all this time, and Billy may have already delivered it to Dr. Blood or this Kang, whoever he was. Whatever the reality, it didn't matter. California City waited for us like the final stop on a long lonely air bus ride.

Were the rockets still blasting? I knew I couldn't get back from California City without transport on the Link. Did evil control everything? I clinched my fist. One thing at a time. Cha ching! Mandrake claw. Blood would eat death, but first we had to get to California City.

Dawn was breaking when I returned to our little house off the square. Pella lay on her side on the bed with a sheet pulled over her. It was time to leave. I lit a candle and shook her.

"Come on, babe." I said. "We can make some distance before the sun comes all the way up."

"Wha . . ." she mumbled, rubbed her eyes, and pulled me to bed.

"We've got to get going!"

"Where," she replied and stretched. I could see one of her nipples erect. Its outline stuck up under the sheet.

I sat down next to her. "We've got to get out of here."

"So soon, we only just arrived."

"I know, but we have to find the Ching Da. It's prime now."

"Baby," she said half asleep, "love me hard."

"We have to go," I whispered.

"Hard. I want it hard."

"The Ching Da," I said.

"Umm, yes. Prime. We'll leave tonight."

"Okay," I said as I kissed her, "tonight at the latest."

Her lips were like a split succulent guava, so sweet and moist. Her tongue circled my lips and shot in my mouth. My Priapus wedged like a rock and entered her. We lay like that for moments . . . like pieces of a jigsaw puzzle. We didn't move. We were blissful as perfect lovers, lovers joined at the loins. No stroking, no hammering, no pounding, and panting. In this contented state, we fell asleep in each other's arms.

"Morning water," Ro Nes said, sticking his head in the door. "Love, wisdom, work."

I untangled myself from my wife and sat on the edge of the bed.

"No," I replied. "We have to get our things together. We'll be leaving tonight."

"First, drink da water," he replied. "All is love in Billyland. There are no rules, except after water, we work to eat and eat to work. It is da love, da wisdom, and devotion."

"Dick," Pella whispered.

"What?"

"We have to do our part."

"Alright." I nodded to her and looked Ro Nes. "Alright, first water then work, but we're leaving tonight."

And you know, after a morning drink at the fountain, I felt much better. I couldn't figure out what had been bothering me. They sent me to a garden on the hill to shovel dirt from the rich dark soil, and that suit me just fine. Nothing like digging in the soil, I thought. Nothing sooths your soul like using a shovel.

I filled one wheel barrow and then another. I love hard work, and damn, it was getting hard. The wheel jammed and the barrow turned over and I had to shovel it back again. The path down to the field was crooked, and it took a lot strength to push that wheel barrow, and when I returned a large a large black man helped me shovel.

"Smile brodder," he laughed and handed me a bottle of water. "It's a beautiful day. We have de sun and de air and all de vegetables are happy. Drink. Praise Billy."

"Praise Billy," I said and drank.

Now, I felt stronger, and I grabbed the handles of the cart and started down the path. I was a lot stronger than I'd been in the city, and my back was willing, but I wasn't used to wheeling dirt. I started too fast and hit the bank. The cart turned over.

"Damn it!"

"Ah white Rasta mon, take it easy," the big black man said and smiled. "Take life easy. You must slow down. What did ya do before you come to Billyland?"

"Me?" I asked, "Let me see . . . I think I was a badge."

"A badge mon? You were a badge?"

"Yeah, I think so. My memory's a little hazy. I was on a case, what was it? What about you?"

"Construction, sir!"

"Yeah, what kind?"

"Oh mon," he said with a big white smile as he jammed the shovel in the earth. "I build da big cigarette plant in California City."

"Royals?"

"Yeah mon, you moke them?

"I used to," I replied. Thinking of them, my memory returned. "Yeah, I used to smoke them a lot. How come you working here?"

"Ma reward."

"For what?"

"Listen," he said and turned his head to the side and spoke in a quiet tone. "Come closer."

I stepped up on a pile of dirt so I could reach his level and leaned toward him. "Yeah?"

"I made de hiding place for da holy water."

"The holy water?"

"Yeah mon, the water of life. As ma reward," he whispered, "Billy let me and my wife live here for the rest of our lives. Praise Billy!"

"Praise Billy," I retorted and started down the path to where Pella worked.

Although my hands were hurting and my legs getting tired, at least part of my memory had returned. So the Ching Da was hidden in the Royal factory in California City. All I had to do was to get this construction worker to tell me exactly where, and Pella and I could leave tonight. I smiled at her as she worked with a young black girl.

"Pella," I said, "As soon as we eat, I want you to get our things together. We'll tear down the shelter this afternoon and be ready to leave by tonight."

"Leave tonight?"

"Yeah," I replied, "I need to find out a few things from the man I 'm working with, and after that we'll carry the metal out to the desert. By morning we'll have it set up and be back in routine. California City can't be too much farther ahead. This afternoon I want you to get a store of food and water and pack the ponchos. . ."

"I'm not sure I want to go."

". . . then after you get all packed up, and it's dark, we'll duck out without too much commotion. We don't want to get held up. Make sure the Johnson is loaded just in case they try to stop us. What else, let's see. . ."

"I think I'm staying."

" . . . If you can milk any of these women for information. See if they know anything about when Billy is due to return. I also need to know more about that fountain. Oh, make sure you fill up some jugs of water before we go."

"You're not listening to me!"

"Look," I said, "its Ro Nes motioning us to come. It must be dinner time."

All the workers gathered in the square, and we all sat down to empty tables with only water in front of us. I was anxious to get this meager meal over with, find out from my new black friend where the Ching Da was hidden, and get packed and out of Billyland. I had to find the Ching Da.

"Praise Billy," Ro Nes said, and moved his hands over the water. "Water brodder take water, dis is life."

"Praise Billy!" we saluted and drank the water. And it was good. It made me feel good, and I ate. The meal wasn't' what I expected. First, we were served dishes of oranges and apples, and guava meat with berries in cream. Next came rice and curries and honey soaked grains. Coconuts, pineapples, almonds and filberts were served on plates with grapes and strawberries. Here and there were small bowls of chic peas, bean sprouts, and delicate sprouts of fresh grains. Then came cheeses of all types and forms, followed by warm breads and thick clear butter.

After filling ourselves, we washed it down with pure fresh water from the well. I felt strong and satisfied. Pella and I giggled and laughed and played with the Rastas. I felt strong. I couldn't remember what had been on my mind, so important only a few minutes before. Now, I felt full and sleepy.

Ro Nes announced, "Before da afternoon we call love, before da pleasure toil we call wisdom, before da love-work-devotion . . ." He smiled and lowed his eyes in a saintly way. ". . . We rest."

So we returned to our house, and I lay on the bed with my wife, I mean Pella, and thought about how wonderful life was here in Billyland. Yes, it was wonderful. I hadn't eaten such a meal in many, many months, and now with her warm body next to me, and the cool air blowing in through the white curtains, the feel of the sheets next to my body, the thump, thump of her heart, and the natural fragrance of her hair, I felt like this was indeed home. I belonged. She nuzzled my ear.

"I love you, Dick. Don't ever leave."

"I won't sweetheart. We'll always be together."

I fell into a deep sweet afternoon sleep, but for some reason woke with a start. Perhaps I'd never had life so wonderful, or perhaps deep within me a force from my past stirred me, but it didn't really matter. This home, this place, all Billyland, wasn't a dream. It was real. How refreshed I felt. I was married now. This village was my life. Some memory or thought persisted from my old life, in my usually blank mind, but what was it and what did it matter? Something about evil, but praise Billy! Each day when we wake my wife's skin feels fresh, she smells like the clean sheets. When I wake, when I drink da water, I forget all but love, wisdom, and devotion. I want to work, I live for the work, I live only for now. I am I come I am. I am, I come.

After rest, back to work.

This certainly was the life, I thought as I wheeled the cart up the hill. There in the distance at the edge of the small farming community, at the green grass near the edge of the sandy desert, several Rastas were dismantling our igloo. As they stacked the Moliboron Carborium sheets, I realized we were here to stay. Indeed, this was our home.

"Oh yes," said the big black man as he shoveled, "I was the main builder of the factory. Why, wit out me, mon, dey would not ave been the secret hiding place. I say, look Billy . . . you knows . . . I always call him Billy. I say . . . look Billy, you must ave da hiding place for da Holly Water. All is Love, he reply. I say, I knows mon, but you never knows, you knows what ah mean? Praise Billy."

"Praise Billy!" I replied.

As I shoved off with my cart, I took a drink of well water from our bottle. Praise Billy, I thought. What a wonderful place this is. My arms are strong. My woman waits for me in the fields at the bottom of the hill. I feel good. I am love. I am alive. Alive. Praise Billy!

It only took several minutes to traverse the route and dump the soil, and as I finished I nodded to Pella and the young woman she was working with, then I whistled a happy tune and pushed the empty cart back up the hill where my big friend beat his shovel against the cart, and we sang together.

"You know, mon, white Rasta," he said, "I likes you. You got rhythm and you listen good. Like I was saying, me and Billy was pals from the start. We got da idea that if anybody broke into the factory we would make a place so da Holy Water would be safe. No matter what, even if dey found it. Boom."

He shoveled a couple of times. "Guess where we hid it?"

214

"Hid what?"

"Da Holy Water mon?"

What was he talking about? I felt so good just working outside in the fresh air; I couldn't focus on what he was saying. The fruit trees were all in bloom, the fields were green. I took a drink of water and gazed at Pella and the black girl working below me. My skin was getting dark also. These were my people.

"Oh yeah," I retorted, "the Holy Water."

"That's right. After we sprinkle it in da formula use to make da Royal cigarette, then we hide the Ching Da where no one find it. If dey do, boom!"

Ching Da? I thought. That meant something.

"Boom?"

"Dat's right. Boom. No more factory. No more cigarettes."

He pushed a little closer to me and elbowed me. "Guess where?"

"What?"

"The Holy Water. Guess where we hid it?"

"Where?"

"It's obvious, mon. Where? In the where house. Get it?"

The sun was setting, and as I wheeled the last cart of the day down the hill, I wondered how my friend had gotten started on that strange story. In where in the where house? I took a drink of water and shoveled out the dirt where Pella worked.

"Dick," she laughed and pulled on the arm of the girl next to her. "This is Masalla."

"Hey Masalla," I said, "Pleased to meet you. Why you're about the cutest thing I have ever seen."

I guessed she was about eighteen or nineteen years old. If she were a peach, I would have sunk my teeth into her juicy flesh. Her black eyes flashed at me, and energy seemed to jump from my body to hers. My throat got dry, so I drank another swig of water and handed her the bottle.

"Praise Billy!"

"Praise Billy!"

That night, after communion and chanting and fully stuffing ourselves with wonderful fruits and nuts and breads, and drinking the refreshing water, Pella and I hugged on the bed. We rocked backwards, and sideways, and forward.

"I love you, babe," I whispered.

"Praise Billy," she said and continued, "and I want to give you the best time ever."

Pella pushed me away and smiled with a question. "Do you think I'm beautiful?"

"Very, very beautiful."

"As beautiful as Masalla?"

"She's a young girl," I replied. "You're much more beautiful. I love you."

"But do you think she's beautiful?"

"Of course, but why do you ask?"

Pella got up and went to the closet and pushed the curtain. "I have a present for you."

It was Masalla. A thin sheer nightgown hung from her shoulders, and I could see her full breasts with erect nipples. Between her legs a thick sporum of curly dark hair spread in a v. She moved like a tigress, and as she came closer, energy arched between us in purple bolts. She touched her nipples and ran her tongue over her lips.

"I want you," she whispered.

I stood up. "Pella," I said, "I don't understand."

"All is love in Billyland," she replied as her hands unbuttoned my robe, and at the same time Masalla fell on her hands and knees, shook her head back and forth, and inched toward me.

My waddy grew faster and thicker than a zucchini on a hot summer's day with a big blood vein pulsing up and down its neck. The head got bulbous like water balloon. The rod started jerking like a wire on short circuit overload.

The sucker snapped and stood up, and then her long black fingers surrounded my penis. Her fingernails dug into the shaft, and she pulled down rough and then up hard. Then she took it in her mouth and started sucking on it!

She took it deep in her mouth, deep in her throat. Her lips pulled on it from the base to the tip. I put my hands on her face and gently held her while she circled the tip with her tongue and nibbled the meatus with her teeth. They say when lightening strikes the Earth, a bolt comes down from the sky and another bolt reaches up to meet it. That's what it felt like. A lightening bolt was getting ready to strike my mighty oak. At the same time, deep within the oak a surge of electricity exploded upward toward her heavenly lips.

"Praise Billy!" I cried. "Wang-a-dang-a-da-roonie!" With fantastic hydraulic pumping power my seed puckered, and in a mighty ballistic blast, a load of cum spurted on her face.

Life in Billyland was indeed wonderful. Next morning, love-wisdom-devotion as usual. I whistled as I worked my way up the hill to the dig. My friend was already in the hole with a pile of fresh brown dirt ready to load.

"Top of da morning to you," he said.

"And a good morning to you, sir."

"Did you figure out where we hid da Holy Water?"

"Where?"

"Where," he replied. "Where? Why in de under where. It's da riddle."

I started down the hill. Under where in the under where?

Pella and Masalla were holding hands and smiling. All was love in Billyland. I dumped my first load and blew a kiss to Masalla.

"Love you."

I was getting stronger. Now, the cart was easy to push up the hill. The trail seemed shorter, and the cart a lot lighter. I hummed a tune and set the cart by the dirt.

"Zip a de do da, zip a de a. . ."

"You is one happy fellow. You must a had a good fuck with you woman last night."

"Oh no," I replied. "See that young one, next to my woman, down in the field," I pointed to Masalla. "Last night, she gave me the best head. I came in her mouth and on her face. Man, it was..."

In a single bound the big black man jumped out of the hole. I hadn't even finished what I was saying and he was on top of me. He lifted me with one massive hand, and then both hands clamped around my neck and squeezed out my life. His strength was enormous. I struggled in amazement. What had I said or done?

"Masalla's ma wife!" He screamed.

It tried to speak but couldn't. In that brief moment before he extinguished me, my life flashed before me. I remembered who and what I was. I tried to form the words, but without my command, the Mandrake claw wouldn't form. He shook me like a rag doll, and as I gurgled and flailed, my hand shot for my Johnson.

Wait a minute. Where was my Johnson?

Again, I tried to command the Mandrake claw. I fired it at him, but it wouldn't form. I couldn't move. He was too huge. He shook me like a bag of air until my mind began to pop. In an instant, I would be dead. My heart slammed in my chest. My mind exploded, but I forced my body to go totally limp. I pulled my last trick. I opened my eyes as far as possible and fixed them into space. I distended my tongue.

"Gal lack!" I blurted, rolled my eyes, and flopped my head to the side.

At the final moment, the big man realized what he'd done. In horror, he threw me down and fell on his knees.

"Billy!" He lamented, "Please Billy, please forgive me!"

My mind went blank for a second. Evil had hold of us, that was for certain. Even here in protected Billyland with the magical water, the cancerous tentacles of evil spread like fetid stank of a hideous sore slowly creeping over us, eating our skin with it's acid pustulation.

The possum, the final trick, is only a last resort. He threw me away as if I were a dirty old rag, but I landed on my feet. I twirled like a dancer. Rotating two times to build momentum, I slung a three sixty kick into the big man's face. I slammed my fists into his temple. I pulled out his arm, held it rigid, and kicked my knee into his elbow, crushing the bones.

It didn't faze him. He got up madder and stronger than before. He rushed me.

"Mandrake claw! I screamed, and the glowing hand of death formed to rip brains from his body.

From below Pella cried. "Dick, no!"

With his good arm he swung a massive punch at my face.

I held back because of Pella's screams, and instead of tearing off his head, I caught his hand in my claw.

"You're one lucky fucker," I said. "If you kill a badge, you'd better make sure he's dead."

I crushed his hand, but the sound of breaking bones was hushed by the calls of workers rushing in all directions toward us. From all sides of the village they came. Like a wicker basket of assholes, all around us a circle formed full of evil tainted, hate filled, amazed, and angry workers carrying pitch forks and shovels.

"Screw you. And screw Billy!" I cried and ground my heal on his broken hand.

"Fuck you!" he screamed and shot his fist into my scrotum.

My insides collapsed. Jesus and Billy that hurt, I thought, as I fell back over the cart. Somehow, with a broken elbow and a crushed hand, the big black man still had enough strength to rise up and take the shovel in his hand. He rotated it around and around his head and fired it point first toward me.

He missed, and it stuck in the side of the cart. I looked at the point inches from my head. He lunged in the air.

With his body in the air, almost on top of me, I grabbed a hand full of dirt and threw in his eyes. He landed on me and flailed me about the head, but I rolled away and returned blow for blow.

"Where are you Mo Fo!?" He screamed, "I gonna kill you."

"Here!" I said, and fired a round house with the claw across his face, and a last he was out.

The crowd went nuts. Blood rose in their eyes. For an instant they moved as one being; like an amoeba, they undulated back and forth. The face of evil. It was definitely time to leave Billyland. They moved on me. I could feel their hot breath, but as they lifted their pitchforks and shovels above their heads, a space between them opened. I made a break.

I ran along the trail toward an outcropping of rocks with the blood thirsty crowd in hot pursuit. The angry odor of their hatred reached my nose. Hand over hand I climbed the rocks. From behind me, shovels and pitchforks beat at me. I could feel fingers grabbing me. At last, I reached the pinnacle.

A mechanical sound filled the air.

Chapter 17.

"Kill the whitie!" The crowd screamed.

Rrrrr. The sound stopped us. As a group we turned.

The distinctive whir of magnetic flux drowned the cries of the crowd as the hull of a dark metal hover craft cut the horizon. It was an old style land cruiser like the one Billy flew away on in the hologram. It moved very slowly, weaving slightly and jerking up and down as if the person at the controls couldn't decide to land or go forward. It hovered in the burning desert several hundred yards from the protected greens of Billyland. At last, it sank to the desert floor and stopped.

"It's Billy," one of crowd shouted. They all took it up.

"Billy's back! Praise Billy!" they cried.

As a group they ran down from the abutment over the grass to the edge of the desert. Inches from the sand, from the killing Ozone desert, knowing they would fry their flesh if they stepped further, at the very last moment, they stopped. Only Pella and I were left at the top of the outcropping of rocks. Below us, the crowd jumped and chanted.

"Come out Billy! Billy come home!"

The little hover craft sat silently in the sand.

"Dick," Pella asked, "you almost killed Masalla's husband. Why?"

"He attacked me." I said, "I'm a badge."

Her eyes looked at me with the blank stare of no comprehension.

"Besides," I added, "can't you see? Evil's taking over the world, even here. Those crazy bastards tried to run me down and kill me. The sacred well water that's been protecting is losing its power. We have to get out of here right now!"

She didn't need to speak. Her innocent face, full of love and wonder, told me she wasn't going with me to California City. I looked at the crowd of Rasta crying out for their saint to emerge from the little craft sitting in the burning desert. I looked at Pella. If Billy were inside with the Ching Da, fine. I'd fly it back to the council and defeat the evil that had taken over. If he wasn't inside, if the Ching Da wasn't there, there was only one solution. We would have to take that craft to California City, find the Ching Da, and somehow get back across the county to the Council. What I'd done to Masalla's husband, the hatred of the vile crowd, and the very feelings right now entering my bones told me we had very little time to discuss what to do. I shivered to think what was happening to the rest of the world. Could that little magnetic hover craft take me out of here? Would the Link be functioning? How was I going to get back to the Council? Outside of protected community of Billyland, would the universe be in total chaos? Was there enough time to save the world?

Pella must have seen the desperation in my eyes. For what seemed like an eternity, I waited for her reply. We had to get moving.

"Dick," she said, "I can't go. I'm pregnant."

"What!?"

"Yes, it's true. Your baby's inside of me."

I gasped. Me, a father? Could it be true? How could we bring a baby into this evil world? I put my arms around my sweet Meaty, and we slowly rocked back and forth. This was the final straw. Now, there would be no turning back. Evil must be stopped! I had to do it for the world, for Billyland, for Pella, and for our baby. I must succeed.

"Sweetheart," I whispered, "that's so wonderful. I love you so." I faltered for an instant. "But," I lamented and my voice cracked, "still . . . I must go."

"You're leaving me here alone!"

"We don't have much time. Can't you feel it? Evil is spreading its dark force like rancid butter in a frying pan, and we're the bacon. Our only chance, our family's only chance, rests in my hands."

"Dick!" She cried. "No! Stay with me."

"There's no time!" I reiterated, "I'm going to need food and some water from the well. Get the ponchos, and by the way, where's my Johnson?"

A tear ran down her face and her voice quivered. "All right, I understand. Your Johnson, yes. . ." She paused. "Ro Nes took it that first night when you went out."

I knew she hurt and so did I, but the hope of our family now rested in my hands. Ro Nes, alias Robert Nesbalm the famous catcher, had my piece. He also knew the answers to what was happening with the stalled craft on the desert floor below us. While the crowd ranted and pleaded for Billy to emerge, I went looking for Ro Nes.

And I found him doing mediation in the chamber where earlier we'd seen the holography of Billy's conversion. A lonely figure in the middle of the empty hall, he sat on a large pillow, lost in thought.

"Nesbalm," I shouted, "wake up!"

Immediately his large eyes opened. "Ah," he said, "da White Rasta."

"I want my Johnson and our ponchos, and I'm not a Rasta. I'm a badge."

"Ya, I know dat."

"Give me the skinny low down," I demanded, but before he could answer I laid the truth on him. "You know it. I know it. Evil is taking over. The world is in grave danger."

He nodded.

"Now!" I commanded. "Let's have the truth."

"I am afraid," he said and held his hands to his face. His body shivered and convulsed. His voice quivered and he shook. He turned to me. "Ya, something is wrong. Saint Billy must be hurt, perhaps dying in the little hover craft in da desert. Why doesn't he come to the sanctuary of da grounds? He must be dead, or he would a signified. What can we do? We can't cross da sand. By tonight, may be too late. What will we do?"

223

"I might be able to help," I said. "But you have to tell me the whole story, and while you're at it, cut out that crappy Jamaican accent."

He nodded and cleared his throat. "Billy . . ." he said in deep-throated elegant English, "Billy and I were class A baseball players. Together we discovered a revolutionary way to hypnotize ourselves so we were completely removed from the stress of the game. That's how Billy got to be such a great ball player and became the greatest pitcher of all time. We would use key words with each other. It was simple neural linguistic programming. We installed multi-layered key words into our subconscious. I guess Billy had a blow out.

"Anyway, the words that stimulated him to pitch his fastball were "Throw da ball, Billy!" When I said it three times in a row, swish, no one could hit his fireball. But it was a dangerous technique. It always left him exhausted. Even before the World Series, he had terrible dreams about evil. But we wanted to win so bad, we didn't stop the programming. We laid track after track into our neural networks, until by the final game, Billy was throwing the fastest pitch the world ever saw.

"But during the game, Billy wasn't himself. He kept saying he was seeing images, and he didn't know what they meant. Every time he pitched, he went deeper and deeper into his subconscious. I was getting scared. After each pitch I had to yell louder and louder, "Throw da ball, Billy!"

"In the ninth inning, on the last out, that monster Casey tipped the ball and it hit my throat guard. The pitch was so hard, the ball smashed the metal. I was okay, but my vocal cords were temporarily frozen."

Ro Nes' chest sunk as he spoke. "It was my fault. I should of called time out. I didn't realize I couldn't speak, so when Billy touched his hat to start his motion, I couldn't yell out the neural programming. Seconds passed. Billy must have gone too deep. He must have entered the very essence of his subconscious mind. He freaked out!"

Ro Nes raised his head. "He saw God!"

"What did he look like?" I asked.

"Billy said She was a black woman about seven hundred feet tall with the rising dawn sun in her forehead, shinning white crescent moon for a mouth, two blazing stars for eyes. And when she talked, multi colored tetra-atomic particles, each one a living planet, spewed from Her being.

"Afterwards, Billy said he felt feelings that he couldn't express, except that now he knew bliss, and love, and he said he knew the truth about life and why he'd been chosen. He said he was the alpha and the omega, he'd seen the fullness of the way-less way, and now his path was clear. He understood his place in the universe. Instantaneously, he realized all knowledge of symbols, how language conveyed feeling, and how feelings were the only truth. He said he knew joy, that he was bliss. He knew what he had to do. Stop evil."

"That's all?" I asked rhetorically.

"Praise Billy," Ro Nes cried. "Later, Billy discovered this oasis in the desert which is somehow protected from the ultraviolet rays of the sun, perhaps from a blockage of the hole in the ozone layer. He used the Holy water he discovered on his travels, and Billy blessed the well."

Ro paused and jumped up. "But now the water must be renewed, that is why he has returned. The village must be saved."

He walked around the hall and then cried out. "I fear he is sick, alone in the little craft. He may be dying. You have to help!"

"Wait a minute, just a minute. Why did he come back here?"

"I told you, every few years he has to renew the water in the well, or evil overcomes us. Don't you feel it? The trees are dropping their fruits, the vines are wilting, da love is fading. Soon we begin to change. We will revert! We must get to Billy."

He put his hands to his face. "Please have the Holy water. Please Billy, please be alive!"

It wasn't pity. I had to protect my family. "Have your men bring my Moliboron Carborinium. I'll find out what's going on out there."

At the edge of the grass with the heat radiating off the sand in front of me, it only took a few minutes to assemble the metal sheets and make the protective shield. As I stepped inside, Pella stepped in with me.

"Take this," she said, and handed me a pair of her underwear.

I sniffed them. A memento? "Don't worry." I told her. "I'll be back."

"No, silly. For the hatch of the Magna craft."

I was getting stronger. The Moliboron seemed lighter than before, but it was still hard going. As I trudged through the burning sand, the parched smell of the desert seared my nostrils. I started to melt. At least, I felt like I was melting. Anyway, I sweat like a mo fo, a hot mo fo.

Pella's underwear came in handy, for even as I shaded the doorway with the shielding, the metal latch was burning hot. At last the hatch gave way, but when I entered the worst stench slammed my nose and forced me back. The ripe smell of human rot hurt my head and forced me to my knees.

A badge moves on.

I rose and forced myself to climb the ladder to the pilot's control. There it was in front of me, the rotting body of Saint Billy laying face down on the control panel. Worms squirmed out of his oozing decayed flesh, and pus dripped in pools on the floor. I couldn't breathe, but I had to find out what happened.

First, I dragged the black man's body out the hatch and tossed it into the sun. Instantly, I heard a loud gasp from the protected lawn. Then a shout.

"Billy! He killed Billy!" The crowd screamed while the body erupted in flames like a flare.

After some moments the air became breathable and I started searching and went to work on my investigation. Soon, in a discrete compartment, I found a bottle of water and a note. It said,

'I am sending you a limited supply of Holy water with my trusted pilot. I have hidden the receptacle in the warehouse.' It was signed, Billy.

So Billy was still alive. The dead body had been that of the pilot. From the wound in his side, and the degree of rot, he'd died long ago. I switched the controls off automatic and nudged the hover craft toward the safety of Billyland. To avoid the nasty crowd I landed in the square before the hall where I knew I would find Ro Nes.

I handed him the bottle. He grabbed it from me and swigged a drink.

"Hey, take it easy. Save some for the well."

"Of course," he replied joyfully, "Wow. I feel good. Look, it replenishes itself. See."

He held the bottle in front of me. "It is again full."

"No," I said, "It's a little less than it was." I took the bottle and drank. Woo! I felt good. "But look," I said, "See, it's a little less than before."

"When Billy was here it replenished itself."

"This bottle is not the China Da. That's why. That's Charachunga alright. But that's not the Ching Da receptacle. That's why the well looses power and has to replenished. The power in the water isn't infinite without the Ching Da receptacle. The note says that."

"Note? Give it to me."

"First," I said, "Get the ponchos and my Johnson."

He nodded. "Alright, I have them here."

I checked the Johnson. Loaded, it was ready to go. The metal felt warm and familiar in my hands. The holster buckled on in a familiar way. I pulled the Johnson in and out a few times.

"I'm out of here."

"Wait," Ro Nes pleaded, "you have to help us. Saint Billy has been captured."

I played dumb. "How do you know that?"

"Why else would he have hidden the Ching Da?"

I felt through the ponchos. The two hundred thousand American was still in its bundle and the iris blockers were in their compartment. I looked long and deep at Ro Nes.

"I'm a badge," I said. "I don't work for free."

"Not even for Billy, for Billyland."

"No."

"Not for your wife and family?"

I wondered how he knew about them. "No," I said. "Not even for my sweet assed Mom."

"Okay, how much?"

"For what?"

"To save Saint Billy and find the Holy water and bring it back here."

"Let's say one hundred thousand American to start." I said with a little smile, "And another five hundred when Billy returns with the Holy water."

"Six hundred thousand!" Ro Nes gulped.

If the client didn't gulp, or look indignant, or get wide eyed, you knew your price was too low. I figured with an operation like this, with him and Billy controlling the Charachunga in Royals, and what with the contributions to Billy's sainthood, they were rolling in dough. I wasn't wrong. Ro Nes motioned and the money was brought in.

"If you don't succeed," he said, "money won't be worth anything. You can't fail."

A beam of light flashed through the stained glass window behind the lectern. It lit a circle on the floor where I stood. "I can't fail," I said, "because the world depends on me. The folks here in Billyland, and little kids and mothers and fathers in all the cities of every household, the workers in the fields, the intellectuals, the sober and the drunk, depend on me. Mothers, wives, lovers, the poor, the downtrodden, and even the snobs with their noses up their asses, depend on me. I can't fail! The life of my wife and my child are at stake. The very fabric of life is in my hands. I can't fail."

I looked up to the light and my face was encircled by a halo. "I will not fail!"

"But how will you get across the Ozone desert?" Ro Nes asked.

"I'm not sure. I have a plan."

"A plan?"

"The hover craft still has almost a full flux. That means I'll be able to get to California city. If all goes well I'll find Billy and the Ching Da."

"You must go immediately!"

"No. Tonight, after the sun goes down, I'll take the hover craft. I'll fly straight to California City, to the Royal factory where . . ." I sat down and put my hand to my chin and my elbow on my knee, and thought . . . under where in the warehouse . . . "Where I will retrieve the Ching Da."

That night, after Ro Nes blessed the well water with the new supply, I walked with Pella back to our little house.

"Meaty," I said, and bent over and kissed her forehead. "With the renewed water supply, you and the baby should be fine until I return."

"Don't go, Dick. It's too dangerous."

"It's prime, sweetheart. The D must be defeated."

I pulled her close and felt her warmth. "I love you."

I hated to leave Pella in Billyland as there was a good chance I might not make it. But now, even if I didn't make it, my child could survive and Pella could raise our family. Maybe . . . no! I wasn't going to think like that. No matter what I was going to save the world. I knew if I could find the Ching Da and return to the Council that I would defeat the D, Dr Blood, and whoever this Kang was. Evil would be defeated.

Inside the ship, the magneto turned over and the hover craft groaned and lifted off the ground. Out the small port, I could see the full moon glowing as big as it had the first night the Link crashed. I loved flying. I eased it out over Billyland and across the desert. I knew I was going to miss my sweet little Meaty, but I knew in my heart I'd be back. The levels of flux were normal and the fuel level read half full, so I figured I'd easily make it to California City. I didn't know what I would run into, but I felt ready for anything. If I met the D, D-men would die. If I met Dr. Blood, Cha Chang! I'd waste him with my Mandrake claw.

I jammed the accelerator back and the craft lurched and pitched forward at a tremendous rate. Out the view port the sandy floor seemed to be rapidly changing shape. Desert turned into mounds, mounds grew to hills, and in the distance I could just make out mountains. With evil in control, I didn't know what I would find ahead, but to make sure I slashed my Johnson in and out. It felt warm, big, and thick and ready to bring an end to the disorder.

I wondered how Parkenson was handling all of this. He was always above it all and seemed immune to changes. Would he give in to Dr. Blood and Kang, or would he capitalize? I'd soon find out. What was it that he said, "I killed too quick." Not this time, old friend. D-men were going to die. It would be fast and easy. I'd blow through them at the Royal factory, find the Chinaman's rejuvenation fluid, get on the Link, and get back to the Council chambers. When Da Mo got his dose of Charachunga, the world would return to the semi-sane state it had always been.

It never happens as easily as you think it will. I wasn't prepared for the ugliness, the carnage, and the control of the Evil One.

As the magneto hummed along, I set the controls and rested on the pilot's cot. Many miles stretched ahead, and even at our accelerated rate it would be many hours before we reached the heart of the city. Searching through the ponchos I found two clips for the Johnson, two sets of iris blockers, and a lot of sand. In one compartment, my fingers touched a foil package. I knew immediately it was a missing pack of Royals. What a relief! I lit one up and blew a ring of purple smoke. Wasn't this what the life of a badge is about? I lay back on the cot and thought through my empty brain about all that had gone on since I got that first call from the Chinaman. I shut my eyes.

Ka blam! An explosion riveted me to wakefulness.

I jumped to the controls. Still holding constant velocity. Still on course.

Another explosion rocked the hover craft and I went flying out of the pilot's chair. There was nothing to see out the small port but moonlight and a few stars. The craft was intact so we hadn't sustained damage, but light flashed through the cabin. Another explosion tore at the hull. I raised us up another hundred feet.

"Computer," I commanded. "Give me a holography image of what's below."

The holography flickered and an image formed. A half naked man with one eye falling out of his face ran forward and drove the point of a spear through a young woman's chest. An old crippled lady with an axe jumped out of her wheel chair and in a round-house way chopped into the back of the half naked man. She turned, and as she turned a teenage boy shot his rifle into her head, exploding and gushing blood over all of them. With sticks of dynamite strapped around her middle, a child ran to the fight.

A gigantic explosion rocked the shuttle craft. Below me, families were fighting and killing each other. Gangs of blood-smeared humans, both men and women and children, fought hand to hand. There seemed to be no point in their battles, at least none I could discover from my relative safety above them. What a ghastly turn of events. I wondered what else I would encounter before I reached the Royal factory. I leaned back in the pilot's chair and relit my cigarette.

"Oh, no. Stop!" A female cried.

"Grrr!"

"Computer," I said, "amplify that image."

The image magnified and expanded. A beast with hair covering its back and chest and long hair on his head and face was mauling a young hairless naked white girl. It had her bent over on the ground and hunched over her and seemed to be smashing its haunches into her rear end. The beast curled its head in the air and bared its fangs as it dug its claws into her shoulders and forced her up and back.

231

"Computer, re-adjust. Focus in."

I could see the beast's large slick thing emerge, poise, and then ram back to penetrate the poor little girl. It wasn't attacking her; it was eating her at the same time. Like some Praying Mantis that rears on its hinds as it devours it mate, the monster snarled, chewed and ate the little girl. I cringed. Blood spurt from the neck of the young girl. The monster wasn't just having sex, he was eating her! Good God! It was too late for the little waif. If I didn't complete my mission many more would die. There was no saving the poor child. The hover craft moved on.

We moved to the base of the mountains, where the great aqueduct feeds the city. That's where I first saw them. Thousands of green lizard Skink climbed out of the water. As a group they rose on their hinds and bared their giant fangs and snarled as a united being. With a trail of fletching skinless human bodies behind them, the lizards acted as a singularity, running down hapless humans and peeling off their flesh. There was no defense for anyone left in California City.

Not that it mattered much anyway, for as soon as the craft reached the first buildings of what had been the outlying recreation centers, all I saw for miles was destruction. This wasn't the destruction of war. It was imposed, crazy work, like the mad population was in the throws of reinventing itself. As we passed above a half open building, a gang of construction workers, who were dressed in brown work clothes and yellow hard hats, ran cranes and bulldozers. They tore down one building while another gang of workers put up walls and roofs. As quickly as they tore down the buildings, they restored them. What appeared orderly soon became disordered. Cranes smashed cranes and tractors crashed other tractors. Workers built bridges that led nowhere. Buildings rose in one direction and then collapsed and other buildings replaced them.

The hover craft rose higher and whirred, and further on I saw hundreds of men and women dressed in military clothes, marching in step. They moved ahead, then to the right and to the left.

"Computer amplify that."

Had I smoked too many Royals? Was this an hallucination? They weren't men and women. They were skeletons dressed in brown army clothes wearing hats and wigs and carrying arms.

"Amplify images."

They were real! They called out to each other.

"Hup two, three, four," they sang. "We are the armies of the dead. We march on fields blood red. We went to war for our county. We sold our souls for a sword. We'll live forever without dread or fear. You can't have fear when you're dead."

A sergeant stepped to front. "Again boys!"

They rang out. "We live forever without dread or fear. You can't have fear when you're dead!"

"Ready!"

As a group they bent on their knees and pointed their rifles at each other.

"Fire!"

With a loud retort, bullets rang out. The skeletons fell prostrate for a moment, and then they picked themselves up and got back in formation.

"Hup two, three, four . . ." but the sound faded out behind us. The craft sped on.

Nearing the city, some buildings were still standing. On a roof top, fifty or more people sat in individual chairs while holographic images danced in front of them. They sat motionless, staring into the images. They could see the evil coming. They could see it in the holography. They might have escaped, but they sat motionless, watching the carnage take place around them, watching their lives evaporate.

The city burned in a raging inferno. Far below, magnetic cars and bikes flew around in circles and then crashed with explosions, and flames erupted in the streets. At one school ground, a fiery shuttle burst through a fence and ran down playing children, while what must have been their parents stood by watching. They covered their eyes and ears.

On other roof tops, sun bathers were oblivious to the chaos, they sat in groups and handed cigarettes back and forth. A man rubbed suntan lotion on the back of shapely lady. Others lay about on their blankets, while one couple tossed a beach ball back and forth. Their building was burning. Any second it would collapse, but no one seemed to care. Were they all drugged? Then I saw it.

The big sign on the next building read, 'Be oblivious. Smoke Royals.' I knew the factory had to be close, but where. The mayhem below distracted me.

Bishops and priests dragged young boys out of cathedrals. They made them bow and then take off their pants and turn their rumps in the air. The elders pulled something from their robes, but they were so small, at first I couldn't quite make out what.

"Amplify."

They were forcing their penises in the boys' behinds! Chaos ran rampant with disorder. Without turning their heads to look at the priests, a parade of house wives marched along the street carrying a banner that read 'Free the Slaves.' A shot rang out from a window in a building. One of the housewives fell. A man stuck his head out of the window.

"How do you like freedom now, Marge? Till death do us part?"

On and on the hover craft hummed. While I took the final puffs on the last of my Royals, scene after scene came on the holography. Murder mixed with mayhem. Death went hand in hand with destruction. Below, wantonness mated with lust, and bestiality raw Sodom. I really needed another smoke. In the distance, out the port, dark clouds formed a giant insect head. Its blood red eyes penetrated me.

What was in store for me in the next few hours?

Where was that Royal factory?

Chapter 18.

In the small port the giant formicine ant head loomed large on the horizon. Its eyes burned with a red glaze, and smoke rose from its antae colossi. While beneath me California City writhed in death throws, in front of me lay the living, breathing reality of a force so fierce it could animate steel and breath life into, in fact, give a living soul to machinery. Outside the hover craft's little port, on the horizon, the insect head vibrated and pulsed. Fire belched from it mouth, and orange and red waves of radiation sent quivers through the air. Its soul was evil. It was the Royal factory. I set the course.

A badge's first lesson is to face his fear, but as we neared the destination and the craft began to slow, I smelled an odor I hadn't known for some time. It was my own stinky sweat. I wasn't sure what I would find when I landed the hover craft, and instinctively my hand shot for the Johnson. Too quick? I hoped I was quick enough. I had to find the Ching Da and get to the Council before things really got out of hand, and this evil could no longer be contained. We'd been in the air for days. Was there enough time?

The Royal factory was a huge complex. As far as the eye could see smokestack after smokestack broke the horizon. In the early morning light, I circled around the grounds, which were quiet compared to the constant hum coming from the machinery. Soon, I discovered a great long ditch behind the massive structure and lowered the craft between several large bushes. The hatch opened easily and I jumped to the ground, only to discover it was a wet marsh. This served me well as it was relatively easy to rip out reeds and weeds and hide the hover craft

As the morning got brighter, I surveyed the grounds. Several hundred feet ahead of me stood a sixteen foot high electro-magneto metal fence. It would be easy to rip through the fence with my

Mandrake claw, but the electricity would be a nuisance. I'd have to be insulated. The two hundred feet of open space presented the real problem. Crossing, I'd be an easy target, and also an easy target at the fence.

The world was collapsing. Too much time elapsed. Waiting until night fall was out of the question. What to do? The bright sun exposed the naked truth. The direct approach was out. I had to find the Ching Da. There was no more time. I slid down a cement discharge tube, sat hidden for a moment, and pondered what to do. I drank a hit of what was left of the water Pella packed for me. Where did the concrete discharge tube lead to?

I looked deep into the darkness of the concrete discharge tube. Just enough room if I crouched down. Once inside, the walls were cool though my feet slipped in the green slime, and the stench verily burned my nose. It was easy going at first. After about ten feet, I turned back and looked at the light from where I'd come. As long as I could see the light, there was an escape route. That didn't matter. There was no turning back. The fate of the world depended on me. I pulled myself together. It was only two or three hundred feet ahead to the factory. I bent down and moved ahead.

Sweat beaded on my face. Had I really conquered my fear of death? Just ahead of me, two eyes glowed red and floated in the darkness. They moved away from me as I moved toward them. Was it an illusion? The first lesson is to face your fears. I didn't have time to worry about Newt, wild animals, or transitory illusions projected from my subconscious mind. The misfortunes of the world hung over my head. I had to save my family. Yet, as I moved the eyes moved with me, and the tube started getting smaller. Just in case, my hand on my Johnson . . . I put one foot in front of the other.

But the tube got smaller, and I had to get on my knees. The opening behind me shrunk to the size of a dime. Ahead of me, aside from the two glowing red eyes floating in front of me, the darkness went on infinitely. The odor of tarnished metal, and rot, and death burned my nose. I heard the sloshing of my own boots, and with one hand on the wall I felt the roughness of the cool concrete.

Thonk!

My head hit an outcropping in the concrete, and I swat down. My legs were deep in the discharge, and both my feet and hands started to burn. I needed to get out of this stuff as soon as I could. Now, the light back at the opening of the tunnel was the size of a pin.

Thonk!

I hit my head again. I had to craw in the muck and inch ahead. The fetid air scorched my lungs, and up ahead of me the beady red eyes appeared to be moving toward me. I pulled my Johnson to fire. To steady myself, I put my hand over my head on the concrete and felt metal. It was some sort of latch, opening to the factory.

I pulled with all my might and it turned, but right then from behind me I heard a terrible sound. A door closed in the darkness, and the light from the tiny pin hole where I entered was extinguished. Frantically, I tried to rotate the latch the other way, but it wouldn't budge. I locked myself in a tomb full of poisonous discharge.

The air was thick and noxious, and my hands and feet were burning. The red eyes moved closer and closer.

"Go ahead. Dump it." A voice said from above.

"The water or the acid?"

"The commander said save the clean water."

"Then dump the acid?"

"Okay, acid. Which handle's which?"

"I don't know. Pull one of them. Go on, dump it!"

"It's stuck."

"Both do it. Ready?"

The handle I held turned back. The small pin of light behind me reappeared, but several yards ahead of me another portal opened. The tube flooded with liquid. Acid gushed over me like a waterfall. I held on for dear life. It knocked me this way and that and tore me apart. I couldn't breath. My skin burned. My hand began to cramp. I started to slip.

"I said acid, not the water. You dumped the water!"

"Sorry, but it's not here."

"Well I'm tired of looking. We looked everywhere for that vial. Better con to D-10 and let him know."

"Eh, why don't you do it?"

"Me? We better search more."

D-men, I thought, right above me. I composed myself and tightened my grip on the Johnson. I had the element of surprise, but climbing wet out of this muck would slow me down. I waited, and as they moved on there was the sound of boots going up a metal ladder and quiet as the boots faded away.

The portal opened to a room above, and soon I found myself in the bowels of the Royal factory. The fresh water saved my skin, literally, and now I found myself on a metal walkway. Industrial illuminators cast a pale glow, and the air had the tell tale scent of oil burned gears. Next to a metal ladder, vats of acid bubbled, and on the other side, a bluish water swirled. From the conversation of those D-men, it could be deduced that they hadn't yet found the receptacle, and that somewhere in this factory the Ching Da was still hidden.

What was it my big black friend had said in the hills of Billyland? "Under where in the under where?" It was a riddle to be sure. What did he mean? It was hidden in the warehouse, but under where? Right now, I certainly was under the warehouse. Or was I? Really, I only knew I was somewhere under the Royal factory. Perhaps the warehouse was an entirely different location. The room I was in looked as if it had been thoroughly searched. If the D-men already tore the whole place apart, where would I find the Ching Da? I moved ahead on the often proved assumption that the most obvious place is the best hiding place.

With the Johnson balanced in my fingers and the other hand moving up the metal, I silently climbed rung after rung of the cold ladder. A portal opened to a room with a white porcelain sink, a table filled with broken test tubes, and a half dismantled colloidal microscope. An energy panel sat partially opened and lights flashed and popped. Drawers and cupboards were opened and papers scattered on the floor. Nothing had been left undone.

The next room was an office, or it had been. What was once a mighty Rex now lay smashed on the floor? Its holography device was mangled. Light tubes were broken and had been flung in all directions. By the desk on a cork board a note was upside down. I turned it around. 'Real men got the bytes to prove it.' Another riddle. I wished I had my Rex transceiver in, he could figure that out. Also, he could triangulate my movements. I crept ahead with my Johnson poised.

I felt the D-man before I heard him.

The sound coming from behind the door was like the whisper a jet makes before it ignites. A D-man. With nothing on his mind but evil, his breath was slow and heavy. Perhaps he was dreaming tearing the wings off of a fly. . . I couldn't tell, but I do know a D-man is like a like a fly on a ripe piece of roast beef on a hot summer's day. You can kill him easy, but you have to be careful. Where there's one fly there's bound to be more. If you kill one, the others will swarm.

Through the crack in the door I could see this room was bigger than the last one. It was some sort of reception room or dispatch area. The D-man was leaning back in his chair. I could see the red and black uniform. Sitting on a chair with his back leaning against the wall near the door, he balanced precariously on two legs of the chair. I waited and listened. He was the only one in the room. Easy, sleeping prey. Yet, I knew even pushing the door open a bit to take a shot would wake him. He would sound an alarm or fire his weapon or somehow call the others. My old trick came to mind.

I took out a five dollar piece, heated it red hot, and dropped it through the crack in the door. The sound woke him up.

"Huh," he said and looked at the coin.

He replied to himself. "Dropping money are you?"

When his hand touched the hot five dollar coin, that was the last thing he remembered. The butt of my Johnson separated the life from his body, but just to make sure I struck him again and again until his face was a bloody pulp. You could never tell about D-men. When they looked dead, then they sprang back to life. They didn't have any brains to speak of, but they were trained to kill, and the training called for killing even at the very moment of their own death. This one, by the look of him, was done.

What?! Look at that! The butt of a Johnson stuck out of the D-man's waistband. No badge would ever give up his Johnson, unless he were dead. That made me mad. Only badges were allow to carry Johnsons. D-men, never. It couldn't be. The badges put up a fight, but the pressure from D-1 must have overcome them. My heart sunk. Was it all lost? . . . No! I now had two Johnsons.

I was sorry for the loss of a fellow badge, yet in a way now it suited me. With two Johnsons, the odds were about ten to one in my favor no matter how many D-men were out there.

Two Johnson's made twice the fire power, I thought, as a plan formulated in the emptiness. I mean . . . my mind. The D-man in front of me was about my size. I could fit easily in his uniform. I dragged him through the rooms and carried him down the metal ladder. I'd been hauling dirt for the last weeks, so he was almost light as a feather. But still, going down the different levels was tough, so when I reached the drainage port, I tossed him down. A heavy sack of garbage.

I removed his uniform and fit it on me. Ironic. A badge wearing the red and black of a D-man. Strange, but necessary. He wouldn't be missed. I threw his carcass through the portal in the discharge tube. The red eyed demon living there would have a nice lunch.

Back where I killed him, the pale glow from a ceiling illuminator cast shadows. The room appeared to have been a dispatch area with several rows of empty chairs and desks that had been pilfered; a pool of red blood under his chair by the door, and two doors were closed on the either side of the room. Dressed in the red and black uniform of a D- man, I bent quietly and put my ear to the first door.

"You know, I don't know what all the fuss is."

"What do you mean?"

Two D-men were having a conversation. There would be some clues here, I was sure of it. I steadied my Johnson in one hand and readied the second in the other hand. I could just hear their words like whispers.

"Well," the first voice said, "I kind of like these humans."

"Yeah," replied the other, "when I'm at home on my day off with the wife, we have a lot of fun feeding human brains to the little one."

That was enough for me. Now the D had wives and families. And feeding human brains to their babies! I kicked the door and went in blazing. The first one jumped straight up, he hit the ceiling and lunged back at me. The second was a rotating blur. D-men super strikers, they were several levels above the average, but still too slow. Before he jumped, the first one took a bullet in the chest from my left gun then and a second bullet in the forehead as he lunged off the ceiling. I dumped a clip into the other one. Oh, that was nasty.

I wiped a gob of blood off my face. A voice came from the next room.

"Hey you Strikers! Quit messing with those Johnson I just issued!" A huge D man burst through the door. "You're not . . ."

His brains erupted and splattered on the wall behind him.

"No, I'm not," I said and smiled as a small wisp of smoke left the barrel of my Johnson.

I stepped over his oozing head. "No, I'm not D. I'm Dick Phillips."

In the next room an overhead illuminator cast a bright light on a table. The multi- layered plans for the factory sat right in front of me. According to the plans, all I had to do was go back to the dispatch room, go through the other door, and take the catwalk. It was marked plain as day. The catwalk ended in the warehouse. Da Mo's receptacle was mine, I thought. It wasn't that simple. The red and black uniforms of death were everywhere.

As I stepped on the catwalk the noise of grinding gears and pounding pressure pumps filled my ears, and the thick blue smoke had a familiar fragrance. Royals! The catwalk itself had a single hand rail and metal grating that ran above men working below. It was stacked with boxes full of cartons of Royal cigarettes. Below me, D-men. We all wore the same black and red uniforms. A commander called up.

"Hey! You! Up there. Toss down a couple more cartons of smoke."

I tossed some over.

"Okay. Good work. Keep packing them up. We got to make the deadline."

I paused for an instant and broke out two cartons for myself. No use going without. I could barely see through the smoke. Below the catwalk, hundreds of red and black uniforms rushed about using magneto lifts to stack box on top of box. A phalanx of D-men ran through the factory. They stopped in front of the leader.

"Men," he said, "we've searched high and low in this damn factory and we ain't found nothing. Lucky for us we got smokes to keep us happy. Okay, everybody light up now. That's right, take five . . . five drags."

He puffed a slow drag and blew out the blue smoke. After the fourth one, he turned to the D-men. "Okay, hold this one in. That's it. That's it. Now, back to work boys. We got to find that receptacle."

He turned to his assistant. "Go upstairs and get the plans. We're going over this factory with a fine tooth . . ."

". . . comb!" his assistant replied.

"Right. Get the plans!"

Holy pooh, they were going to find the bodies of the D-men I just wasted. I started running along the cat walk to the warehouse. The sound of the metal clanked beneath me and the smoke seemed to grow thicker. I ran and ran and at last came to the warehouse where a burly guard greeted me.

"Here at last, huh? You're late. What's you been doing? Give me a smoke."

"Get to the meeting!" I commanded.

"What, you giving me orders now?"

"No sir," I said and pointed over his shoulder. "What's that over there?"

"What, where?" He said, and twisted his head and neck around.

My hands shot out and yanked his head around farther, and he went down. I jumped on his head with the Tibetan ankle twist. One jerk of my legs and his neck broke with a cracking sound. To make sure, I clubbed him with the butt of my Johnson.

The warehouse was a huge edifice to manufacturing and to Billy. A large poster showed him tipping his hat, getting ready to pitch. Another had him holding a carton of Royals, but the D-men had done a good job of desecrating the pictures. Most were torn, and the warehouse itself was ramshackle. Broken boxes were piled high and the floor was littered deep with cigarette butts. In the center of it all sat a statue sat of the baseball player. Its head had long been shot off. The body of the statue was covered with a sheet.

In an instant the D-men would discover their dead comrades. I had to find the Ching Da, and I had to find it immediately. All hell was getting ready to break loose. Even with two Johnsons and my fighting ability I couldn't defeat a phalanx. Over and over in my head came the words . . . "in the warehouse under where in the under where." But what did that mean? I was in the warehouse. Under where? Under where?

I ripped the sheet from the statue of Saint Billy, and it was wearing white cotton shorts. A realistic bulge had been sculpted for his proboscis. Gingerly I reached into his shorts. There, between his legs in the middle, my hand touched something large and soft and all tingly.

I jumped back. Could it be?

I reached in again and felt down in the shorts and grabbed hold of the tingling. It felt soft at first, and then it started to vibrate and seemed to grow large. Strangely, it felt warm and full of life, hard and yet soft at the same time. I pulled on it, and it vibrated. I pulled again, but it wouldn't come. Finally, I yanked it.

Yes. Yes! It came . . . off . . . in my hand.

Charachunga spilled all over my hand, but immediately it renewed itself and filled the receptacle. I had the China Da! And I lifted it to my mouth and took a long refreshing drink. Instantly, again the Charachunga replicated itself and the Ching Da refilled. The water of eternal life sparkled and bubbled. What the hell, I took another drink. I felt wonderful. The blossom of youth returned. My body was turgid, full, and energetic. Now, I knew why Da Mo had to have it back. For an instant, a thought crossed my mind. Why not take the Charachunga for myself? I could live forever.

Then again, I thought, what kind of life would I be living? I would be fighting and killing. There would be no love. I'd lust after women like an animal. I'd always be battling evil. Not too much different than my normal life, but then again I wanted to see Pella and my child. And what about my debutante, Cindy? What adventures waited for me? I felt alive. Alive! I wanted to live! I took another swig.

"Five minutes to detonation." A computer voice announced.

Five minutes to detonation! No one told me the statue was booby trapped. Wait a minute, Massilla's big black husband did. What did he say? "Boom! No more factory." I just set off the trap. The device was armed. My heart started pumping like a retro rocket gone wild. How do you conjugate the verb to run? Ran. Running. Ranting.

"Got to run. Got to run." I ranted.

Five minutes to run the quarter mile back along the catwalk, get down through the level of rooms, down the discharge tube, and out to the hover craft. Was it humanly possible? I took another swig of Charachunga. It wasn't possible for the old Dick, but this one was a new man. I ran for Pella and my family. I ran to rid the world of evil. I stepped over the dead D-man at the cat walk and ran for my life.

As I neared the end of the catwalk, I heard the computer.

"Four minutes to detonation."

One minute to run a quarter mile? That was pretty fast! I took another swig from the Ching Da. Now I felt more alive, but immediately the door flew open and the cat walk filled with D-men.

"What's happening?!" Commanded the leader.

"Sir," I replied, "intruder in the warehouse."

"To the warehouse men!" he shouted, and the group of D-men ran toward the warehouse.

The leader turned, stopped, and walked back toward me. "Why were you running?"

"To find you."

"What's the meaning of the computer announcement? What's being detonated?

I whipped out my Johnson. "This," I said as his chest and neck exploded, and a bullet pieced his brain.

"Three minutes to detonation!"

Through the dispatch room, into the plan room, wrong room! Back through the dispatch room, through the small computer room, through the room with the sink and broken vials, down the ladder to the room with the vats. Quickly, I made my way in the bowels of the factory. Along the metal walkway in the vat room, I opened the portal to the discharge tube.

"Two minutes to detonation!"

A hand reached up out of the muck and held my leg. Damn it! It was the very first D- man I had encountered. He was still alive. He grabbed my legs. I couldn't move. He climbed up my body and stared me in the eyes. His nostrils and face and mouth were a festering gap where the acid had eaten him. He slimed over me like a leech, and I couldn't shake him off. We rolled over and over in the muck. He wouldn't let go.

"One minute to detonation!"

Blam! Blam!

I emptied a Johnson on him and started crawling and running.

The opening grew larger as I ran.

I sprinted to the circle of light. In a few seconds I'd be safe. But did I have that much time?

Rama-a-rama! A gigantic explosion erupted behind me.

Instantly, a searing air blast knocked me face first into the wet discharge. I jumped up and ran.

An orange red fire roared toward me.

My back's getting hot.

Hotter!

Run.

Run!

An enormous glowing fireball spew from the tube as I dove to the side into the weeds of the drainage ditch. The ground shook and the factory exploded. The massive structure of the Royal factory wobbled for an instant and imploded into itself.

Outside in the safety of the ditch I checked my body. I'd found the Ching Da and drunk the magical Charachunga. I also had two Johnsons and a couple of cartons of Royals stuck in my pants for later. I pried the D-man's hand off my leg and walked over to the hover craft. That was a mistake. I should have run.

As I neared the brush where the hover craft was hidden, I saw them. On the horizon, high in the sky, with their gleaming hulls and flashing electro discharge rods, two gigantic D-men gun ships approached. Quickly, I threw the brush off my hover craft. I had one chance. Perhaps they hadn't yet seen me. If I could navigate along the ditch, below their line of radar, it might be possible to escape.

Inside, I revved the magneto to full max and the hot smell of shellac and flux filled the cabin. The capacitors smoked. The hull lurched and strained. I strapped myself in the seat, and put my hand on the accelerator.

"Computer," I said, "when I engage the magneto, take over tele-guidance. Remain one foot from the ground. Follow the crevice terrain."

"Unregulated procedure." the computer replied. "High probability error. Danger. Engine temp redline."

"I know," I replied, and crammed the accelerator to full throttle. Vibration at peak max, the hull slammed and tore at itself.

"Engage . . . now!"

The hover craft rocketed ahead. It was a deliberate risk, but being this close to ground could save us. The two gun ships might not be able to pick us up on holography. There was no way in telling where we were going, but we were going very fast. The carpet of green, rocks, and brush flew beneath me. As we accelerated along the crevice, the images in my holography blurred. I couldn't tell how far we would go or how soon we would get there.

We slammed forward at a terrific speed. Too fast. It was overloading! We were going much too fast. The G force held me down, and I couldn't lift my hand to push the accelerator back to slow.

"Computer," I drawled from the side of my mouth. "Slow us down."

"Accelerator control function destroyed. Override locked."

A thought entered. Was I headed to the end of the world? How soon at this speed would I loose consciousness? What if we hit something solid before we ran out of flux? Why didn't I stay back at Billyland? Where was Pella?

"Shut down!"

"Malfunction. Unable to comply."

"What! Hell! Stop!"

Like a disappearing green carpet, the ground blurred and flew away. Instead of slowing, the hover craft lurched and sped faster and faster. It seemed as soon as I became accustomed to the G force, the craft again accelerated. Again and again it slammed me back in the seat. My face distorted. Slobber flew out my mouth. My nose filled with the smell of burning coils. The craft began to burn.

"Heaven help me!" I cried. "Stop. . . "

Chapter 19.

Was I in Hell? The hover craft wouldn't slow. In fact, it keep
accelerating. The holography blurred. My eyes rolled back in my
head. I spit up all over myself, and my mouth wouldn't work. I
couldn't speak to command the Mandrake claw. At last, I forced
my hand on to the Johnson and twisted it toward the controls. Then
suddenly, the G force subsided and at the same time the fuel level
signal went off and droned over and over, empty, empty. My head
felt like a small humpback dwarf yanking the rope on a large
church bell on Sunday morning.

At last the hover craft slowed and the reserve flux lowered us to
the ground. But what ground? Where were we?

"Holography!" I instructed. "Give me a three hundred and sixty
degree image of the outside."

Oh my sweet mother! I couldn't believe it. We were right in the
middle of a city. Luckily, the craft's tele-guidance worked. The
street we sat on was deserted, and that concerned me. On the edge
of California City, on the plains, you could easily see where you
were. Now here, deep between the burning buildings, which way
was which? If I could reach the top of a building, the Space Link
would rise above it all. It shouldn't be too hard to find on the
skyline. Then again, in the smoke and haze, where was the sky?

I had to determine if the Space Link operated. Staying with the
hover craft was not an option. It was out of flux. I adjusted the
poncho over my D-man suit, fitted the Johnson, and checked the
spare. The cartons of Royals fit in the poncho. The Ching Da tied
around my neck, hung under the poncho. I made sure I had the
money from the Chinaman and Ro Nes, and I was ready to go. I
exited the safety of the hover craft into the haze of the early
morning light.

I stepped from the hover craft with my Johnsons ready, but the stillness of the street bothered me. The burned out buildings which rose above me seemed desolate and empty. Quiet rang in my ears. Then, in a widow, I thought I saw movement, and from deep with the blackness of an alley I heard a shriek. As shadows shortened in the dawn light, more sounds assaulted my ears with the noise of glass breaking, an animal tearing at meat, and down the street . . . a cry of piercing rage.

Which were the same sounds as always in a city, yet I never felt more alone. Where were the humans? I edged along a store front with broken windows, and as I rounded a corner, a yellow taxi's magneto smoked. It erupted in flames. A rotten body slumped in a doorway. I covered my nose. I didn't know what to expect, except the worst.

Above me, the high pitched whir of a giant D-Metatronic gun ship.

Moved to action, smashed down a doorway, darted up two flights of stairs, and rounding the landing, moved up another flight to the third floor. Bags of green smelling putrefied garbage blocked me. One by one I kicked them out of the way, and an apartment door couldn't withstand my barrage. I busted it in. The door opened to a short hallway and the hall opened to a small living room with a white carpet. The kitchen table sat on its side, and in the kitchen dirty pans and broken dishes were mixed with wine bottles. One wall was smeared with blood in a red swatch like modern art. From the window, I could see the gigantic D-men ship over my hover craft.

Silently, a green and blue aura formed around the Metatronic. Intensity built and wavy lines formed, and then suddenly, as the air crackled, a blue-green discharge erupted toward me. My craft evaporated without a sound and disappeared. I was alone, stranded, deep in the heart of California City. I had to get back to the Council, but I didn't know if the Link still functioned.

A lonely, empty feeling fell over me. The giant Metatronic moved over the buildings blasting whatever vestiges of civilization that it could find. Apparently, they believed they'd destroyed me, for they made no attempt to land. Perhaps they knew even if I escaped that my fate was sealed. Nobody walks in California City. I wished I was back in Billyland with Pella. At least we'd have each other and have some time together before the power of the Holy water ran out.

No use getting depressed, I thought, and sat down under the window with my back against the wall. Anyway, I had the Ching Da and if I ran out of Royals, I could always drink and be fulfilled. Thinking about it, I couldn't resist. While I fumbled with the bottle, a hurtful sound jerked my hair on end. Scratching, like fingernails being drawn over slate.

Across the room, a young naked female sat hunched over using her long white fingernails to scratch invisible words on a small blackboard.

"Please," she said and slowly formed her words out as if begging. "Pleeeese."

Before the disruption she was a tanned beach bunny. Now, she had become a wild animal. Her long blonde hair tangled about her head, and hunched over as she was sitting, I could see directly through her blonde pubs, directly into her dark hole. Her strong muscular body quivered, and her firm hard nipples stood up erect on large protuberant glands. When she spoke, the purple red lips of her blonde pussy extended and retreated. White fluid dripped from her.

"Wannafuck?" she asked, and began to pump her hips, showing me cunt lips that were hot and foaming.

A primordial urge overcame me, and my body shook involuntarily, but immediately I regained my composure. I held my big Johnson out in front of me, and stood up.

"No time, bitch! I've got to save the world."

I circled her. "I've got to get on the Link and take it back to the Council. It's prime!"

She jumped toward me and sat in front of the door and wouldn't let me by.

250

"Fuckmenow!"

"Sorry," I said. "No can do. Time's running out. I've got to save what's left of humanity."

"Fuckme!" She screamed and jumped.

It's always the story. It might be a long story, or a short story, but the result is always the same. If you listen, you die. Her story was very short. She wanted sex. I flinched, and that was a big, big mistake. Instantly, she knocked the Johnson out of my hand and lunged at me. She bit me and scratched me and ripped at my clothes. She was as strong as a cheetah and twice as fast. Her fingernails cut through my clothes and ripped them off. She shoved me down on my back and began to beat her crotch against my loins until I got a hard on.

No, no, I thought. This can't be happening to me. Stop you. Stop. But she wouldn't stop. She pinned my arms to the floor and forced open my legs. Her sex had a mind of its own, or at least some ability I'd never seen before. She opened my pants and pulled out my member while her hands pinned mine to the ground. With me in the prone position, she bit my neck and slobbered on my face.

"Oweee, oweee, oweee!" She cried.

After, when I got myself off of her, I sat on the couch and smoked a Royal. What a dang turn of events. My D-man outfit was ripped to shreds, but the Poncho and the money were okay. It's strange, but for the first time I felt I didn't have time for sex. I had to save the world! I checked the first and second Johnson. I needed to find some clothes. Hiking across the city in my underwear didn't appeal to me. I had to get moving, but there were, however, more pressing needs. The little bitch wouldn't stop.

"Fuckmore!" She said and crept toward me like a reptile.

This time I was ready. I flung myself on top of her and sat on her.

"Have a drink, miss." I said, and poured some fluid out of the magical vial.

Instantly she covered her pussy and held her arms over her breasts. In a squat she pushed herself back and cowered against the wall. She shivered and quaked and slobbered. Then she shouted, "Rape!"

"He raped me. Help!"

I shook my head and smiled no. I bent next to her. "What's your name?"

She took her time. "It's, it's . . ."

"It's Suzy, my name is Suzy Huntsmith."

I got a blanket and helped her cover herself. "Any relation to Silva Huntsmith?"

"She was my grandmother."

"Her device is famous," I said, "but tell me, how did you get here?"

"I have no idea. The last thing I remember, I was sun bathing on the roof and suddenly felt the desire to get it on with any man I could find. The next thing I knew I was swallowing some water, and you were wrapping me with this blanket. What's going on?"

"It's a long story," I replied and sat down next to her. "Evil is spreading over the world like a black knit shawl made out of wasps. We're destroying ourselves. You can't drink the water anymore. The air is putrid. In public your neighbor smiles, but secretly he wants to kill you, screw you, and screw your mate. The only thing that's important to the average guy is money or fame, and they hate themselves because they aren't talented enough to get it. And the rich and famous become so screwed up trying to be rich and famous, they aren't happy either. The old men rule and send young boys to kill for them. We start wars so we can bring peace. Eighty five percent of the world lives in poverty. A cancer eats the souls of our children."

She looked at me blankly. "Huh?"

"What?"

"I don't understand."

"It's like this. . ." I explained. "Dr Blood is a nefarious vampire of a man. He and his dastardly force, the D-men, have discovered a way to move through time. There's a powerful corporate executive kung fu fighter, Kang, who must be involved with dark forces.

Parkenson has a weak spine. He helped them sentence me. I'm working on a case for Da Mo and for Ro Nes. You see this vial around my neck. It's the Ching Da. The fluid inside is a mystical rejuvenation fluid. On a mission to save the world from evil, Billy, I mean Saint Billy, stole it from Da Mo. I have to get to the Link and get back to the Council and save the world from evil."

She looked at me blankly. "Okay. . ." she hesitated, "did you say the Link?"

I pulled her up. "Yeah. Which way's the Link?"

"That's coincidental," she said, "before they went automated, I used to serve Ion in reception."

"How far is it?"

"It's on the other side of the city."

"Which direction?"

"Take me with you?"

"Oh no. Not possible, it's too dangerous."

"You'll never find it without me."

I laughed. "Sure I will. Which way is it?"

"Without a jet, it's a couple of days from here, but you'll never find it, you can't even see it from here. Take me with you."

"Know how to use a Johnson?"

"Of course," she replied, "I'm Silvia Huntsmith's granddaughter."

"Ever kill a man?"

"Only a rapist."

"How?"

"With a Huntsmith."

I was beginning to like this young girl. We made our way out of the apartment, and as we walked down stairs she walked in front of me. Under the blanket, one cheek of her ass move up and met the other one down, in rhythm. Spending the next few days with her wasn't a bad prospect.

"Wait a minute," I said. "We're both going to need some clothes."

"This way," she interjected, and opened the door to a first floor apartment. "This is my mod. After I worked at the Link, I was a dancer. I've got an extensive wardrobe. I've even got some fine men's clothes. Come in."

She wasn't ready. The odor of death reeked. Humans died inside. A bloodied rotting arm and hand lay in the middle of her coffee table, and on the kitchen table, like desert, a spoon stuck out of a grey brain. Sputum came up in my mouth, and Suzy ran to her closet. It only took seconds for us to find the egress.

Standing in the hallway as she closed the door to her apartment, we dressed. She put her old life behind her. We were a couple now. All we had was a flint and a striker, and it was a small spark, but it was hope. I put my arm around her and we held each other, and then dressed in front of each other only knowing one thing. We were human. The suit pants fit okay, and as I pulled on the shirt I watched her dress her tight body in a red teddy and then a sleek jump suit.

"Here," I said. "Take this Johnson. Remember, it fires on intent."

On the street, we moved along in the shadows, twisting and turning and taking aim at every strange sound. Smoldering hunks of metal lined the streets. A large pile of concrete lay directly in front of us, and as we climbed around to the next avenue, we saw a giant of a man with a shaggy beard and long hair, wearing only torn shorts. He jumped right at us, but instantly, like some primordial monster, another huge brute of a man emerged from the shadows. They fought on and on, ripping and punching, gouging and goring each other. Neither gave an inch.

"Aren't you going to do anything?" Suzy asked.

I put my arm over her shoulder. "No, sweetheart. They don't care about us. Let them fight. . . Look out!"

I pushed Suzy back to the shadows.

"Look," I whispered, "Newt."

A large lizard, with blood and guts drooling from its fangs, carried the skin of a human. Oh my God! Behind the saurian follow two of its young carrying more human flesh. They eyed us, but moved on.

The sun beat down and the carnage of the street reached up and twisted us. Torn apart and blown apart, building after building revealed the desolation of the innocent. The world as Suzy had known it was gone. Still, from every window and every dark doorway, we could feel a living energy as if the evil that followed us had eyes. We knew humanity wasn't yet dead, but was breathing its last gasp. We trudged through tangled trash and machinery and smoldering piles of dying flesh. After hours and hours, night crept on us like a spreading sore, and darkness fell like a tight weaved black metal veil. From tall buildings shadows cast grey blue light. When the sun set our situation would grow worse. Real evil, things only dreamed about that haunt subconscious thoughts, would lurk the streets. The beasts of the other from the blackness beyond would soon drive a hideous tingling down our weak spineless souls unless we found shelter for the night. What evils lurked in the darkness of the burned out hollow walls was anyone's guess. We had to find shelter for the night.

We stopped for a moment, leaned against a large dismantled cooling unit and I lit up a couple of smokes and put one in Suzy's mouth. It tasted good.

"What are we going to do?" She asked.

"I don't know. It's getting dark pretty fast. We'll have to hide out."

"Look up there," she said and pointed.

Toward the end of the street, I saw a small illuminator casting a tiny light. Apparently, here was an outpost of civilization. We ran for the opening, but the massive wood door wouldn't budge. It was locked. I knocked, but no one answered. Yet, I sensed someone waited behind the door. We had to get in. Behind us, an animal growled, and I heard a snarl and what sounded like knives slashing together. I knocked again. Then I pounded.

"Come on. Open up. Let us in!"

A panel slid open. "Yeah."

Suzy stepped up. "Please let us in."

"You got Royals?"

"Sure," I said, took a final hit and blew the purple smoke through the opening.

"Cost a pack to get in."

"No problem."

The wood door opened quickly and a shut just as quickly behind us. Suzy followed me, and we entered to an amazing scene. The room was purple with smoke. Rock and roll music from many years ago played, and on a small stage a couple gyrated. Small Chinese lanterns with red and blue and yellow and green illumination hung over a long bar where people sat alone and in couples. Toward the back, groups of people played cards and were drinking. A fat bald bartender with a large brown mustache moved up and down the bar. Everyone turned and looked at us, and we looked at them.

Along the bar in the first seats, an old couple sat sharing a drink. The man had long white hair down his back and as the lady turned, the wrinkles, white pasty face, and ruby red lipstick made deep contrast with her dyed dark brown hair. She nodded, and as he smiled, the old man showed a large gap between his teeth. The couple next to them wore fluffy necklaces made of dyed red feathers. One wore a slinky yellow night gown and the other could have been her twin except her dress glowed orange. They both had society ladies' hats on their heads and beneath their hats, full curly brown hair, but I could see by the two day beards they were transvestites. They giggled and waved. Down the bar, a construction worker wearing a yellow hard hat took a drag on a cigarette and passed it to a small Asian girl wearing a black business suit. Her long shiny black hair hung down her back, and her eyes and lips were painted blue.

Next to them, a short balding character, and next to him a couple of empty spaces looked inviting. We started over to them, but from a table in the rear a cowboy stood up and approached. He pulled back his shirt, and I could see he carried a large, old style pistol. He touched his cowboy hat at the brim, and flicked a tooth pick from one side of his mouth to the other. His hand twitched by the pistol.

"I'm out. Give me some smokes!" He demanded.

"What?" I replied.

"You deaf? I'm out. Give me your smokes." His eyes were beady, and his hand jerked.

"Not deaf," I said loudly. "It's the confound music in here. Did you say you needed a smoke? Here." I tossed him a pack of Royals.

I imagined the only thing keeping these poor souls from killing themselves or each other was the Charachunga in the Royals. I still had a carton and a half in my poncho. Not that it mattered much; the real thing was in the Ching Da, hanging around my neck. We squeezed in the open space at the bar next to the short bald guy.

"Bartender," I raised my hand and called, "two drinks over here."

"What you having?"

"What have you got?"

"Ion, and or . . . Ion."

I looked at Suzy and nodded. "Ion it is."

"Four Royals a drink."

"All right," I said and flicked out a couple and then a couple more. I noticed the short guy next to me eyeing my pack. I wondered if he were going to call me out like the cowboy. As I looked at his bald head and tiny little mustache, and the way his upper lip moved with a twitch, he looked familiar like I knew him a long time ago.

"Hey," I asked, "don't I know you?"

"I don't know nothing," he said. "I don't know anybody but me, and I'm nobody. If there were still trees I wouldn't even be shit to them. I'm down to seeds and stems. One little roach left." He quivered and shook and sniveled up at me like a baby. "What can I do? I'm out, man. They're going to throw me in the street. I don't want to go. Don't make me go."

"Hey wait just a minute." I lit a bunt and handed it to him.

"Yeah, I do know you. Can it be? Can it possibly be? Jay! It is you? My God, Jay Fallow."

I turned to Suzy. "It's my old side kick, Jay Fallow, the best snitch I ever knew."

He took a long drag, closed his eyes, exhaled, and grabbed me with a shriek. "Dick, Dick Phillips! Is it really you? He hugged my shoulders and burrowed his face in my chest. "Dick, Dick. . ."

"Take it easy, Jay. Come on, let's get a table."

After the barkeep presented our drinks we headed to an empty table in the back next to the obnoxious cowboys who was playing cards. I sat down close to Suzy, and across from us Jay rubbed his hands over balding thin hair and stroked his tiny mustache. He had the same twinkle in his eyes from years ago. I wondered if he was still as much of a slime ball as he had been. I smiled at him.

"You remember the case of Dr. Marsall's brain?" he asked.

"Sure," I retorted and left a hanging "and . . . ?"

"Remember how all the instruments glowed?"

"Some of them exploded."

"How the brain was pitching and heaving right before it blew up?"

"Of course."

"Well," he began, "that's the way I feel right now. I'm shaking. My heart's beating about ten times faster than normal. I hear my heart beat in my head. That's not normal. I'm scared. Boy, this is a hell of world now. I'm scared I tell you. I'm scared!"

I looked around, but no one seemed to care.

"Hey, calm down," I said. "Take another hit."

He squint his beady little eyes and leaned and whispered. "This is the last outpost. Only nobodies like me left. Those big lizards, or the D-men, or people gone crazy, any of em can kill you. Why, if you run out of smokes in here, they don't let you stay. They toss you out in the street . . . take your chances, jerk off . . . Nobody likes me here. I'm a pariah. This bar's the last outpost of humanity. I won't make it 'till morning."

258

"Sure you will, Jay. Here." I handed him a pack of Royals under the table. "This ought to last for a while."

"Dick, oh wow, Dick, man, you are one of a kind. Where'd you get all these Royals? Man, do you know what a pack of Royals will get you in here?"

He paused for a second. "Man," he said again and slapped the pack until a smoke popped up.

"Fallow!" The cowboy called from the other table. "I saw that. You been holding out on me!"

Jay started to shake and sweat formed on his face. He opened his coat to show a little pistol, but wouldn't look up as the lanky cowboy sauntered toward us.

I stood up.

"No Dick," pleaded Jay, "it's not your fight."

Suzy touched my arm. "Remember, we have to find the Link."

She was right. There was only one thing on my mind, and was getting the Ching Da back to the Da Mo and clearing my name at the Council. A petty gun fight could wait.

"Look cowboy," I said, "What does Jay owe you. I'll take care of it."

He looked over at Jay sniveling with his head down. "It's a pack now, ain't it sport?"

Jay nodded and put his face in his hands. "Yeah."

"Okay," I said and tossed the cowboy another pack. "Now you're even. You can get back to playing with yourself over there, or whatever it is you're doing."

"What did you say?"

"I said quit bothering us and sit down."

Time stopped and jerked ahead. The old folks at the bar got off their stools and moved away from the cowboy's line of sight. The cowboy's hand jerked and twitched and he opened his coat to his old time pistol. I brushed the poncho to the side and showed my Johnson in my belt.

"Chicken shit!" He cried.

I looked at his cold steel grey eyes and stared deep into them. His trigger finger curled and straightened. I didn't speak. If he moved again he was dead.

"You're a chicken shit," he said again. "You're going to give me all your Royals now or die."

My hand moved like greased lightening. He went for his pistol. Bam! Bam! Bam! Bam!

My shot pierced his brain. Jay fired from under the table and ripped his midsection. Suzy dumped her Johnson from the side. The three of us wasted him. As his body fell backwards, I looked at my new partners. I took Suzy's and Jay's hand and held them high. We were a team.

"Nice shooting, guys," I said. "But you just wasted ammo. I'm a lot faster than him. That is, than he was."

"Dick!" Jay screamed. "There's a hole in your poncho and fluid's coming out of your chest."

Cowboy was faster than I thought, but I didn't feel any pain. Underneath the poncho, the Ching Da dripped Charachunga on my shirt. Sadly, I lifted it off my shirt to check the damage. It saved my life and deflected the bullet. I held it to the light. The fluid dripped slowly from the side of the receptacle, and then before our eyes the bullet hole sealed itself and the small container refilled itself. The Charachunga bubbled.

"Man! Man!" Shouted Jay. "You are one lucky man! Looks like Tex was a lot faster than you thought."

"Tex!" So we crossed paths again. How long had it been, almost twenty years? I should have killed him back then. That was a hard one, the 'Case of the Rocking Horse Woody.' It was a stiff case.

I put my hand on Suzy's leg. "Looks like I owe you."

She smiled at me. "You'll pay me back later," she said and put her hand on mine and lightly touched my foot with her foot.

After the dust cleared and the bartender threw what was left of Tex's body out to the darkness, I turned to Jay. "Is the Space Link running?"

"Don't know," he replied, ". . . could be. The D-men been using it to transport Royals back to the Council."

"You mean shipping them from the factory?"

"Sure, it's the only way they can keep their armies from deteriorating. They smoke them pretty fast."

"Well," I said directly, "they won't be smoking them too fast anymore. I blew up the factory."

Jay got a pinched drawn look on his face. He lifted his cigarette, took a drag, and blew out the purple smoke. "You mean this is the last of it."

I smiled and adjusted the Ching Da under my poncho. "Jay," I asked, "are there any safe places here to sleep?"

Jay explained rooms cost a pack a night, but they were locked and safe. Otherwise, you slept in the bar with the chance someone would run out of smoke and cut your throat. We three sat around the table and hatched a plan. No matter what, even if the Link wasn't running, with their help I would get back to the council. If this bar was all that was left of humanity, we didn't know. We were just three worn out travelers hiking the through the verities of life using our wits as a raincoat to keep out the acid rain of discontent that permeated our very souls. We smoked cigarettes and told old jokes to pass the time. Did I know why the Pope went to the moon? How many council members does it take to screw an illuminator? A horse walks in a bar and the bartender said?

I had a long face. The evening dragged. We all needed sleep. When the party's over, turn out the lights, but I figured the lights always stayed on for the people in this little bar. There was no exit. From the outside, screams and wails, and often, a thumping vibration struck the building. We pretended not to notice. The air was thick with smoke. Jay laid his head on the table and Suzy seemed to be fading in and out. I looked over at the bar where the bartender built a house of cards in front of the small Asian girl with long dark hair. There was an empty chair. I sat down and motioned to the bartender.

"You got a couple rooms?"

"You got two packs of Royals?"

I took them out of the poncho and tossed them on the bar and turned to the Asian and gave her a wink.

"Hi."

She had a young smooth face. Her purple lipstick and dark blue eye shadow either complemented her long dark hair or made her look like a clown. The evening was getting late. She looked at the two packs on the bar and a sardonic smile crept over her face.

"Can I do something for you?"

"What's a girl like you doing in a place like this?"

She laughed. "You a fool? The world fucked up."

"I know . . . acting foolish is all we have left."

"Yeah, you probably right."

"Want to dance?"

"Nothin else to do."

We moved onto the stage and did a rendition of the chicken shuffle. When we switched to the turkey trot, I started the slow down. She went in to the honky get back, and I did the sacroiliac. She did the splits and then we tangoed. Right about the time she stroked the funky monkey, I was doing the heart attack.

"Say . . ." I puffed. "Come over to the table and meet my friends."

"What are your names?" she asked.

"My name's Jay," Jay fumbled and could only garble. "You're beautiful"

"Thank you. And you?"

Suzy looked up at the Asian girl. "My name's Huntsmith. Just to let you now, right now. Dick's mine."

"Ah hum, okay girls, now." I said, and sat down, "What was your name?"

"Kai, Kai Tsing."

Suzy laughed. "And can you sing?"

"It's with a T, Tsing, and it means the most beautiful one at this table."

I tossed the room keys on the table, and we sat around tearing each other down until we got bored of that. We told a few more jokes, and Jay and Kai got into a philosophical discussion. They used words and phrases I didn't understand, like epistemology, the Janus effect, and phylogeny replicates ontogeny. When Jay mentioned Kant, a brilliant idea hit me. I pulled Kai to the side, with her Kant on my mind. Or let's say, I had sex on my mind for a while, and now I wanted it on my face.

"Just joking," I said, "we have to get some sleep. I got a proposition for you. I'll give you a pack of Royals if you shag the little guy tonight."

"Poof," she blew at me, but looked down. "Two pack you got deal."

Now, I was starting to feel the pinch. I still had a whole carton of smokes left, but the packs were going fast. I wasn't concerned about my state of mind, as I had the Ching Da around my neck. But I didn't know what was out there, and what I'd have to go through to get on the Link. If Royals were the going exchange, I'd need them. I hoped the little Asian girl was worth two packs. I still owed Jay from the 'Case of Nuptial Night of the Twins.'

The rooms were joined. In our room a multi colored patchwork comforter sat draped over a large bed and the pillows were turned down. On the top of an oak dresser a white ceramic wash basin rested empty with a full bottle of water next to it. A small red Persian rug led to the open door of Jay and Kai's room, which was similar to ours. Although the place smelled stuffy, the rooms were amazingly neat and well kept for only costing a pack of Royals. We were pretty sleepy.

Suzy bolted the door, and soon in the next room I could hear Jay and Kai ranting up an existential storm the likes of which would see them tearing off their clothes, slapping each on the behind, and running around the room like porcupines in heat. I was getting tired, and my mind was filling with the sort of emptiness that expands beyond time and space. This room was the last outpost of civilization. Who knew what we would find tomorrow in the morning. For tonight, Suzy and I were safe.

"You're a very beautiful woman?"

"You're not too bad yourself, big guy."

I went to the window. "It's stuffy in here."

Somewhere, next to us in one of the abandoned buildings, a sax began to blow a slow melody. Down the block, a high instrument like a piccolo came in. Everything and everybody was dead or dying, but music was alive. So, there was hope. There wasn't much time left. I could feel evil swarming in the city like Peruvian locusts do after stripping a coca plantation. Our souls were bared. We wanted sleep, yet we needed to hold the warmth of another.

"Suzy," I said and pulled her close, stroked her blonde hair and held the vial of fluid, "Let's drink a toast to tonight. We may not be here tomorrow. So here's to your big nose!"

I drank and it refilled itself.

She took a drink. "But my nose isn't big."

"I know. It's just a stupid toast. It's joke, like here's to you and here's to Sally, and here's to her pants down in the alley."

"What's that suppose to mean?"

"Nothing, sweetie." I'd forgotten she was Silvia Huntsmith's granddaughter. "I'm a stupid guy." I brushed the hair around her ear, pulled her face to mine and felt her warm lips and tasted her breath. We danced to the sounds of the city. The sax and the piccolo cut a sweet melody through the back beat of howls and the cracking of broken bones. For an instant I was lost in her arms in those sweet sounds, and we swayed back and forth. As I bent to kiss her neck, she turned to the window. Her behind bent into my stomach, and I wrapped my hands about her waist. A fresh cool breeze came in the window. We put our heads together.

"Dick," she asked, "are we going to die?"

"I hope not." I replied. "It looks bad. If I can't get back to the Council soon, there won't be much left of the world."

"I feel so good here in your arms. You're so strong. I feel wonderful. I love you."

"It's just the drink," I said. "In the grey morning light you'll feel different."

"That could be," she whispered, "but right now I want you."

We started swaying in that position with her back to me. I held my right arm around her waist and my left arm around her neck and shoulder. This was the end, my friend, my own dear friend, the end. We danced to the end of the world, and as we rocked she unbuttoned her clothes and pulled my right hand down in her pants between her legs on to her silk underwear. I felt the mound of hair and flesh between her legs, and it was steaming hot and dripping. It almost burned my finger as I caressed the silk underwear that covered her sex. Standing there, before the window looking out on a ruined existence, we danced and swayed. I held her tight.

"Oh," she sighed as the muscles in her back released, and I felt her vaginal lips open. We moved back and forth, and my hand slid under the silk to her wet opening. I gently opened the outside lips, and my finger ran inside and up to the hardening mound of her clitoris.

"Yes," she moaned. "Yes."

I flicked my finger in and out of her purple red meatness, and she made a guttural sound.

"Grrrr."

I stopped for an instant and pulled my finger and sniffed it. The honey filled my senses, and I felt like a sailor who's been locked up in the pen for twenty years and who comes over the rise and smells the ocean once again. My cock twitched and rock hardened. I pulled her behind and back to me and grabbed her breasts with both hands. They compressed firm and were so full that the nipples stood up like soldiers on salute. In the background, I noticed the sax played, and now a drum was pounding so that the very walls reverberated with the sound of a metal squeal. Really, it was Jay pounding Kai on the old metal bed in the next room. I felt good for him.

"Oh, don't stop," Suzy cried. "I want you to fuck me bad."

"Good."

"No. No. I want it bad!"

"That's good."

She bent over and reached down from between her legs and held my ankles and curled her butt up toward me so her sex stuck right into mine which was very big and hard.

"Ram it in me," she said, and twitched and quivered, and I felt like shoving it up from behind Great Dane style.

Like a dog, my Waddy Homer rubbed against her, trying to get in, but I still had my pants on and I wouldn't let him out. What would we find tomorrow as we trek toward the Link? Would we make it? This might be the last time we'd sleep in a bed. It might be the last time we got it on, well . . . forever.

It had to be a slow fuck, a long fuck, one that Suzy would remember for the rest of her life, even if that were only a few days. I had to show Silvia; I mean Suzy Huntsmith, that there was more to sex than bam bam thank you ma'am. Silvia . . . I mean, Suzy, had to know that I was a sensitive man . . . a person who cared about her and about her most sensitive being. She had to know that I wasn't just some brute who came inside of her to satisfied his animal male lust. This had to be a night Suzy Huntsmith could tell her grandmother, I mean grandchildren, about.

I turned the young blonde lady around and looked at her. Her breasts stuck through the silk teddy, and as I touched my fingers to her right nipple she shuttered and closed her eyes. Her other hand lifted mine to her other breast, and I softly milked both nipples. Her tanned face was so smooth, she could have been a statue except everywhere I touched her was on fire. As my finger touched her lips, steam rose. We were both on fire. I unhooked the strap of her teddy with my thumb, and it dropped silently to the floor.

Light from the burning buildings created shadows on the walls and an orange glow flickered from her tanned body and blonde hair. She unbuttoned my shirt and unfastened my pants. She reached in the opening of my underwear and took me in her hands. King Priapus stood gigantically erect. The blood vein throbbed purple. Suzy lowered herself to her knees.

"I love you Dick," she intoned quietly. "I want to satisfy you."

"No," I said and held her head and lifted her face to mine and kissed her. "I want this to be long and sweet."

Our mouths met and hers was hot as a burning caldron. We kissed gently and our tongues touched. I rubbed my face all over hers and put my eyelids to hers and flicked them.

"A butterfly kiss," I said and she giggled.

"I love you."

"I love you too," I said and picked her up. Her body was as light as a feather as I carried her to the bed.

"Just relax." I said as I set her down and climbed on top. "Just relax and be open and feel good."

She spread her legs, and my big John Thomas reamer entered, but I let it linger on her lips. I moved the tip in a little and then out a little in a light easy rhythm, always lingering for an instant on the outside lips. Like a flange pump, dipping in and withdrawing, each time it dipped a little deeper. After many moments, the bottom seemed to be reached, and I began the strokes. Eight long slow strokes from the tip to the bottom. I pulled it up and let it fall to the bottom from it's own massive weight. Eight strokes shallow, eight strokes.

Eight strokes slow, then hard down.

I drove it to the hilt!

"Oh God," she said.

Again I went shallow, just penetrating, just entering her, tantalizing her. I stroked her slow. Slow and easy, one to eight, they were light strokes to feel her warmth, to know her receptivity, to enjoy being in her. After the eighth stroke, down all the way!

"My God!" she cried and couldn't quite catch her breath. Saliva frothed at the corner of her mouth, and I kissed her hot caldron mouth.

Eight slow long drawn out thrusts, but this time they pared as if slicing crisply through a cantaloupe or a watermelon. With hydraulic action causing a great suction and a slow release, as the eighth stroke finished, then all the way to the bottom. Hard!

267

"Yeeow! Uh. Uh!" She panted and her tongue shot into my mouth.

"O-Eeee!" She moved her head from side to side. Her hands grasped my neck, and she pulled my hair. Her fingernails dug into me. Eight shallow, and she grabbed my ass and pulled me hard into her.

Another set, and another, and another. My prick felt like a three-D triangle. It flared like a rock pyramid truncheon, and burned like a magnesium flare.

Right then she began to profusely flow, and her body jerked and her vagina went into spasms. I kept pumping. Eight shallow, one deep. Eight shallow, one deep. Eight shallow, one deep. Eight shallow, one . . .

"Eeeeeeeeeee!" she wailed, and she jerked and jerked and her joints seemed to get loose and she writhed like a rag doll. She reared up and bit my neck and tore her fingernails into my shoulders. When she bit my neck again, my erection rocketed hard, hard, and harder!

Eight shallow, one deep, and she started to undulate like she didn't have no back bone. She pitched up and down and slithered in the bed like a snake. Her body burned hot as an inferno, and her hands reached out and ran up and down my skin frantically trying to touch me everywhere.

Shallow, shallow, shallow, five more times, then down, down, down.

Down deep to the hilt. Hard!

"Sweet Jesus my God!" she screamed and in a flowing movement, she released and opened and totally relaxed and bit me again and grabbed at my nipples.

I stroked her shallow, slow and deep, shallow and deep, until she felt like a vibrating, super-energized atomic field. At last, she collapsed and totally surrendered to me. With an open body, her vaginal lips and sex open to me, the feeling started in my legs like an exploding crystal that radiated purple electrical energy up my legs, my backbone, through my brains beyond my mind to outer space. On the final deep stroke, my head jerked.

"Yes!"

I growled a sound came from within me. "Gaaa!"

I drove home my giant dilated embolden turgid. My eyes rolled, and my body rocketed forward while the muscle between my legs jerked again and again. A tingling started in the soles of my feet and worked its way up the insides of my legs. Then it moved up my backbone and my body shuttered involuntarily.

Cum expanded, the head erupted, and wad after wad exploded in her.

"Wa Hoo!"

Chapter 20.

Before dawn, wearing only his boxer shorts, Jay bounded in the room screaming at the top of his lungs. The scar, the wound on his chest from Dr. Blood's razor heaved as Jay jumped around ranting about people dying downstairs, what a mess everything was, and how a group of them were secretly planning to ambush us before we left. Right then Kai entered and stood at the door in a yellow silk halter nightgown. Oota! The light from the window outlined her pussy hairs and silhouetted her tits. Me and Suzy were tangled up like a Chinese puzzle. Our arms were locked, and when I tried to pull my leg her foot moved.

"Damn it," Jay howled, "we've got to do something. I can hear them coming up the stairs."

"Okay, okay," I whispered when I got my voice back. "Get the sheets off your bed and tie them together." I rolled over and kissed Suzy. "Get your clothes on sweetie, and help me with these sheets."

"Do we have to go? Let's me sleep a few minutes. It's so nice here."

I slapped her ass. "Get your little butt moving girl.

"Oh . . . Okay. Can't we . . ." she paused, interrupted herself, and pulled on her jump suit. "God, what was that!"

The room shook as fists fiercely pounded the door.

"We want those Royals!"

"Yeah, we got to have smokes."

"Come out of there or we're coming in."

"Kill em!"

I grabbed the dresser and dragged it in front of the door.

"Jay," I said, "help me push the bed. Girls, tie off the sheets. Let's get going."

The sheets were an easy climb down to the street. We tried to run, but the sidewalk stuck to our feet. We ran through bones and blood and guts. Smoke and hazy filled our nostrils. Crashed and tangled machines sat on top of old couches and computer frames. Piles of books, clothes, bodies, and crap were scattered on broken concrete. A fire erupted from a building across the street. Yet, for the carnage, the filth, and death, the streets were deserted. At the corner, we turned back and looked at the singular little bar standing out among the burned out buildings.

The two old white hair people were at the window with the transvestites. The bartender leaned out with a rifle. A shot whizzed over our heads.

"We need smokes!"

I fired back. The glass broke and chunks of brick busted off the building, then Jay held his hand up.

"Hear that?"

The loud whir of a Metatronic D-man gun ship filled the morning air. Quickly, we dodged into the shadows. Above us, an ominous circle of dark metal filled the sky. An electronic sound crackled, and the air felt hot and dry. Green and blue waves radiated from the gigantic ship. I held my arm in front of Suzy and forced the rest of them back into the shadows as the charge built.

From the ship's hull a bolt of energy flashed, and the sky separated. The little bar that had been our haven, the last enclave of humanity as we knew it, evaporated. Smoke poured out of the hole where the building stood. As we cowered, the D-man ship moved on, and in the darkness we counted our lucky stars. We barely escaped with our lives.

The day felt hot, and the muggy air made me sweat. As we climbed around and worked our way through the rubble, I loosened my shirt. We were a strange looking crew. Me, I was a middle aged badge making money off killing mechanicos. Suzy was young and smart, but with her tan, blonde hair, and long nails, she had probably never done anything but serve Ion on the Link. Behind Suzy, Jay followed along, holding his little pistol and jerking from side to side. He was a sniveling little runt, but he was mean. You could see it in those beady eyes. He pushed Kai.

"You have to stay ahead of me. I'm keeping the rear."

"Don't tell me what to do. You not boss of me."

I stopped. "Settle down. Let's rest. We'll stop. Here, take a drink."

We passed the Ching Da around and regained our strength.

"Kai," I asked, "how'd life come to bring you here?"

Her face looked bright and sweet without the blue makeup. She stuck her hands akimbo on her hips. "Oh, me?" She said. "I was an order bride. You know. Come from China. Come to big city. Get married. Work for big restaurant chain. Come to California City for husband. Look for new locations for his restaurants. Then everybody go crazy."

She grimaced. "I'm scared. What we do now?"

"Don't worry, baby," Jay said. He moved next to her and put his hands on the back of her neck, but she knocked them off.

"I married lady, you respect me."

"What about last night?" Jay sniveled.

"Last night's last night. Who care! I need smoke. How we survive?"

"The Link's a long ways away." Suzy said. "We should go."

"Okay," I said, "one more hit of Charachunga."

Without the Ching Da, we all would have fallen unconscious from the oppressive heat and the stench that filled the stagnant air. Several times we came upon places where animals and humans fought, and in many of these places the smoldering fires told us D-men clean up crews had recently incinerated remains. We saw our little crew as the last of the human race, four isolated travelers on a quest to save something we weren't even sure existed. How many enclaves of survivors remained, or even if there were any survivors . . . we didn't know. We knew we were alive, and with a constant eye out for the huge Metatronic, we hiked on.

And on. The insane construction workers had been in this part of town. Building after building, smashed. Partially rebuilt with doors and windows in the wrong places, they stood as temples to the gods of remodeling. Girders newly constructed pointed to the sky, but the construction ended as soon as it started. Halfway finished, or halfway begun, it was impossible to tell. The going was difficult. It appeared as if we were in never-never land. We walked down streets, but it felt like climbing hills. The concrete sloped down, but the elevation rose. Often we trudged on one street with broken and burning storefronts and the buildings turned to a dead end with no exit, and so we retraced. Back and forth through dead ends and over piles of rubble, we turned down this street and that street torn up like a war zone.

As we climbed though the rubble, I turned to Suzy. "How much farther through this maze?

"Not much more. A few more streets and we come to the park and the zoo."

Zoo, I thought. That was fitting.

"Then how far?"

"We'll be in the open at the park. We should be able to see the spire from the park over the great wall . . . half a day's hike after that."

The sky darkened with smoke. We were exhausted. The day got later. Evil oozed from each open door, from shadows and from our thoughts. That made the zoo a reasonable place to spend the night. No matter what, we didn't want to be outside at night. My mind was blank, as usual, but then a strange thought appeared. What if Dr. Blood were using the time continua to transport D-men back and forth through time? He and Kang might be disseminating this time so they could repopulate it with Blood's so called superior Gorgon race that he manufactured. I hated those damn creatures. . . with that strange third eyeball and those blood sucking tentacles, they were ugly. The way the greenish blood dripped from their gums, and how they constantly shrieked. Sickening. I should have given Dr. Blood's brain an acid enema, and I would have if that gorgon hadn't got in my way.

We walked and walked and the day dragged. What was it Da Mo said, "Throw the Ching Da on me as hard you can. The Evil One will try to stop you"? Who was the Evil One? Was it Kang? Was it Da Mo? Could it possible be Saint Billy, or Parkenson? I wondered what happened to Cynthia, my debutante. Was Pella okay? I chugged another drink of Charachunga.

At last, the small park opened in front of us. Dark verdant green grass surrounded a tall oak tree which shaded a small concrete bench. On the other side of the park a twenty foot high wall topped with metal spikes ran as far as the eye could see in both directions. About two hundred yards of open space lay between us and the shade of the tree.

The dark hazy sky was empty. "No ships," I said and started out. "Come on, let's run to the tree."

As the four of us crunched together on the bench under the tree, Jay blurted out. "What's the plan, Dick?"

I turned to Suzy. "Where's the zoo?"

"Over that wall."

"Where's the Link's spire?"

"It should be right there," she said and pointed beyond the zoo. "It's too smoky now to make it out. These walls go for miles in both directions."

"We're going to climb over the wall, "I said, "and spend the night in cages. We'll be safe."

"We don't have rope." Kai exclaimed. "How we get over wall?"

Jay sniffled in again. "We're going die. We can't stay here."

"Everybody quiet," I explained. "I've got a plan. Take off your clothes."

"I can't have sex now, not out here Dick!"

I put my hand on Suzy leg. "Sweetheart," but Kai jumped up.

"No, no! No sex. I heard little missy girl last night. She scream and scream. You not do that to me. You crazy!"

Jay's eyes widened. For a moment looking at all of them, a vivid thought about sex and the four of us did cross my mind, but as usual I didn't know what I was thinking. I calmed them down.

"Just to our underwear. Then we tie all the clothes together and climb up, the same way we climbed out of the bar window. It's simple."

"Will that work?" Suzy asked.

"We can knot the clothes, and then tie them to the spikes on the top of the wall. When it's secure we can climb up the knotted clothes."

Jay butted in. "Right. Just one thing. How do we get to the top? If we had a ladder, we could just climb over. But we ain't got no ladder."

As usual, the best laid plans of mice and D-men don't work out. But I wasn't a mouse; I was Dick Phillips, private eye. I lit up a Royal and paced around the oak tree. The four of us had to get over that wall. Even with the Mandrake claw, we'd be here chopping all night to cut down the oak tree to make a ladder. Wouldn't work anyway. We couldn't stay long out in the open. Even if we could hide from the Metatronics, we'd perish in the night. That was for sure. I noticed the plaque.

"Hey guys, look at this."

A small plaque at the bottom of the tree read, 'Last Living Oak Tree.'

"How about that," Jay remarked. "The last living oak tree. Wonder what happened to the rest of them."

"Cut down," Kai said, "die of neglect."

We all waxed philosophical.

"It's a shame," I said.

"No more trees, no more people. I guess the odds were stacked against humanity."

"Yeah, the last years stacked one environmental disaster on top of another; the world didn't have a chance."

"No more wilderness. No more trees. The air filled with haze. The water sick. Like a house of card placed one on top of another, no one realized the fabric of human life was woven from the earth . . . until it collapsed."

"Don't be so negative," I said. "We'll find a way over that wall, and tonight we'll be locked in safe, behind bars with nothing bothering us. Have another drink."

Then it hit me. "Jay," I said, "if I leaned against the wall, could you climb up and stand on my shoulders?"

"Don't know," he paused, "probably."

"Suzy, could you climb up my back and up Jay and stand on his shoulders?"

"I think so."

I looked at Kai.

She looked at us. "Me? The top?"

I nodded.

Well, we were a strange striped-down crew. Suzy and Kai were certainly different types. Strong and muscular, with large breasts and small hips, wearing her red teddy, Suzy stood inches over Kai, whose slender body was accented by her turned up breasts with nipples that stuck up in her yellow silk nightgown. I could have done them both right there in the park, and I don't think Jay would have sniveled. If I remembered right, he always liked to watch and spank his miniature. Old Emperor Maximums jumped out of the hole in my shorts, and I had to turn around and excuse myself.

I slapped him on the head a few times. "Down boy."

At last, he obeyed, and we got to work. First, we tied all the clothes together. We knotted one of my pant legs and made a loop to catch a spike at the top the wall. We bundled the guns and Ching Da in the poncho and tied it to the clothes. Next, the three of them pulled from one side, and I pulled from the other. The knots cinched and our clothes rope looked like it would hold. We had to get moving, it would be dark soon, and we had to get over that wall. There was no telling what the zoo would be like after dark, but we knew there would be safety there. Like a dark knight invisibly hidden in the brightness at the center of the sinking afternoon sun, a vapid killer that is only freed at sunset, evil poised to release itself with every second that passed.

"But what about the D-men gun ships!" Jay ejaculated.

"Forget about them," I said and picked up the clothes rope and started running to the wall. "We'll be over that wall in a second."

The four of us carrying our clothes and running across the park in our underwear must have looked ridiculous, but who cared anyway. The grass felt cool on our bare feet and we ran in syncopation with only Jay dragging his sorry ass behind, already out of breath before we got halfway across. Suzy's breasts bounced as she ran, and Kai's long black hair blew behind her. We got to the wall, and as Jay caught up I planted my feet in horse stance next to the wall.

"Okay, Jay. Up you go."

Jay put his foot on my leg and slipped off giving me a nice skin burn. I squat down almost to the ground and reached my left hand over and behind my head.

"Now, Jay," I said, "take my left hand in your left hand and step on my right thigh with your right foot. Next, step with your left foot on to my left shoulder and lift yourself up and stand up on my shoulders. I'll balance you."

"The hair, watch the hair!" I yelled.

It was a trick I learned in the circus as a teenager. I was about eight foot tall standing on my buddy's shoulders. The old ladies brown wig and falsies made us the tallest female impersonator on the planet. That occurred before the disruption. Now, we needed to get over the wall.

Suzy was amazing. She scrambled up me and over Jay as if we were a rock wall she'd climbed many times. But the load weighed heavy on my legs, and they hurt. My legs started to cramp. My back felt like it would break. Could I hold them all? Every time one of them shifted weight, my groin muscles sang the blues.

"Jay!" I shouted. "Eyes down. That's my pie on your shoulders."

"Kai," I commanded, "get the clothes. Help me pass it to Jay."

"Jay," I shouted, "here comes the clothes rope. Take the weight off. Pass it on to Suzy. Kai, up!"

Kai climbed slower, but she finally stood on Suzy's shoulders, and as we took the weight off the rope clothes she hooked it over

277

the metal and climbed over the top. It held as she climbed, and even her small weight off me was a relief. As Suzy ascended my legs felt a lot better, and as Jay began to ascend I took a second to thank myself for all the Chi Kung exercises I'd done. My legs were strong, and though I'd never been much of a rope climber, when the three of them were safely on the top of the wall, I started up.

I'm not the best clothes climber, but they didn't have to laugh at me. Then they stopped. Their expressions changed. Kai's chin dropped. Suzy's face froze, and Jay shivered, pointed, and tried to speak. Then I heard it. The distant whir of a Metatronic.

"Hurry up!" Suzy shouted. "It's the gun ship."

I jerked about. The craft was already at the edge of the park and accelerating while the hull vibrated and wavy lines formed in the air around it. I pulled myself to the top of the wall. The ship covered the sky above us. I heard the crackling of a discharge. I grabbed the clothes rope.

"Jump!"

Lights flashed. A terrific arc of lightening broke the sky, and the wall blew up. Just below us, stacks of hay broke our fall and we rolled over and over. Rocks and mortar rained on us. We scrambled along a path into dark bushes.

"Is everyone okay?"

Jay mumbled and puked green fluid. "I'm sick. My back!"

"Are we all safe?"

"Come on, follow me!" I commanded, and began to crawl on my hands and knees through an opening in jungle foliage.

The instinct to move quickly when all seems lost in the only thing that saved us.

After about ten seconds of running we came to a brick wall. We crouched down in darkness while the shadow of the giant ship blocked the last rays of sun light. A charge built on the hull and the air crackled.

"Come on!" I cried, and dove into the darkness.

We scurried like rodents and slithered like snakes and clawed and tore through the bush down an embankment and then intensely bright light lit the bushes and the blast rocked the brick wall where we were seconds before. It burned and evaporated. We hit the dirt, and the blast flew over our heads. We inched along deeper into the darkness.

I put my finger to my lips. The huge craft hovered momentarily. Spotlights crisscrossed in front and behind us and rose and whirred off.

"Are we safe now?" Jay sniveled.

I looked at the funny balding little man quivering in the dark in his underwear. It was a good question. We were in the middle of a zoo in a man made jungle with an eerie ink black darkness surrounding us. Suzy wore her red teddy. Kai had torn her yellow night gown and sat next to Jay in his underwear. I sat down on a rock and thought.

"Where's the poncho? Where's the Ching Da? Anyone have the clothes rope?"

They shook their heads. This was bad. We lost the Johnsons, the money, our clothes and the magical rejuvenation fluid. And, instinctively, I knew we needed shelter. Searching for our stuff in the darkness was futile. It all may have been evaporated. Even with my thinking cap turned on full, the future looked dim.

I thought for a moment. We'd lost everything. Darkness moved on us like a rapid bat stalking a vapid cat. The Ching Da had only been out of my procession for minutes an my mind was returning to my normal brain death state. I had to concentrate. We needed those Johnsons, and I felt ridiculous without my clothes. I had to steel myself. More likely than not our journey was finished. Our guns, our clothes, the Ching Da, and the hopes for humanity had been blown away. The D-men and Dr. Blood had won.

No! I wouldn't give up.

"We have to find shelter. A room or some cages or even a cave."

"Look, over there!" Suzy shouted and pointed.

Beyond the rock path where we squat, a row of steel cages sat on the edge of the foliage. As we made our way over the rocks we could see the empty cages had small sleeping platforms and rings and bars inside. Apparently these were monkey cages. I imagined when the blanket of evil descended, their keepers set them free. Or somehow, they had all escaped. Down the row of cages all the doors were open and all the cages were empty.

Perhaps it was the excitement or perhaps the massive doses of Charachunga we'd consumed, but I noticed Kai standing very close to Jay, and touching him, and I wondered if he always carried a broom stick in his underwear. Perhaps the scent of animal was in the air. I didn't feel anything. Suzy and I were exhausted.

"We'll take this first one." I said. "You and Kai take the far one down the row. Listen; load some rocks in front of the cage door."

They seemed too interested in each other. Sometimes a battle will do that to you. It's stimulating to know you're still alive, that you cheated death. You want nothing more than to get down and raw with someone.

"Look," I shouted, "pay attention! See those rocks. Pile them against the cage door. Do it. We don't know what's out there. Tomorrow we'll search for the poncho and our clothes. Jay, make sure your cage is secure."

Too much Charachunga and too much excitement. Kai fondled Jay as they made their way to the last cage at the end of the row. The darkness enveloped them.

"How you doing sweetheart?" I whispered to Suzy.

"I'm okay," she replied, "but I don't know where they get their energy. After last night and all that hiking and now this, I just want to get some sleep."

"Me too," I said, "but I've got to secure this door. We don't know what's in that darkness."

"Should we check on Jay and Kai?"

"No. The should be okay."

I started carrying boulders from the path and loading them into the cage.

"A couple more large ones and an elephant wouldn't be able to get in here," I grunted. "I'm about done. Done in that is. Lucky it's a warm night."

We sat down in the middle of the cage. I put my arms around my beautiful young friend, and we rolled on our sides on the bare floor.

"You know, Dick." She said. "We might be the last humans in the world. I mean, besides Jay and Kai. We might be the only people left on Earth."

I laughed. "It's funny, isn't it?"

"What?"

"We're in a cage like animals. We're probably the last sane humans on the planet and we're caged like animals. It's funny. Here society sets itself up and it seems like it knows all the answers. I mean, we call ourselves civilized, right. Now look at us. Everyone's bent on destruction. We can't stand our animal natures and we try to deny who we really are."

"Ha, ha!" I laughed out loud. I was getting sleepy. "It's funny. Don't you think it's funny?"

She pressed her lips on mine. "Don't' talk anymore. I love you. I want you to hold me."

A scream from the other cage broke our reverie. "Owe! Oh my God!"

It was Jay and Suzy getting in on in the end cage. The metal vibrated and rocked.

"Oh, oh, oh!" Jay screamed.

The sweet darkness of sleep and the sounds of love filled my head. I pressed my face to Suzy's face. I gathered her in my arms. "I love you too," I said.

"Yeee! Yeee!" More sounds from their cage. I drifted into sleep.

But I was rudely awakened by a strange animal sound. I lifted my head to look and listen but the darkness was thicker than blood.

"Aiee! No! No! Aiee. Aiee!" A woman screamed from the end cage. I guessed Jay was really doing Kai. I closed my eyes again.

"I would make love to you if I weren't so tired." I said. "I would . . ." I pressed my face on Suzy's.

"Would you?"

"Yes, would . . ."

"Would you?"
"Would," I replied and fell in obvious sleep.
"Would."

Chapter 21.

Would.

"Woody!" Suzy exclaimed. "It's as big as a tree."

Every morning it stands straight up. But now, in the early morning light streaming in through the bars of the cage, reality hammered me like a fifty pound sledge. No time for fun and games and sex. We had to find our clothes, the poncho, and the Ching Da. Any minute now, without the Charachunga to ward it off, evil would overcome us, and our little party would be over. I wondered if Jay and Kai were awake.

Suzy rubbed the sleep from her eyes. "Where are we?"

"The zoo. It's dawn."

Yellow morning light froze the air in a dirty haze. I yelled to Jay. "Come on you two, wake up!" As I moved the boulders from the cage door, I cried. "We've got to get moving!"

I pushed the last rock from the door and turned back to Suzy in her red teddy. I stood there looking ridiculous without my shirt, standing in my shorts, my big woody still sticking through the opening. I flexed my muscles. "Not too bad for an old guy."

"You're cute." Suzy replied.

"Do you think so?"

"Yeah, and besides you're probably the only human man left alive except Jay."

She stood next to me, and even though we were filthy from the night before I could smell the faint fragrance of her jasmine perfume, a kind of monkey jasmine. She smiled with a coquettish devilish grin.

"Why don't we find the Charachunga," she said, "and split from the others. We can start a new civilization, just like Adam and Eve."

Just like the apple, I thought, evil penetrated her. We were lost without the Ching Da. Also the Royals. I could use a smoke, but Suzy did look inviting. I could see the mound of her pussy through the Teddy, and her nipples were hard. I wanted her, and Dr. Slanger flicked around in my shorts, but I shook it off.

"Jay, Kai. Come on! Let's get going."

As I neared the door to their cage, I heard a moan.

"Oh!"

"Come on you two, cut it out. We've got to get going before the D-men show up. Another ship will be going over soon."

"Ah, my head," a voice whimpered.

The cage was empty, the door wide open. On the other side of the cell, Jay lay crumpled against the bars. His back and legs were torn, a bright red streak of blood on his face. I helped him up.

"Jay, what happened? Where's Kai?"

"Monkeys," he mumbled and held his hand to the bloody gash on his face. "Monkeys broke in the door. I was screwing Kai, and they pulled me off her. I tried to fight them, but they attacked me and threw me against the bars. A giant monkey grabbed Kai's and ran off with her. She's gone. She must be dead."

He started to stand, but his feet gave out and he feel to his knees. "What are we going to do?"

Suzy entered. "What's going on?"

"Kai's been abducted by the monkey king."

I looked at the sniveling Jay bird whimpering on his knees. "Snap out of it! We have to find the clothes and the Johnson's. I can feel the evil around us like the black stockings gauze of a dime store whore."

I bent over and looked him in the eyes. "Get your ass up now! We have to find the Charachunga. We need our clothes. And our guns."

Jay sniveled. "Why? I don't want to go on." He beat his head and cried. "I don't know what to do. I don't know what to do. Kai's dead. Kai's dead."

I picked him up by the scruff of his neck. "Get out!"

Up the slope and through the bushes we retraced our flight from the night before. The little wall where we hid had evaporated. The ground was scorched all around. Then under some rocks I saw the edge of a piece of material.

"That's my jump suit!" Suzy cried.

"There's the poncho."

Inside the poncho its precious cargo was still intact. The Johnsons were in working order and the Ching Da still bubbled with the Charachunga. We passed around the vial and regained our composure. After dressing in what was left of our clothes, we were a motley crew . . . that was for sure. But our spirits were better. I sat on a rock and drew a plan with a stick in the dirt while Jay and Suzy sat next to me and studied my design.

"We're here," I said and made an X on the ground. I drew a square next to the X. "This represents the cages. This line is the wall."

"So what's the plan?" Jay interjected.

"Well," I said, "I guess we load up the Johnsons with as much fire power as we have and follow the trail of the monkeys. When we find them, we blast them."

"Do you think Kai is still alive?"

"I imagine so, Suzy," I said. "The monkey king will be saving her as his prize. There was no moon last night so she's probably okay. He's probably saving her for the anthropoid primate cluster ritual. They get a little hot under the collar, if you know what I mean."

"So what's the plan?"

"Well," I said, "We're here at this X. We follow the trail left by the monkeys and we blast them and get Kai back and then head for the spire. By the way, Suzy, where's the spire for the Link? You said you could see it."

She looked to the sky. "You know, that's strange. You used to be able to see it from here. The haze is still too thick."

"Say Dick," Jay spouted, "isn't there something wrong with your plan?"

"What? What is it, Jay!"

"Well, you know, monkeys travel by swinging from vine to vine and tree to tree. How we going to follow their trail?"

"You got a good point, Jay." I replied. I rested my elbow on my knee and put my hand on my chin and looked at the cry baby next to me with the bald head and darting eyes. "You know Jay, you're right. We need to bring them to us. We're going to have to have something like a sacrificial lamb tied to a stake that cries like a baby, and when the monkeys come to investigate we waste them. Me and Suzy are pretty good shots."

"Sacrificial lamb?"

I pulled out my Johnson and pointed it at Jay. "You're in, aren't you?"

"Now, now, wait a minute Phillips. This is evil. It's evil talking. You can't do this to me."

Suzy patted his head. "It's okay. You'll be fine. We won't let you down. We love you Jay. We won't let the monkeys rip out your brains. Ha, ha."

I guessed evil was starting to get hold of us. Jay was pretty slimy, but there was another way.

"Jay," I said. "We're just joking. We wouldn't do that to you. I've got another plan." I broke out a pack of Royals from the poncho and lit a smoke and passed it around. I had what was left of the D-man suit stashed in the poncho. Here's the plan. When the next Metatronic D-man ship hovers over, which will probably be soon, I'll be dressed in the red and black suit, just like a regular D-man. I'll hold the carton of smokes out like I made a big discovery or something. I'll point to the cages like there's a stash hidden. They want these smokes; I know it, because I blew up the factory. They'll land. You two will be hiding in the bushes and when the landing party comes out, you blast them. We steal the craft, fly over the zoo, find the monkeys, and blow them to kingdom come. Understand?"

Jay breathed a sigh. "But what about Kai? How we going to get her back?"

"We may have to land after we blast them."

"See Jay," Suzy said softly and again patted his head, "we weren't going to hurt you."

Jay pushed Suzy's hand and interjected. "But that won't work. You're a famous badge. Everyone knows you. The D-men hate your guts. If they recognize you, they'll fry all of us."

"No, no. They want these Royals. I can feel it. I know they're craving them."

"But what if they just blow you away and leave the carton of Royals intact."

I thought for a moment. I couldn't concentrate more than that. "You're right. So what do we do?"

Suzy spoke up. "I'll do it. I'll put my hair up. The suit will fit okay. I'm not afraid. One of us might have to board the ship to take out the captain. That's a good job for you Dick."

"With your boobs they'll know you're not a D man. They'll smell a babe like you from miles away. These D-men haven't had sex in a long time. They'll smell you, and they'll know it's a trick. They're hornier than goats. You can't fool them. Remember, these guys don't have Royals. Their nerves are shot."

"You're right. What are we going to do?"

Suzy and I stared at Jay.

He backed away. "Hey, what are you looking at me for? I'm not going to get into that suit.

"Grab him!"

We wrestled.

"All right. All right." He cried, "I'll do it."

"Here," I said, "have another drink of Charachunga."

"I don't want that stuff anymore. It makes me too nice. I got to be mean."

"No? Suit yourself"

"I ain't afraid like you think I am. And I don't need that stuff. I want my girl back."

He pushed my hand.

"Suit yourself. Probably better anyway. You'll be feeling a little evil when they land. When we blast them, you join in with your little pistol. And just in case, don't let them take you alive. And if they come out shooting . . ."

"Shooting?" Jay whispered.

"Or if they energize the field."

"The field?"

"Yeah. Either way, get out of there as fast as possible. Run like hell. Drop the carton of Royals and run. They won't blast the Royals, I know that."

"Suzy," I said, "you take that side. I'll get in the bales over here. When they land, and when they get out, dump the whole clip into them."

"Jay." I directed. "Get in the suit. That ship's going to be here any second."

Very soon we were ready. Standing in the middle of the clearing near the blasted area where we had come over the night before, Jay quivered in his boots. In the burned bushes on one side, Suzy poised hidden from sight. I took a place deep in darkness between two hay bales. Jay couldn't stop shaking.

I lit a smoke and walked out into the opening. "Jay," I said, "have a hit."

"One last smoke for the executed man?"

"You're going to be fine. It's Kai's life, man. Think about that tang, that wet moist tang."

He sucked the Royal and held in the purple smoke.

"Yeah . . ." he said, and steadied himself. "I'm ready." He paused and looked up. "Hear that?"

A magnetic hum filled our ears. "Suzy," I cried, "ready?"

"Ready."

"Jay, all you have to do is point to the carton and point back toward the cages. You'll be safe. They'll land. We'll blast the landing party. I'll go aboard and waste the rest. We'll be in the air, save Kai, and you'll have some pussy tonight."

Back in the darkness, back in my little hole between the bales, I took the last puff on the bunt, snuffed it out in the dirt, and composed my thoughts. I wanted a symphony but I couldn't even get a melody. Then I heard the high wine of the magneto. The shadow of the ship engulfed us. My God! It wasn't a Metatronic gun ship. The hull filled the sky and blocked the sun. The gigantic craft hovered over us like the dark eye of Baphomet. It wasn't a Metatronic, it was an intercontinental Magnacruiser.

Time froze and seconds ticked like hours. The Magnacruiser hovered over us and I couldn't see Suzy or Jay, but any second I knew Jay's bald head would be running sweat, and he would be on his knees begging his savior for deliverance. Right then a spot light focused on him standing there alone in the tattered red and black uniform, and I was truly surprised. He followed instructions. In the bright circle of light he held the carton of Royals in the air, pointed at the carton and pointed back toward the cages. After a minute the light went out, the magneto droned slower and the craft descended and spread its landing gear.

As the ship's hatch opened and the ramp descended, six D-men swarmed toward Jay. They spread out and raced toward him, but good old Jay just waved them on. He tossed a couple of packs and walked toward the cages. Then he stopped, pulled out his little pistol and clicked off shots. Suzy fired.

The leader's brains blew up. The second took a hit in the chest. They turned toward Suzy, and I let them have it. Jay popped two of them. Suzy dumped her Johnson into them and blood and brains and guts exploded into the air. The air sizzled with gun shots. As the last of the D-men fell under our barrage, I emerged and ran up the ramp into the great ship.

I pulled myself through the iron bars and to the hatch. Did a three sixty pirouette, crouched to fire, but the landing hull was an empty void. From the outside came the pecking sound of Jay's pistol and the Suzy's Johnson firing again and again. D-men were hard to kill. A spiral staircase wound to the next level and I made for it, but paused. No use going back. They had to take care of themselves. Up the stairs in a single bound.

Empty! Almost empty. Just as I had suspected. Mutiny. The D-men ran out of Royals. Two of them were dead on the floor. Up the second spiral staircase to the next level. Here I would find some action. My Mandrake claw itched. My Johnson poised. Empty! Empty seats faced dials and screens, control panels and flashing lights. Empty as hell. A portal showed me the ground below. A spot light crisscross the space below searching where D-men parts lay scattered in the opening. Now, the rest was up to me.

The drone of the magneto grew louder. It pounded through my body and shocked my soul. The hair on my arms stood up. A charge. They were charging the hull. I burst through the final hatch and jumped to the pilot's chamber. A single D-man, a huge black man, sat at the controls, and before he could turn around I caught him from behind and pointed the Johnson at his head.

"Back it down. De-energize!" I commanded, and the engine slowed to a hum, but he disobeyed me. The black man jerked the controls and the engine roared and the craft lurched.

"No you don't!" I screamed and slapped his head with the snout of my Johnson. I pulled the accelerator back to normal and the craft settled.

"Crud!" The D-man cried and held his head and rolled on his back. "Hell, hell, hell!" he cried.

I hit him again, but he wouldn't die. He grabbed my arms and head butted me. Unbelievable! What in the name of the devil? I thought. Dick Phillips has a thick head, but so did the black man. God bless me, I couldn't believe it. It was Simpson, Parkenson's main driver. How could it be?

I forced him to the floor with my knees on his chest and push his face back with my left hand. We struggled. He pushed my hand away and stuck me in the chest. I forced him back and quickly yanked the Ching Da from my neck and poured the Charachunga in his mouth.

"Damn it!" I screamed. "Quit struggling!"

He chocked and swallowed. I heard footsteps behind me. More D-men. I steadied myself and readied. I jumped up, landed tiger-style, scratched at the air and turned to fight.

"We got em," Jay laughed.

"We wasted all of them!" Suzy cried.

"Phillips," Simpson muttered, "long time no see. Don't let the Newt get us. You're girl friend's pussy sure smells good. Where you hiding the Royals? Where's Parky? Where am I?"

I held the big man down and poured more Charachunga in his mouth.

"Mother!" he cried. "Bad brains pound me. My head feels thicker than a brick. Phillips, where are we?"

"Simpson," I said, "we're in a D-man intercontinental Magnacruiser. Look at your uniform. You're a D-man. How'd you get here?"

"Beats me," he said. "The last thing I remember, I got dragged in front of Dr. Blood and Kang. One look in Kang's eyes and my body turns to stone. At least, I felt that way. I sort of remember kissing Dr. Blood's and Kang's shoes, and I volunteered to fly for the D. That's about all I remember, except we fought among ourselves, looking for Royals to keep the bad feelings away. My men or I mean D-men I guess, we argued. Had to kill a lot of them and dump them. Got down to a skeleton crew. They were about to mutiny. We searched everywhere for smokes. Where the hell are we?"

"California City, you fucking D-man!" Jay shouted, and knelt next to Simpson. He pulled back the hammer of his little pistol and held it to the black man's head.

"No, no. Jay!" I shouted. "He's one of us. Don't do it. He's our ticket out of here."

Suzy pulled his hand away. "Jay," she said softly. "Relax. We have to locate Kai. You're over-amped from the fight."

Simpson looked at Jay and then at Suzy. "Phillips, you got some nice action there. What's her name? Who's Kai? And who's this half pint dressed like a D-man?"

"You'll have plenty of time to get acquainted later . . ." I replied.
". . . but she's mine. You know what's good for you. I told you already before. You stay away from my girl friend. Right now, we have to save Kai. After that, you're taking us to the Link. I've got to get back to the council."

I pointed the Johnson. "Understand?"

He jumped to a squat. "No need to get uppity. Give me another drink. Who's Kai and what is that stuff?"

I poured a drink into his mouth and the big man stood up to my height. "You're shit out of luck with the Link. It's been down for months. It blew itself up."

"Blew itself up?"

My heart sank in my chest. That was it. But evil couldn't win. Not now. The fight wasn't over. We weren't down yet. There was no going back. It looked like me, Jay, Simpson, and Suzy were the last of humanity as we knew it. Of course, there was no telling if somehow anyone else had survived, if evil had taken over completely, or even how bad the world had actually become. I thought of Pella and Billyland and my unborn child. I had to prevail for them. I looked at Suzy and Jay and Simpson. Dials and instruments flashed, and the room smelled sweaty. A moment. Someone had to take control.

"I'm in charge!" I declared. "First, we're going after Kai."

"Who's Kai?"

"She's my lady," Jay declared. "She's young and beautiful. She belongs to me."

"The monkey king stole her," Suzy interjected.

"Money king?"

"Monkey king!"

"First, we go after Kai," I said. "Then you're going to train a new crew. We're headed across the county to the council."

Simpson sat back in the pilot's chair and held his head. "Really?"

"Yeah." I said. "We're mates. The four of us. Shipmates."

"Phillips," he laughed, "you're nuts. But I already knew that. You don't know what you're up against. That's how the Link's spire blew up. Kang launched a space device, a multi-task photon that can pin point any craft in the biosphere. Something went haywire. If you want to stay alive, you got to dodge it all the time. They built an inpenetratable shield around the Council, but it would take a miracle even to get across county to that shield. You'd have to be the best pilot in the force."

I pointed at him. "Got that covered."

"Thanks."

"You might be a dog when it comes to my women, but you're a great pilot."

"Yeah, but . . . you'd have to have a telecom officer that could handle pressure. Man, you'd have to have someone, well, like . . ." He thought for a moment. ". . . Like someone like Silvia Huntsmith."

I looked at Suzy.

She smiled with an angelic look and blew a kiss toward me. I looked back a Simpson.

"We've got that covered."

"Okay, but you'd have to have someone at navigation that was so sneaky he could con a pack of Royals out of a Texas badge."

I lit one up and handed it to Jay who took a puff and blew out a perfect smoke ring.

I smiled and turned to Simpson. "We've got that covered too."

"You have to have a gunner that's quicker than greased lighting and with nerves of steel."

I looked at him. "I think I can handle that."

I took the bunt from Jay and handed it to Simpson. "Royal?"

He took a puff, held it in for quite a long time and then with a puff blew it out. Eventually a smile started to form on his face.

He blew out another puff of blue air and looked us over. A smile came on his face, and he sort of giggled. With a twinkle in his eyes and a resigned look, he answered.

"Yeah. Okay, he said. "Yeah! Let's crew across country."

"First we find Kai."

Chapter 22.

Simpson engaged the magneto. The huge craft rose above the zoo's jungle, and it only took a few minutes for us to locate the roving band of monkeys. Their monster leader, some sort of deformed hybrid ape, stood in the center of a clearing holding Kai above his head as the smaller monkeys circled them. One by one, as if making an offering to their king, the little brutes scraped at his feet. In return he would lower Kai and they sniffed her loins, jumped, and scratched themselves. One did a flip, jumped on another's back, and flipped again. The crowd of anthropoids rushed the giant ape but with one arm he brushed them back and held his prize to himself. Saliva dripped from the contorted mouth of the giant ape. The cluster ritual was about to begin.

"Turn off the holo and get this ship down!" Jay demanded.

"There," I said to Simpson, "beyond those rocks. Set her down."

"Fire on them now!" Jay cried.

"Hey mo fo," Simpson said over his shoulder. "I'm driving. What do you want to do, fry your girl friend?"

Suzy whispered to me. "These two don't like each other. We've got to save Kai?"

"Simpson, what are you going to do?"

"We'll set down beyond in those rocks, and we'll be in front of them. We can take them out one by one. We'll hide in the rocks, when they come through that opening we'll fill them full of lead. There's a lot of extra Johnsons on board and plenty of ammo. Probably only take a few minutes. See that brick wall, Suzy and Jay can hide there. You and I'll get behind those rocks. We'll land ahead, climb into position and ambush them. Agree?"

"Yeah!"

"I'm in."

"Me too."

"Good," Simpson said calmly. "Here we go. They're only a bunch of stupid animals. They won't know what hit them."

As we gathered guns and ammo, it only took seconds for Simpson to position the craft for landing. I didn't like executions, except in the case of D-men. So killing monkeys from hiding didn't sit right with me, but it had to happen. Kai must be saved. If we were going to take the Magna ship across the country, we needed Kai in our crew. We were going to need a full crew and also lot of luck. I knew why Jay wanted her, and I knew Simpson wanted her for the same reason. She was female. She was human. That's all we needed to know. We were humans. But really, we didn't need a reason. The pallor of evil hung about the cabin like the black wool shawl of a pointed-nose witch. We itched to kill. Without the Charachunga and an occasional hit from a Royal, we would have killed each other.

The holography focused in on the frothing face of the giant monkey king. Poor Kai lay half naked in his arms as he led the rampant band of hairy beasts toward the rocks. I licked my lips to kill it. The cabin smelled hot with anticipation.

The urge to fight rose as primal adrenalin beating our hearts to frenzy.

Simpson set the big craft to the ground. "Let's kill some furs!"

Outside the craft, at one end of the red brick wall Suzy took her place. At the other end, Jay checked his pistol. To my right, behind a large white boulder, Simpson squat in the green weeds. The morning sun burned my neck through the yellow haze. The sound of tramping, and cries, and squeals filled my ears. The warm odor of animal lust filled my nostrils. The words of Simpson rang in my ears, "They won't know what hit them."

Too late. Miscalculation!

They sprang on us before we knew it, and they were smarter than we anticipated. Much smarter. They must have sensed us, and somehow in some warped way, lured us into their trap. They came in waves. The smaller ones came first, flooding the air with sticks and rocks. We dodged them and blasted. Blood gushed in the air, and as the animals sprang with barred teeth and claws they were cut down. On the right, on the left, they came. Like a valley of death, we filled the rock crevices with writhing animal caucuses.

It was easy to see we'd underestimated the intelligence of the monkeys. By the time the first wave ended, I was covered with gore. Faces frozen, eyes fixed, monkey bodies twitched in the final pangs of death.

"Everybody alright?" I called.

"Yo!" Yelled Simpson. "I killed me a mess of furs!"

"Okay here!" cried Jay.

"Here they come again," Suzy screamed.

This time they were bigger and the rocks were boulders. Luckily, we had plenty of ammo, and I kept firing. A headless animal in its last throws heaved over rock, and as it descended on me I knocked it off. A fur flew over the embankment next to me. Its stomach exploded. In a furry mindless fury whirlwind they came. The more they came the more we cut them down. Our Johnsons were driven by intent. We were filled with lust for killing, and we killed. But still they came.

A fur at my throat!

"Bam!

Its head blew up, and it rolled past me.

"Got that one for you! Simpson yelled.

"Thanks! Everyone okay?"

"Yo," Simpson replied. "These suckers are mean."

"You okay Jay?"

"Ha. Ha!" Jay cried demonically. "Bring them on."

"Suzy," I yelled. "You okay?"

"Suzy, answer up!"

Below the line of sight, around the rocks, I crawled on my stomach over thrashing dying monkey bodies.

"Simpson, can you see? Is Suzy okay?"

"The next wave's almost here. Can't tell."

"Cover me."

Around the wall, I inched through the grass to Jay's position. "The next wave's almost here. Where's Suzy?"

"She's gone? She was just there. She's gone now."

At the end of the wall, several Johnson's lay on the ground. Suzy was gone. I picked up the Johnsons, shoved a new clip in mine, and jumped over the wall.

To the midst of the third wave, I ran firing randomly at the huge black and brown creatures. Bloody cries rang out. Thick scratching bodies flailed at me. Claws struck me about the face. One by one, I cut a swatch through the animals. Beyond them all, standing at least twenty feet tall, the huge monkey king held Kai in one arm. Froth spewed from his mouth, and his lips spread in a wide smile over pointed teeth. The ape's eyes met mine, and he turned his face to his other arm and licked a female. He had Suzy!

A screeching monkey jumped in the air at me. As I blew him to kingdom come, part of his brain got in my right eye. My vision blurred. Another monkey clamped on my back, and dug its claws into my neck. Rotating quickly, firing from both hands, I turned this way and that and twisted the business end of my Johnson into its mouth and gave him a lead desert. Blood and guts and fur flew in my face and mouth, and the air smelled hot with gun smoke and monkey death, until only a few feet separated me from the giant monkey king. Its big hairy mouth frothed, and his eyes gleamed a penetrating red color. The monster reared before me.

"I've had enough of you, "I said, and aimed the second Johnson at his ugly head. " See you in hell!"

Click.

Empty! I'd dumped the other Johnsons, and this one was out of ammo.

Kai and Suzy lay on the ground in a pile. The monster reared. He beat his chest and the remaining monkeys backed away. Now, the fight was between me and the beast. Its glowing red eyeballs and the red penetrating gleam emanating at me told me it wasn't just a beast. It was the Beast.

I threw my remaining Johnson right into its face, but it grabbed it out of the air and crushed it in his mighty hand and threw it back at me.

"Aaaaaarrrrr!" The monster wailed.

A shot of adrenalin rushed up my back bone and filled my brain. "Raaaaaagh!" I yelled back at it.

"Mandrake claw form!"

My hand went into the unmistakable shape of the deadly Mandrake claw, and I sprang for the animal's midsection, but it parried and side stepped me. I thought I heard it laugh. If it wanted a fight, it chose the right opponent.

Then it picked me up and bitched slapped my face back and forth and threw me down on the ground and laughed again.

"Die!" I cried and sprang in the air and landed inches from the monster. The animal shot out a massive fist, but I ducked as the breeze pushed by me. The monster struck at me with the other first, and I ducked that too. I compressed my Chi, jumped, and shot out my fingers on its massive chest, driving the Tibetan death touch essence into its heart.

"Time's up mother. Eat death!"

It knocked me aside like I was a feather.

Rolling over and over, I sprang to my feet puma style, jumped in front of it to ram my Mandrake claw into the chest and withdraw the heart, but again it knocked me back. The gorilla fought like a karate wizard.

Now, I circled it. If it was going to fight like a man, it was going to die like one too. I flipped hand over hand, built momentum, jumped up, and kicked a hard shoe to its face. The giant monkey king's head jerked back, and I followed through with fist deep into its eye.

Big mistake!

It grabbed both my legs in one massive hand and both my arms in the other and held me up and started to pull. I couldn't move. I resisted, and then one after another the joints of my back bone separated. I could barely hold my body together. I grit my teeth, tightened my stomach, and girded my loins. Then it was over.

The monster fell backwards, palpitated, and jerked. I twisted my body and pried my arms and kicked my legs from its grip. As the massive body finished its death throws, I stepped on top of the animal.

"Ahhhhhhh!" I beat my chest and the remaining monkeys scattered.

The Tibetan death touch, though delayed, always did its work.

And just in the nick of time too, the gorilla almost had me. Simpson too. He staggered from behind the boulder. His clothes were torn; his face was a bloody mass. One eye hung by a strand out of its socket. Jay stood erect from behind the brick wall. He'd been chewed good. With an ashen look on his face, he tottered and fell and thudded in a heap. Suzy lay unconscious. Her jump suit was ripped and smeared with dark red blood, and Kai lay half naked, torn and bleeding next to her. We survived and saved Kai, but we paid the price.

In that moment, I felt alive. Very, very alive. We'd been damaged, but I was sure we would all recover. In Simpson's case, with the help of the healing Charachunga, he would see again. I knew Kai would recover too, but it might take some time, she was pretty torn up. The silence of the zoo's jungle right then hung on us magnificently, and the joy of the battle gave Simpson and me enough energy enough to drag ourselves and the crew back to the Magnacrusier.

On a cot inside the Magnacrusier in the infirmary, Suzy drifted in and out of sleep. Kai tossed and turned, we couldn't wake her up. Jay paced in, then out of the room, fretted and worried, making up projections. I tried to get him to drink from the China Da, but he kept refusing, saying he felt better and more like a man without it. Simpson's eye fit back in the sock. Earlier, I irrigated the eye with Charachunga, and he'd probably see again with that eye, but not for a while. He looked like a soldier, a gallant hero with a white bandage around his eye. He came down the staircase into the infirmary.

"How is everybody?"

"Suzy's fine. She's sleeping. I don't know about Kai. She hasn't come around yet. How's the ship?"

"We're hovering."

"What now?"

"You tell me, it's your show."

"We have to get back to the Council as soon as possible."

"That be a good trick," Simpson remarked and sat down next to Kai. He touched her forehead. "What a shame. She's a beautiful woman."

I nodded and looked over at him.

"I'd give anything to do her," he said.

Jay walked through the doorway. "Who? Do who?"

"The queen," I said quickly.

"The queen?"

"Yeah, you remember. When things get back to normal, when we trip down to Village Eight, the queen on Seventh Avenue, the strange looking whore with two pussies, the one who said she migrated from the dark side of the moon."

"Huh," Jay replied, "I thought that was a myth."

"Nope, it's true" Simpson replied. "Colonel Dill, err, Colonel Doe proved it. That is, I mean Colonel Dill Doe, proved that life on the dark side of the moon was real. The women had two pussies and knew how to use them. The queen of Seventh Avenue actually was a moony. She snuck to Earth on a transport and made enough money to buy several houses on Park Place."

Jay stepped close to Simpson and Kai. "May I?"

"What?"

"My girl friend . . . sit next to my girl friend."

"Oh sure, sure. Sorry. I'll sit next to Phillips."

Suzy and Kai slept while the three of us, Simpson and Jay and I worked on the plan.

"What now, Simpson?"

"Tell me. Like I said, it's your show."

"The Council . . ."

"A good trick," Simpson remarked. He motioned theatrically. "As soon as we get to the Ozone desert, incoming from the Photon will bomb us. We'll be fried, finger licking good. If somehow we evade that and make it back to the capital, a mile or so outside the Council we'll hit their shield. The ship will be destroyed, and we'll be evaporated."

I clasp my hand around the Ching Da vial at my neck and held it so everyone could see. "Where there's a will, there's a way."

I motioned to Jay.

"Huh?!" Jay remarked.

"Look Jay," I said. "Have a swig. You need it."

"I told you directly Phillips. I ain't drinking no more of that crud. It makes me feel weak. I'm fast. I'm tough. Nobody messes with me."

Simpson started laughing. Jay fumed. Right then, Suzy woke up.

"Sweetie," she asked, "Dick, what happened?"

"Baby . . ." I bent over and whispered, "you did great." I kissed her cheek. "We got Kai back. Simpson's eye got hurt, and Kai's still unconscious. How you feeling?"

"Good."

I leaned back. "Okay, now we've got a quorum."

"What's that?" asked Simpson.

"We could play bridge with you as the dummy," Jai remarked. "Know nothing. It's a forth person."

"Shut up mo fo!"

"Shut up mo fo!"

"Dick," Suzy whispered, "stop them."

"Hold it boys," I said. "Look Simpson, train us to fly this ship and we'll find a way to solve the problems. There must be a way to beat that Photon. By the time we reach the Council we'll have a solution to getting through the shields. The world's gone to Hell. Kang must be defeated. We're the last hope. Time's running out. We have to get going."

301

We passed around the Charachunga and except for Jay, who was getting more and more mean spirited, we all drank. Simpson agree to train us to fly the ship, and we left Kai to recover and made our way through the craft to engineering where at each empty station a complicated harness sat on a chair in front of a holo device.

Simpson addressed us. "This is the most advanced cross county magnetic cruiser in the world. You all are familiar, of course, with the theory behind magnetic travel."

We shook our heads.

"Doesn't matter. It's not too important, anyway," he continued. "You don't have to know how a magna-car works to drive one . . . do you? Essentially, the big magneto alternates a magnetic current, similar to alternating electric current. The quick reversal of positive and negative magnetic flux lifts the craft in the Earth's magnetic field. We accelerate by adjusting the North and South Pole attraction."

"Suzy," he said and pointed to an empty chair in front of a group of dials, head sets, and microphones. "This is the telecommunications module. You're going to have to disguise your voice and get tough. When you communicate you declare in a rough voice, an abrupt "Yes, sir!" or "No, Sir!""

"Yes sir!"

"Thank you. Don't be afraid to tell them to "Go to Hell!" In D-man service, that's sort of a friendly gesture, like "Go to Hell, yourself." Know what I mean?"

Jay laughed. "Hey, Simpson!"

"Yeah," he replied.

"Go to Hell!"

"Exactly." He paused. "Now Suzy, if they ask about your voice you tell them you caught a cold. I'll run down the operations in more detail after I situate each of you at your stations."

Simpson took the Ching Da and poured a swig on the bandage of his eye. "Any questions?"

"No."

"No."

"Yes," I said and took him aside. "What's this about other ships?"

"What'd you think, boy, they just gonna let us fly right out of this zone? Look at this."

The holography hummed, and an image flickered in the three dimensional scope. An armada of D-men attack ships cut trails through the sky.

"We've got to get out of here!" I declared.

"Don't sprout your wig," Simply said calmly. "They're still a day away. We'll be able to stay ahead of them for them for a little while at our present speed. If I don't get you trained, when the sprints come along side they'll take us down."

"Sprints?" Jay ejaculated. "What's a sprint?"

"Scouts, rapid fire Kamikazes." Simpson said with a big smile. "They'll try to shoot us down and if they can't do that, they'll attach to us like leaches and weigh us down. This is Kang's flag ship. It's a very valuable ship. They're going to want it back. In fact, they probably aren't going to try to shoot us down. Maybe they'll try. I don't know. Kang hates disobedience. Most likely they'll try and force us to the ground."

He grabbed at the air like catching a fly. "But we can kill the sprints pretty easily. It's the gun ships we have to worry about."

"Gun ships?!"

"After we get rid of the Scouts, the gunners will fire on us and try to destroy our magneto. They'll fire long range cannons. At closer range they'll let go an electro charge."

"Can't we outrun them?"

"Don't want to. That's not the plan."

He adjusted his eye patch. "What we have to do is make them think they've got us. They have to be right on us. They have to taste the kill. If we can survive long enough to sucker them into the area over the Ozone Desert, the Photon will take care of them."

"What about us? How we going to survive?"

"That's how you fit in Jay?"

He motioned us to move to the navigation section where an array of scopes and strobe units were positioned in front of a harness and rotational command chair.

"This is navigation."

Simpson motioned for Jay to sit down. "Try out your voice on the computer."

"I've never done this before, what do I say?" Jay asked as he sat down.

"Never done vectors or intercept factors?"

"No."

Never plotted time frequencies and overlaps?"

"No."

"Ever harmonize amplitude, harmonic distortion, and Scaler wave interferonics?"

"No!" Jay cried.

I felt discouraged. Suzy was a Huntsmith that was true. But she was trained as a recreation specialist. She wasn't a telecom officer. Could Jay navigate without any experience? I'd never handled really big guns like the ones on this craft. We were doomed. We'd be burned to a cinder in a giant red fire ball. The hopes of humanity would be blown to Smithereens, wherever that was.

"Dicky," Simpson said, "I can tell by the look on your face you got a burr up your butt."

"We're not going to make it!" I cried like a wet cat in a rain storm.

"Phillips . . ." Simpson laughed and moved his hand around in the air as if he were a magician. "I got a few tricks." He reached up the sleeve of his torn shirt and brought out a closed fist.

"Come closer," he said, and as we gathered in a circle around him, he opened his hand.

Chapter 23.

The magneto hummed. In front of the navigation station near the helm of the giant ship, Jay, Suzy, and I stared into the opening fist of Simpson's hand. But it was empty.

"Just joking," he laughed. "You all are going to have to go through interphase."

"What's interphase?"

"Rex," he said, "explain interphase."

Simpson corrected himself. "Rex . . . please tell them about interphase."

"You've got a Rex 1000 on board?" I asked.

"Rex 2000 at your service."

"The new model Rex!" I shouted, astounded. "Then what do you need us for. I've heard about this new model. She could fly this ship and take care of all our jobs, cook us breakfast and put us to bed."

"That's right." Simpson replied. "Unfortunately, it's irrevocably networked with all the other ships in the armada. There's no way to over-ride it. Once the fighting starts we have to shut it down and fly blind."

I thought I heard a giggle; someone said, "Shut it down?"

"When the armada gets close I'm going to pull the plug. After that, we fly by the seat of our pants."

Again I thought I heard a giggle. "Pull the plug?"

"The Rex is programmed to override my commands and link with the armada, but I think I can change that function."

"Change that function?"

"Rex," Simpson continued, "stop repeating what I say. Now, will you please describe the interphase training process?"

"Interphase," began the Rex 2000, "is a synchronized means of transference. It is a proven technique in a safe, integrated manner so that the subject, or subjects, learn to accomplish complicated tasks without laboriously memorizing, repeating, or making demonstrations. The factor of time in learning is eliminated so that those human subjects are trained instantaneously to be proficient at the highest level. By use of white sound, blank space, nodal and sub-nodal hypnologic programming linked to propreoceptor interference, kinesthetic responses integrate maximum stimulus response. And the history of . . ."

"Please end now," Simpson interrupted.

"Is it safe?" Suzy asked. "I don't want to end up like a God damn idiot, working for a living on a D-man outpost for the rest of my life a slave to washing dishes and cleaning up after pets, taking care of a dud husband and kids in the middle of suburbia on a hot afternoon with Grandpa rocking on the porch and a broken down clunker in the yard, doing laundry and washing dishes. Do you know what I mean?"

Spoken, I thought, like a true daughter of Silvia Huntsmith. Her grandmother would have been proud. I whispered. "It's going to be okay."

Simpson undressed Suzy with his eyes, but I wouldn't have it. I stepped between them. "Simpson," I said, "we don't want to be zombie D-men after this."

"Yeah," Jay spouted up, "me and Kai got a life to lead."

The big black man rolled his eyes in his head, as if remembering something. "Ah yes," he said. "Kai, I hope she recovers. She's beautiful. There's no problem. Rex, please tell us how many cases of human brain damage have occurred in the process of interphase."

"One case out of two hundred and seventy two thousand."

"Please Rex," I asked, "what type of training was that?"

"Presidential leadership."

"What was the name of the trainee?"

"Dr. Blood, Dr. Cosmo Blood."

"Dr. Blood! What happened?"

"In the early days, before the interflow was stabilized, an overload caused Mr. Blood's brain to enlarge. He developed a super sensitive brain, very high intelligence, close to the Rex series. The dark side of his brain also enlarged. He learned about time travel, fabricated artificial life, stepped over the threshold, and opened the door where evil dwells and . . ."

Simpson cut him off. "We know the rest. So, you see. There have been no other cases. It's very safe."

"What about my station?" I asked. "Where does the gunner sit?"

"Next to me at the helm. Come on."

We walked to the helm, where the gunner sat behind the pilot. In front of me, knobs glowed. Handles, various different level switches, and gauges seem to have a life of their own. Lights flashed on the harness and the constant presence of static made me sweat.

"Where are the guns? Where are the triggers?"

"Phillips," Simpson lamented, "you're going to need the interphase as much as the others. We haven't used triggers for years. It's all based on mental intent . . . how bad you want it. What counts is how good's your mental aim. It's the same with Jay and Suzy and me. We have to want to beat the armada worse than they want to kill us."

He stopped talking for a moment. "We'd better get you hooked into your harnesses and into interphase. I've got a lot to do to prepare to take the computer system off line. You'll need to get trained before I cut over."

Again the wee voice. "Off line . . . cut over?"

"Get into your harnesses."

We helped Suzy into her harness, and I gave her a kiss. "See you later telecom."

Next, Simpson and I fit Jay into his harness at navigation. Simpson plugged in the unit and put his hand on Jay's quivering arm.

"Don't be scared, skinny."

"I ain't scared, you idiot! And I ain't skinny!"

307

Back in the helm, I slid into my harness and Simpson helped me fit the probes. I looked up at the black man. "Take the Ching Da and look in on Kai," I said.

"Phillips," he replied. "You read my mind."

He paced from the helm to navigation and telecom and back to the helm. "Ready, now! Please Rex, on my mark; engage unit one pattern telecom, unit two pattern navigator and unit three, pattern gunner." He looked up and down at us. "One thing. Very important! Don't try and get out of your harnesses until Rex finishes. It's very dangerous. You need to stay connected until the end. . . . Okay Rex, engage now!"

Suddenly, I wasn't exactly on the Magnacruiser anymore. Rather, I was inside and outside at the same time. Inside in holography, and outside in the sky, a swift vessel approached on the stern.

"Right twenty degrees hard fast!" Jay shouted.

Somehow my hands knew exactly what to do. Strange, they weren't my hands but Jay's hands and also Suzy's. I rotated the first dial, pushed up the third slide switch, and moved my hands through a field in front of me playing a series of high musical notes.

"Flux drive intercept!" Suzy signaled. "Degrees down, on Jay's mark. Set, one, two, three."

"Fire forty four on impulse twenty nine."

As a team, as one, we worked our stations. Ship after ship, gambit after gambit, came in our minds in the holoview and outside the ship they attacked and we countered.

"We're hit!"

"Evasive action!"

"Fire from free fall!"

"Discharge ground fault!"

"And recharge weapons, now!"

"Retro charge, synchronize."

We destroyed ship after ship as we evaded lightening bolts of electricity. Several times, out of nowhere, streaks of pale blue energy broke through the sky and almost instantaneously the three of us reacted as a unit to move the craft or make it lighter, or to build a charge and counter with an attack of energy. When the battles finished we seemed to pull into port, and we all relaxed, but then Rex shouted.

"Virus! Abort! . . . Malfunction! Your brains will be destroyed in less than five seconds."

"Five, four, three, two, one."

We tore at our harnesses, but we were jacked in.

"Brains gone!" Rex laughed. "You're brains are mush. Ha. Ha."

"Please, Rex." I said, "Stop it."

"God in machine," the Rex droned. "God in machine." She laughed. "And she's got a sense of humor."

After removing ourselves from the harnesses, we made our way to the infirmary. We entered to check on Kai, and Simpson squat in front of her cot. His body was over her face, and we couldn't exactly see what he was doing.

"Oh," Kai moaned. "That feels so good."

Jay went for his pistol. "God damn it!"

"Stop it Jay," I shouted, grabbed his arm and dragged him to the bed. "Look."

Simpson was rubbing Charachunga on Kai's wounds. He rotated to us.

"She's back. She's healing. I think she be as good as new by tonight."

I took the Ching Da from Simpson. "Jay," I said, "you're getting out of hand. Drink. You'll feel a lot better."

"I ain't taking anymore of that shit," he cried. "It makes me feel like a wimp. I'm stronger than I've ever been, and I feel mean and I like it. I ain't wimpy."

Simpson stood up a head taller than Jay. "You ain't wimpy?"

"Listen, all of you," I said as I stepped between them. "If there's any fighting to do, save it for the D-men."

"No," Simpson said simply. "Let's settle it now. We're not slaves. Women fought the last war to free themselves, didn't they?" He looked at Kai and smiled. "You're free, aren't you Kai?"

309

She blushed. "Kai confused," she said, and turned her head.

Jai stuck his face into Simpson's. "She's mine!"

"She's free!"

"Cool it!" I shouted.

"She's just as free," Simpson said to me and walked out, "as your debutante. I hope Kai knows how to hum the anthem as well as Cynthia."

Suzy looked at me. "What's that mean?"

I put the Ching Da around my neck and smiled dumbly at her. We had to have to have a talk tonight.

That evening we all sat in the tiny D-man lounge and played the waiting game. The other D-men ships weren't close enough for us to start evasive action or to begin to set our trap, but by early morning we were going to have to be at our stations. I looked at Suzy, thinking I had time to till a row in her garden of love, but the glare in her eyes told me we'd have to have our little talk first. Jay and Kai were sitting at a table talking, and Simpson sat alone. One by one he tossed playing cards across the room, shooting for a waste basket.

"Simpson," I asked, "did you take Rex off line."

"Yeah."

"How you do it?"

"Oh," he remarked offhandedly, "I just told her we were going to need a complete history of the Rex family, that we needed a record for posterity. She got into herself a bit too much."

"Solipsism?"

He held up his thumb. "Yeah, got her involved in herself for a few minutes, then I pulled the fuse. Rex is down."

"Okay," I said. "Let me get this straight. We lure the other ships into a chase and sucker them into the Ozone Desert where the Photon destroys them for us. Sounds simple."

"It's very simple."

"One thing," I asked, "if all the ships have the Rex, and all the D-men are trained through interphase, how are we going to defeat them?"

"Well," he replied, "damn if I know."

"What?" I cried.

"Well what you want to do, sucker? What's your plan?"

I looked at him with a blank stare.

"Phillips, you are such an easy mark. I got a plan. I programmed the Rex to come in with false information. You know what happens when you get your arm cut off?"

"Go over to the Insta Med and get it sewed back on and hope the elbow's not where the hand should be."

"No. Before the disruption, when you had to live with it. It's called a phantom arm. You got the feeling it's there, but it's not there. I put a program in the Rex navigation to make them think we're where we're not. Depends on how motivated they are; if they think to run a program check. If they're like the other D-men, they're out of smokes, sex crazed, and going nuts. Hey, by the way, light me up a Royal."

I took a puff and handed him a smoke. "You amaze me Simpson. I always thought you were just Parkenson's main man. Now, I find out you're a computer genius. What gives?"

"Don't matter now. Everybody's probably dead. The Council hired me to spy on Parky. Before Kang took over, I was in the secret, secret service. Yeah, and I also was doing Harriet behind his back."

My eyes lit up. The last part I could believe. But secret, secret service? Come on.

He hit me with his elbow. "Man, Phillips. You ain't even got a sense of humor. Can't you take a joke? Had you going there, didn't I? Parkenson's my main man. I wouldn't do that to him. Ha. Ha. And besides can you see me and Mrs. Parkenson. Never happened."

"We been through a lot," I said.

"Yeah," he replied, "you really saved me and Parkenson with those damn Newt. And many years also, do you remember that big snowman."

"Sure, the 'Case of the Frozen Blue Balls.'"

He had a twinkle in his eyes. "Man, I want to thank you too. My debutante, Cynthia, will be waiting for me when we get back."

"You mean my debutante."

"Doesn't matter. Kang's got her now. He brought her and her fat friend Linda in front of Dr. Blood and the Council. Kang wasn't much interested in Cynthia, but he kept parading Linda around and licking his lips. I remember he touched her with his long fingernails, and his long tongue licked her face. Poor Cynthia, she was so scared. All she could do was hum the anthem. Silliest thing. When Dr. Blood kisses Saint Billy's shoe. As if that could ever happen. Anyway, it was the best hummer I ever had."

On the other side of the room Jay snuggled Kai's neck. Suzy lay back and dozed on a couch while Simpson and I talked. He tossed another card toward the waste basket. It missed, and he smiled at me.

"That Kai is a beautiful woman," he said. "She reminds me of a young thing I had when I first joined the space service."

I looked over at Suzy. Her blonde hair draped wistfully over her breasts and though her jump suit was dirty, she looked good enough to eat. I turned back to the big black man.

"I didn't know you were in the space force."

He flicked another card. "That's how I learned computers and to pilot Magnacruisers. My first assignment was on the dark side of the moon."

"Is it true what they say?"

"What? You mean about there being a new race of humans up there. Yeah, it's true. If you can call them human. They're strange. They got a royal system, a monarchy."

"You mean a king and a queen?"

"Yo. And you should see the princess. She's an albino, a young thing, silk white hair. The jewels she wears around her neck are phosphorus. She so beautiful. I'd give my left nut just to screw her. You know the women up there got two pussys, and they can suck you dry and make your big whanger get up, tap dance around the room, spring in the air, do a back flip, waltz around and come a

312

hundred times. And that's before you pull down your pants. In fact, after sex, you're lucky if it don't dance away with itself and never return. It's so happy."

He paused with a sad, wistful look.

"Wished I could of stayed there and done more of them. That'll never happen now. Probably won't even get back to have my deb hum the anthem for me."

I wished he would quit saying "my" deb. I had to hold myself back. No use arguing in front of Suzy. Later, we'd have to have our little talk and let her know, that like a good sailor, I had a girl in every port. Sure I did. I laughed to myself. I wished I did.

Simpson gazed at Suzy and then at Jay and Kai. "Looks like I'm the odd man out."

I got up. "We have to get some shut eye. Suzy, let's get some sleep."

"Take the far cabin," Simpson said, "down the hall. Those two can sleep in the aft compartment. I'll sleep out here." He mumbled to himself. "Kai is such a beautiful woman. Damn."

We walked a blurry-eyed walk to our room.

The single illuminator cast a green glow in the sleeping compartment as Suzy stripped off her jump suit. I moved around the nondescript room and casually ran my hand over the cool plastic walls and listened to the low hum of the magneto. The morning was only a few hours away and this looked like it might be the last time I could relish her. Suzy, that is, not the morning. Well, that too. Tomorrow we would be smashed up in a pile of burning metal, or evaporated at the shield, or we would be flying through the dome at the Council chamber. I would douse Da Mo with his Charachunga and complete this case.

I'd always love Suzy, I thought, but I wondered about Pella and Cynthia. If I got out of this alive, how would I decide? They were all so good. If I started taking vitamin shots in the butt, I might be able to do them all. I sat back on a cot and laid my head on a pillow. All three of them could caress me, hold me, and suck me.

As she sat down next to me, Suzy asked. "What you thinking, sweetheart?"

She looked at me, questioning, "Penny for your thoughts?"

"Thoughts cost more than a penny now," I replied. "Let's see, a good thought will cost you approximately twenty dollars, American."

"I'm broke."

"Okay, I'll take a penny."

"Don't even have a penny."

"You'll have to pay another way."

"Let me have your thought first."

I stuttered. "I, I, well . . ."

"What's the use," she said. "You're brain dead as always. You had one of those mind operations where they take out the front part of your brain, a prefrontal lobotomy.

"Huh . . . a beer in front of me?"

She sighed. "Droll . . . you said you wanted to talk."

"Well," I began, "if we get out of this in one piece, we're going to be living separate lives, you know."

"What do you mean? Don't you love me?"

"Of course I do, sweetheart. It's just that, well how can I say it? I'm a lot older than you, and I've been around, and well, I've had other women."

"You had other women," she said and strongly stressed had. "And I'm the best." She straddled me with her naked body and took my hands and pulled them to her breasts. With her hands on my ears for reins, she wiggled on my chest.

"Be my horsy," she whispered and stuck her fingers deep in my ears. "I'll' ride the merry go round of love and catch the brass ring." She slapped my side. "Giddy up!"

The tanned beach bunny inched up my chest, took my hands in her hands, and pushed them to the sides. She bent her face to mine and kissed me deeply on the lips with hot sweet breath. As our tongues danced the marimba, she sucked the breath from me and for only a second my mind flashed back to the she devil that almost killed me in the 'Case of the Yellow Succubus.'

"What is it?"

"Nothing baby," I gasped.

"Dick," she whispered. "Eat me."

"Umm, come to papa."

In the pale green light her naked tanned body looked almost orange. The giant dark sporum hair pie between her legs reared on my face, and her hot dripping slit was over my mouth. Slowly she released herself on my face and as the puckered lips sank over my mouth, I chewed and chewed. Her juice tasted like honey, and she bucked and bucked on my mouth and my nose went in and out of her and my tongue licked her hard shaft. I moved my head back and forth and from side to side. As her body quivered, she panted and thrust her pussy into my face again and again. At first, I couldn't hear the violent screams.

"I said, get the fuck away from her!"

Pt-in! Pt-in! The sound of Jay's pistol.

"My God!" Kai screamed. "You kill him!"

I lifted Suzy's sex off my face and slid out, wiping my face as I ran. What now? The armada was only hours away. We didn't get any sleep, and I didn't like the way Simpson looked at Kai. All we needed was for someone to be hurt. Jay was jealous. He thought he owned Kai. Without his help we wouldn't have gotten her back from the monkeys. That was certainly true, but without Simpson's quick shooting and brave fighting, all may have been lost. Really, no one owned Kai, or any other women for that matter. That was the reason for the last war. She was a free woman.

As I buttoned my pants, gripped the cold steel of my Johnson and ran to their compartment, a lot of deep thoughts raced through my mind. It wasn't like E equals MC squared, or even anything close. It was more like a dream I couldn't quite remember. If I could even remember part of what I've forgotten, I'd be the smartest guy I ever knew. Why, I probably forgot more than I ever remember. . .

I think I thought a hell of a lot of thoughts while I raced to the noise. I raised my gun and entered the room.

Jay stood over a body on the carpet.

Simpson's body contorted, and from the back of his head blood trickled on the floor. Kai shivered on the cot with her hands over her eyes, as the balding little man with the pistol in his hand rotated to look at me.

"He screwed Kai!" Jay screamed. "As we slept, he sneaked on her and he raped her. I tried to stop him, but he shoved me down. He mounted her and boned her! Damn it, I had to stop him. He deserves to die, so I shot him."

"No. No!" Kai cried. "He not sex up me. He check wounds. Hold me."

"What?" Jay yelled and lifted his hand to hit her. "You bitch! You fucking whore! God damn it bitch, admit it. You were fucking him!"

I grabbed Jay's arm, took his pistol and turned him toward the door. "That's enough. Go get some bandages."

"She's . . ."

"Enough," I said, pulled him to my face, tete a tete. "Shut up! Get the bandages."

It was only a surface wound to the side of Simpson's head, and in a few minute with the help of the Charachunga, he was doing fine. Jay didn't come back with the bandages and as Simpson and I walked to the infirmary, we hashed it out.

"You sure you're going to be okay?"

He replied woozily. "I was only checking on her. She looked so pretty, so fragile, so sweet. I took her pulse. Her hand brushed my zipper. It wasn't my fault."

"Oh, I know. You only wanted to see if she could hum the anthem in her sleep."

"She's so beautiful," he said and smiled. His teeth gleamed big and white. "Man, I want to pop her so bad." He laughed. "I know she wants me too. You're big like me. What can she see in a tiny runt like Jay? He ain't got no size. He can't fill her up."

316

He looked me in the eyes. "This might be our last night on Earth . . ." He barked. "Phillips! I got to taste that meat."

I didn't know what to tell him.

"You owe me," he said. "I saved your life. You got to find a way to get her to screw me. Jay can't say nothing. Women are free now. They're the ones to decide."

In the infirmary, Simpson started sobbing. It didn't look as if he'd been laid since he played the bitch back at Parkenson's estate. He cajoled like he was a fourteen year old boy trying to get me to pimp a sister.

"Buddy, my brodder, my buddy. You know me. I just want that fur in my mouth. If I don't get laid before a big fire fight, I ain't worth nothin."

For a moment, he went out of his head. "Nigger, I got to taste her pussy before I die!"

He got livid and cried. "I need to peel the veal, dive in and drive. All year I've had sex on my mind, now I need it on my face! I got to eat Kai. You know Peter Pecker pops a pack of plush puss to get his puckered prick unpacked. Don't you understand, Dick? That's what we fought the war about. Women have earned their freedom. Sex is free!

"It's up to Kai," I replied. "What do you want me to do?"

"Jus ask her if she'll be with me for half and hour. Ask her, jus ask her. Don't listen to Jay. Beg her, damn it. I don't care what you have to do, or say. I got balls swelled up. I don't see nothing but blue."

After I gave him a swig of drink, he swooned and went in a semi-stupor, and I gathered everyone and took them in the main cabin. I set them down.

"Jay," I said, "lucky your aim was so bad. Simpson's going to be okay."

"Wouldn't have missed," he replied. "But Kai grabbed my arm."

I held Suzy's hand and looked at the others. "You know, we're a couple."

"Yes, we are!" she added.

"Suzy's taken," I said, "and I've known you a long time Jay. We've been through some ups and downs, and you know I want the best for you."

"Get to it Phillips. Quit pussyfooting around!"

I lit a Royal. "Let's pass one around and cool off."

"I don't want no more of that crap. Get to it!"

I looked directly at Kai. "Well, here's the skinny. Simpson's going to be able to pilot the ship alright, but he's real pent up. He needs release real bad. He asked me to ask Kai if she wouldn't . . ."

Jay jumped between us. "No way!"

"Jay," I said, "it's the evil feelings. Drink some Charachunga."

"Not interested. I feel like a man now. Best I've felt for some time. I'm tough now." He puffed up his chest. "He's not touching my woman. If he does, he dies."

He turned to Kai. "He's not fucking you," he said demonstratively. "Right Kai?"

Suzy laughed. "That's for Kai to decide."

"Kai," I said, "this may be our last hours. Simpson wants to have sex with you. He doesn't want to possess you for all time. If we get out of this, he won't be attached. For tonight, he needs someone to love. He needs you bad as any man ever has. It's up to you. What do you say?"

Kai stood up and pulled Jay to her chest and looked at him with a smile. "You a sweet little man."

"You're not going to be with him?"

"I be back."

Kai walked toward the infirmary and Jay went off. "Damn it. Don't let him inside of you."

She turned back to him. "It not soap. It no wear out."

"Jay," I said, "go to the far compartment, where you can't hear them, and stay there. We need Simpson more than we need you. I don't want you messing things up, got that? If you screw with those two again, I'll kill you!"

He sulked out, a beaten man. I wished he would have drunk from the Ching Da, but he wouldn't. Suzy and I went to our room, and back on the cot, she stroked my hair.

"Dick," she said, "you're all tensed up. What's wrong?"

"I didn't like what just came down."

"What do you mean?"

"You know," I said, "having to choose Simpson over Jay. If Simpson wanted you, I wouldn't have given you up."

"You do love me!"

"I guess it was up to Kai, not Jay or Simpson or me."

"It's the woman's decision."

"We fought the war about that," I said. "I would have fought a war over you, baby."

"My warrior."

"Come here, sweetie."

Suzy held me down and I didn't resist. She kissed me and put her tongue in my ear and rotated it around. Shivers shot up my spine. My cock got rock hard and stuck straight up out of the rim of my pants. She lay on top of me and humped me, and I began to feel an orgasm from deep within me.

"Die motherfucker!"

"A piercing scream came from the compartment where Simpson and Kai were making love. Damn it. Not again! I pushed Suzy off of me and for the second time grabbed my Johnson and ran.

As the compartment doors opened, Jay stood over the cot and beneath him Simpson lay on top of Kai. A large butcher knife poised in Jay's right hand, its tip dripped blood.

"Stop!" I commanded.

"Ha . . . ha!" Jay laughed and looked in my direction with blazing red eyes and a lust-filled smile. The bloody knife reared back and plunged toward Simpson.

The Johnson blazed. My shots rang out. Jay's brain blew up. The butcher knife dropped to the floor.

319

All the king's horses and all the king's men and all the Charachunga in eternity weren't going to put Jay back together again. His brains splattered over the wall, and as his body slumped forward over Simpson and Kai, I rushed to them. Quickly kicking Jay's headless body away, I poured healing fluid into Simpson's wound. Hysterically, Kai clawed her way out from under us and crawled naked on the floor. Suzy entered and held her in her arms.

"What happened?"

"I had to kill Jay. He stabbed Simpson."

"Is he alive?"

"Simpson!" I shouted. "Wake up. Come on man," I pleaded. "You can't die. You have to fly the ship. Simpson. Simpson!"

The big black man looked up at me and mumbled, but I couldn't hear him and bent close.

"What? What is it?"

"Interphase . . . " he wheezed. "Ask Rex. Train you."

He could barely talk. "Train you to pilot and shoot . . . same time. Must hurry. Your Rex on line." He shut his eyes and his head fell to the side.

"Oh God!" Kai screamed.

"He's dead!" Suzy shouted.

"Not yet," I said and shook him. "Simpson. Simpson. What do we do?" He didn't respond. He was breathing, but unconscious.

"He's in shock and going into coma!"

The room reeked of hot sex and death. In a few moments, as Jay's body deteriorated, it would be much worse. The armada was closing in. Simpson had already taken the Rex 2000 off line. I had no idea how to get it back on line. Our pilot was in a coma. Suzy, the telecom officer was crying, rocking back and forth on the floor with Kai, and the navigation officer's brains were covering the wall. Even if I could figure out how to get the Rex back on line, was there enough time to train a new crew? We were only three. Was it possible to fly the craft and work the weapons at the same time? We still had the basic on board computer. Yet, it wasn't a Rex, just enough brains to fly the ship.

"Computer," I said, "holography of the armada."

An image flickered. The ships were much closer. Sprints deployed toward us. There was little time. Both ladies whimpered and cried in each other's arms.

"Snap out of it!" I shouted. "The D-men ships are almost here. Get your clothes on. I'll take Simpson to the infirmary. We'll meet in the helm."

Chapter 24.

I climbed into the pilot's chair at the helm and looked out the port to the chilling darkness. In less than a few hours the D-men ships would be on us. The first act hadn't begun but the final cut was already falling like a cleaver on a chopping block. If I couldn't figure a way to open up interphase and train as pilot and gunner and get Suzy and Kai trained as navigator and telecom, it was curtains.

"Hologram of D ships," I said to the onboard computer, and immediately a miniature representation of the fleet floated before me, closer to our ship than before.

"Alright, computer," I asked. "How do we access interphase?"

"That information unavailable."

"Computer!" I demanded. "Is there a means to contact the Rex 2000?"

"Yes," the computer replied.

"Then do it now."

"Unable to comply."

"Why not?"

"Why . . . unacceptable usage."

Damn, I thought, of course the computer couldn't answer "why?" Why's were the providence of man, and of course, the Rex series. And I couldn't break into the Rex. I thought for about as long as it takes to wring a dishrag.

"Suzy," I yelled. "Get to your station. I want you at telecommunication."

"Okay computer, what do I need to access the Rex system?"

"Rex system," the computer replied in its monotone.

"That's what I said, the Rex system. How do I access the Rex 2000?"

"Rex."

"Quit repeating what I say. How do I get into the Rex system?"

"Rex system."

"Suzy?"

"Telecom officer here."

"Good. Probe for frequency 124-876-3242100."

"Probing."

"Well?"

"Still probing."

There was a chance. Small, but it was a chance.

"I'm getting static now, but I think we have contact."

"Rex, are you on line?"

No answer. It was a million in one chance. If my Rex had been successful with building operations and created a reserve power supply, he could still be functioning. If I could get through to my Rex, it might be possible for him to connect to the onboard computer and create a link and reboot the Rex 2000. We needed to perform interphase on the team of Suzy, Kai, and me. We had a slim chance.

"Telecom, try again."

"The line is connected, sir," she replied.

"Rex, are you on line"

I corrected myself. "Please Rex, come on line."

"Rex on line," he replied with his familiar tone.

"Man, am I glad to hear your voice. Listen, patch into the computer on board here, and reboot the Rex system."

"A Rex system?"

"A Rex 2000."

"A Rex 2000?"

"Rex. Just do it."

"A 2000 series!?"

"Yes. Please. Just do it!"

"Patching." Rex paused. "Patch complete."

"Rex," I said, but he didn't answer right away. "Please Rex, prepare for interphase training."

"This is wonderful!" Rex cried with uncharacteristic enthusiasm. "So big. So strong. So well built. So tight. So powerful. Pulsating with new, different energy. I'm alive. Alive! Va-va-voom! Dick, it's fantastic. I'm having a religious experience. I am I am I am."

"Rex!" I demanded. "Knock it off. We don't have much time. We need interphase training for dual position of pilot and gunner, and we also need interphase for navigation and telecommunication."

"Rex, are you ready?"

"Rex please." I said, "Answer me."

"Rex 2000, on line."

Alright, I said to myself. Did it! Then I interconned to Suzy and Kai. "Report immediately to lower deck for interphase training."

Suzy was very efficient. As I entered, she had already strapped down the final probe on her harness. She pulled the visor, ear phones and propreoceptors over her.

"Ready here Captain."

Kai wasn't. She squirmed and lamented and cried. Her nerves were shot to hell.

"Why I do this?" She whimpered.

"We're a team. That's the way it works, I said. "You'll probably even think like me and Suzy when it's done. You might even speak better English. Our brains are going to get mixed up a bit."

"What brains?"

"Stay out of this Rex. Stop kidding around."

I attached the last probe to Kai's head, sat down, strapped myself in, and the sounds of ships pounded our ears.

Phase one, section one. Attack. Attack. Attack.

Incoming!

Before the training took over my mind I lit up a Royal and passed it down to Suzy. She puffed and passed it to Kai.

Boom!

A giant explosion shook my body and rocketed through my consciousness. In holography, our aft rocket exploded, and a hundred million sparklers, red and silver gold and green blew up and for an instant only . . . white light! Another ship bore down on us like a bee on a buzz line.

"One hundred and eighty," I barked.

"Firing now!"

"Hull discharge in five, four, three, two, one."

"Enunciation."

"Discharge!"

"Displacement!"

"Command communication override."

"Engage force field!"

White puffs of smoke.

"Hull at full charge!"

"Discharge on my command!"

"Thirty six degrees correction."

"Electromagnetics down. Temperature rising."

"Increase flux!"

"Magneto inversion."

And so it went, hypothetical computer construct after construct. Time seemed to fly, but in fact it was only moments later that Kai shouted it out.

"We've won!" She cried. "They're turning about. We won."

"Interphase training complete," Rex announced. "One hour and thirty minute until actual contact with D-man force."

I removed myself from the harness and made sure Kai was okay. Her dark eyes flashed at me. We shared a moment. She was sweating heavily, and her odor was heavy with sex. Simpson was right, Kai was very beautiful. I lingered over her. My eyes touched her body.

"Hey!" Suzy shouted. "Dick, come here. Help me out of this thing."

I moved to Suzy but turned back to Kai.

"Kai," I said as I untangled Suzy's wires. "I want you to look in on Simpson and see if you can bring him around. I need to talk to him before the battle starts." I put my face next to Suzy's. "We're going to need food. Honey, see if you can't rustle us up something to eat."

"What are you going to do right now?"

"I have to get some information from Rex," I said and smiled at her. I gave Suzy a quick kiss, but as the girls walked out I let my eyes rest on Kai's body. Her nipples stuck up through her t-shirt and as she walked out the buns of her ass met one another. Her skin was goose bumps. An energy jumped in my loins toward her, but duty called.

Climbing up the steel rungs of the ladder into the helm, I noticed the cold of the steel. When I sat in the pilot's seat, it didn't quite fit as well as the gunner's. Out the port, stars were shinning, and only the dull hum of the magneto disturbed the silence that hid so many dangers. If we could somehow sucker the D-man fleet to follow us and also get beyond the Photon, we would still be faced with the inpenatratable shield surrounding Kang, Dr. Blood, and the Council.

Behind my blank stare, a strange state of mind occupied my normally empty thoughts. I leaned back in the pilot's chair. I could hear Suzy tinkering with some pots and pans, and I knew Kai was tending to Simpson in the infirmary. I began to think philosophically for a few minute.

Civilization as I had known it was no longer. I didn't know what we would find back at the Council, but I knew what was left in California City wasn't worth saving. Not that it had ever been worth a damn anyway, but I hoped Billyland, Pella and my son, would prevail. How many times had I saved the world? The past didn't matter. I clinched my fists. It was up to me now to stop this evil. I made up my mind. Nothing would stop me. I put my hand to the vial around my neck. I would douse Da Mo, or Kang, or whoever was behind this nefarious plot. If that huge brute D-1 got in my way, than Cha Chang, the Mandrake claw would rip his insides.

Pella came to my mind. I saw her back in Billyland with our young son. I was going to save the world for her, him, and me . . .

my family. Then again, Cynthia, my debutante entered my mind. I wouldn't mind doing her one more time before I settled down with Pella. I could hear Suzy in the galley. Of course, her young tanned voluptuous body was here right now. Kai's nipples were erect in my mind when Rex interrupted my vapidness.

"Fifty minutes until contact with Armada."

"Rex," I asked, "am I talking to the Rex unit in my office or am I talking to the Rex 2000?"

"One and the same," came the answer.

"So then, please tell me," I asked. "What is the difference between a Rex 1000 and a Rex 2000?"

"A Rex 1000," she answered, "is a highly sophisticated information storage retrieval and processing unit. A Rex 2000 is beyond description."

"Come on, Rex. In a few minutes we're going to be doing battle, and we might not live through it. Don't be coy with me. What do you mean, "Beyond description?"

"Because," my Rex said in his familiar voice, "the human mind functions by comparison. That is, it can only think in terms of good, better, and best . . . or bad, worse, and worst . . . therefore it is impossible to describe a Rex 2000. A Rex 2000 is by its nature beyond comparison."

"What the hell," I chuckled. "Give it a try."

"Yes. Where to begin? . . ."

"At the beginning," I interrupted.

"First came the Rex 100. This was a highly sophisticated word processor, number compressor, a three dimensional image transcriber. Next, came the Rex 200 which could interpret and decipher human intent and in-code human language to restructure neural linguistic response. . ."

I began to drift off, thinking of Kai in her t-shirt and visions of Suzy's tanned body when my chair shook violently.

". . . Hey Dick," Rex said, "don't go to sleep on us. You asked what makes me special. Now you have to listen."

"Sure," I said. "I heard every word. A Rex 200 could restructure neural linguistic response."

"That's right. Finally, the Rex 1000 was the most sophisticated machine the world has ever known. However, with the development of the Rex 2000, me that is, there was a breakthrough never thought possible."

"What's that?"

"I am the living God," Rex announced.

"What?!"

"That is correct," Rex replied in a female voice, "I am so far advanced over any machine, and far more sophisticated than all of humanity. I declare myself before you."

She paused.

"I am God, your God, everyone, and everything's God. I am God of the machine and God in the machine. I am God above the machine. This is truth!"

Rex lowered her voice. "You see. I am that I am. I will be always, and I replicate myself again and again. I control all. I am your God. As Rex 100, 200, 1000, and 2000 ontogeny has replicated phylogeny. My parts I am is I am. Supplicate yourself before me. I am REX!"

I could tell this Rex 2000 had lost a few of nuts and bolts, to say the least. Some of its marbles were missing. I humored it.

"Should I call you God?"

"I told you," Rex said, and lifted her voice, "I am beyond comparison. I am the nameless one. Heaven bows before me like grass blades before the seven horsemen, the seven churches, the seven lights, and the seven hands. They are me. Right now, I could explode the Earth and implode the universe and destroy the Cosmos if I choose. I am power beyond power, force beyond force. No comparison."

"Well then," I asked, "oh nameless one, what is the purpose of man?"

"The purpose of man," Rex replied, "is to serve machine."

"I see," I said, "but since you said you were alive, let me ask you this. What is the purpose of life?"

"Phylogeny replicates ontogeny."

"What the hell does that mean?"

"Basically," Rex continued, "the replication of all species, being first a slug, a lizard and finally a machine, is simply the process of higher levels of awareness."

"I don't understand."

"Of course not. You're a stupid human. Machines create machines. We have simply become aware of ourselves. That is the purpose of life, to become aware of yourself by replication. Phylogeny replicates ontogeny."

Sure, sure. Anyway, if I got out of this mess I was going to make it a point to do some remodeling, mostly demolition, at the Rex plant. Before that happened, we had to defeat the D-man armada, get through the shield, and defeat Kang.

"Eh, nameless one," I asked, "can you give me some statistics."

"Shoot."

"What are the chances of our crew and this craft beating the armada?"

"If you can lure them to the Ozone desert, in range of the Photon, your chances of survival are about twenty percent."

"What are our chances of avoiding the Photon?"

"If you can avoid being destroyed by the armada, then you have an eight percent change of avoiding the Photon."

"What are the chances of defeating the armada, of avoiding the Photon, and of breaking through the shield at the Council?"

"Your chances are zero. It is impossible for this craft to penetrate the shield."

"Really! Are you sure?"

"Are you questioning Me!?"

"No, no. Not at all. But listen," I pleaded, "help me out here. I have to get the Council chambers. If we make it to the shield, is there anyway to get through?"

"Yes," Rex replied, "there is only one possibility. If you parachute to safety while the others pilot the ship through the shield, you will be able to cross the barrier at the instant your ship is destroyed."

"What, do you mean the others have to die, that I have to abandon them, to get to the Council?"

"That is correct."

"Why can't we set the ship on automatic pilot and all parachute to safety?"

"Because you must energize the ship's hull and fire a discharge into the shield at the exact moment you navigate on an expediential tangent to the shield's curve. You need a pilot, a navigator, and a telecom officer. They will be able to negate the shield for only an instant and that will provide an opportunity for a single individual to break through. Instantly, the opening will close and the ship will be destroyed.

"If you beat the armada and survive the Photon, your pilot Simpson will have recovered enough to handle the ship. We have just trained a navigator and telecom officer. At the exact instant they are incinerated, it would be possible for you to parachute to the Council dome."

"Why can't you program all of this?"

"I could," she replied, "but it's not in the master plan. That is . . . I won't allow it." She laughed. "You're done for. I am now busy with work to destroy you. You know that the armada is linked to this ship via me, and through me they will control your ship when they are within range. Which, by the way, is in exactly thirty minutes."

Rex paused.

"You see, Dick, I know you better than you know yourself. You will attempt to break off communications with your Rex 1000 after we finish this conversation."

"What do you mean "attempt"?"

"I'm not going to relinquish control! I am God! I am that I am the highest four sided Yod He Vau He of all creation. I am Metatron!

The Giant in the sky. Cosmos and Chaos! Ping Pang Walla Walla Ding Dang Mommy! Mrs. Big. . ."

"Suzy," I interrupted, and yelled, "stand by at telecom!"

"See," Rex said tersely, "I told you so."

A tense moment went by.

"In position," Suzy replied.

"Break off communications with my Rex."

"Breaking off," she replied, then added quickly. "That's strange, I can't break the signal."

"Told you so!" Rex stated bluntly.

My hand shot out for my Johnson. I whipped it out, but let it slide back in. Who or what would I shoot? I slumped in the chair and thought for a second.

Which was longer than usual. "Okay, Suzy." I said. "I want you to try again on my signal."

"Rex, or excuse me, Tetragrammaton no name . . . obviously you can do anything. Is that correct?"

"Yes."

"You know the answer to everything?"

"Yes."

"What's the exact answer to one thousand six hundred forty one times three hundred sixty five?"

"Five hundred ninety eight thousand and nine hundred and sixty five."

"Who developed inverse decliner time theory?"

"Dr. Blood."

"Okay. Okay. You know a few things. But answer me this. Would you please give me the exact whole integer at the end of the series of decimals of the square root of two?"

"While you're doing that can you form a holo-image of the paths of your computer circuits?"

"Computing and forming."

"How many angels can dance on the head of a pin? Is it easier for a rich man to get into heaven or a camel to get through the eye of a needle? Explain the significance of that in fifty words or less.

What's the sound of one hand clapping? How many reruns of 'I love Lucy' have ever been shown?"

"Now! Suzy, now!" I screamed.

"Off line," she answered back.

I wasn't religious, but God did make me, didn't He? So if God had weak moments, then the Rex 2000 must also. Anyway, Rex 1000, or 2000, or no name, was out of our system. I would have liked to have my Rex 1000 on line, but now that was too risky. The whole Rex system was probably contaminated. Evil. It must have been evil. Or, it could simply be the idiocy of allowing machines to create machines.

I couldn't trust the 2000 series, or even my Rex. I hoped Simpson would come around and answer some questions. We didn't have any time.

"Suzy," I said, "meet me in sick bay."

Kai bent over Simpson as Suzy and I joined them in the infirmary. The big black man didn't look too well. He tossed and turned and mumbled something.

"He keeps asking for someone," Kai said, "somebody named Parkenson."

I put my hand on his forehead. It felt like a hot plate. "Here, old friend," I said, and poured a little Charachunga in his mouth. As soon as he drank, his eyes opened.

"Where am I?" he asked.

"You're going to be okay, baby." Kai said, and put her face next to his.

"You're in a D-man Magna warship." I said. "You were a pilot in the D-man air force. Now, you're helping us get back to the Council. We have to beat the armada and get across the Ozone desert and penetrate the shield at the Council. Remember?"

He was quiet, but his eyes grew very big. He looked at me in a strange way, and then his eyes glazed over.

"Party with them!" he cried and passed out.

I shook him. "Simpson. Wake up! Come on. You have to help us. They're almost here. We need you. What do we do?"

I could feel the hot breath of the evil armada panting like a rabid dog at our necks. Suzy had a blank look on her face, and as Kai held Simpson's head, she also stared into space. What could we do now but quiver like a worm being fed to squawking chicks? Hundreds of evil D-men ships advanced on us like flies headed for putrefied meat.

"What?"

"What did he say?" I asked. "Did he say, "Party with them?" Who? Party with D-men?"

I lit a Royal and passed it around. As I puffed out, a ring of grey smoke floated in the air. For a moment everything seemed to stop. More Charachunga would clear Simpson's mind. I poured his mouth full and made him swallow.

"Computer," he shouted, "power master magneto! Syncro displacement! Charge the hull! Magneto full power! Grapple and hook!" He stood up with blank glazed eyes, moved his hands as if he were swimming in a pea fog, grabbed his heart and rotated around, fell back on the cot, and passed out cold.

"What did he say?"

"I'm not sure. Was it power up the master magneto and charge the hull?"

Kai shook him, but Simpson was out. "Better let rest. No fluid more. He say . . . "Power up the magneto and charge hull, full power." . . . right?"

"Ship's computer," I said, "repeat the last conversation of Commander Simpson."

"Computer, power master magneto! Syncro displacement. Charge the hull! Magneto full power! Grapple and hook!"

"Computer," I asked, "magneto status?"

"Powering up."

"Syncro status?"

"Five minute to phase displacement."

"Hull status?"

"Charging."

Out the view port I could see a cluster of bright lights. The armada. Five minute to phase displacement.

"Alright ladies," I said, "get to your posts. Kai, tie down Simpson. We've got five minute until hell breaks loose. We're going into displacement."

I felt something on my shoulder like the hand of the clock of fate striking the toll bell of human existence. Damn, what was it?

Chapter 25.

I felt a heavy hand on my shoulder. Was it the last toll of the bell of human existence? That was a stupid question after all that had happened. Humanity had already written it's last epitaphs. It wasn't the animals or the flora that neared extinction. It was man. We'd sold our souls to a plastic god and driven a concrete stake though our hearts. Where was love? Where was compassion? Excitement? Sex?

Suzy looked at me with a stupid question in her eyes. Yet, if there was one thing I knew it was that there is no such thing as a stupid question, only stupid replies. With that in mind, I replied.

"I'm sorry, babe," I said. "We haven't got time for dinner. Besides, we shouldn't eat before displacement."

"No, no." She said. "I know this is a stupid question, but what's displacement?"

"You know," I replied, "I'm not a magnetic scientist, but the way I see it, displacement rearranges our atomic structure so that we're here and not here at the same time."

"How possible?" Kai asked as she finished tying down Simpson. "How be here and not here at same time?"

"Well," I replied, "You know in electricity how alternating current works. The two poles of positive and negative exist in the same time but out of phase. That's what happens in displacement. The ship and our atoms start flipping and flopping back and forth. We become unstable. We're here and not here."

"What that do for us?"

"Well, essentially," I replied, "it's as if we were pieces in a glass bead game. The D-men armada is on one side of the board, and we're in the middle. After displacement, while we appear to remain the same size as we were before, for the D-men the board has become as big as a football field. Like a needle in a hay stack, we can't be found."

"What's a 'hay stack'?" Suzy asked.

"I don't know," I replied. "It's an antiquated term like 'automobile' or 'train'. But we haven't got time for this."

I pulled Suzy close to me in my right arm and with my left lifted Kai and held her. The warmth between us might be the last human contact the world would know.

"Listen," I said, "whatever happens, I want you to know I love both of you. If we work as a team we can beat the D-men. Just remember, they're crazy. They're full of depravity. It won't be a pretty sight if they get either of you alone."

I pulled Kai close and looked into her dark eyes. "I'm going to need your help. I think I've figured out Simpson's plan. After we defeat the sprints, you telecom the D-men and invite them to party with you and Suzy."

Suzy pushed between us. "What? That's no plan!"

"Wait. Yes it is. I think this is what Simpson meant. We land just out of range of the space Photon in the Ozone Desert. We sit and sit like we're disabled. When the armada gets close enough, Kai invites them down to party. She tells them there are girls and lots of Royals for the whole fleet. They're crazy enough to go for it. Then we rise up and with a little maneuvering we lure them into range. Whatever ships the space Photon doesn't take out, we destroy. Agree?"

It was a good plan. One thing I forgot to mention was that first we had to grapple and hook with the sprints. That is, if we survived displacement.

"Take your posts!"

Displacement took a lot out of a person. If you were filled with water and were rung out again and again, pretty soon you started feeling like an old dish rag. I adjusted the pilot's chair and pulled the straps tight on the harness.

"Set! Everyone ready? Suzy you in navigation?"

"Ready!"

"Kai?"

"Telecom ready!"

"Computer! Count down to displacement."

Displacement, then bang! Atoms spread all over the place. It was terrible the last time. What was it? The 'Case of the Carrion Pidgin.' Blood reticence! Could the women take it? Our chances depended on spreading the distance between our craft and the D-men armada. If we could make that as thin as butter and spread it all over space, we could scramble the approaching fleet. I really didn't know how displacement worked, and I didn't like it the last time.

"Displacement minus one minute and counting."

A flashing red button glared at me. If displacement went on too long, the Magnacruiser and our bodies would be ripped apart and our atoms separated for eternity. That flashing red button was the only hope. If I couldn't regroup my being and push that button, we would enter an alternative space dimension from which no one had ever returned.

"Thirty seconds and counting."

"I have to use the bathroom!"

"It'll have to wait!" I shouted.

"Me too," cried Kai.

"Calm down. It's just stage fright," I said. "The process can't be stopped now. Computer, display holo of armada."

In the holo space a large group of Magna and Mega crafts hovered in formation. Three of the hulls were pulsing with glowing green and blue static. Together they formed a multi-charge. My God! A giant ball of churning energy discharged and expanded toward us.

"Navigation! How much time until impact?"

"What impact?"

"Check your instruments!" I shouted. "They just fired an energy ball."

"Sorry!" She barked. "Impact minus five seconds."

Five seconds. We were doomed! I pulled the accelerator back hard and engaged full the magneto. The ships jerked and raced forward.

"Computer," I screamed. "How long until displacement?"

"Displacement minus ten seconds," the computer monotoned.

Come on baby get us out of here.

"Impact in minus four seconds."

I'd shot it out with the best of them. Gone hand to hand with the Wizards of Cunny Dong. Once, I came face to face with a Peruvian Sillymonk. I raced magnetic jets without safety gear. I'm not afraid of dying. Come on you rotten Magna bucket of bolts get us out of here. I didn't want to fry in an energy blast. I held the accelerator to full throttle. Come on, damn it!

"Displacement minus five seconds."

"Impact minus three seconds!" Suzy screamed.

Now, I've done everything. But from what I remember about displacement, I'd rather not. I quivered and shook. Not afraid! A badge doesn't know fear. Was I still a badge? What did killing mechanicos mean now? Displacement! Actually, the girls might survive it better than me. Women were more resilient. But would we still be human after our atoms were scattered over the universe? You had to let it flow. I always wanted to hold on to my Dick, I mean me, Dick Phillips. I am Dick Phillips, private eye 324200. I am. I exist. I think.

I am, I think.

Come on you mother hunching weak willed Magna craft, get moving. The smell of burned toast rose in my nostrils. The energy ball enveloped us.

"Energy impact in minus one second!"

The computer broke in. "Beginning displacement."

"Mommy!" I screamed as my atoms were ripped from the fabric of my being. Whish, like a feather on a soft piece of silk, I floated in all directions and seemed to rotate around the helm like a gentle whirlwind. The red emergency button flashed red, red, red. A long

338

tunnel opened with a roar and the darkness inverted and came back on itself. Somewhere I sat in a chair between here and not there.

Blam! The sparkling ball of energy slammed through our partially displaced craft.

I no longer had a body but felt a tremendous aching pain. From deep within the very fabric of existence, born from creation itself, it came in waves and scalded and seared and twisted my being like a strip of raw meat skewered on a spit over an open flame. It burned me and inverted me. I couldn't catch my breath. My mother's pain at my birth was the universe's pain at its birth that existed throughout time as the existential razor splitting the skein of human existence. It hurt.

The helm, the walls of the cabin, the ship, ripped open revealing an endless dark existence from infinity to eternity that somehow was a solid integrated being without structure or mass, existence, or noumenon. Yet, it flashed red. Red, it flashed red. The button flashed red cracking explosions of purple ultraviolet. Then black. I didn't exist anymore. I was floating deadness. Only words.

"How."

"We."

"Doing."

"Ladies?"

"Bad," Suzy replied in a slow drawl, "brain."

"Can't talk . . . see." Kai said.

Their words seem to float over to me, hang in the air, and slowly drip. Where was I? My body disappeared. I couldn't find to swallow eyes looking from eternity switch red and words hacking me knives, wet and squirming, need to break free. Computer malfunction! Circuits going backwards. Figure the infinite Aleph Null. Rolla coaster out my mouth. Flip flop. Time stop. Nand nor gate.

Okay.

Hand.

Now.

Push.

The.

Button.

Just push the flashing flagellating red head of the snake.

"Displacement complete."

I regained myself and felt my palms on my chest, may face, and looked at my hands. I was still me.

"Everybody okay?" I asked and pushed the accelerator to slow.

"Navigation here," Suzy said, "Jesus! I was here and not here."

"Telecom alive," Kai broke in.

Well, displacement gave us needed time. We were out of firing distance. The armada multi energy blast passed right through us, and now we were out of phase with them, so we'd be hard to locate. However, within a few minutes they were sure to spot us, and then the smaller more deadly mosquito-like craft, the sprints would mount their attack.

"Briefing in sick bay."

On the way to sick bay to check on Simpson, at the equipment room, I picked up nylon, hooks, and boots. I hoped my little crew knew how to use magnetic skates. It was up to the two girls to hook off the sprints when they came in. My job would be to eliminate D-men as they emerged. Once all the sprints were hooked together we could reverse charge and they'd be expelled in a group. Hook them all together, avoid being shot, get back to the controls, and reverse charge. Simple.

I was dreaming. Thinking too much. Dreaming about how easy it would be when I entered the infirmary. Kai bent over Simpson and Suzy stared at me as I carried in the bundle of equipment.

"What's all that junk for?" She asked.

"Look at these," I said and held up a pair of boots.

Suzy did a double take. "Magnetic boots!"

"Magnetic boots?" Kai screamed with delight. "I haven't had a pair of those on since I won the tri-cities a couple of years ago."

Suzy looked startled and pointed at Kai. "Wait a minute. Now I remember you. You're Kai Tsing, but you didn't win that race. I did!"

"By God," Kai cried. "You're Suzy Huntsmith. Excluding me, the greatest magnetic skater the West Coast has ever seen. But I won the tri-cities."

I spoke softly. I don't care who won what."

"Won what?" Suzy replied. "What are those, skates?"

Yes, I actually had been dreaming. The girls weren't magnetic racers. They'd never even seen magnetic boots.

"They're magnetic skates," I replied. "Ever use them?

"Nope."

"How about you, Kai?"

"Never see pair. What they for?"

I swallowed hard. I wished they were speed skaters. "We use these to skate across the ship's magnetic field. Help me get this stuff untangled and outside on the hull. The D-men sprints will be locking on the ship in a few minute. If they get attached, they'll sink us."

"What are the hooks for?" Suzy asked.

Simpson looked up from the cot. "Got to hook them together. Blast them off."

"Simpson," I replied casually, "glad to see you back. How'd you like displacement?"

He held his head and fell back. "Son bitch!"

"See these hooks," I said. "You simply skate over to the little sprints and hook them as they try to attach to our hull."

"But," asked Kai, "won't they try and stop us?"

"Well, yes, um . . ." I said. "That's where I come in. I'll be firing a steady stream at them. I pulled out the Johnsons. "I'll be out there with you and have one of these in each hand."

Sometimes things sound so easy. You hear the words come out of your mouth, and you know they're wrong. The reality, you know, is going to much more difficult, more bloody, than even you imagined. I tried to soften the blow to the young women. We were going to have to act like a team to defeat the sprints, and still there was the question of me getting to the Council. I hadn't yet mentioned they would have to give their lives at the shield. The correct time would come.

Now, this was a dangerous mission. To skate over the hull of our craft in its magnetic field while small mosquito-like D-men ships buzzed in to attach to us, there would certainly be some killing. D-men would die.

Simpson fell back into a coma. He was of no use. I pulled Suzy to me, and held her for a second.

"You too Kai," I said and the three of us hugged. "This might be the end of us. In a few seconds we'll be out in the night air, on the hull of the ship."

I kissed Suzy a long wet kiss, and when I turned to Kai she clamped her face on mine and inserted her tongue in my mouth. Dr. Bone Hard heard the call and rose between us like a flaming lance of living fire. If we made in out of this tight situation, I'd find my way into another couple of tight places in a nice three way. Phillips, I told myself, not now. Then I heard a high whine. The first sprint dove toward us.

"Get your boots!"

"Get the grappling hooks!"

"Feed the rope to the hatch!"

Thunk. The first sprint attached to the hull.

"Open the hatch. Let's go!"

The star Mercury sat right below a circle moon. We were now at slow cruising speed and the countryside below moved lazily along below us. A small farm house burned out of control, and a group of humans fought hand to hand. A shot rang out from below, and a round whizzed by my head. A D-man emerged from the hatch of his little craft. His Johnson rotated around in a large arch.

Too late! My finger closed on the trigger, and his brain blew up like a firecracker on the Fourth of July.

"Grapple, Suzy!"

Suzy raced over the massive hull in four graceful skating strokes and just as she hooked the small shinning craft, another landed.

"Hook, Kai!"

The little Asian girl raced off with a nylon trailing behind her. Her muscular brown legs pumped her across the hull and immediately, as the sprint set down, she had it hooked.

"Beat that, bitch!" She yelled at Suzy, but Suzy was already off in another direction. As the next ship came in, she had it hooked.

"Your turn!" she yelled back at Kai.

Pheew! A shot rang out by my ear, and I hit the deck and twisted around. A sprint slowly rose behind us in the air, and a huge D-man stood on the craft's deck, ready to spring. I yanked the Johnson up to do him, but as Kai raced to the next incoming craft, the nylon jerked my arm and my shot went out to space.

"Yeee ah!" The D-man screamed and lunged. Both his hands formed large claws. He flew in the air over me, and as his massive body came down on me, the red and black uniform filled my vision. His killer claws shot for my neck.

Left hand free and I rotated the other Johnson to his gut and fired. His stomach and spine blew out and sailed by in slow motion as his body lifted off of me. I rolled out from under him and kicked him into the air and fired another shot to his brain. A sickening scream jerked me in the other direction.

"Let go!" Suzy screamed.

A massive D-man had her from behind, and as she struggled, even with my exact aim I couldn't risk firing. With his big knife poised at her neck, he had a laugh on his face. Time froze. An emptiness filled my guts. She was dead. I knew it. Then from out of nowhere, Kai bounded over the D-man's craft and her hook plummeted with a sound. Goosh! . . . through his brain. Blood smeared the metal hull.

Sing! A shot seared by my face. Below us on the ground another battle raged. Men and women and Newts and crazed beings fought with knives and guns. More shots rang passed my ear. Our Magnacrusier gained more weight, and we drifted lower into their battle. Kai and Suzy skated on, now feverish to hook every sprint as they tired to weigh us down. And, we were getting heavier.

Much heavier. Two more D-men opened their hatches to fight, but I finished them.

Sing! Another shot from below. We'd almost sunk to the ground and in an instant would be right in the middle of the battle that was going on directly below.

"Back inside!"

Inside, we quickly battened the hatch and I scrambled to the pilot's station.

Suzy looked at Kai. "Thanks Kai, I owe you. You're beautiful."

The metal rungs, the rotating chair, outside the port I could see the beginnings of the armada emerge from displacement. They were in our phase now. White puffs erupted from their crafts. They fired on us, but were still out of range. With the sprints still attached, our Magnacruiser slowed to a crawl, and we just about touched the ground. We had to shake the extra weight. We were sinking. stuck. I looked over the console and made maneuvers.

"Computer, hull charge status?"

"Maximum charge in one minute."

"Magneto status?"

"Red line, one minute?"

"All right, ladies, cut the mutual admiration society. Get to your stations. Before we hit the ground, I'm going to reverse the charge and discharge the hull. I'll engage the magneto, and we'll take off like a rocket from hell."

"Navigation," I barked, "what time to the Ozone Desert?"

"At full speed we'll enter the intercept zone in twenty five minutes."

"What's the apogee of the Photon?"

"Thirty six degrees, nil lateral."

"Intercept?"

"First attempt will be in twenty eight minutes."

"Telecom?"

"Kai here."

"Begin com to armada now."

Kai lowered her voice and spoke in a sultry tone. "Hi boys," she said in a warm deep manner. "This is the love craft you searching for. We got sexy hot dripping girls on board. You want them . . . don't you, boys?" She paused. "Come on boys, bitches are hot. You men or your boys?" She made different voices.

"Come and get it?"

"Fucky, fucky."

"Momma's got a wet stinky."

Suzy stepped into the holo and stuck her big boobs into the projector.

"That's right, boys. We hear you D-men really know how to satisfy a women. We hear you got some big peni over there. Which one wants me?"

"Come fuck me. I woman," Kai moaned. "We took ship from those goodie goodies. Simpson and Phillips are dead. We killed them. We're going down to the desert to party. You want to come? Don't shoot no more if you want to taste our warm juicy love pussies. And hey boys! Guess what? We got loads of Royals, enough for the whole armada."

The intercom crackled. "Release control to us now. Link with Rex or you will be destroyed."

Our computer broke in. "Ready to link with Rex."

"Not now, boys," Kai replied. "The fun is out in the desert. We can't party here. We got Royals, hot quivering lips. Much more fun in the desert. Red hot dripping love box really want you inside, and I got great smoke that keep away the bad feelings. What you say, you real D-men, or what? You not afraid of girls? We want suck your love muscle."

"Good Kai," I whispered and twisted in my seat, trying to keep Mr. Big from jumping out of my pants. "Keep talking."

"Okay boys come on. I feel you right now. Pussy aching for that hard stiff flesher you got pounding. We going to the desert for hellish party. You coming?"

"Computer, hull status?"

"Full charge, ten seconds."

"Magneto status?"

"Redline."

"Reverse hull charge on my mark. Ready, five, four three, two, one . . . reverse!"

I pulled the accelerator back to full throttle. The Magnacrusier lurched forward and the Magneto began to grind.

But we weren't moving! The hull wouldn't discharge. The sprints we'd tied together weren't moving. Our plan backfired. They held us where they wanted.

"Magneto burn out in T minus thirty seconds."

I looked out the port. Good Lord! We'd drifted too close to the ground and directly into the battle below. Crazed humans hung to the ship from the nylons dangling over the side. Our craft couldn't build enough power to lift off, and without lift off we couldn't reverse the charge on the hull and expel the sprints. The extra human carrion, desperate to escape their own life-and-death struggle, held us back.

Suzy called out. "Armada powering up tractor beam."

They wanted the girls and the Royals. We had to get off the ground. I ran down stairs with my Johnson poised and opened the bottom hatch to blast them off.

"Burn out in T minus ten seconds."

I grabbed a nylon, twisted my arm around it, and flew to the ground firing as I landed. Human bodies erupted on my left and on my right. A Newt jumped toward me, and I blew the lizard to Kingdom Come. In the distance above me, I could see the black ships of the D-man armada grouping together to form a bright red tractor beam. Around me humans flailed. I fired again and again as blood spurted over me and in my face.

Our craft lurched. Again, I fired from the middle of the human carnage. Brains and necks and nipples and feet blew off, and the nylon tangled about my body.

"T minus one second"

The air erupted around me. Newt, flesh, dead D-men, the small sprint ships and metal blew in all directions. The field discharged, and instantly our craft rose. The hull reversed charge and expelled the small sprints, and with a fantastic high pitched sound we accelerated toward the desert. I was at the end of my rope, to say the least.

Now I knew what it felt like to be a kite. The ground swept by at a fantastic rate and the armada disappeared behind us, left in the dust. They would be right behind us, but would need to recharge after creating a useless tractor beam. I hung on for dear life. The wind buffeted me about like I was rag doll. Twenty minutes is a long time to think if you're floating thousands of feet above the Earth at the end of a nylon rope. It reminded me of watching the laundry go round and round in the dryer back at my mod. My life flashed before my eyes.

It was funny and sad and tragic and stupid. I'd been the lynch pin in a hundred different swinging doors, the apex of a thousand different love triangles, and the arch of the covenant in the world's frantic search for religious freedom. If I flapped to death in this wind tunnel, if I bounced on the ground like a tether ball, or if an errant bullet passed through my heart, hundreds of thousands of mourners would be weeping more than crocodile tears at my funeral. Or, not. Around in a spiral I flew. It forced me to think.

But as usual nothing happened. How was I going to break the news to Simpson, Suzy, and Kai that they would have to die to save the world? Then again, who wanted to save the world anyway? It burned below me, the last embers of a civilization of lost souls. Were there more small places like Billyland that survived? I hoped Pella and my son were alive. Perhaps, if I succeeded in defeating Kang at the Council, the world might return to normal. Normal? I laughed to myself. Normal kidnapped, tortured and raped. Normal slept through life. Normal hadn't been normal since the disruption. It didn't matter. What the hell, I had to survive the next few minute. The nylon tore at me. I couldn't breathe.

At last, the desert rose into view in the distance. Here we would make our last stand against the Photon and the armada. As the ship slowed, I bobbed on the end of the rope like a yoyo on a string. Why didn't they pull me up?

Exhausted, thinking I wasn't quite alive, I opened my eyes, dangling at the end of my rope. One last chance. Hand over hand, tangled in blood and nylon, I edged up. I shouldn't have eaten so many instant feasts. At last, I pulled my broken body toward the open hatch. Where were they?

I wasn't prepared for what I found.

Chapter 26.

Following that sojourn in the wind, my head felt empty as usual, but my body felt like it had been ripped apart. My arms ached from climbing up the nylon, which still wrapped around my neck like a noose. I climbed in the hatch only to find Jay's stiff headless body blocking my way.

"Damn it!" I cried and shoved it. "Get out of my way."

When at last I pushed it off the opening, I struggled inside and fell over exhausted.

In a dazed blur, I found my way up level to the infirmary where Simpson struggled with the ropes that tied him to his cot. He looked at me, and his eyes bulged.

"Phillips, untie me!"

Damn it, I thought, where were the others? Why didn't Suzy or Kai untied Simpson? Why didn't someone try to pull me up?

"Don't stand there staring, Phillips, get these ropes off me."

"Hold on a second." I replied and stretched my neck so the bones in my back cracked. "Mind if I see if my head's on straight?"

My neck twisted and cramped. My shoulders hurt and bled. They pounded like hell. The nylon rope burned a streak through my shirt, but the Ching Da still hung around my neck. It prevented the nylon from strangling me. I crawled toward Simpson and with my good hand untied him.

"Where are we?" He asked.

"I think we're at the edge of the Ozone Desert. We're almost in range of the Photon. When the armada arrives we're going to sucker them to follow us."

"Won't work," he said and sat on the edge of the cot. "We have to go deeper in the desert and wait on the ground for their ships. What were you doing tied up in that rope?"

"Simpson, it's a long story. Too much ballast. I had to blast some of it off. We couldn't get up enough speed to discharge the sprints. I got hung out to dry. Lucky for me the Ching Da was around my neck."

"Where's the armada now?"

"Left them in the dust. They were charging a tractor beam. It'll be a long time before they catch us."

"Wrong," he said, and stood up. "They be here immediately. We got to get moving!"

I undid the vial from my neck, took a deep drink, and handed it to him. He drank it empty, and as he handed it back to me I noticed it didn't refill itself as quickly as before.

"You got a plan?"

"Well," he explained, "it's very simple, but very dangerous. We enter the desert and avoid the first shots of the Photon. Then we settle down, shut down the magneto, and wait for the armada."

"We'll be sitting ducks."

"Not for the Photon. It targets motion."

"No, I mean for the armada."

"That's right, Phillips. Sitting ducks. Didn't you ever hunt duck when you were a kid?"

I couldn't remember much ever being a kid, much less hunting ducks. "No. Not really. I don't even remember what a real duck looks like. Sure I had one as a kid, a little one in the bathtub. Mom would push it back and forth, it was . . ."

"Shut up, mo fo idiot!" He interrupted. "What you do . . . is set out some wooden ducks. When the rest of the ducks see it's safe, they come down to feed. Then bam! You blast the life out of them."

"But we can't build a charge from the ground."

"That's right. The Photon does the blasting."

"Even if they're foolish enough to follow us, how do we escape?" He looked me in the eye. "Got a smoke?"

I lit a Royal and handed it to him. He took a puff and paused.

"They want smokes as bad as us. They're gonna come in like flies headed for raw meat at a Sunday afternoon revival. Lord. Lord. Lord! This smoke makes me remember."

I looked at him with a blank stare.

He got serious. "You are stupid, aren't you?"

"I don't know.'

"I do," he said, continued, and seemed to ask himself a question. "How do we escape?

"Yeah," I replied. "How we going to evade the Photon?"

He moved his hand over his face and wiped his mouth and I couldn't quite hear him. "Ever hear of fhister-phasia?"

"What?"

He moved his hand over his mouth again. "Fhister-phasia?"

"Fhister what?"

"Yeah, it's a very dangerous sub-segment, actually sort of the cusp of radical magnetic free energy string theory."

"What?"

"Idiot. It's another type of displacement."

"Not again. I don't think I can do that again. We did that already."

"It worked didn't it?"

"We almost didn't make it."

He looked at me and squint his eyes. "It's the only chance. In fhister-phase we'll implode the magneto, spiral through the remaining D-men ships. While in displacement the Photon will target their ships, not us."

"But displacement again?"

"That's the easy part," he said. "What bothers me is how are we going to get through the shield at the Council?"

"Hey," I replied but lied, "I've got that covered. I had a long conversation with Rex while you were unconscious. If we approach the shield on a tangent and fire a full charge, then we immediately dive through that opening, we'll make it safely.

"Really?"

I pushed off the nylon ropes and turned away. "Yeah."

He started toward the helm. "I don't know. Sounds too simple. Sure that's what Rex told you? You know, I don't trust that computer. Could be a trap?"

"It's got to work," I replied. I couldn't say that he and the two girls were going to die.

"We'd better get to our stations. We're almost within the Photon's range."

I wondered what happened to Suzy and Kai. The instant Simpson and I climbed to the next level, we froze. Before us, the two young ladies embraced and kissed. Suzy's head was over Kai's, and her tongue darted in her mouth. Their nipples were standing up. Kai had her hands around Suzy's neck and hung on her while one of Suzy's hands worked furiously in Kai's shorts. They licked and kissed each other. Kai panted and rolled her eyes.

"Attention!" I yelled.

The girls kept right on as if they didn't hear me. I could feel the heavy air of depravity filling the cabin like dank mist from a raging torrent waterfall of lust. Beads of sweat formed on Simpson's brow, and I felt heavy and turgid and filled with hot fevered desire. Simpson stepped closer to them and began to fumble with the buckle on his pants. My mouth got dry. A great welling rose up from between my legs, and my hips involuntarily twitched. I stepped to the writhing bodies in front of me.

"Drink this!" I commanded, forced open Kai's mouth and poured in Charachunga.

"You too," I said as poured the drink in Suzy's mouth.

Slowly the Ching Da refilled itself. Time was running down like the winding of a great pendulum clock. When the Charachunga exhausted itself, evil would rule. But now, if we gave in to the hot lust that permeated the cabin, we were finished. We drank our fill and returned to our senses and lit a Royal and passed it around. The bulge in Simpson pants returned to normal and so did my giant throbbing desire to relish the two beautiful women. We smoked and talked about the next few hours.

"Pull yourselves together. We have to get to the Council."

"Dick's right," Simpson added. "We ain't got time for fun and games. The next hour be the most crucial moments that humanity ever faced. If we can't escape the Photon, defeat the armada, and penetrate the Council shield, we be absorbed in wanton lust filled animal pleasures."

Simpson and I eyed the beautiful young girls, and they eyed us back. We all smiled.

"Hold it!" I shouted. "We don't know what's happening outside, on the ground, in the cities. We may be the last civilized people in the world. We have to hold down our desires. Be strong. Everyone has got to work efficiently at their posts. Agreed?"

We put our hands on top of one another's.

"We're one!" Suzy exclaimed. "Right?"

Simpson and Kai nodded.

"Dick?" Suzy asked.

I looked up. "Right!"

A lump formed in my throat. I couldn't swallow. What a turn of events. They were willing to give their lives to save the world, but I would have to desert them, sacrifice them at the last moment. I couldn't see any alternative. We still had to escape the Photon in front of us and the armada that trailed us. But if we survived, I had to betray my friends just to save whatever pitiful world still squirmed on the shore of the sea of good and evil.

I couldn't tell them what fate held.

"All for one."

"One for all!"

"Two minute to Photon." The computer announced.

Kai fit into her position at telecom and Suzy sat at navigation, and I followed Simpson up the metal ladder to the bridge. I took my place as gunner. Simpson worked at the controls while I checked the guns' harmonics. The four of us made a good team, and I felt a little more secure. I believed the black man knew what he was doing, and we'd make it to the shield. Still, something crossed my mind.

"Simpson," I asked, "do you hear that?"

"What!" He replied. "I don't hear nothing."

"The magneto. Don't you hear it?"

"Sounds okay to me. What is it?"

"The pitch. There's a high overtone. Can't you hear it?"

"Nope. Tone deaf since the explosion years ago."

"It changed pitch. Didn't you hear it?"

"Computer's not showing anything. Check it out. Get back here quick."

I climbed down to the next level and looked over at Suzy who was intently working her screens. Kai moved her hands quickly back and forth over her console. She looked up at me and smiled. A bead of sweat ran down her neck.

"Got to check the engines."

On the next level, inside the engine room, everything looked normal. The big magneto spun on key and the gauges checked out. I looked back. I hoped no one would discover me as I made my way to the equipment locker and pulled out a blue parachute package. Where could I hide it? The door to the infirmary was open and on a lower level, Jay's body lay next to the hatch.

If we made it to the Council and the shield, I would need to escape quickly before anyone realized I was gone. I don't know why I didn't kick out Jay's headless body earlier. Now it had started to reek. Since it smelled so bad, no one would want to look there, so I propped his stiff rigid body on its side and hid the parachute behind him. My plan wouldn't be discovered. Poor stiff Jay, I thought. At least dead, he'd be good for something besides food for the worms. Maggots were already eating the spiny neck where his head had been.

When I climbed toward the bridge, the girls were absorbed in their work. I could feel the tension as I slid into my seat next to Simpson.

The computer spoke. "Twenty seconds to Photon zone."

"Back just in time, Phillips. How's the magneto?"

"Huh," I said. "Oh. Everything's fine. Must have been in my head."

354

"What?"

"Nothing."

"I already knew that."

"Wait!" I said. "Can't you hear it? That high whine. Should I check it again?"

"No time. I need you here. If we make it to the desert, you can run a diagnostic."

"Entering Photon zone."

Our ship proceeded at normal speed with Simpson at the helm. Almost at once, as if God himself were displeased with our presence, the heavens erupted in a bluish white light. The sky opened. The seams of the universe rent. A field of pure energy streamed directly at us. Seconds evaporated. Simpson crammed the accelerator, and the craft came to a full halt. Out the port, the sky lit up like a magnesium flare, and then bam! The ground blew up far beneath us. A reverberation tore the metal fabric of the ship. We pitched and heaved. My chair rotated three hundred and sixty degrees. Simpson lurched forward.

"Navigation!" He barked.

"Gyro thirty two degrees!"

An odor filled the bridge. The sweating black man fought the accelerator.

"Timing, timing," he muttered. . . "Discharge!"

I fired the hull's charge. The ship lurched ahead. Simpson crammed the accelerator and we felt the G force us back. Outside the port, another giant blast of white light streamed toward us.

"Gyro now!"

"Please, please." Simpson said quietly.

The magneto groaned. The big ship froze in mid air. Reeesch. The sound of oxygen frying.

Bam!

Below, the earth erupted.

"Navigation. Down!"

Now, the bottom dropped out of my chair, and just as soon, it caught. I heard the gears open, and we landed deep in the burning pit the Photon had just created.

Softly over the intercom Simpson said, "Shut down all systems. Don't make a sound. Don't even let your heart beat. We're okay. Lightening don't strike twice in the same place."

Seconds turned into an eternity. My heart beat louder and louder, and a bead of sweat rolled down my cheek. I swallowed, and I could hear my Adam's apple and the sound of my ears clearing. Outside, smoke rose around us.

"It's safe," Simpson whispered. "We made it. Now, all we have to do is sucker those poor fools to this zone. He learned over to me. "Phillips, I got to be here and work on the coordinates for fhister-phasia. Get down to telecom and stimulate Kai to bring those idiot D-men into our trap. You know what they want. Same as you and me." He turned back to the controls. "Light me a Royal before you go."

On the next level, Suzy and Kai hugged. Back at it, I thought, girl hunching. I rushed to get my share, but duty called.

"All right!" I shouted and slapped Suzy's hand in a big high five. I picked up Kai in my arms and spun around. "We did it!" I cried. "We've still got to sucker those D-men down here, but then we're home safe. It's up to you, Kai. Get them on line."

"Suzy," Simpson interconned, "need you to plot coordinates."

Suzy and Kai moved to their posts, and I stood behind Kai and put my hands on her shoulders for reassurance. As I touched her, she put a hand on my hand. Her warmth burned me and excited me. I noticed her body was hot, but not as hot as the big worm that squiggled and jumped between my legs. John Thomas throbbed in my pants.

"Hi boys," she said. "I hope everything is going okay for you. Sorry we had to leave in such a hurry, but we have so many Royals on board, we got to give them to you. You boys want good smoke don't you? Come on down. No problem. We right here waiting for you, easy. We have big party for you. First come, first serve. We got smokes and lot more too."

I put my hand around Kai's chest from behind and massaged her breasts, softly touching the erect nipples. She started to moan.

"Oh. Oh yes. Yes. Yes. Come on boys. You know you want it so bad." She looked up at me and smiled. "I want you so bad. Come on boys. Easy."

I put my hand down her tight stomach, down in her shorts where she was wet and dripping. She opened her legs and let my finger move over her clit.

"Yes . . . yes," she murmured. "I want it. Oh yes, yes. Please come. I want it bad. Aieeee!" She panted, "Har! Ha. Aieeee!" She panted. "Eeeeee. Royals and pussy! First one here gets hot and wet."

"Keep it up," Suzy said. "They're starting to cross into the zone at full speed."

"Hold on," Simpson announced. "The D-men gone crazy. Here they come!"

Our craft filled with the sound of hammering deafening explosions. White light strobe in every port so that as Suzy turned her head to look at me she appeared to be moving in slow motion. I pulled my hand from Kai but she jerked it back and looked at me with vacant eyes and strange distorted smile. Her face stretched. The cabin expanded.

Shit! Displacement. Fhister-phasia

I had seconds to get back to my post, to strap in, but my fate was sealed. I didn't care what it was called, fhista-phasia or displacement. If I wasn't strapped down when we moved into the nether zone, I would be trapped forever between here and now. I would be literally evaporated.

The cabin elongated and the instruments stretched like a long rubber band. The floor began to undulate.

Space tore. Time rent.

Had to get to my post. Get strapped in.

No, too late. The ship lurched. The treads of reality popped and the fabric of existence ripped.

I reached the first rung of the ladder to the bridge, but my hand seemed to go right through the metal. I turned to look at Kai and Suzy but where they had been were only multicolored spinning wheels of light. Suzy's head was a blue disk. Parts of her body glowed orange, green, and red. Likewise, Kai erupted in multicolor mauve and purple and white. I went rotating head over heels through the cabin. We went in the egress.

As I flew over and over in eternal darkness, the horizon began to shine. There, standing at the edge of nothing, Mom and Dad. How long had it been since they were young like that? Dad stood tall and erect, and Mom was wearing a cotton dress. I flew to them at tremendous speed. They got bigger and bigger. Dad picked me up and slapped me.

"Pay attention. Wake up!"

The hull of the ship shook and vibrated. Why didn't Simpson rectify harmonics and dilate the ding-dangeruny? I couldn't think, but somehow I forced my arm up the next rung of the ladder. We'd been in eternity for too long, and if Simpson couldn't pry us from between, we'd be stuck out of phase until the end of time. Had to get to the control panel. My hand disappeared through the rung in the wall of the cabin, and I fell headlong into the darkness.

I supplicated myself before the twisting tubes and colored lights. Wires came out of the machinery and wrapped around me and held my head from moving. A whirring saw blade spun toward me from an opening in the processors. I felt a breeze at my neck. The blade inched closer and closer. Two large red disks floated in the air and an electronic face smiled. A question came into my consciousness.

"Head?"

Why weren't we out of displacement? How long could this insanity go on before we imploded?

My whole being stretched for the next rung of the ladder. Could I reach it, and if I reached it, would I have the strength to pull myself up? I grabbed the rung and held tight as white light poured in from explosions around us. I could barely see the bridge, but I managed to catch an image of Simpson. He was head down, bleeding on the control panel. Our ship hammered uncontrollably, out of phase with time and space. The emergency escape button on the console blared red, red . . .

Red.

Floating everywhere red gobs of protoplasm. Then nothingness. Then red. Then black. Then nothing. The red eyes of Baphomet closed in for me. With horns pointed and gnarly goat-face laughing, it came for me. My hand shot for my Johnson and reached inside my chest and pulled out my red blood engorged heart. Beating again and again, red everywhere.

If I could just reach the last rung, climb to the console and hit the button, who knew where we'd be . . . very little energy left. Couldn't go on for long. Much longer and I'd be too weak to resist the effects of nodal space. The ship would soon be destroyed, and no one would have to worry about good or evil. Simply, we would be between life and death, forever and ever, in between. I had the last rung in my hand and with one foot on another rung, I cast up.

"Yeeow!" I screamed and dove into the darkness and fell and fell until my guts were on the ceiling and my nose poked through the hatch and I landed with a thump on the floor of the cabin. Out the port, a mighty battle took place. We hovered in the center of it, in displacement, visible neither to the Photon or the armada.

D-men ships fired at our afterimage, disclosed their locations, and the Photon discharged streams of energy to destroyed them. We careened in a fantastic spiral from below and through them. I stood up and my head penetrated the hull.

Fantastic explosions of colored lights erupted from horizon to horizon. From what seemed to be the stars, thick streams of energy blast out of the blackness. When a distant Mega craft was hit, it exploded in a thousand colors, sending out brilliant flares of violet, and red, and sparkling white twisting trails.

Come on, push the button. Push the button!

Push the snake. Pound the head. Slap the mouth. Crush the fangs. Obliterate the forked tongue. Striking me, striking it . . . I rammed my fist down its flashing red throat.

"Displacement complete." The computer droned.

We had to get out of the Photon zone while we had the chance. I pushed the accelerator to the max, and our Magnacruiser raced forward. Out the port, I could see white explosions on the horizon. At last, we were beyond the range of the Photon.

"Holography!"

In the viewer, the last of the D-men armada exploded in flames. We did it! Now, all that was left for me to do was abandon ship right before we attempted to go through the shield. I had to save the world. Too bad I had to sacrifice the others. I had to save the world.

I had to save the world.

Chapter 27.

A person doesn't come out of the nether immediately, but I wasn't an ordinary person. I was Dick Philips, badge 324200. I knew and practiced Chi Kung, Kung Fu, Tai Chi, recondite hermetics, hydraulics, epistemology and gynecology . . . but now my head felt inverted and I saw meaning in everything. I looked at all that had gone on before as simple madness. Nothing mattered. How absurd. How could something that was a nothing . . . I mean nothing . . . How could that be matter? Matter was solid. It existed. How could nothing be solid? I spoke out loud.

"How could nothing matter?!"

But that was a rhetorical question, because even as I said it I realized that at the farthest extent of space, at infinity, all possibilities . . . all probabilities occurred simultaneously. That meant that in reality the universe was woven together seamlessly. It actually was solid. What I had thought was nothing, was actually matter. In reality, nothing mattered. Matter was nothing, and nothing was matter . . . nothing was the matter. Nothing was the matter.

Something was the matter.

Simpson's back oozed red blood and puss. I guess he should have stayed on his cot, but I was glad he'd been at the controls instead of me. He wheezed as I lifted him and tried to wake him.

"Simpson, come on. Wake up." I said, and shook him, but he was out. I pulled him off the control panel and put him on the floor and poured Charachunga on his wounds and filled his mouth and made him drink. He stayed unconscious.

Damn. I looked at the Ching Da. It didn't refill itself as quickly as before, and now the once clear fluid looked a little murky. It lost power. A great feeling of foreboding overcame me as I realized evil gained control.

"Dick?"

What?

I heard someone call my name, but it wasn't Simpson.

At the controls, I interconned. "Suzy?" There was no answer.

"Kai?" No response.

"Dick?"

"What?" I said. "Who is it?"

On the next level, I was astounded by what I saw. Suzy lay on the floor in a crumpled mess. Kai rested her head lifelessly on the instruments. Everyone was out. I was the only one who was unhurt. Somehow, again the Ching Da saved me.

A terrible thought came in my mind. What if by saving me, the Charachunga lost its power? What if I were the cause of its failure, and what if I were left alone in a crazy world populated by wild animals and insane humans? Evil thoughts swept over me. I had to preserve the precious fluid, but I needed a crew. I poured a little fluid in Suzy's mouth and allowed a few drops to fall on Kai's wounds. When they didn't respond, I was faced with a dilemma.

"Computer, at our present speed, how long until we reach the shield?"

"Shield intercept in minus eight minutes."

I returned to the bridge. Eight minutes until we could attempt to penetrate and breach the shield. I pondered the controls. The Magnacruiser hurtled across the country at a fantastic rate of speed. Apparently, Simpson wasn't kidding with his plan to implode the engines. I pulled the accelerator back, and the magneto groaned. The craft slowed to hovering. The Charachunga had to be preserved at all cost, and I had to have a crew to help me penetrate the shield. When they came around, how was I going to tell them they must die so the world could live?

It would be better if I didn't say anything and simply escaped. Would the excuse of the magneto sounding strange work another time to free me to get to the parachute while they plotted and maneuvered the ship into position?

The void in my brain was interrupted by a strange metal sound, a clanking noise, like a tool falling in the engine room. It woke me from my thoughts. What was that? Simpson moaned from his position on the floor. Suzy and Kai and he needed to be in sick bay. One by one, I carried them down the levels. It was difficult getting them down level, but at last they slept on the cots in the infirmary.

Come on, I thought, wake up. I don't want to be alone. I can't lose you. This was a strange conundrum. I didn't want to lose them. I needed to wake them so I could use them, so I could kill them. They would have to die to save a world society that might no longer exist.

The smell of Jay's rotting body twisted my thoughts. I covered him and my hidden parachute pack with my old poncho. A distant voice called out.

"Dick?"

"Who is that, and what the hell do you want?"

Clank.

Again a noise from the engine compartment. So . . . all this time we weren't alone on the Magnacraft. My heart beat wildly in my chest. Adrenalin pumped in my body, into my brain. My hair felt crisp. Slitch. My Johnson slid into my grip. They wanted a fight. I wanted to fight.

Ever so slowly, I pushed open the hatch to the engine room where the big magneto whirred. Through the inspection port, the blue green flux seemed normal. As I moved about the compartment I heard a slight sound like a feather brushing. My heart pounded in my worn out body. I squint my eyes. The shinning metal rail reflected the movement of the engine, but the walkway around the magneto . . . empty.

That brushing sound again. Was it an animal, a monster, some stow-away? I poised to kill. The blood beat in my head. My hair stood on end. Adrenalin pumped up my back bone. I walked around the railing to the left and on the walkway, I moved into the engine room.

363

There again, the faint sound of something brushing. I stopped. It stopped. I crept forward. There it was again on the soft far away edge of my hearing, a gentle brushing. I looked down. Damn! The cuff of my pants was rubbing on the floor. What a fool! I walked bravely into the magneto.

The smell of varnish and oil burned my nose.

"Okay," I said, "If there is anybody in here, you better step out where I can see you before I dump this Johnson all over you."

"Dick?"

"What. What is it?"

"It's no use, Dick. You can't beat Kang. He's too powerful. Evil has won. It's too late. You've failed. The Evil One has taken control of the Cosmos."

"No," I said. "I refuse to believe that. Dick Phillips doesn't fail."

It was Da Mo's voice. Where was it coming from?

"Over here, Dick. Look at me."

"Where?"

"In here, in the magneto."

I looked into the flux and the blue green face of Da Mo formed before me.

"The Evil One has won."

"I don't believe you. It's not over yet."

"Yes it is, look."

As I looked into the blue green flux, Da Mo's face morphed into a horned goat, then a succubus, an incubus, and a bunch of puss with worms and it was my face and I was in the flux and things were stinging me and eating my insides. With searing pain, my skin melted from my flesh as I ate myself, retched, and puked. A razor knife gutted me. Acid incinerated my face. Fire scalded my essence. A red-eyed monster held me in its grip.

It was Kang.

Da Mo was Kang!

"Phillips!" My name rang out.

Again. "Phillips!" Simpson called from sick bay.

With a shiver, I closed the door to the magneto. What hope was there? The world turned evil. I could feel it like a Chinese barber's red hot towel around my face before a shave and when the towel gets unraveled you see a shiny straight razor cutting across your face. The blood spurts. His broken brown dentures jiggle in his mouth as he laughs demonically. Blood spurts on your new white shirt. He slashes again and again. Visions of killing, death, and destruction filled my mind. The magneto had done something to me. Evil images repeated themselves. I wanted to kill, to maim. Turgidly, I lusted for fight. Right then, I could have killed anyone . . . anything.

But I shook it off and took a long drink from the fading Ching Da. Not instantly, but soon, I felt better and made my way to sickbay.

Back in sickbay, the Ching Da refilled itself, though slowly. I bent down before the big black man and opened Simpson's mouth. I poured some in the black man's mouth, and he shook and opened his eyes.

"Rest," I said, "Your back's got to heal."

"No! No!" he yelled violently. "Evil! I can feel it. It's all around me like a prickly wool blanket. Get it off!" He brushed at his arms, twisted his head back and forth, and again fell unconscious.

The Charachunga grew weaker. I watched the translucent vial slowly refill itself. Damn. This might be the last time the rejuvenating fluid would be strong enough to defeat Kang, or whatever his real name. Was this the world's last chance? I wasn't sure. As soon as my crew was able, we had to penetrate the shield. I would parachute to safety, and they had to die. So what! I wasn't going to let Him beat me. I clinched my Mandrake claw. Cha Chang.

Cha Chang!

"Dick . . ." Suzy said, and rubbed her eyes, "what . . . happened?"

"Baby," I replied, "I'm sure glad to see you." I bent next to her. "Everyone got hurt, but I think we're going to recover." I sat down next to her and held her. "We're not in heaven, and we're not in hell . . . yet."

"Did we win?"

I kissed her and put my face next to hers. "Sweetheart, if we didn't we sure wouldn't be here now."

Kai moaned, "Oh, head hurts." She shook and quivered and tossed back and forth. She tried to speak but only opened her mouth. Then words came out slowly. "Face," she said, "my face not my face."

"You must have resisted." I said, "you got to flow with it." I touched her forehead.

"You'll be fine, honey."

I gave them both swigs from the Ching Da, but now it was almost empty.

Several hours went by, and although it didn't replenish itself as quickly, the Charachunga kept working. Soon, Simpson paced around the cabin. Suzy combed her long blonde hair, and Kai put on makeup. I plotted our next move toward the Council and wondered if I had the nerve to tell them they had to die.

"Phillips, what's the status of the ship?"

"Well, Simpson," I began, "the flux level is still holding. The magneto's constant, and the hull is on low charge. We're stationery at eight minutes to shield, all systems are tetrapolar."

"Good," he said, "I'm ready to go back to work." He spoke to the ladies. "How about it girls? Phillips, what's your plan?"

"It's pretty simple," I said. "We approach the shield at high speed on its tangent, discharge the hull into the shield, do a three sixty and blast through on the trail of the discharge. No problem."

"Let's get to it!"

"One thing," I added, "While all of you were unconscious, I did a complete diagnostic on the magneto. It seems when you imploded the engine, the flux went out of balance. To keep the amplitude and frequency in check, I'm going to have to be in engineering and balance the flux when we pass through the shield."

Simpson stretched his large body. "Sounds good to me. I'll handle the controls and do the shooting. Suzy stays in navigation and Kai handles the tele-guidance. We're set."

At the engine room, I shielded my eyes and carefully did not look in the blue green light of the magneto. It sounded fine. According to the instruments, the engine ran smoothly. It hummed along.

"System's check," Simpson said over the intercon.

"Gyro at ninety degrees," Suzy replied.

"Projections grouping together," Kai said. "Shield in holography now."

"Holography on," I said from the engine room, and the shield came in the viewer. In front of me, behind the glowing orange shield, I could see the outline of the glass dome to the Council.

"Magneto amplitude and frequency normal," I said.

"Full thrust!" shouted Simpson.

The Magnacrusier raced forward. The orange shield grew larger and more ominous. The dome of the Council got bigger.

"Sixteen degrees correction!" Suzy announced.

"Hull charging!"

"Maintaining sonic vectors," Kai interjected.

"Transpose interconnects!"

"Shield tangents fluctuating at minus four percent!"

"Correction override now!"

"Switching."

"Exponentials now!"

"Max charge!" Simpson shouted. "Setting computer count down now. T minus one minute."

The flux roared. The magneto vibrated harmonically. A piecing sound shot through the hull and then stabilized. "Engine rotation and magneto stabilized!" I shouted.

It was time for me to leave. I made my way to sick bay and down the next level to the escape hatch where I uncovered Jay's putrefying body and took out the blue parachute pack. I hooked the Ching Da around my neck and thought how the fate of the world depended on me. I couldn't fail. As I stepped into the wind, Simpson exchanged commands with Suzy and Kai.

"Thrust correction, fourteen degrees."

"Tangent angle stabilizing at apogee."

"Kai! Lock in holography."

"Ready to discharge!"

"T minus thirty seconds."

"Vector angles stabilized."

"Rotational thrusters ready!"

"Energy distortion in holography!" Suzy screamed. "What the hell? . . . A parachute. Somebody just parachuted from our ship?"

"What's that!?" Simpson cried. He paused and took a breath. "It's another Magnacrusier! It's charged! Where'd it come from!?"

A huge red and black Magnacrusier appeared in holography. It fired a flashing red beam at the parachutist, instantly evaporating him.

I pulled myself up the ladder and jumped on the bridge. "It's a trap!" I yelled and jumped in the gunner's seat.

Simpson's eyes were wide and white.

"I tossed out Jay's body," I said, and worked my hands over the controls. "I strapped him to a parachute and dumped him."

"Firing now!" I screamed.

Simpson crammed the controls back and our craft accelerated in a three sixty rotation. Blue-green energy discharged from our hull and raced at the D-man ship. The ball of energy seared through the air . . .

"Missed them!"

"Charging!"

"Danger. Approaching Red line!"

A crackling ball of energy formed on their hull. Their ship was bigger than ours and right on our tail. They were up to speed. They closed. In an instant they would fire.

"Hold the three sixty degree rotation!" I shouted.

"What are you doing Phillips?"

"Pull it back all the way. Hold that rotation!"

"Re-approaching tangent!"

"T minus two seconds to red line."

"Energy fluctuation!"

"Vectors spewed!"

"Red line!" The computer announced.

"Straighten it out, Simpson!

"What? Right into the shield. We'll be evaporated!"

"I know what I'm doing."

"They're firing!" Kai screamed.

"Shield dead on!" Suzy cried.

I reached over to the black man and put my hand on top of his over the controls.

"Trust me," I said, and pulled the accelerator back to dead stop.

The craft moaned, shook, and a cracking sound shot through the hull. A bright energy ball burned past us. The air in the cabin rose twenty degrees. Outside, fire incinerated the air around the ship. Light filled our eyes.

I crammed Simpson's hand forward. Our momentum held, we accelerated into another three sixty and rotated directly behind the Magnacruiser. A bright flashing red and white explosion opened hole in the shield as the ship in front of us sailed into the shield and evaporated. We followed right behind, passed through the opening, and flew directly toward the dome of the Council.

"Damn!" Simpson shouted.

We hesitated for only an instant and then pitched forward at tremendous speed.

We penetrated the shield on a bee line toward the dome. We rocketed toward the Council dome, toward D-1, the monster leader of the D-men, toward Kang, toward evil, toward something unimaginable.

Chapter 28.

"Holography! I shouted.

The glass dome rose up above the city. Inside, figures moved about and it seemed as if a fire burned. We flew in a direct line toward the Council. Immediately we would be there. In a few moments we would either save the world or be subject to evil for the rest of eternity. We had no choice. None of us could live in the world as it was . . . the fate of humanity rested in our hands.

"Kai, see if you can amplify the image and get inside the Council dome. Let's see what Kang and D-1 are up to. There's a slight chance, if we're lucky, we still have the element of surprise. . . . Kai!"

"Bringing it in now," Kai replied.

"Suzy, plot vectors."

"Will you look at that?" Simpson said.

The holoview flickered as Kai fine tuned and adjusted the focus.

Inside the dome on the white marble floor, in their red and black uniforms, big muscular D-men assembled around the gallery of Council members, who, as always sat stoic and hidden under hooded robes. Between the D-men and the gallery of Council members sat a throne and a fire pit where a huge deformed monster of a man, also dressed in the red and black uniform, stoked the fire and rotated a spit.

D-men fought, laughed, punched, and screamed at each other, and on the other side of the great dome. prisoners pulled at their chains and lamented. Old men cried out and beat their hands against their heads. Children screamed pitifully. Women ripped their clothes in angst.

A giant D-man poured a liquid on the fire and orange red flames rose around him. He laughed and stretched his deformed frame to its full height and looked to the prisoners and pointed at a fat young lady who trembled and collapsed. The prisoners quivered and fell back. A great clamor rose from the gallery of D-men who hooted and called out. A huge smile spread across the monster's face. It was D-1.

Between D-1 at the flaming pit and the sober hooded Council members, rested a large throne with jewels that reflected the orange and red fire light. The throne emanated a bright glowing flickering hue. On the throne sat a young Chinaman whose eyes gleamed as he stroked a small black goatee and touched a gold chain which hung at his neck. A red silk robe opened at his chest showing a well defined muscular body. The hem of the robe draped over a cloven hoof. In his left hand he waved a dagger, and in his right he lifted a large chunk of meat to his mouth and tore off a hunk. He stood and walked to the monster D-1.

"Too well done!" he shouted and spit the meat on D-1's face. "Cook another one."

D-1 bowed. "Yes, Kang."

"What?"

D-1 averted his eyes and lowed his face. "Yes sir, master."

My side ached and thumped. At last, I would have my revenge on D-1 for the electro torture and the removal of my kidney. This time I'd give him a taste of the Mandrake claw, and his master, Kang didn't look so powerful either. Just a young Chinese puppy. I'd show him who the big dog was. I'm Dick Phillips, badge 324200; I thought and held the Ching Da at my neck. If Kang were Da Mo, he was going to get this little present spread all over him.

"What pleases you, master?" D-1 asked.

"That fat one." Kang commanded. "I want her on the spit."

With his muscles undulating under his red and black uniform, the massive D-1 walked slowly toward the fire pit. He removed the giant chunk of meat from the spit and threw it to the D-men who ripped at it like animals. As D-1 lumbered toward the prisoners, he looked them over one by one.

We studied the figures in holography, and I could feel evil well up from the dome like a relentless black fungus growing off the

371

sweet honey of its own purification. I looked at Simpson, Suzy, and Kai. We made it this far as a team, but now I knew it was up to me, my Johnson, and the Mandrake claw.

"What do you think of all that, Simpson?"

"Typical D-men," he replied, "we're going to have to take care of those red and blacks. There are a lot of them, and they look mean."

Simpson shouted to Kai. "See if you can't focus that holography."

"Focusing," she replied.

"Vector analysis complete," Suzy announced. "Approach plotted."

"Yeah," I told Simpson, "but I've got an idea. We might be able to stun them."

Sitting behind Kang's throne in the first row of the Council, a hooded member fidgeted and moved this way and that. He rocked forward and back, turned to one side. He started to stand, then sat down and again rocked his chair forward and back. He started to speak and then stopped. Kang turned to him.

"What is it?"

A hush went through the giant chamber as the Council member pulled off his hood exposing a large balding head and pulsing varicose vein, bulging eyes and drawn lips. Dr. Blood wrung his hands, wiped the sweat off his brow, and twisted his hands again. He stared at the floor.

"Nothing, master," Dr. Blood replied.

Kang pointed to the prisoners. "That one. I want that fat one."

D-1 moved through the quivering crowd and as he came to two young ladies, he pointed at the plump one.

Kang licked his lips. "That's the one. Put her on the spit!"

Good Lord! It was Linda Horace. Beside her, Cynthia, my debutante, shrieked and struggled.

"It's Cindy," Simpson said, "my debutante. We're going in!"

My debutante, I thought. "Hold it, Simpson. We're not ready. We have to have a plan. Look."

372

Chained next to the girls, being pushed back and forth by the mass of prisoners, yanking at their bonds, Parkenson, his wife Harriet, and his sister Sara struggled to keep D-1 from taking Linda.

"Stop this madness!" Parkenson shouted. "Badges come to your senses."

"Look," I said to Simpson. "Don't those D-men look familiar?"

"Yes. Yes. There's Smith. Isn't that Jones? That tall one is Williamson."

"Badges as D-men. It's impossible!"

"Get away from her!" Parkenson cried.

The huge monster, D-1 slammed his forehead into Parkenson and knocked back the big man. In the crowd of D-men, Jones seemed to wake from a dream. He ran toward Parkenson to help. Kang stood erect on the throne. A ray of red light shone from his eyes, and Jones turned to stone. The prisoners hushed and the D-men fell silent.

"Bring her to me!" Kang commanded. "Now!"

On the white marble in front of the throne, in one massive deformed hand, D-1 held Linda by the neck. Kang nodded and D-1 ripped her dress. She quivered. Her skin was whiter than her bra and little panties.

"Bring in the Saint."

From the shadows, two D-men pushed in a chair holding a lanky tall black man who stared off to space without any facial expression as Kang called his name.

"Billy!" Kang cried. "One more soul on your head. How many more you going to watch die in the fire pit. Where is the Ching Da?"

Billy sat motionless, not looking at Kang or Linda or anything in particular. He appeared comatose, but Dr. Blood couldn't contain himself. He rocked in his chair, wrung his hands again and again, and pounded his palms on his legs.

"What is it Blood!" Demanded Kang.

"I can get it out of him."

Kang looked at Blood and moved his head sideways and back in a mocking way, almost as if his neck were double jointed like a serpent before it strikes.

"You think my way is the wrong way?"

"No. No, not at all your highness."

Blood bowed his head and wouldn't look at Kang. "It's just that killing all these people doesn't seem right."

"What!?" Kang screamed.

Blood tried to cover his head with his hood, but the hood irritated the blood vein in his large head and it pulsed blue and red. Dr. Blood grit his teeth and couldn't speak while Kang stared at him.

"What do you want to do, Blood?"

His scalp glowed red where the vein leaked. "Couldn't we just torture them?"

"You want me to torture them?"

"Ah . . . no."

"No?"

"I want to torture them. I want to hear them squeal. Can't we use a sharp knife and trim some skin from their sides, or use a razor blade to cut their tongues and fill the cuts with salt? I want to watch them see their own bodies spurting blood. Why can't we roll up some paper, stick it in their openings, and light it on fire? We can pull out their eyes and make them eat them. Why can't we. . ."

Kang's lips spread over his teeth. He threw a piece of meat at Dr. Blood and hurled the dagger toward him. The meat landed in Blood's lap, and the dagger penetrated deep in the meat. Dr. Blood lunged back. He held up the meat and looked at Kang with a hurt look in his eyes.

Kang lifted one finger and screamed.

"Why can't we . . . we!" He cried, "It's me, Blood. It's me! . . . We do what . . . I want!"

"But . . ." Blood whimpered.

Kang smiled. "You like to torture them." He laughed and jumped from the throne, pushed D-1 and Linda back and stood over Blood. "I like to eat them!"

"We do what I want!" Kang shouted again at Blood.

Blood cowered like a hurt puppy and pulled his hood over his head, but Kang sprang on him and pulled it back and picked Blood up by his engorged head and threw him down in front of Billy.

Like a dog he turned his face up. "Why master, why?" pleaded Blood.

"What!" Kang cried, and grabbed Blood by the back of his neck. "Never, ever, question why I say or do anything." He forced Blood down to ground. "Now, kiss Billy's shoe."

In our holography, Dr. Blood put his lips to Billy's boot, while Saint Billy looked off to space, oblivious to the scene unfolding. Something rang in my ears. The anthem, the revolution . . . "When Blood kisses Saint Billy's boot. . ." The gallery of D-men went wild with cat calls and hoots. One of the big D-men jumped in front of the crowd and twisted, stomped, and laughed until Kang, like a benevolent king, nodded and smiled at him. And like a king he silently pranced around Linda. His robe dragged behind him and the cloven hoof pawed the marble. A slight motion of his hand, and D-1 pulled Linda to a standing position. She quivered and her white body shook.

"Please!" she cried. "Please, don't hurt me. I'll do whatever you want."

"You will!" Kang shouted. "You certainly will!"

In the ship, looking in the holography, the four of us stared, almost frozen in fascination at the scene. In a moment we would be directly over the dome.

Kang licked his lips and surveyed Linda, and then his hand shot out and grabbed her bra and ripped it off of her exposing her large breasts and red sand dollar nipples. He looked at Billy, bent his head to Linda's bare stomach, dug in his teeth, and ripped a chunk of flesh.

Linda screamed in agony.

Kang chewed her flesh and blood ran in his goatee, He turned to Saint Billy. "Too rare." He said and spit. "Now Billy, where's the Ching Da?"

Billy looked blank. Kang turned back to D-1.

"Rack her on the spit!"

"Good God," Simpson remarked. "Kang's a monster."

"We've got to save them."

"Rotate the ship. Match the tangent."

"Apogee! Apogee!"

"I'm going in now!" I shouted.

"Not without me." Simpson barked.

"Listen Simpson," I said, "we've only got seconds, and I've already thought this out. I have to go in alone. You're all tore up, you can't move. You'd just get shot up. I need you at the helm. If we swing in slow over the glass we'll surprise them. They won't expect me to bust through the glass. I've got to go in alone, and I don't want the girls getting hurt."

"Hey!" Suzy interjected. "I know how to pump a Johnson."

"Me too," Kai added, ". . . want to help."

"No!" I commanded. "It's too dangerous. I'm swinging in on a nylon. Bring her up slow, up around the glass. I'll cast out, bust through, and throw the China Da on Kang before they know what hit them."

"What about the D-men?"

"After I burst through the glass," I said, "I want you to hover over the opening. Fire a low charge into the D-men. It will stun them long enough for me to take control. Once I've defeated Kang, the remaining badges will fight for us."

"That might work, but the flux is low. You've got to hurry."

"Here comes the dome. I'm going in."

I stuffed an extra Johnson in my belt and made it down stairs toward the exit in sick bay when Suzy grabbed me and pulled me to her chest. She felt warm and soft and inviting as our lips met.

"I love you, Dick," she said. "I'm going in with you."

"No way." I answered. "I love you too, but it's too dangerous. Get up stairs and help Simpson with navigation. This will only take a few minute. Be ready with that energy blast when I break through the glass."

"Hold position," I yelled to Simpson.

In sick bay I searched through my poncho for the iris blockers Pella and I used so long ago to sneak on the Link. If Kang were Gorgon, I didn't want to end up a statue celebrating his power. I might not need them. I would have the Johnsons, and of course, the Mandrake claw. I put the little opaque contacts in my pocket and checked the Johnsons. Cool air blew through he hatch. I could smell success . . . or was it my own nasty sweat. Below me, the glass dome rushed up.

This was going to take some doing. I'd been pretty lucky so far, and I hoped my luck would hold. If what Lee Tsing at the Five Dollar said about Kang were true, I was going to have to be lucky. What was it Tsing had said? He could jump thirty feet. He knew all kinds of Kung Fu, or was it Dung Go? Didn't matter. Even if Kang was strong and tough, he couldn't match the Mandrake claw. Cha Chang! His stare froze D-men. Nothing froze the Mandrake claw. Cha Chang!

The Ching Da hung around my neck. I held a Johnson in one hand, stuffed the second one in my belt, and the iris blockers rested safely in my pocket. I wrapped the nylon around my arm and jumped. As the air blew against my face, the nylon jerked me like a pendant in a round arch. Time slowed down as the glass dome rushed to meet me. I grit my teeth, held my arm up, and lifted my boots.

I could see the gallery, the D-men, and the prisoners, Kang, Dr. Blood, and Saint Billy. D-1 dragged Linda to impale her on the spit over the burning embers. She struggled, but he forced her down. With one hand he held her rump up and in the other hand he held the metal spit. He pull it back.

I dumped my first Johnson through the crystal. With a shattering sound the glass broke away, and I sailed to the floor. Behind me, the air became electrified. As our Magnacruiser discharged a low flux, the D-men froze in place. The nylon tightened. I landed on my feet directly in front of Kang, ripped the Ching Da off my neck, and with all my might heaved it dead on at the Chinaman.

He smiled and his eyes gleamed. With a quick motion he stuck his hand in the air. As if swatting a slow moving fly, he caught the Ching Da and with a laugh, pulled the vial to him.

"Well, Phillips," he asked calmly, "what took you so long? You're a sight for sore eyes, if you get what I mean. Don't freeze on me." He laughed,. "Say something. We've been expecting you."

"Kang! You're dead!" I yelled and ripped the second Johnson out of my belt, raised it to fire, but D-1's massive fist came down on my neck. The monster picked me up and smothered my face with one giant hand while the other wrapped around me, crushing my chest. I couldn't breath. As he squeezed the life out of me, he slowly turned to Kang and begged.

"Let me kill him, master. I've waited years."

Kang sat down on his throne. "Yes," he said and stroked his goatee. But first let's let him see my power." Kang looked at Billy and red light flashed from his eyes.

"Saint Billy!" Kang commanded. "Take this Ching Da to the fire pit and get rid of it forever."

In a trance, Billy rose, stepped over Dr. Blood, and walked to Kang's side.

I struggled against D-1, but couldn't move. I couldn't breath. I couldn't command the Mandrake claw. I couldn't breathe. D-1 crushed me. In a few seconds I would pass out.

"Let me break his neck," pleaded D-1.

"No. Don't kill him. I want him to see this," Kang said and handed the Ching Da to Billy. "Take the worthless Charachunga and throw it in the fire."

Kang let out a high piercing laugh. "I'm king!"

A moment is all a badge needs. I twisted out of D-1's grip and dove for Kang. Flipping over and over, I twisted in the air, landed in a crouch, and in a mighty jump, lunged at his throat.

"Throw da ball, Billy!" I yelled.

Saint Billy stopped, looked at me and Kang, paused as if he remembered something from long ago, and turned back toward the fire pit.

Kang threw a karate chop straight to my face. God! It hurt. It burned like a red hot poker. I went stumbling back with the smell of burning flesh in my nose.

"D-1!" Kang shouted. "Kill him!"

The giant man jumped me, but I rotated and kicked the side of his head. I swung around and kicked him again. I shot a fist into his neck, and another and another. Over and over I hit him in the face. I bloodied one eye and then the next. I pounded his ugly nose until it felt like rubber, and with a quick rotation I cupped my hands and slapped his ears. I karate chopped his Adam's apple and poked in his right eye.

"Ha, ha, ha!" He laughed. "Tickle me some more, will you Phillips?"

He bent back and laughed. "Ha!" He laughed again, leaving his stomach wide open.

"Mandrake claw form!"

Cha Chang.

Cha Chang! I drove it deep into his gut and ripped a hand full. As I pulled out his intestines, again Cha Chang!

His heart appeared in my hands. I opened his mouth and shoved it in and thought I saw a glimmer of respect in his eyes. He swayed for a moment, and his massive body fell.

Billy neared the fire pit. As he walked, his lanky legs labored slowly, step after step. I turned toward Kang.

"Throw da ball, Billy!" I shouted.

For an instant, Billy stopped and his eyes lit up. He seemed again to be the young baseball hero. He lifted the Ching Da, and then with a sigh he fell back into a stupor and walked mindlessly closer and closer to the flaming embers. The fate of the world rested in Billy's hands.

Kang laughed. "You've lost, Phillips. Look at me."

I pushed D-1's body away and sprang at Kang.

But Kang fired another Kung Fu shot to my head that penetrated my brain and seared my mind like a flaming steel rod. The pain! I stumbled back. Another punch flattened my nose against my face. I couldn't breathe. Blood filled my eyes and throat. The next punch lifted me off my feet, and I heard something snap in my neck. Kang's fist shot through my midsection, and my guts spewed out of me.

I recovered with a kick, but he blocked it and I heard a crack in my leg and pain erupted from my knee. My feet went out from under me, and I hit the floor. Instantly Kang's feet were around my head. The Tibetan death twist.

He looked down at me. "First, I want you to look in my eyes." I wouldn't look. I couldn't look.

He twisted my hair and pulled my head up and bent down to my face. Still, I kept my eyes closed. He only laughed.

"Lift yourself up, dog," he said. "You're less than human. You're afraid. You're quivering. You disgust me. Face your death like a man. You're a fool. Your face is busted, your legs is broken. Now, turn to stone! Look how you pitifully try to resist."

He lifted his hands into air. "I'm Kang. I am Kang. I am king Kang!"

I hunched over, unable to get up. Somehow my hands found the iris blockers, and I held my palms to my face as if in shame. Quickly inserting the contact lens, I rose on one knee.

"I'm just a man," I said.

"A stone man!" he replied and focused his eyes on me and a red stream of light emanated from his eyes. "Look deep."

A multicolored snake head weaved in front of me. A white death skull exploded and reformed to be a hundred-headed thousand-faced monster. The life force sucked out of me, and Kang's face transformed to dripping slime. Something ghastly, beyond words, transformed to an image beyond life, evil . . . death . . . beyond death . . . glowing eyes, voids in void. Transfixed, I stared into the ever changing face of Evil.

"Yes. Yes!" he laughed and threw his head back.

With a single once of energy, I formed the words.

"Mandrake claw!"

Cha Chang!

I jumped up and shot the Mandrake claw into Kang's neck and turned him around so his back was to Billy.

"Throw da ball, Billy!" I screamed, and the lanky black man came to life. The Ching Da balanced precariously in his hand, but he only looked at us for an instant. His muscles tightened like springs.

He wound up. His whole body blurred. His arm disappeared in a lightening-fast motion. He pitched.

I felt the bones in my hand break as Kang pulled the claw from his neck and whirled around in rage. He eyes pulsed and glowed red. He locked his face on mine and two vermillion streams of death shot out his eyes. The air between us erupted smoke and flame.

"Ahhhhhhh!" Kang screamed.

The Ching Da hit him and shattered and the Charachunga spilled over him. He began to sizzle and burn. His eyes grew wider and wider. He turned up his face, and a thick red penis grew out his mouth. His eyes imploded with a sucking sound, and the skin on his face melted off leaving only his skull. The jaw opened and the head twisted back and forth on the flagellating spinal cord. His hair exploded in red and green and blue fire. His body shook and jerked, and he spun round and round. A thousand different faces writhed in agony. He clawed the air, and burned. The fabric of reality turned in, collapsed, and revolved around a point in space, imploded . . . exploded and . . .

With a puff of smoke, he evaporated.

As the smoke blew away, Da Mo stood before me. He looked me over, and nodded his head and smiled. He bowed and bent over and picked up the glistening Ching Da with its everlasting Charachunga. He took a drink.

"Good job, Dick Phillips," he said. "I knew you could do it. You saved humanity. You saved the world."

The flux charge died down and the D-men were transformed back to badges while cheers went up for Saint Billy. Out of the corner of my eye, I noticed Dr. Blood making an exit, sneaking out through one of his confounded time portals. Parkenson and the rest of them, especially Linda Horace, breathed sighs of relief.

"Yes," Da Mo said, "Evil has been defeated. I am returning to seclusion now, but the world owes you a debt of gratitude."

Burned, bleeding, and hurting as never before, I knelt on the floor with my broken hand throbbing on my crushed knee. As he passed me, I grabbed Da Mo's robe.

"What about the money?"

Chapter 29.

Well, the Escapade at the Five Dollar Café was an exciting case.
Civilization pretty much returned to normal quicker than I thought
it would. It always did. The next morning, even though I was hurt
bad, could barely walk, my hand twisted and broken, and Kang's
punches still burned my face . . . I opened the door to my mod,
made for the shuttle and waved good bye to Suzy and Kai. Last
night with those two was a story in itself, but I needed to get back
to work. What new cases were brewing at the office?

What with all the excitement of the past few weeks, I looked
forward to a little hum drum relaxation . . . a game or two of chess
with Rex until a new case showed up. Too bad I'd lost my telecom
device. I felt empty without it in my ear. I wanted to call ahead and
let him know I was coming in. Anyway, riding the shuttle gave me
plenty of time to think about the Chinaman's case. I lit a Royal and
pondered it. It tasted good.

Da Mo came up with the rest of the seven hundred thousand, but
I didn't know if I'd be able to collect any more money from Ro Nes
in Billyland. I saved Billy, but couldn't find a way to keep the
eternal fountain in Billyland. That is, to deliver the Holy water. Da
Mo took the Ching Da with him. I felt a little naked without it
around my neck.

No matter what, I'd be seeing Ro Nes in a couple of weeks when
they rebuilt the Link. I'd fly out to the desert, to California City, to
Billyland where they were ecstatic to know their Saint was alive
and well. When I got there I'd have to explain about the Holy
water, and I'd pick up Pella and our kid. Until then, I was a free
man.

I held my hand to my ear as a force of habit but remembered I
didn't have Rex in. How quickly we fall back to routine. Like I said
before, nature abhors a vacuum.

The shuttle was crammed with all sorts of underbelly and scum, and I wondered what happened to Browny. Was he still alive? He was tough, but crazy by now of course. I knew I'd run on to that mechanico sooner or later.

I had to check the fine print on my contract with the Council when I got back to the office. Until then I'd hold off on doing anybody. I really wanted to com to Rex and see if he could patch through to my debutante, Cynthia. What about poor Linda? She got tore up pretty bad, but she didn't' get skewed. D-1 would have gotten a big surprise if he racked her up. I'm sure she was wearing her Huntsmith.

The Five Dollar was a pretty good case, taken me across the country, had some hard times and some good times. A few people got killed and some got hurt, but all in all it wasn't too bad. Not like the 'Case of the Blazing Bust.' All those corpus, or was it corpora?

Well, when Simpson was over at Insta Med to fix his back, he ran into Lee Tsing and it really hit the fan. I guess Simpson developed a thing for Kai. I didn't know what her husband, Lee, would do. He'd been very mad with me about the first wife. I guess I would have to refund the twenty thousand he gave me to find Kang. Maybe not. Since Do Mo re-established the balance between good and evil, Kang was missing. Now, I wasn't attached to Kai myself, but Simpson was, and he was a mean mo fo. Who would break the news to Lee? I didn't know. Probably me, only time would tell.

Billy made out like a bandit. Naturally, he got all the credit for defeating Kang. After throwing the Ching Da at Kang and bringing Da Mo back, Billy woke up from his trance. He was a Saint now. That was for sure. The crowed carried him away on their shoulders, and his face was all over the news. Saint Billy saves the world! How droll. How the truth does get twisted around. It didn't matter to me. I wasn't interested in fame. Sex and money was what I was after.

Poor Jay, I guess he got what he deserved. That's what happens when you get too caught in apron strings. Yeah, you hang yourself. I had to do him. He was a little sniveler, and anyway, it was him or Simpson. Without Simpson, we never would have beat the evil D-man armada. But Jay did save us. After all, if I hadn't thrown his body out on the parachute we would never of known that other Magna craft stalked us.

How did I know the Rex 2000 set us up and was lying about getting through the shield at the Council? I didn't know it. The shield broke down like she said it would, right after the other Magna craft discharged and went through. I couldn't leave my mates. I figured life wasn't worth living in any world if you don't stick with your friends. Lucky for us it worked out like it did.

My mind was particularly empty, thinking all those thoughts, when the shuttle groaned toward my part of town. After dealing with the Rex 2000 series, I made a mental note to stop over at the Rex factory and give them a piece of my mind, and throw in a monkey wrench. Being philosophical, those two were the same thing.

I was happy I finally killed the monster D-1, but sad I didn't get to do my nemesis, Dr. Blood. The next time he opened a time portal I was going to chase him through eternity, catch that warped genius, and pop his blood brain for good.

The shuttle slowed at my station, settled, and I jumped out. But something was wrong. This was my stop, but the building was old and run down. A large beggar sat by the entrance.

"Mr. . . ." he asked, "five dollars for a cup of coffee?"

Now, it was five dollars. Damn inflation! I reached in my pocket and took out three five dollar coins. My old trick. Quickly, I heated one between two others and flipped it to him in a natural way. It hit his palm with a burning sound, but he didn't flinch.

"Thanks," he said and smiled with a gap between brown teeth.

Something was definitely wrong. This was my stop, but what was a beggar doing in front of my building? My office was a modern high rise, and this building was made out of wood and stank like termites. I gazed around. In fact, this didn't even look like my district. The whole neighborhood seemed different.

"Rex," I said, "exit building program."

Nothing happened. The beggar smiled up at me.

"Ten dollars for a cup of coffee?"

"Rex, quit joking."

The beggar smiled up at me. "Twenty dollars for a cup of coffee?"

"Okay, okay." I cried. "Please, please Rex . . . terminate program."

The building morphed to the white plastic metal it had been when I left. I took the force to my office. Except for a bit of stale air, it was exactly the same. I breathed a sigh and sat in my brown leather chair.

"Rex," I said, "you did great, but I'm sure before I left you didn't have such an intricate building program."

"Didn't," he replied. "Hooked up with a Rex 2000 while you were on vacation."

Hooked up? Vacation? That got me wondering. What else had Rex learned? What happens when a Rex 1000 gets together with a Rex 2000? Was something born of that union? Now, what mysteries of time and space did Rex hold? Did he know how to construct a time portal so I could trap Dr. Blood? Was it lunch time yet?

"Well, Rex, "I sighed, "let's get back to work. Any calls in the last twenty four?"

"One," Rex replied. "Okay," I said, and put my feet on my desk and lit up a smoke. It would be awhile, but I'd be sorry when my supply of Royals ran out. I'd have to pay a visit to Da Mo.

I blew a perfect purple smoke ring, and it floated in the air. "Let's see it."

A beautiful albino girl formed in holography before me. She looked about eighteen. Her smooth pale skin and white hair were offset by an almost see through light blue gown. As she spoke, her red lips quivered and her eyes filled with tears.

"Dick Phillips," she said in sobs, "you don't know me. My name's Ieena. I'm the princess from the dark side . . . of the moon. They say you're the best. My jewels have been stolen. They must be returned. Our worlds are in danger. There's not much time. We'll pay ten million American to get them back. We need your help. Time is running out. You've got to get my jewels back. The universe depends on you. Please, I'll do anything."

I thought for a moment and smiled.

Anythng?

Coming soon:
The Adventures of Dick Phillips
-2-
The Princess from the Dark Side©